SAM CRESCENT

EVERNIGHT PUBLISHING ®

www.evernightpublishing.com

Copyright© 2019

Sam Crescent

Editor: Karyn White

Cover Art: Jay Aheer

ISBN: 978-1-77339-879-2

ALL RIGHTS RESERVED

SAM CRESCENT

Sam Crescent

Chapter One

Cassie Love gritted her teeth as her afternoon of sunbathing just got a whole lot more sexual. She held the paperback book in her hand. It was an old-style bodice ripper book, but she liked freaky shit like that. The sun was shining, and it felt like a million degrees outside. It was a random day off from working as a receptionist at the sheriff's office.

Growing up with a deadbeat dad who was in trouble with the law every single week, had given her a knack for knowing one or two things about the law. Of course Daniel, the sheriff in charge, didn't mind giving her a job either. She was super organized and had never caused a problem in her life.

She knew he considered himself a bit of a stepfather figure to her, and she didn't mind. He'd helped her get a job in the diner, and then the library while she was studying at the local college. When his receptionist had retired, he'd given the job to her.

For Cassie it had been an amazing vote of confidence. The sheriff had been on first name terms with her for some time. She hadn't been able to escape that. Her father's drunkenness had meant he was thrown in jail every week.

"Oh yeah, Slade, oh fuck, yeah. That feels so good."

Being drawn out of her pity party, Cassie rolled her eyes. Slade Coal was the thorn in her side at home and at work, as he was the deputy working beneath Daniel. He lived right next door to her. They were the only houses at the bottom of the street. She had wished her other neighbors were closer, but on either side of their houses was an abundance of trees dividing them from the rest of the houses. If she walked outside her front door, she could see the entire street, and wave at her neighbors. The trees had been one of the reasons she'd bought the house. She also loved the space, the kitchen, and it was so completely different from the trailer she had grown up in.

This was her own domain, and she loved it.

What she hadn't known was that at the same time she'd moved in, so did Slade. They lived side by side, *and* she saw him every single day at work. It was like she couldn't catch a break. Then when she'd bought this place, the previous owner had told her to keep an eye out for the guy next door. Being the curious woman that she was, she'd asked why. It would seem these two houses had a fifty-year history of the single occupants getting together.

"That's the freaky curse that I was told about, and you know what? I'm happy about that. We're married, and we're expecting a baby."

Cassie didn't believe in stuff like that. Clearly, the couples before had started out with an attraction to each other, which evolved over time. The way she felt about Slade was *not* attraction.

The guy was fucking another woman in his backyard. She had asked him repeatedly and nicely, if he'd keep *that* business inside. Each time he'd give her a smirk and tell her to grow up. Fucking outside was the best. He also owned a pool.

Her afternoon of reading and catching a few rays had gone. There was no way she was sitting out here listening to this.

"Oh, Slade, you're the biggest I've ever had. Give it to me. Please, please."

Getting up from her seat, she went inside, opening the fridge to grab the peach iced tea that she had made. Pouring herself a generous glass, she took a sip. Her body was hot. Her were nipples tight, and her pussy was slick. She refused to be affected by the sounds that had been coming over the fence, or the way he'd chuckled.

Slade Coal was a horrible human being. He never fucked the same woman twice. In fact, she'd been at the desk when women he'd been with had been waiting. Every time he broke up with a woman, Cassie had a front row seat to that disaster, and she hated it. The women all acted as if he was this mega brilliant, hot guy. They didn't see that he was an asshole that used them to get what he wanted. Besides, Cassie was a much better woman than that.

When her telephone rang, she welcomed the reprieve.

"Hello," she said, wondering who'd call her.

"Hey, Cassie, it's me, Jessica."

Cassie laughed. "Hey, honey. It's great to hear from you. What's up?"

"Can I bring the kids over? They're wanting to

spread out, and it's hot as hell in here."

Biting her lip, Cassie looked out toward her garden. Yet another thing she loved about her home was that even though it was a modest, two-bedroom house, it came with a lot of land, which she loved to tend to.

"They're, erm, my neighbor, he's at it again."

"They're screwing?" Jessica asked.

"Yep."

"Let's see how long he lasts with a bunch of kids screaming for mommy?"

This had Cassie smiling. It was time she started fighting fire with fire. "Sure. Bring them over. I'll get the barbeque set up, and we'll have a blast."

"You're a lifesaver, Cassie. Love you so much."

Jessica was one of the few friends in her life that had never judged her. Living in a trailer, Cassie was used to being called trailer trash, and dumpster, and a few other things. Her clothes had always been too small, and that didn't help her much fuller figure. She'd been the big kid, or the fat girl at school. She still was a big woman, size eighteen, and she loved her body. There was so much in life to be concerned about. Cassie didn't think her weight mattered. She did work out and walked to work. She didn't own a car, and rarely took a cab, but she loved to cook and bake. She also grew some of her own vegetables out in her yard.

Finishing her iced tea, Cassie made her way outside. They had stopped for the time being but knowing Slade and his little visits the way she did, it wouldn't be long before they started up again. Running fingers through her hair, she removed the protective cover from the barbeque, and then headed back inside, to start preparing some food. She loved cooking kabobs outside, and taking some of the vegetables and chicken, she prepared them.

Within twenty minutes, she had everything ready. Her doorbell rang, and she heard Slade and the woman at it again.

Opening the door, she gave a warning that they were having sex. Jessica shrugged, and after her three kids threw their arms around Cassie, they rushed outside.

"Still no luck on the home front?" Cassie asked.

"We saw ten places last week, and none of them fit. William thinks we may have to move towns, and I don't want to do that."

"You'll find a place soon."

"Yeah." They left the kitchen, carrying trays of their prepared food. Her three kids were already running around, playing chase and screaming.

Jessica moved toward the fence, and Cassie rolled her eyes. Her friend was listening to what was going on. She couldn't believe it when Jessica found a hole in the fence and was peeking through. Still, she didn't tell her friend to stop. Jessica was the kind of woman that just did what she wanted to do.

Everyone had told Jessica to wait between kids, and to not have them so young. Before they even graduated, she was pregnant. Now at twenty-five, Jessica was married with three kids, but William was a good guy.

Cassie placed the food on the barbeque as Jessica came over.

"They're trying to be quiet."

"I really don't need to hear this."

"Sometimes you are such a prude, Cassie. I'm surprised you've not taken a chance at Slade. You've got to admit, he's hot."

She turned toward her friend and frowned. "Join his endless queue of women vying for a spot on his bedpost? No thank you."

"Not everyone is going to be like Andrew, okay?"

Cassie sighed, and didn't say anything else.

Andrew was a sore subject for her. He was the guy that had used her for a bet with one of his buddies. Cassie hadn't known all of his feelings were fake. Not only had she given him her virginity, she'd also told him that she loved him.

Her final year of high school had been a nightmare.

The truth had come out on that first day when they returned. Andrew had used her in a popularity contest. He'd gotten the fat, trailer girl to love him.

Since then, she'd not been with anyone, and refused to even date. Men were all the same. After seeing her father, and then Andrew, she'd observed men at the sheriff's office, and decided none of them were worth it.

****

Slade drank his coffee while watching the receptionist organizing the main area of the department. They were a little town, so besides some of the drunk and disorderly, the occasional break in, or some parents wanting to teach their kids a lesson, they were rarely busy. Still, Cassie Love had to keep things pristine. He'd noticed this about her, and Daniel didn't have a problem with having a clean environment.

Even his own desk had been cleaned when he'd been out at a job. Sipping his hot coffee, he watched as she bent over, admiring the fullness of her ass. The skirt Cassie wore molded to every single curve, as did the white blouse, enhancing her large tits. He'd give anything to have her bent over the desk, or at least to mess up all of that neatness.

Cassie was made to be fucked, to be worshipped, but he had yet to see that ever happen.

"Is there a reason you're ogling the staff?" Daniel

asked, standing at his own doorway.

Slade wasn't even embarrassed that he'd gotten caught. It wasn't the first time.

"Yeah, she looks pretty today." But then he thought she looked pretty every single day. Coming to work, knowing he was going to see Cassie was a highlight of his day.

Daniel sighed. "Don't upset her."

"I never do."

"Really? Because I've been hearing talk in town that you're not the most considerate of neighbors."

"What? Has she complained?" Slade moved across to go into Daniel's office. Cassie would come if they were needed.

"Just what I heard in the diner for breakfast. Jessica, her friend, was gossiping about you screwing some woman in the backyard."

Slade smiled. Darla had kept him entertained over the weekend. She was a regular at the gym and had been panting after him for some time. He'd needed the release, so it was just easy to take home what was offered. Of course, when Sunday night came, and he'd had his fill, he'd kicked her ass to the curb.

He hated it when women seemed to get dreams in their eyes that they had no right to get. Slade was honest and upfront with every person he was with. He fucked, and he loved to do it. His dick liked a variety of pussy, and there was no way he was settling down. At thirty-six, he'd tried to settle down, but it just wasn't for him. He'd never cheated on a woman in his life, though. The relationship had gone sour when he was younger because he just couldn't handle turning into a bore. His girlfriend had gone from kinky to straitlaced sex the moment he'd put an engagement ring on her finger. His parents' marriage had been a shambles. His mother was miserable with his father's constant cheating. His father hated his mother because he felt trapped in the marriage. It always pissed Slade off because his father was just as much to blame, and yet at times it was like his father blamed him and his mother.

Growing up in that shit had been a nightmare. When he saw the same thing repeating for him, he had to get out, so he broke off the engagement, and hadn't been serious about a woman since.

"I wasn't seen." And the moment he'd heard kids, he'd lost all desire to fuck. Taking his little party inside, he'd been unable to focus. Hearing Cassie laugh had drawn him to watch her in the garden. He wondered if she even knew that from his bedroom there was the perfect view of her backyard. Many nights he'd spent watching her. She was the one woman who didn't fawn all over him or try to impress him. She was always polite to him.

He'd done everything he could to try to get a rise out of her. Fucking women in his backyard when he knew she was out there had been part of it as well. Just once, he wanted to see her lose control.

"It doesn't reflect well on me or that badge. I don't want my office to be made a laughingstock, do you understand me?"

"Yes, I do, and I won't. Good. It just so happens that Jessica is a gossip, so it's not that big of a deal, but please consider me when you act next time."

Slade took pride in his badge, and he'd never do anything to disrespect it.

"So, erm, what's Cassie's deal?" he asked.

Not once had she complained about him, and it made him wonder whether or not she was even real. No one was that good, or that ignorant. There had to come a point where she'd just snap at him.

"What do you mean?" Daniel shoved a file into a stack.

"You know, she's very secretive, and I notice you're protective of her."

Daniel sighed. "It's ... complicated."

"I can handle that." Slade took a seat and looked across the desk. Daniel rubbed the back of his head.

"She didn't have the best time growing up. Her mother bailed when she was ten, and the only good thing her dad could do was get drunk and arrested. Most of her weekends were spent here. Each time her father would promise it was the last time, but still she was here. I watched as her belief turned to acceptance. He'd say the same stuff, and I knew she didn't believe him. The light in her eyes died a little more. It didn't help that kids could be cruel. After a time, I think Cassie just stopped caring."

Slade saw that Daniel felt responsible for her. "She doesn't trust easily."

"No. I don't ever expect her to either."

"Is the dad still in the picture?"

"No. Cassie's a good woman."

Slade knew she was a kind woman. No one had anything bad to say about her, apart from the whole trailer trash comment. He didn't really listen to that shit. Cassie was a hard, dedicated worker.

Daniel trusted her, and so did Slade.

"I'm not paid to gossip about my employees. Get to work, Slade."

He was dismissed. Leaving Daniel's office, he made his way to the coffee machine. His own drink was cold. Cassie was staring at a computer screen with a pen in her hand. She had on a pair of glasses, which made her look so damn sexy. Her brown hair was tied into a bun at the base of her neck.

The way she looked reminded him of the librarians in porn flicks. Any minute now she would let out a sex tigress, but alas, that didn't happen either.

"Do you need anything?" she asked, her gaze landing on him even though her head didn't move. She had that way of assessing that seemed to turn him on.

Yeah, your lips around my dick.

"I hear Jessica was gossiping about me today," he said.

"What about?"

"The noises coming out of my house over the weekend."

Her cheeks went a nice pink.

"Did I disturb you?" he asked, trying for innocence.

"Not at all. You've done nothing to disturb me."

She'd heard him all right. What he'd give to just have her come out and say shit to him. He wouldn't mind at all.

"Really? Because I thought those kids that came around were a little loud." He loved kids, and he'd not minded their presence. Hearing Cassie's laugh had been refreshing. Of course, seeing her in a bathing costume had also awakened a fire in him that he couldn't put out.

Cassie sat back, staring at him. "You're really going to complain about my friend's kids?"

"Why not? They were loud. Next time keep the noise down."

She didn't say anything. Her eyes didn't even shoot a glare in his direction. Turning his back toward her, he headed back to his office.

"Sure, the next time I hear you screwing, I'll make sure to have it reported. I'm sure there's some violation you're participating in."

Her fighting talk made him smile, and it gave him

exactly what he wanted.

Walking back toward her, he leaned against her desk. Slade wanted her to be interested in him. He didn't know what it was about her, but she got right under his skin, and made him ache in ways no other woman ever had. He never played where he worked, but not only was Cassie near him during the day, she was there at night. They lived right next door, and it was hard to ignore her, especially as she had this raw sexuality about her that made him want to get down and dirty. She tried to hide it in her conservative suits, and tight buns, but he saw it. Even as her cheeks went a little pink, she licked her lips, and he knew she was curious about him, even if she didn't want to be.

"You know, at any time you want to be the woman making some noise with me, all you have to do is say so. I've got room on my schedule."

"With all due respect, Slade, you're a walking, talking, advertisement for sexual diseases. I'd rather never have sex again." She turned her back on him, dismissing him.

She said that now, but she was fighting a losing battle.

Chapter Two

Cassie couldn't deny that Slade was a good-looking guy, but he also knew it. He was way too cocky, and she didn't like him. Even though he was pretty to look at, she wasn't falling for him. She knew he was a player as well, and she had heard the evidence with her own ears.

Running the pen along her lip, she couldn't help the way her body awakened at the thought of his touch. It was wrong. After being with Andrew and losing a part of herself to him, she'd vowed to never be with anyone else. Growing up all she had ever wanted was kids and a family, a home, but she had changed her mind. There was no way she could trust a man again.

"You're still here?" Daniel asked. "Don't you go out to lunch?"

She jumped as she turned to look at the sheriff. Seeing that a couple of hours had passed, her cheeks heated, and she jumped up. "I'm so sorry. Time flew by, and I didn't even realize." She'd been too busy daydreaming about Slade, and she was going to snap right out of it.

He was a player, and she meant what she said, a walking, talking sexual disease.

Leaving the sheriff's office, she made her way toward the diner where her meatball sub was waiting for her. She loved meatballs with pretty much anything. Paying for her sandwich, she left the diner and headed toward the park near the lake. Taking a seat at the bench, she unwrapped her lunch, and took a bite. Closing her eyes, she released a moan as the flavors of the onion, garlic, tomatoes, and beef exploded in her mouth.

She loved her food, so much.

"This is where you come to?" Slade asked.

Opening her eyes, she watched as the object of her thoughts took a seat beside her. She frowned. "Did I invite you to eat lunch with me?" she asked, feeling like a bitch but really needing to keep him away from her.

"Nope. I invited myself, and I have to say, I'm not disappointed. I've been curious about where you disappear to." He looked around at the other families that came to the park to each lunch.

Taking another bite of her sandwich, she tried to ignore his presence. Lunch was something she enjoyed so much. She loved her food, and right now, he was invading her space.

"You're not going to talk to me?" Slade asked.

She glanced at him as he unwrapped his own sandwich, which looked like roasted beef with onions and peppers, and lots of cheese.

"That's fine. I can deal with the silence. It makes a refreshing change actually. Women usually talk my ear off. It can get quite irritating."

Gritting her teeth, she kept on ignoring him, refusing to say a word to the man beside her even as she felt rude.

"I mean, women love to talk a whole lot, don't you think? Usually it's them begging me to do stuff to their bodies, to make them scream a li—"

"Don't you have anyone else to each lunch with?" she asked, caving as the images he was giving her were just too much.

"So you *do* speak. I knew I'd get something that would make you give in. Talking about sex unnerves you. I find that really interesting."

She sighed, and slid down the bench to try to put some distance between herself and his very hard body. She was never affected like this by anyone else, and right now, it was driving her crazy that he was getting under her skin.

Was something in the air? Had there been some gas released? Her hormones were all over the place, and she was hating it.

"It doesn't unnerve me. I don't need to hear about what you do with other women, or any woman." She took a bite of her sandwich, and watched the families as they were having fun. Lunchtime always evoked these feelings inside her. She felt like she was missing out on something. Her father never brought her to the park, or taken her out to lunch. From a young age, she'd had to learn to do everything herself.

The pain struck her hard, and she rubbed her chest, aware that the dreams she had as a little girl would never come to pass. In all of her twenty-five years, she had learned one thing: men were never to be trusted.

Daniel was the only exception to the rule. He'd been like a father figure when he needed to be. Still, it didn't help that it only served to remind her that her own father preferred the bliss at the bottom of the bottle. For many years she'd thought she could help him, to get him to stop. He'd not always been addicted to the bottle. Sure, when her mother was mean, he'd drink, telling her it was easier to numb the pain. Her mother was her dad's greatest weakness.

"Then come out on a date with me. I'll show you what a really good time is."

She turned toward him, and glared. "I have no interest in dating you, Slade, nor being anything other than neighbors, or colleagues. Please, try to bug someone else." Thinking about her father had taken her appetite. Wrapping the half uneaten sub, she stood up, and carried it back to work with her. She couldn't throw anything away, food especially.

"Wait, wait, wait."

She hadn't made it more than three steps when Slade stopped her, grabbing hold of her arm.

It was then that she realized neither of them had touched before, and she didn't like how good his hand felt on her elbow. Using every single ounce of strength she owned, she didn't flinch away from his touch. She stared at him and waited.

"I don't want to make you uncomfortable."

"Then stop screwing women while I'm in the backyard." She watched his reaction, and she just knew in her gut that he did it on purpose. "You know I'm outside relaxing and yet you do it anyway. Why?"

"I'm an asshole."

"That's no damn excuse. Do it again, Slade, and I swear I'll call Daniel!" She went to storm away, but she tripped on a patch of earth, and would have landed face first if Slade hadn't caught her.

"Women are always falling at my feet, but you do it so gracefully."

Her heart was racing, especially as his muscular arms were wrapped around her, holding her close. Licking her lips, she stared at him, and hated that her body felt alive with his touch, and they hadn't even been touching anywhere inappropriate.

"I wasn't falling."

"I know. You were trying to make a really good exit, and you have a really nice ass to watch walk away."

"Is this what you're all about? Laughing, joking, not being real?"

"Life is too short not to live it. You need to stop being that virginal goddess that you like, and start being adventurous."

"You mean taking you up on your offer?" she asked, already hating that she'd fallen in front of him.

"I can show you a few moves that will make your

head spin."

"You're the best thing that has happened to me, Cassie. I'll love you for the rest of my life."

Those were the words she had believed of Andrew when he'd spilled them from his lips. She had believed him, and that had been her biggest mistake, and it wasn't going to happen again. Her vow of being with no one would stay. Even if her body did want Slade, she wasn't going to have him.

Pulling out of his arms, she didn't even say anything. Grabbing her wrapped sandwich from the ground, she left him standing there, refusing to say another word. When she was back behind her desk, she tapped her fingers on the desk, and wished she could think of somewhere else for her to be.

"You okay?" Daniel asked, coming out of his office.

"Yeah, I'm fine. I had lunch." She stared at the screen, knowing that Slade would be coming in any minute. "Actually, I'm not feeling so good today. Is it okay if I take off early, and head home?"

Daniel nodded. "Sure. You keep hours that I can't even pay you for. You're a hard worker, Cassie. Go home, relax, and enjoy the sun. I heard a storm is heading our way."

"Thank you."

She grabbed her bag, and was out the door, already walking home. Her stomach was twisting, and she didn't like how Slade had gotten under her skin. She wanted nothing to do with him, not now, not ever.

He was a dangerous man who used women for his own amusement. She'd seen some of the women he played with come to the office with a cake, or some other concoction in the hopes of tempting him.

Cassie wouldn't be that woman, no matter how

much he could make her body sing.

       ****

Rubbing his chin, Slade watched as Cassie dragged out a chair, and then took a seat. She had sunglasses on, and a book rested on her stomach. The one-piece bathing costume was still so conservative, but it showed off her figure nicely. He never saw her wear it anywhere else but in her backyard.

If he ever told her that he'd seen it, he knew she wouldn't wear it again. What was it about this woman that seemed to have question marks all about her? Daniel rarely talked about her, and no one would gossip with him as he was still considered an outsider, given he'd only been in town for a few years. All he did know was that she had a deadbeat dad who was no longer in the picture. She'd grown up in a trailer park. Maybe that was it. He needed to visit her old home and see if anyone would like to talk.

He'd gladly pay for the information because he wanted to know as much about her as he could.

She tucked her long brown hair behind her head and settled down. He loved the little wriggle she did, her hand going to the book on her stomach as her knee lifted up. She hadn't started reading yet, but she would.

There was nothing else for him to do today, so he was just going to enjoy the view.

Actually, he wanted to talk to her, and he knew how to do it without her moving an inch. He entered his backyard, and went to the bottom at the far end, where the fence panel lifted up. He'd discovered this a few months ago when he'd been painting.

The previous owner had told him about the little curse or blessing, whichever it was, of the single people who moved into these houses, ending up together. Slade didn't believe in bullshit like that, and he lifted up the panel, entering her garden.

Now he was trespassing, but he needed to know why she had left work early yesterday. He had every intention of talking to her about it after he'd given her time to cool off. When he got back to the office, Daniel said that she wasn't feeling well.

It was probably the first lie he had caught her in, and he was shocked. He didn't think for a second that Cassie could lie to Daniel. Still, Slade wanted to know if it was him, and he wanted to make shit right between them.

There was a seat beside her, and he took it.

"Why are you here?" she asked, surprising him when she spoke, and didn't freak out.

"You knew I was here?"

"I saw that fence when I first moved in. The previous owner told me all of its secrets. I didn't expect you to use it." She pushed her glasses up onto her head. "What do you want?"

He watched as she folded her arms, trying to hide her curvy body from his gaze.

"You can relax. I'm not a rapist. I only do willing women."

"I didn't think for a second that you'd do anything like that."

"You didn't?" he asked, somewhat shocked by that revelation. He figured she thought the worst of him no matter what.

"Just because I think you're a jerk doesn't mean I think you're a rapist. I've heard the women you've been with, Slade. They're there because they want to be." She shrugged. "What I don't understand is why you're in my garden." She sat up, leaning forward, and it caused a little gap between her breasts. Damn, those beauties had his cock getting hard.

He usually had a lot more self-control than this.

"Why did you run?"

"I don't know what you're on about."

Slade stared at her and saw she was lying. Her cheeks were red. "You didn't want to see me yesterday after what was said. Why?"

"I don't feel comfortable being around a guy who can only make everything about sex. That's not who I am. I'd really like for you to go now." She moved her legs to the side and stood.

He got up as well and noticed how much smaller than him she was. She was so curvy, and he wanted to get his hands on her. He liked that she wasn't afraid to eat either. Before he invaded her lunch the other day, he'd seen the enjoyment she had of her food. Some of the women he'd been with had all done the whole calorie counting and refusing to eat food. He really didn't give a fuck if a woman wanted a dressing with her salad, or if she wanted the last piece of fried chicken.

Life was too damn short to put everything off or to deny yourself what you really wanted.

He loved to play, and he intended to live every single day to the fullest.

"I noticed you don't go on any dates."

"You're confusing me right now. You're invading my garden because you want me to go on dates?" She frowned at him, holding the book to her chest as if it was some kind of lifeline.

"Look, I know that your dad was this big, giant asshole, but you don't need to keep walking around with a stick up your ass."

Slade regretted it as soon as he said it.

When he was around Cassie, he didn't seem to get his shit together, and now it was making him put his fucking foot in his mouth.

"Wow, I mean, really, wow. You think because you've talked about me to random people that you have a right to tell me to live *my* life the way *you* think I should. What's the matter, Slade? Not used to a woman not being interested in you?" She looked him up and down, and smirked.

"I don't have a problem with a woman not wanting me, but believe me, you're not one of them." He stepped toward her. "You want me, which is what pisses you off. You don't want to, I'll give you that, but make no mistake, Cassie, your pussy wants me."

Before he could stop her, she slapped him around the face. "Get out of my garden. You're a pig, and there's no way I'd ever fall for you. You're a horrible excuse for a human being." She turned on her heel and stormed into her house.

Gritting his teeth, he was about to head back to his own garden, when he stopped. He couldn't allow that to happen between them. She was his neighbor, and he knew she was a nice woman. He'd seen it himself with other people, how she'd always help anyone in need, from helping an old lady across the road, to listening to people moan even when she didn't have the time.

They had gotten off on the wrong foot.

He wasn't a monster, and his mother would be so pissed at him because of how he'd spoken to Cassie, no matter how she reacted to him.

Come on, Slade, get a fucking grip.

Before he could question himself, he made his way back into her house, and found her in the kitchen, pouring herself a drink.

"I'm sorry," he said. "I don't know why I said that stuff, but I didn't mean it, and I'm sorry."

She turned toward him with a glass to her lips. He watched as she removed the glass and licked those beauties that would look so good wrapped around his dick.

Wrong thought.

"I'm sorry for hitting you." There was a pause, and he saw her cheeks were a little red. "Would you like a drink? I made a fresh batch of peach tea."

"I'd love some."

She got him a glass and handed it to him. "Here you go."

He took the glass and had a drink. It was really nice, sweet, fruity, and refreshing.

"I'm not always so rude."

"And I'm not always so blunt or violent." She moved so that the island was between them. He watched her as she drank. Her gaze kept landing on his. "I'm kind of embarrassed right now. For some strange reason, our conversations seem to move to sex."

"I'm a jerk. Blame me." This made her smile. "Did you hear about the supposed curse with this house?"

"You mean the couples before us? The ones that have ended up being married?" she asked.

"That's the one."

"I think we're safe and sound with that. We can barely stand each other." She stared at her glass, and he hated it.

He didn't like the silence or the awkwardness between them. They were both better than that.

"Look, I know we got off on the wrong foot, but we also work together. I'm sorry for being mean, and I appreciate that you didn't call Daniel about the noise. I won't do it again."

She smiled. "Thank you. I do appreciate that. I won't ignore you, and I want to apologize for being a bitch. I'm not usually like that."

"I also want to say sorry about commenting about your dad. I don't know who he was, or anything about you. I'm sorry."

She held her hand out. "Then it's very nice to meet you, Mr. Coal."

Slade didn't hesitate. He took her hand and gave it a shake, smiling as he did. "Friends?"

"More like neighbors without attitude," she said.

"I can live with that." He finished his tea, and then let himself out of the back of the house.

There was no way he was going to be fixing that fence piece. Something told him he was going to be using it a whole lot more.

Chapter Three

A few days later

Cassie left the grocery store. Her trolley was completely full of groceries, and she may have gone a little overkill on some of the bargains. Oh well, she could bake up a storm to take to the care home, or the diner. There were plenty of people at her old trailer park that would appreciate the food that she made.

She loved cooking. The biggest problem was she couldn't eat it all. This was another reason she had hoped to have a huge family someday. Her love of cooking and baking would come in pretty handy. As it was, that didn't look like it was going to be anytime soon.

Pulling her cell phone out, she started to scroll through her contacts until she found a cab company to come and take her home.

"What are you doing?" Slade asked. He stood in front of her, a small brown bag in his arms.

"I'm calling a cab to take me home."

"I'm right here. I can take you home."

It had been a few days since their little encounter in her backyard, and everything seemed to be going smoothly between them. His asshole comments had diminished to almost nothing. Of course, when women came into work wanting to speak to him, she had to listen to him very politely explain his situation. He didn't date … ever.

There was a time she'd felt bad for them until she heard from Jessica that Slade was known for being very upfront. He offered a good time, and nothing else. It was the women determined to change his mind that seemed to be the biggest problem. This only served to make her feel like the worst human being in the world for judging him. She hadn't known anything else, and instantly assumed the worst of him.

Still, she found it sad, but then she knew why Slade was going through it. After what happened with Andrew, she wouldn't believe or trust anyone else with her heart. Yet, she didn't have much choice in the matter, not really. She'd love to have an experience where there was no risk of falling in love. Was it possible to just have fun? To find a guy and to literally fuck?

"Are you okay? You look all lost in thought?"

Pulling out of her own arousal, she smiled. "A ride would be great, thank you."

She pushed the trolley toward his car, and was surprised as he took control, placing her bags in the trunk of his car.

When the trolley was empty, she moved it back into one of the bays, and then climbed in the front of his car. This was the first time she had been in his car, and it was kind of strange to her, and yet completely intimate.

"So, how have you been?" he asked.

"I've been good. You?"

"Great, really great. Did you walk to the store?"

"Yep. I enjoy the walk. Especially as it felt like it was going to be a really nice day." She lowered the window to allow some air in the car. He pulled out, and they were heading back to their own home. She waved at a couple of people as they passed. "I saw a couple of women stop by your place yesterday. Why were they going to trash your car?"

She'd held the phone in her hand, when she saw one of the women begin to kick his tire. It was kind of scary, the evil look in their eyes.

"They didn't take kindly to me turning them down."

"Ah, I can understand that."

"You can?"

"No woman wants to be turned down."

"I didn't the first time, but I'm always clear. It's sex, and nothing else. I'm not a bad guy in this."

"I didn't say you were, Slade. Ugh, okay, I thought you were, but I was wrong, and I'm sorry. Yes, I'm getting to eat humble pie, and I can see from that look on your face you're very happy with all of this."

"Totally. It's nice to hear a woman admit when she's wrong about someone."

"I've heard that you're a very open and honest kind of guy. Some women just want to be the one that changes your mind."

"You ever done that?" Slade asked.

"What? Changed someone's mind? Nah, nor would I want to. That's up to someone else."

"So you don't do relationships?" he asked.

"Nope." She hadn't done one for a long time.

He pulled up onto his drive, and they climbed out.

Cassie waited for him to open the trunk of his car, and when he paused, seeming frozen in time, she looked at him. He was staring at her.

"What?"

"You know about the whole neighbors to lovers thing?"

"Yeah."

"Do you think it started with a car ride?"

Cassie burst out laughing. "Nah, I think it started out as a hell of a lot more. Maybe there were some car rides, and then spending time together, being with each other every single day, decorating. Before long there's no dates appearing, and then bam, they're the ones having sex. I wouldn't worry, Slade. I do not for a second think that one car ride home, and we're heading down the aisle."

He started laughing as well. She grabbed several

bags, and as she went for a third, Slade waved her off.

"I'll bring them in."

"Excellent, thanks."

She entered her home and went straight to the kitchen. The natural light was something she loved about the house. Opening the back doors to let more fresh air in, she placed the bags on the counter, and began to empty them out.

"Are you expecting a party or something?"

"I know. I'm a sucker for a bargain, and all of this cost me like half the price." She was used to growing up with nothing, so she had a thing now that she made sure there was enough to eat in the house. "It'll be fine."

"If you need any help eating your way through this, give me a holler. I'm an expert eater, and I love food."

She giggled. "I may hold you to that."

"Right, I better get my own steaks in the fridge." He was just leaving, pulling open a door when the handle snapped off. "Well, shit," he said.

She winced. "Yeah, that's been wobbly for some time. I have to say repairing door handles is not my forte."

"I've got a spare. Let me go and grab one. I'll fix the damage."

"Okay. I'll leave the door unlocked."

By the time Slade got back with a little toolkit in hand, she had put everything away, and was making herself a salad.

"Do you want some lunch?" she asked. "I could grill up some shrimp, and make it something a bit more than some leaves of salad?"

"Absolutely. I'm starving."

While he fixed her door handle, she finished up the tomato-mozzarella salad, with a basil dressing. She quickly cooked up some shrimp and tossed it through the mixture adding some arugula to finish. She served them up just as Slade got done.

She placed their meals on a plate, with some iced tea, and they agreed to eat in the yard.

Cassie sat down, pushing her hair off one shoulder before reaching for her plate. "The only problem with the summer is keeping up with everything." She had to mow her lawn and weed through her vegetable patch.

"What do you do with all your vegetables?" he asked. "There's more there than you can use."

"I can." Her cheeks heated as she admitted to the old-fashioned skill.

"Really? Wow, you can. I thought that was still pretty outdated. You know we have stores all around with canned goods."

She started laughing. "There is just something about homemade. Also, I'm kind of a doomsdayer at times. I worry that if I don't learn that skill, one day soon, I'm going to need it. Besides, I enjoy it. On the last day of harvest, I gather my vegetables, and take it indoors, planning over the weekend how I'll do it. It's fun." She tried not to cringe for a second time that day. Canning is fun? It's like saying taking glass out of your foot is fun. Her hobbies were lame to the average person.

"You know what, I may have to see this in actual action."

"You want to see me canning?"

"I'll have to see it to believe it."

"I could show you my pot, and my jars." They were all in her pantry ready for the day.

They finished their lunch, and she took him inside, showing off the big canning pot, and then she moved a bit further down, for him to see some of the jars from last year's canning event. "See, I told you. I'm kind of weird like this."

He picked one up that read salsa. "This was made from all ingredients you'd grown?"

"Yep. Pretty awesome if I do say so myself. It's great with tortilla chips."

"Can I take it?" he asked.

At first she was going to say no, but then she realized she was only being silly. "Sure. I hope you enjoy it."

****

The salsa had been amazing with tortilla chips. He'd eaten the entire jar by the time Monday arrived, and he had to ask for more. Before heading into work though, he took a little detour toward the trailer park area. Slade had been around here a few times, and it didn't seem real to him for Cassie to have grown up here.

She was always so neat, so tidy, so clean. He'd noticed that her house didn't even have a speck of dust. Her pantry was the cleanest he'd ever seen. She was even better than his mother at organizing stuff.

"Is someone in trouble, deputy?"

He turned to see an older woman sitting in the shade, knitting something in her lap.

"No one is in trouble. Have you lived here long?" he asked, moving toward her.

"My entire life. You can have a seat. No one is afraid of you. It's been a long time since we saw you out here, deputy."

He took a seat opposite her and stared out across the entire park. "Do you remember a Cassie Love?"

"The Love family. I do remember them. Her father was such a nice guy when he first moved here. His wife … not so much. I mean, everyone thought the wife was a sweetheart, but she wasn't. She always had men over every single day, and on occasion Bill caught her."

"Bill?"

"Bill Love. It's Cassie's father. Of course, they would scream, and rave. Her mother would throw stuff around, and Cassie would sit out on the grass over there as they fought. Bill would forgive, and then it would all happen again. Then one day, a car came. Something fancy, and I watched as Cassie's mother took a bag, kissed her daughter on the head, and left without a backward glance. It was a really fancy car as well. She had left for a better life, not even taking her daughter."

Slade wasn't liking this little tale.

"Not long after that, Bill started to get drunk. He wasn't physically mean, but sometimes we'd hear him rant and rave at Cassie. Saying it was all her fault. I never saw a man go downhill so fast. Cassie had to live with a lot." The older woman tutted. "Then one summer before senior year, we saw a nice young man coming 'round. He was treating her all good like. We knew Cassie was falling in love, and that she had it bad for this kid."

Slade didn't like the jealousy that sprang upon him at the thought that Cassie could love someone else.

"What happened?"

The older woman sighed. "He broke Cassie's heart. Told her it was all part of some bet, and not only did he get to fuck the trailer trash, he got to pop her cherry. Ray made sure that boy didn't come around again." She pointed to another trailer, three down from hers. "Cassie still comes around. She's always bringing us her baked goods."

"What happened to her dad?"

"Don't know. He skipped town when Cassie graduated. A couple of us went to see her. Me and Ray included. We saw her graduate, and it was a proud moment."

Slade saw how proud she was. There was no hiding that look.

"Well, I think I've said everything that needs to be said. I need to go and take a nap."

Before he could ask for any more information, she was gone.

Seeing no point in staying, he made his way back to the sheriff's office. Daniel had promised him that he'd be sheriff as soon as Daniel was ready to retire. Of course, Daniel had also warned him that he needed to get the town to love him, and to want him for the position first. Slade had a lot of work to do to get where he wanted to be, but he loved the challenge. Slade had no intention of leaving or finding a job elsewhere. He was content to be a deputy in a small town.

Entering the office, he saw Cassie was on the phone, so he gave her a smile, and headed back into Daniel's office where he found his boss signing off on a few things.

"You had a productive morning," Daniel said without even looking up. "Talking to some people in the trailer park." He finished signing a sheet of paper before looking up.

Taking a seat, he stared at Daniel. "I was asking some questions is all."

"What about?"

Gritting his teeth, Slade got up, and closed the door. "I was asking a few questions about Cassie. She's my neighbor, and I was curious about her."

Daniel tilted his head to the side. "Why didn't you ask her?"

"I didn't want any trouble."

"You think talking about her behind her back won't cause trouble?" Daniel leaned back in his chair.

"You have no idea about women, do you?"

"I know a great deal I'll have you know. What do we know about the asshole that hurt her?"

Daniel laughed, and Slade didn't know why. As far as he was concerned, this wasn't any laughing matter. He wanted to know what the fuck the bastard found funny.

"Wow, do you believe in that little curse that's on your two houses?"

"No, I don't. I wanted to know more about Cassie. She's so uptight, and she doesn't date. I just … can't a guy have some curiosity?"

Daniel sighed. "I guess you're right. The fucker's name was Andrew. He doesn't live around here anymore. His dad still does. They own one of the big factories."

"They're one of the rich families?"

"You got it."

Slade sat back.

"And I don't want Andrew back anytime soon. I saw what it did to Cassie after that bastard broke her heart. He used her for what he could get, which was points in a damn game. Last I heard, and from what I've seen, Cassie has never dated since."

"I don't like the fucker." And Slade didn't even know him.

"You don't have to like him. You want to know why Cassie doesn't get close to anyone, then I'd say Andrew is a pretty big reason. After being dumped, and your entire … experience gossiped about time and time again, I'd say you'd be very … careful next time."

"What about her dad?" Slade asked. He wanted answers, and he wanted them fast.

Daniel leaned forward. "You want to tell me why you're asking all these questions?"

"I told you. I want to know more about my

neighbor." There was no other reason.

"Right, okay. If you must know I tracked Bill down myself."

Slade waited, curiosity eating away at him.

"He's dead. I went and identified him myself. Got into a fight in the city, and it went ugly. Ended with a bottle being smashed and jammed into his throat. It was an ugly way to die, but I had a feeling that Bill was making sure someone killed him."

"She doesn't know?"

"Nope. She doesn't."

Running a hand down his face, Slade couldn't help the feelings that were rushing through him. He felt bad, and angry, also sad for her. She hadn't lived a great life. In fact, from everything he'd been told, her life had been incredibly shit.

"Is this why you're protective of her?"

Daniel shook his head. "I'm protective of her because behind all the bullshit you see, and the bitchy attitude, she's a very kind woman. She gets hurt way too easily."

The phone on Daniel's desk started to ring.

Without being told to leave, Slade was already gone, closing the door behind him. Moving up toward the main desk, he saw Cassie eating some kind of pasta salad.

She was staring at her screen and doing some typing.

"Mrs. O'Ryan called again. She said that aliens are attacking her field, and that if you don't come soon, they're going to impregnate her." Cassie smiled over at him.

"Just another day in the office."

"She went into a great deal of details. You'd have loved it." Cassie held out her food. "Want some? It's a

Caprese pasta salad. Really good."

He took the bowl and the fork from her hands and took a bite. The flavors were amazing, and he leaned against the wall.

"So, I was wondering what you're doing Friday night?" he asked.

"Me? I don't know. Probably read or something."

"Well, I know this really great movie that I picked up the other day. It's supposed to be really good."

Cassie turned to look at him. "You're inviting me to watch a movie?"

"Why not? I'm being generous here. It could be a scary movie."

"Very true." She chuckled. "Fine, fine. I'll grab some popcorn. When will you be playing it?"

"At around eight o'clock. You think you can make it for then?" he asked. Why was he doing this? Asking her out to watch a movie. It wasn't a big deal. Not really. He could ask a woman out to watch a movie.

He'd intended to spend the night by himself, drinking a few beers, and just relaxing. There was nothing wrong with having a bit of company.

"I'll be there."

Slade handed her back the empty bowl. "I can't wait." What made it even worse for him, was the fact he really couldn't wait.

Chapter Four

The movie was great, Cassie thought the following day. She had gotten a couple of bags of popcorn, and it had been funny as well. Slade took care of the ice cream, and it had been a lot of fun.

She released a chuckle as she took out another weed, thankful she had on gloves as it looked like another stinger. Her vegetable patch hadn't been cared for the past week, and she was regretting it. The fruits of her labors were doing really well, but she should have taken care of those weeds. She didn't like to use chemicals though, so that wouldn't have done. The sun was shining, but there was another storm heading their way. She wanted to get as much done this afternoon as she could so she didn't have to worry.

"What are you doing?" Slade asked, opening the loose fence.

"You really need to fix that."

"Why? It's not like you're answering your front door. This came for you?" He held up a box, and she frowned.

"I've not ordered anything."

"I guess you won something?" Slade asked.

She shrugged. "Not that I'm aware of." Moving out of her vegetable patch, she took the box, and began to open it. When she couldn't open it, Slade took a blade, and ran it across the edge. "You carry a knife?"

"It's not that big, but it's perfect for opening pesky packages."

Opening the box, her cheeks heated, and she quickly closed it up.

"What is it?" Slade asked.

"It's a gift from my friend Jessica." Whom she would kill when she next saw her.

Slade took the box from her, and she tried to stop him from looking inside, but the damage was done.

"Who would send you a vibrator?"

There was no way she could get any redder than she already was, was there? "It's a joke."

"I don't think it's a joke."

She groaned.

"Are those the sounds you make during sex?"

"No. They're not." She grabbed the vibrator from him and left the box in his hands. Entering her home, she placed the packaged vibrator onto the kitchen counter. She was tempted to throw it in the trash, but Jessica had told her she needed to loosen up a bit. Could the vibrator help with her dreams?

Just recently Cassie had been having a lot of sexual dreams. The guy was always blurred out, but when she was with him, she was happy. The way he touched her body would drive her crazy with even more need.

"Why do you need a vibrator, and who would send it to you?"

She grabbed them both some iced tea. It was way too hot for a conversation like this. "My friend Jessica sent it to me, like I just said, and now that you've overreacted, how about you mow my lawn?" The weeding was a job that was taking her a lot of time. She needed a little bit of help.

"Why would your girlfriend get you a vibrator?" he asked.

If she didn't know any better, she would think he was jealous, which would have to be completely wrong. There was no way he'd feel like that. He had so many women at his beck and call.

"She thinks I need to lighten up. We were talking, and she said that a vibrator would do the job." She patted his chest. "No need to worry."

Leaving the house, she put some distance between them as Slade was starting to look more appealing. She had to remember that he was the fucker that lived next door. He was a horrible man, and yet even as she was thinking all of those things, the past few weeks had been so much fun. They'd even talked. Then she remembered Slade wasn't an awful guy at all. He was a man that women wanted but didn't like that he didn't want them long term. He was no longer such a bad person.

Still, it had only been a couple of weeks, and she imagined he still fucked random women.

He followed her outside, and didn't even wait as he grabbed her lawnmower, and started to help her out. She finished weeding through her vegetable patch, and then checked on her plants to make sure they didn't have any pests or diseases. Happy to see that they were growing, she made her way toward the furniture.

She folded down the deck chairs and carried them to the shed. By the time the sun started to set, her garden was spick and span, and they had finished on Slade's garden. He'd mowed his lawn, and she put down furniture. She wore gloves as she did his garden though. She didn't know what he'd done on the furniture, and it kind of scared her what she'd catch.

"You know I've not fucked on any of this," Slade said, coming out with a bottle of beer.

Cassie took the beer and sipped at it. She wasn't a big drinker. She had seen firsthand how bad alcohol could make a person, and she never wanted to be weak like that.

"You're really crude." And she was happy that her cheeks hadn't gone red. There was a time she would have. The vibrator was a different story.

"I call it what it is. I'm not in the habit of avoiding shit."

"Fair enough. I think we're done. We shouldn't be too badly damaged by the storm." She then glanced at the trees on either side of their property. Some of them were really tall, and it always made her nervous. They had been really lucky so far.

"Will you use it?" Slade asked.

"Will I use what?"

"The vibrator."

She frowned and turned to him. "Isn't that a little personal?"

He shrugged. "Don't care. I think it's important. We're friends, aren't we?"

"Yeah, but I wouldn't ask you if you used a vibrator. Do you use a blowup doll?" she asked.

She didn't like the image of him screwing some poor defenseless doll. It was just not happening for her. "Forget I asked."

Slade burst out laughing. "No, I don't and have never used a blowup doll. They look like something out of a horror movie."

Covering her face, she laughed. "I really, really, shouldn't have asked. I'm sorry."

"Nah, it's fine. It's what friends ask each other all the time, right?"

"I don't know. I've never told Jessica stuff like that before, and I don't think I'd want to know if it was true." She sipped at her beer. "Our work here is done."

Slade looked up at the sky. "Yeah, and it looks like they're going to open up, any second."

"I'm going to head back home. Have a good night."

He was there to lift the fence, helping her.

"Thank you." She gave him one last smile before

heading inside where her phone was ringing. Closing her door, she rushed toward it and picked it up off the cradle. "Hello."

"About time. I was worried there."

"What's up, Jessica?"

"I wanted to make sure you're okay. You know these storms freak you out."

Rain had already started to come down, and Cassie moved to the window in her living room, which overlooked the entire street. Within a matter of minutes, it had gone from being a light drizzle to pouring it down with rain. "I'll be fine. I've handled storms before." She hoped this was the last one of the season as she really hated storms. When she lived in the trailer, it always was louder than ever before, and of course there was a fear she'd be burnt alive if lightning struck the trailer.

Most of the time she spent storms alone, and now wasn't any different.

"What did you do today?"

"Cleaned the garden. Slade helped me, and then we moved to his place, and we cleaned his garden. It all looks great."

In the background, Cassie heard one of the little ones screaming.

"I better go," Jessica said. "If you need me give me a call."

"I will. Thank you."

She replaced her phone and paused as the lights flickered. She would be fine. There was nothing to worry about at all.

Heading upstairs, she took a quick shower. Changing into her pajamas, she settled into bed, turning on the television. She held a pillow tightly, trying to calm her nerves, but nothing was happening. The storm was getting stronger with every passing minute.

When the lights went out, and the electricity went off, she couldn't just stick around in one place. Reaching out for her flashlight, she flicked it on. Her heart was racing as she made her way downstairs.

Every now and again, she released a little scream as another wave of thunder crashed.

Finally, when her doorbell rang, she rushed toward it.

There was Slade, completely soaked, but she threw her arms around him.

"Don't like storms?" he asked.

"Nope. Not at all, and right now I'm totally freaking out."

He carried her inside, closing and locking the door.

"I heard your screams, so I guess it makes sense for us to hang out for a little while. Or at least until the storm dies down."

"You'd do that?"

"Of course, I would. You clearly don't like them."

She shook her head. "I never have. I'm sorry if I disturbed you."

He laughed then. "I wasn't doing anything other than watching a movie, which totally cut out on me."

"Me too. Upstairs."

"Come on, let's grab some of that iced tea you like to keep on hand, and play a game or something."

****

Slade sat in his office and couldn't stop thinking about Cassie. He'd stayed with her the entire night. Every time there was a wave of thunder, he'd seen how nervous she was. In the end, he'd fallen asleep with Cassie in his arms.

When he woke the next morning, she'd still been

there. He'd not freaked out. In fact, for another hour while she slept, he'd simply held her, enjoying the feel of her in his arms. Not for the first time he'd wondered if that was what got men going first. The feel of their woman in their arms.

"You survived the storm?" Daniel asked, standing in his doorway.

"Yep. The power was out, but not for long. Nothing went bad in my freezer."

Cassie had also been concerned for hers. Knowing that when she was growing up, food was often scarce, he'd not said anything. Her freezer had been full, carefully labelled, and was a top quality one that had been able to retain the cold.

"I know some water pipes burst, and a few cables came down. The entire town lost power. Not for the first time, I'm going to recommend you and Cassie getting a generator for your houses. They can be expensive, but if you split the bill, it'll keep your homes running."

"We handled everything quite well." He didn't want to give her power when she was more than happy to accept him into her home.

"Is it starting?" Daniel asked.

"Is what starting?"

"You know, the fall."

"I have no idea what you're talking about."

"The guy before you started out screwing around, having a shitload of fun, and that changed quite quickly when he realized the gem he had living next door."

Slade rolled his eyes. "Nothing is going on. I'm just more of a love thy neighbor than hate her. I don't want her throwing shit bombs over my fence."

Daniel laughed. "Cassie would never do that. Oh well, we'll see. I've got to head out to the old pastor's place. He thinks someone has broken into his church again."

"Okay. I'll man the office." He smiled at Daniel, and watched the older man walk away. There was no way in hell that he was falling for Cassie. He was a guy that loved a variety of women, that loved to fuck.

So he'd not been with a woman in a couple of weeks. That didn't mean anything. He needed time to recuperate. There was no way a guy could be this damn handsome and not need time to gather his strength. He wasn't falling for his neighbor. Sure, he found her cute, and sexy, but that was what he felt for a lot of women. They were cute and sexy.

Running fingers through his hair, he sighed. He was losing his mind, and he had to get laid.

"Four across, something big," Cassie said, coming to his door, and holding a newspaper.

She wore a pair of black pants, and a white shirt. Whenever she was working she always wore something conservative. He'd seen her in jeans, and even a dress when she'd been at home.

Why was he obsessing about what she wore?

Why did he even care?

"My dick. That's big."

She rolled her eyes. "I misread. Something else for big—huge. That's four letters across, and that goes with height, which is down. Yay."

"My dick is huge, just so you know."

"Why does everything have to be about sex with you?"

He shrugged. "Because sex is the what the world revolves around."

"Sounds quite shallow to me. Just saying." She held her hands up.

"Really? You think two people connecting in the most basic way is shallow?" he asked.

"All those women you … dated, did you feel connected to them? Did you have a baser instinct to mate with them? For them to be the mother of your child?"

"Fuck no."

"Then it's all really shallow. You used them to get off."

"And I liked it, and so did they. I have a way of making a woman scream for more."

"Cool. I'll leave you to that."

She left his office and went back behind her desk.

Gritting his teeth, he was determined to prove to everyone that he was not falling for Cassie. She was going to stay in the neighbor column of his life. He didn't want to connect with anyone. He'd seen firsthand what it did to his parents, and he was determined to never settle down.

When it was time to leave, he headed home, and without going to Cassie's place, even though he saw Jessica's car there, he got changed into some jeans, and a shirt, before heading out.

He drove toward the best bar in town, which was out on the high road, and served people from at least five different towns. It was a huge place, that also opened out onto the back, in the summer. Howard's joint served food, beer, and had a live band as well.

Slade had picked up many of his conquests here.

Getting to the bar, he slapped his hands on the counter, and gave Bethany his sexiest smile. "Hello, beautiful, how are you?"

"Well, well, well, I didn't think I'd be seeing Slade Coal again. It's been what, a couple of months now?"

"I've been busy. Had a lot to do."

She smirked, flicked her dyed blonde hair, and winked at him. "Well, honey, you can certainly do me any time you like. You know I love it dirty as can be."

He certainly did, and that woman had taught him a thing or two. She was in her fifties and been divorced seven times already. The irony was, she had divorced her men for cheating on her.

She was also a sweetheart, who saw nothing wrong in having a good time.

"Anything new going on here?" he asked, taking the bottle of beer.

"Nope. Just regulars, and a couple of townies here for a good time."

He checked out the bar, and nearly spat out his beer when he caught sight of Cassie. She was sitting at a table with Jessica, William, and some other guy. He had to wonder who was looking after the kids.

"You know that guy sitting at Jessica and William's table?"

"That's Chuck. He's a rancher that has just been dealing with his cattle. Good friends with William, and rarely comes out to play." Being behind the bar, Bethany was a wealth of information. "It's good to see Cassie here on her own. She was here many times as a young'un, trying to get her father to go home. Of course, he'd send her out, and men would be pissed at how upset she looked. She's doing well for herself."

Now his curiosity was piqued once again. "You know Cassie?"

He turned toward Bethany, wanting all the information he could get.

"Everyone knows Cassie. Her mother was a whore and trapped one of the sweetest men in town."

Slade knew Bethany well enough to see pain in the woman's eyes. "You loved Bill?"

Bethany sighed. "That man was … he was a darling, Slade. He was hard working, and he doted on his little family. Loved Cassie's mother so much. It always broke my heart when I'd see her here, drawing men's gazes. I was emptying the trash out once, and I saw six men taking turns with her, and she was loving it. I was going to make them stop, until I heard her screaming for more. That she wanted it." Bethany shook her head. "For the first time in my life, I really thought I could have been a good woman to Bill and given Cassie an amazing life. She deserved more than the mother had given her. Bill did as well. Anyway, he turned to drink when she left town, and that sweet, hard-working man ceased to exist. He was a fucking nightmare. It broke my heart seeing him fall. I guess in that moment, I realized the power some women have over men. Wow, you've got me gossiping like an old woman, Slade Coal. Now, tell me, why are you so curious about little Cassie?"

"No reason. She's my neighbor, and I work with her. I guess she's a bit of a mystery to me."

That, and he couldn't stop thinking about her. It was starting to drive him insane.

Chapter Five

"You know Slade is here, don't you?" Jessica asked.

"Nope. I haven't seen him."

"Is that because of Chuck? Do you like him?"

Cassie touched up her lipstick and rolled her eyes at her friend. Being on this double date hadn't been what she wanted to do tonight. A good book and some hot chocolate had been on the cards, but Jessica had ordered her out of the house. If she hadn't arrived, her friend had promised to burn her entire bodice ripper collection, not to mention her erotic romance. Cassie did own an e-reader, but she also loved paperbacks, and they were part of her proud collection.

She wasn't risking anything happening to those books, so she was here now, touching up her lipstick, and trying to have a good time. Chuck was nice and all that. He was a rancher, was sweet on the eye, kind, but she also knew he was just after a cook for his ranch.

The last thing she wanted to be doing was stuck on a ranch all day. She loved cooking, cleaning, and relaxing, and none of that included working on a ranch. She had no interest in it, even though she didn't mind Chuck talking about himself.

"If you're hoping for wedding bells, you're so totally wrong." She turned to her friend.

"Chuck doesn't do it for you?"

"He's nice, and I don't mind the dates, but I'm never going to be what he needs."

"A cook?"

"You got it. Sorry. I've not got what it takes to be with him."

Jessica sighed. "When are you going to get over this Andrew nonsense?"

"I have no idea what you're talking about."

"Yeah. You do. From the moment that asshole hurt you—and I get that he did it in the most despicable of ways—you've not let anyone else in. All men are not like Andrew. They're not all going to hurt you."

Cassie blew out a breath. "I'm not doing this because of what happened between me and Andrew. I'm just … I'm not going to lead a man on because of it, or even pretend something could happen between us. I hope Chuck finds what he's looking for. I'm just not it."

They left the bathroom, and Cassie bumped into a large body. Before she fell back, strong arms caught her, and when she looked up, she smiled.

"Well, Jessica told me you were here?" She couldn't help the happiness that flooded her at the sight of Slade, and even his cheeky grin.

"You're here on a date?"

"Yes. Some of my precious possessions were threatened, so I had no choice but to come and party." She patted his chest. "I better go. Have a nice night."

She made her way back to their table and found just William and Jessica there.

"Where's Chuck?" she asked.

"He's stepped outside for a smoke."

Cassie nodded.

"We're going to have a dance. Is that okay?" William asked.

"This is your first time away from the kids in a very long time. Go and have fun. I can amuse myself." She waved them off with a big old smile. Jessica was a great friend, and she loved her so much.

Matchmaking was not Jessica's forte, even though she really was convinced that she was good at it.

Tapping her fingers on the table, Cassie watched the happy couple, and was pleased she had come out, even if being here wasn't exactly something she wanted to do.

"You know, I've always been a sucker for a woman on her own," Slade said, dropping down beside her.

"What are you doing here? I thought you'd be picking up your next bedpost fling."

He covered his heart and looked all wounded. "I'm here to keep my little neighbor company. I was surprised to see you here."

"Shocked that I could actually have some fun?"

"You got it. Totally surprised me."

This caused her to giggle. "I can have some fun."

He stared at her, and she really didn't like what that look he was giving was doing to her body. "You can? How about having a dance?"

"I can dance."

Slade held his hand out. "Then come on. It's a party out there, and instead of being on the sidelines, let's get in."

She placed her hand in his, and within seconds she was on the dance-floor, laughing in his arms. At first, he held her hands, and they did a kind of two step. She was so busy laughing as they were stumbling over their own feet. She forgot everyone else on the dance-floor, as they were suddenly doing some kind of sixties dance with a twist and pull thing. When he pulled her against him, her back was to his front, and his hands were holding her close.

They were swaying their hips, and she was able to look out at the bar, seeing people watch them, and in that moment, she didn't care.

"You know Chuck's after a cook for his ranch, don't you?"

"Yeah, I know. Don't worry. I'm not easily

smitten. I didn't mind coming out on a date though. Sometimes it's nice to dance."

He turned her around, dropped her down with a spin so that her hair grazed the ground, and by the time she was up, chest against chest, the music had changed to a really slow number.

"I have to tell you something, Cassie," he said.

"What is it?"

"I can't dance."

This she found so funny, and she threw her head back laughing. He joined her, and for at least a minute that was all they were doing.

"Well, for a terrible dancer, I'm having a good time. My feet don't hurt at all. You've not stepped on them once." She glanced down, and then smiled back up at him. "See, you're not doing so bad. Don't always be so hard on yourself."

She was loving the feel of his arms being around her, and how much fun she was having. It didn't matter that she was here on a date with someone else. Chuck had left her to have a cigarette, and Slade had asked her to dance. She found him really sweet for asking.

"I, erm, I struggle with men."

"What do you mean?" he asked.

"The whole talking, and dealing with them, and having to … I don't know. I guess I try to put on this show, and it can make me uncomfortable."

"You don't need to put on a show."

"I don't?" she asked.

"No. You can just be yourself, and guys will like you."

Maybe it was the dancing, or the beers she had enjoyed, but Cassie didn't know why she told him about Andrew. Yet she did.

"Before my last year of high school, I, erm, I fell

in love with one of the guys at school. We'd been hanging out all summer, and he was so nice, and sweet. He told me that he loved me, and I'd never felt that way. He didn't judge me, or at least I didn't think he did. It had all been a lie." Cassie looked at him. "I've struggled to trust anyone else after that."

"I don't blame you. Some kids are assholes."

"I've made this really depressing."

"You haven't. I don't think so. Thank you, Cassie, for trusting me with this. It means a lot to me."

The song came to an end, and couples began to make their way onto the dance-floor.

"Thank you for the dance, Slade."

She was leaving when he caught her arm, stopping her.

"Would you like to go shopping with me tomorrow?" he asked.

"Shopping?"

"I need to get my parents an anniversary present. I was thinking of taking a trip to the mall. You don't drive, so if you'd like to go with me, the offer is still there."

"That would be fantastic. I'll be ready."

She pulled away and sat down in her seat. The stench of cigarette smoke was around Chuck, and she found it turned her stomach a little bit. She didn't like cigarettes. Many of her mother's lovers had been smokers. Once they had visited with her mother, fucked her, and stood outside to have a smoke, Cassie had seen them, looking all smug. At the time, she didn't know they were having sex. The rocking of the caravan and her mother's screams had been a game, or so her mother had told her.

"What were you and Slade talking about?" Jessica asked.

"Just some stuff."

"You've got to be careful of Slade. He runs through women faster than pack of wolves chasing a bunny," Chuck said.

She turned to Chuck. "We work together, and I'm aware of how he treats women."

Chuck moved closer and placed an arm across the back of her chair. "So, what do you think of a tour of the ranch?"

****

"How long have they been married?"

"Thirty-six years," Slade said. He glanced over at Cassie, who was scrolling through her cell phone. She had just gotten a text, and he was curious about who she was texting. Instead of asking, he gritted his teeth.

"So, it's not a milestone or anything?"

"They've done the milestone, even though that was a relief in itself." He always found himself cynical around his parents' anniversary. Every year he tried not to be, yet it still happened.

"Why is it a relief?" she asked.

"Because they shouldn't have gotten married. There are a lot of the times when I don't think they even love each other. They put up with each other."

"Thirty-six years is a long time to put up with each other."

"They got married because my mom was pregnant with me."

"Oh."

"Yeah."

"So, you're thirty-six. Ha, I never knew."

He found this funny. "You didn't know my age."

"Nope."

Slade knew her age, and her date of birth, along with the fact that she loved daisies. There were so many growing in her garden, and he had watched her stroke the cute flowers. They were not the small plants either, but the large ones with the huge blossoms.

"They must love each other to still be together."

"My father has had numerous affairs," Slade said. Just saying the words out loud left a bad taste in his mouth. "He didn't love her enough to keep it in his pants."

"And your mother forgave him?"

Slade sighed. "She didn't want me growing up without a father. I don't know. There were so many times that I asked her to just cut and run. She didn't need to stay in a loveless marriage because of me, but she stayed."

"I guess that means she loves him even if you don't see it."

"My mother is quite the looker. When I saw men flirting with her, it's crazy, but I hoped she'd step out on my father, just so he could have a taste of what he did to her." Slade shrugged. "She never did."

"Is this why you sleep with random women?"

"There's no sleeping involved."

This had her chuckling. "Sorry, screw random women."

"Your experience with Andrew keeps men at arms' length."

"I'm not judging you, Slade. Just trying to make sense of who you are. You like sleeping with women, I prefer baking and reading. We all have our ways of coping."

"Your way must be very lonely," he said.

"And yours is any better?" she asked.

"I have sex. That's intimate, close."

"You screw them. I'm not a virgin, Slade. I know there are many different ways to fuck, and many different positions. There are also some that mean you're not close at all. It's just an action, mechanical even. Besides, screwing doesn't make for a connection. Time spent, and enjoying each other, the foreplay in between sex, that's the real deal."

"Now you're quoting one of your romance books?" Slade wasn't entirely sure if he was right or not.

"I'm not. I truly believe that sex isn't just about the whole fucking thing. I think it's about building up. The foreplay."

"This coming from a woman who won't let a guy near her?" he asked.

She laughed. "I've let you, Chuck, and Daniel near me. And there's William of course."

"I'm talking about men who'd get through that icy exterior you like to keep so much."

"Don't worry, Slade, you don't have to do that with me. I can take care of myself."

He glanced over at her as she put her cell phone away.

"Who keeps texting you?"

"Chuck. He wants me to take a tour of his ranch. I told him another time and that I was busy with a friend."

Slade liked that. She had blown off the other guy to spend time with him.

"Did you find any women to give you a good time last night?" she asked.

"Why are we talking about this?"

"You asked about Chuck, and with our newfound friendship, I think it's only fair that we share." She rested her head on his shoulder. "Besides, you know how my night was."

Chuck had offered to drive her home, and she'd accepted. Slade had also arrived at the same time, and he'd made a big show of waving, putting his trash out, and by the time he got into his home, she had already been inside.

"And you know how my night ended. No woman came home with me." He didn't want to think about the why either.

There hadn't been a woman who interested him. When he wasn't talking with Bethany behind the bar, he'd been watching Cassie. He'd not liked the feeling of watching Chuck dance with her. Many times while they'd been dancing, he'd wanted to snatch her out of the fucker's arms.

Finally making it to the mall, he parked on the top carpark where the sun was beaming down.

Cassie was wearing a summer dress, and when he'd seen her this morning, he'd been shocked by how beautiful she'd looked. Her long brown hair was down, and her face was free of makeup. To him, she had still looked so utterly beautiful.

"Do you have any ideas for your parents?" she asked, closing the door, and placing her bag over her shoulder.

"A divorce lawyer."

"What about a picture frame, or some kind of trinket to mark the occasion?"

"I usually send them a figurine of couples dancing." He rubbed the back of his head as they entered the busy shopping mall. "Actually, there's something else I want to ask you."

"Go ahead. You have my complete attention."

"My parents are having a meal, and they've invited me along. I don't want to go alone, and seeing as we're friends and all, would you come to my parents' anniversary dinner?" he asked.

"Are you sure? Isn't an anniversary dinner a more personal affair?"

"If you don't come there is a chance it will just blow with how prim and proper they are. It's like they want some big applause for their achievement."

"And you don't think they deserve it?"

"I don't. They got married, and it has been up to them to stick it out. I don't like it."

She sighed. "You're really pushing this new friendship to the limit, but I'm not the kind to see a friend suffer, so you've got it. I will be there."

"Great. I'll let them know there will be a plus one."

Cassie chuckled. "Well, if we're going to be there together, we're going to get them something decent. What about a waffle maker?" she asked.

"I think that's what you give to newly married couples, isn't it?"

"I don't know. I've never been married, and I don't intend to." She grabbed his hand, and before he knew where they were, they were in a cooking shop.

"My mom has all the stuff she needs for her kitchen."

"I don't, and I happen to have broken my spatula so I need a replacement."

"You're hijacking my mall trip?" he asked, watching as she grabbed a basket.

"Do you have anything more important to do for the rest of the day?"

"Nope. I can't say that I do."

She handed him the basket. "Then be a good man, and hold this." He watched as she put a pie plate, three spatulas, two lots of baking tins, and finally some kind of parchment paper inside.

He had never seen so much excitement on a woman's face before just because she was shopping for her kitchen.

"Right, now that I've done that, any ideas?"

They stopped at a jewelry store, and Slade forced her inside. He couldn't believe how she turned her nose up at the beautiful pieces.

"Every woman loves diamonds," he said.

"I'm not most people." She moved to a box of engagement rings, and she looked across them. There were several beautiful diamonds.

"Are you looking for something particular?" the lady behind the counter asked. Her name tag said Jules.

"No. We're just looking," Cassie said.

"This is not our only selection of engagement rings. If your fiancée would like, I could show her more pieces." Jules looked at him as she spoke.

"We're not—"

He placed his arm across her shoulders, pulling her in close. "We'd love to see whatever you have to show us. Only the best for my girl."

The woman smiled, and left them.

"What the hell are you doing?" she asked.

"I'm having fun. You know it's that thing you do when you have a laugh?"

"I know what fun is all about. Why waste time like this? We're not engaged, and we're never going to be."

"Now you're just breaking my heart. Don't ever presume our fate. We'll always get it wrong. Come on, you can't tell me some of these are pretty."

She looked at the cases, and shook her head. "They're pretty, but they're for women that are with boyfriends, or engaged."

"Then for one morning, you're going to pretend." He stood behind her with his hands on her shoulders. "And I won't take no for an answer."

Chapter Six

Slade wasted an hour in the jewelry story making her try on piece after piece after piece. Cassie wasn't and never would be a jewelry girl. At least, never again. There were a few rings she had liked, and they had felt amazing on her finger. Andrew had used jewels and told her every woman loves them. She refused to be drawn by such lies again.

She wasn't in love with Andrew. Yes, he'd broken her heart, but he had also taught her some valuable lessons in life, and they were lessons she intended to stick to.

Taking a fry, she popped it into her mouth, and refused to look at the man opposite her.

"Are you still pissed at me?"

Cassie ignored him.

"Look, it was just a little fun."

Again, she ignored him.

"We made that woman's day."

Finally, she glared at him. "Telling her that you'd invite her to our wedding was not funny, Slade. I don't like lying, and what you did was just plain old stupid."

"I didn't pick the ring, now did I? You liked the large diamond with little stars in the band."

She stuffed another fry into her mouth, and glared. "Is everything such a game to you?"

"It's not a game. Not really. I don't see anything wrong with having a bit of fun."

"I didn't think it was funny."

He pointed his own fry at her. "I'm getting that. You're very uptight. Have you ever just let loose?"

"Yes, I have. I got a broken heart, and mocked every time I walked down the school hall. Believe me, I know what it's like, and I don't intend to relive the experience." She dipped her fry into some ketchup, and took a bite, releasing a sigh.

"Not every single guy is like Andrew."

"I know that."

He reached out and took her hand. "I want you to believe it. I know I have fun with these women, and you think I'm an asshole, but I never promise them more."

"I don't have a problem with that. I mean, yeah, I thought it was cruel, but I can see you're not a complete ass." She stared down at her plate. "I just … I guess I still let what Andrew did to me rule some of my decisions."

"Have you ever been with a man other than him?"

Her cheeks heated even though she didn't want them to. She shook her head. "No."

"I don't know what it must have been like to be a girl in high school like that."

She shrugged. "The school hallways were the worst. I hated it more than anything else. They would pin panties to my locker, and words like slut, and whore. Trailer trash pussy. I don't even know why I'm telling you all this. If it wasn't for Jessica and William, I wouldn't have gotten through that last year. In the beginning when I saw Andrew, he'd always have a new girl on his arm. He'd make sure that I knew he was having a much better time with her than he ever would with me."

"This guy sounds like a total fucking jerk."

"He was, and he is. His parents own half the town."

"Do you still love him?"

She shook her head. "No. I don't even think it was love back then. I think I was infatuated with him. He made me feel special, and with a father like Bill, well, it was hard to ignore that." He stroked her hand, and she smiled over at him. "Thank you, for listening to me."

"I think if I ever see this Andrew, I'm going to beat the shit out of him."

"He's not worth it. By the end of the school year, I had no feelings for him. I'd look at him, and instead of feeling hurt or heartbroken, the mere sight of him pissed me off. It was like I had finally woken up to the loser that he was. It was just too late."

"Is that when you promised yourself that you'd never fall for another guy again?"

"Yep. I think I'm doing okay. I've been on a couple of dates. Not many. Chuck was my first one in a long time."

"Daniel's very protective of you as well."

"I know. He was like a father to me when my own was a waste of space." She tucked some hair behind her ears. "I think I put him through hell for a little while. With my parents gone, I started my … monthly cycle while I was in the sheriff's office toilet. I was waiting for my father to be cleared, and I must have screamed or something. Daniel came, and he did everything he could to explain to me what happened." Her cheeks were on fire now. She didn't know why she was telling Slade this stuff. She covered her face. "You're so horrible."

"Why am I horrible?" he asked, laughing.

"You make me comfortable, and then I start telling you all these embarrassing things about myself." She looked at him through her fingers. "Is this some kind of deputy spell? You get me to spill my innermost secrets?"

"This is no way a secret. You've got someone alive who knows what happened."

"I know. For the longest time, I couldn't look at him I was so embarrassed."

"Daniel's been a good friend to you."

"He has, and I appreciate everything he's ever

done for me." She grabbed her burger, and took a large bite. "What about you? Any interesting tales to tell?"

"Not a chance. I'm a cool as they come." He winked at her.

"I don't believe it."

He rolled his eyes. "Okay, there was one time … I screamed when I first woke up. Many years ago."

"Why?"

"Well … I was hard." He pointed down at his dick, and she started to smile. "I didn't know why, and I kind of panicked."

"Wow, I never, that is just … so funny. You didn't even realize you had a hard-on?"

"I didn't, and you know at times when you talk it makes me forget that you're this little innocent virgin."

"I have never said I was an innocent virgin. You can think what you like." Some of the books she read were downright dirty. Just because she kept everyone at arms' length to protect herself, didn't for a second mean that she didn't want to connect to others. Andrew had hurt her in a really bad way, and she didn't want it to keep affecting her, but she knew she was going to have to change something in her life to be able to find some kind of happiness.

****

In the end, Slade settled on a cruise for his parents' anniversary present. He and Cassie had picked up a few trinkets, a picture frame, a photograph album, and a vase for them to take to dinner.

He had a month to go until the dinner, but everything was booked, ready, and he was all set.

Sitting in his backyard, soaking up the sun on a Saturday morning, he tried not to listen to Jessica, Cassie, and William as they spoke about online dating. The kids were playing around, and he didn't like not being there, being part of it.

Finally, after twenty minutes of only hearing little snippets of conversation, he lifted up their fence, and entered her yard.

"Isn't that trespassing?" Jessica asked. William and Jessica were sitting on either side of Cassie as she had a laptop perched on her knees.

"No, he calls it friendship access," Cassie said, smiling up at him.

Damn it. He was really loving her smile, and he found himself giving her reason to. "What are you all doing?" he asked, moving behind Cassie, to see a dating website was pulled up.

"Jessica said I needed to meet new people, so I started a page for a dating website." Cassie pointed at it.

The picture was a cute one taken when she'd been gardening in her little vegetable patch.

Slade didn't like the stab of jealousy that washed over him at seeing her picture on a dating site.

"Anyone pinged you yet?" he asked.

"Three guys. One is an accountant—"

"Boring. Those guys do nothing but talk about numbers, taxes, and rules. Next one," he said.

"A teacher of science—"

"You do not need to get lost in chemicals and shit. Move on."

"You're being a pain, Slade. This is serious, and if you're not going to take it seriously, you can make your way through the fence." Cassie looked up at him and glared.

"Fine, fine, fine. The next one."

She did some clicking, and then pulled him up. "A firefighter."

He couldn't say anything about the firefighter.

"I think we have a winner," Jessica said.

"Organize a date, and make it close so you're safe. William will watch the kids, and I can drop you off for your date."

"I'll drop her off," Slade said. "I'll even stick around so if the guy turns out to be a total loser, and dangerous, he doesn't know where she lives. Can I get some iced tea?" he asked.

"Sure, it's in the fridge. You know where I keep it." He nodded, and left, going toward the fridge to fill a glass. Jessica followed him into the kitchen, and he gave her a smile.

"You know, Slade, you're acting all jealous of Cassie."

"I'm not jealous, just being cautious. Do you know how dangerous those online sites are?"

"We all know how dangerous they are."

He took a sip of the lemon tea, and stared at Jessica. She had her arms crossed, and was staring at him. "What is it?" he asked.

"You know, if you like Cassie, you could just ask her out on a date."

"I don't date, and Cassie and I are friends. Nothing more." He didn't like the bad taste he had in his mouth from saying those words.

"How long has it been since you had a woman, or went on a date?"

"I'm taking a break," he said.

"You know, this house and your house, have seen many single couples find—"

"Romance, I know. I've heard the rumors, but it's all bullshit. Cassie and I are friends. I care about her, and I don't want to see her get hurt." He took another long drink of his tea, and glanced out of the kitchen window.

Cassie was chasing after one of the children. She wore her bathing costume with a pair of shorts. His cock thickened at watching her tits bounce, and his gut twisted at seeing her pick one of the girls, and swing her up in her arms. In that moment, Slade could see her doing that with their children.

Yearning unlike anything he'd ever known woke up inside him, and he no longer wanted to watch other couples with their kids be happy families. He wanted it himself. He wanted it so much that he had to hold onto the counter as the reality began to set in.

He'd not been with another woman, and he'd found himself drawn to Cassie, more and more.

Shaking his head, he refused to believe that he was falling for her.

"No," he said, turning to find the space where Jessica had stood was now empty.

There was no way he had any feelings for Cassie. They were friends, and other people needed to stop thinking they could interfere with them.

Leaving the kitchen, he took a seat on Cassie's chair. William sat beside him, and for several seconds neither of them spoke.

"You've got a wonderful family," Slade said.

"Thank you. When Jessica and I realized we were pregnant at such a young age, we were scared as well."

"You're only twenty-five?"

"Yes, and we've got three kids. My parents own one of the businesses in town, and I've been working my way up since I was eighteen," William said. "I would do anything for my family."

Jessica and Cassie were running around laughing.

"You know Cassie tried to give me and Jessica this place," William said.

Slade turned toward him. "She did?"

"Yes, put the down payment on it, and came to our house, about to hand over the keys. We both knew what this place meant to Cassie. As much as we wanted a bigger place, we've finally found a place of our own. We're in the process of getting all the documents in order. We told Cassie to keep this for herself."

Everything he was finding out about Cassie was just proving to him how damn good of a woman she really was.

Chapter Seven

"Do you need to wear the dress?" Slade asked.

Cassie gave a twirl and chuckled. "Do you like it?"

"I think you look beautiful."

"You don't sound happy about that."

"I am. I'm very happy for you."

"Then what's the problem?" she asked, tucking her hair behind her ears. "This is my very first official date."

"What about Chuck?"

"That was a double date. So not the same thing. At least I don't think so. We're meeting at an Italian restaurant."

"I know. I've got all the details, and I will be sticking around to make sure everything is okay."

Cassie moved toward Slade, and threw her arms around his neck. "I really do appreciate you being an amazing friend." She pulled away, and when she went to move, he grabbed her tightly.

Closing her eyes, she tried to ignore her own reactions to his closeness. She didn't want him to pull away, or leave her alone.

He released her, and she didn't look straight at him. She couldn't, not right then.

"If at any point you're not happy, I want you to let me know."

"You want me to give you a kind of code?" she asked.

"Yes." He stared at her for several moments. "I want you to wave at me." He lifted his hand and gave a wave.

She laughed. "You want me to do that."

"Yes, and then I'll come to your rescue and get

you out of there."

"You're such a good friend." She was so nervous. "Are you ready to go?"

He hesitated, and she waited. "Yeah, I'm ready. Let's get this show on the road."

"I'm so nervous."

"What is this guy's name?"

"He said it's Greg."

"And you don't believe him? If you don't believe him now, there's no chance of you ever doing so."

She laughed. "I don't know. I guess right now, I'm kind of freaking out because all I'm seeing are all the horror stories of what other women have gone through." She also didn't like the fact that she was feeling guilty.

That one hug from Slade had caused a lot of mixed feelings in her.

Pushing some of her hair out of the way, she licked her lips, and then clasped her fingers together. All the time she was aware of Slade sitting next to her.

They spent a lot of time together now. When they were at work he'd often join her while she was finishing the crossword. For lunch if he wasn't out, they'd eat together. Somehow their grocery shopping had also come together. In fact, she spent more time with Slade than with anyone else.

Daniel had even commented on how they finished each other's sentences.

"So, erm, any special woman going to be paying a visit?"

"Nope. No woman."

She hadn't heard any of his sexy adventures in his backyard for some time. He always found a reason to visit her, and they'd sit for hours, chatting, laughing. He'd even helped her maintain her vegetable patch.

He found a parking space near the restaurant, and

they walked together. She wore a modest heel, and a really tight dress that showed off her curves. This had been a luxury purchase that Jessica convinced her to buy.

Once inside, she told the maître d' that she was waiting for someone, and it turned out Greg was already there.

"I'll be at the bar," he said.

The maître d' took the lead, and then she was moving toward the window seat of the restaurant, but still close to the bar. Out of the corner of her eye, she saw Slade take a seat, and it helped her to relax a little.

"You're Cassie Love?" the man said, standing tall.

"Greg?"

"Yes, that's me. Your picture didn't do you justice." He took her hand, and pressed a kiss to her cheek. He moved the maître d' out of the way, and pushed her seat under the table.

She felt a little uncomfortable, but she had put that down to all this newness.

"I'm really sorry. I'm so nervous. If I say something stupid, please ignore me," she said.

"Is this your first online date?" Greg asked.

"Yes, it really is. Does it show?"

He laughed. "Just a little, but that's more than fine."

"Is this your first?"

"No. You're my fourth."

"Oh, well, then you should be a pro, and can totally lead the conversation, right?" She smiled, and this made him laugh.

"I wouldn't call myself a pro. Fourth date could mean I'm really bad."

"Or I'm really lucky. Fourth time's the charm." She grabbed her water glass, and took a sip.

Why did I let Jessica talk me into this?
I'm so fucking nervous.

She was so nervous she was even thinking curse words. Her heart was racing, and at the same time, she felt like she was betraying Slade. She looked toward the bar, and saw him playing around with his cell phone.

He wasn't paying her all that much attention.

"Would you like some wine?" Greg asked.

"No, no, thank you. I'm not much of a big drinker. I think it said that on my profile."

"Yes, it also said you worked as a receptionist in a sheriff's office. That must be exciting," he said, leaning forward.

She didn't know what to do with her arms. Should she cross them, and lean forward, showing interest? That would put her elbows on the table, so wouldn't that be rude? What about if she crossed her arms? No, that would show that she was defensive.

What were the damn rules?

Resting her hands in her lap, she forced a smile.

"I wouldn't call it exciting. It's a small-town sheriff's office. A couple of drunk kids, or the occasional, erm, graffiti person. The odd drunk, that's about it. What about you? You're a firefighter. That must be really scary but rewarding."

He nodded. "It is. For the most part, it's scary. Running into burning buildings isn't easy, and then when you lose people, that's even harder."

"I can imagine. I wouldn't ever be able to do a job like you do."

There was a topic that Greg was more than happy to talk about, and she sat listening to him. He spoke of some of the people he'd saved, and showed her a few pictures of cats he'd rescued. There was even a dog as well, a rabbit and a guinea pig.

They enjoyed their meal. She had some kind of pasta dish—she couldn't even remember the name—while he had a large steak. By the end of the meal, she was ready to go home, and she knew there was no way a second date. It had been fun, but there wasn't a spark.

"Do you need me to call you a cab?" he asked.

"No, no, my friend is here, waiting to drive me home." They stood from the table and smiled. "This was fun."

"Fun but not again?"

"I…"

"Don't worry about it. We didn't have that spark really." He nodded toward her, and left.

It was a strange end to one of the most uncomfortable experiences of her life. She took a seat beside Slade, and ordered herself a shot of whiskey.

"He's gone?" Slade asked. "What did you say to him?"

"That you're my pimp and if he doesn't get gone, you're going to beat him to a pulp."

Slade laughed. "What did you really say?"

"That it was fun, it wouldn't be happening again, bye."

"Really?"

"Pretty much. It was so uncomfortable, and I didn't know what to talk to him about. We'd read each other's profiles, and it all just felt so cold. It was so weird I didn't even know what I ate." She shook her head. "Never again. I'm not doing the online dating. Jessica even mentioned speed dating as well. Not happening. This has been a real eye opener." She thanked the bartender, and knocked back the stinging liquid. "Ready to go home?"

"Yep. I certainly am."

****

Slade had wanted to do a victory dance when her date had got up and left. He sat down in her sitting room, waiting for his iced cold beer that she'd promised him. His shoes were already kicked off, and he placed his feet on the coffee table in front of him.

They had sat in her sitting room many times eating a box of cheesy chips, and drinking a cold beer.

Cassie entered, carrying two bottles of beer, and a tub of chocolate ice cream.

"Hold on a second."

He watched as she kicked her shoes off and sighed as she made her way toward him. She handed him a beer and a spoon, taking a seat beside him. Her bottle of beer was on the coffee table. Her feet were curled up underneath her. She rested the ice cream tub on a pillow, and then they were diving in.

"I don't even know why I let myself be talked into it."

"You wanted to date," he said.

"That wasn't it."

Slade looked at her, and he saw her cheeks were already bright red. "You can't just say something like that and not elaborate. I'm a guy. I don't know what the whole blushing thing means."

"It doesn't matter. Forget I said anything."

He sighed. "What is it? If it wasn't for the date, then what was it for?"

She took a bite of chocolate ice cream, and her brown eyes stared at him. He saw the conflict in her gaze, and he held his hands up.

"You can say whatever you like, and I won't judge. I won't say anything. I'll keep my opinions to myself."

"You promise?"

"I promise. I don't say shit I don't mean."

She bit her lip, and he watched as she squared her shoulders. "I'm twenty-five years old."

"I know."

"I've only been with one guy, and he completely smashed my heart."

Slade stared at her. "You're looking for someone to fuck?"

She nodded her head, surprising him. "I'm a woman. I have needs just like everyone else. I don't want, nor do I need, forever. I just … I want to make memories, different ones than what I remember with Andrew. He wasn't that great, and I was blinded by lies. I want to feel something. I heard you with those women out back. It sounded like it felt good, and I guess, I don't know, I figured I'd find someone to do it with."

Slade honestly didn't know what to say. His cock was rock fucking hard. Hearing Cassie's need, and knowing what she wanted, it turned him on.

Sitting at the bar tonight watching her with another man, it had made him assess his own feelings for her. He wasn't in love with her, and he didn't for a second see a marriage in their future. She was his friend, and he didn't want that to change.

What he couldn't do was deny that she aroused him. He was attracted to her, and had been for a long time, even before they were friends.

Putting his hand on her thigh, he stared into her eyes.

She was never going to take that next step, and it was down to him to make the move. He took the ice cream and the pillow from her, placing them on the floor.

Cassie didn't stop him.

If at any moment, she told him to stop, he would. Putting his hand back on her knee, he caressed beneath the dress, but didn't go far. Resting his arm across the back of the sofa, he stroked her neck, pushing her hair out of the way. Running his thumb across her lip, he slowly slid it inside her mouth. He watched as her tongue came out, and licked it. He pulled out, and then replaced his thumb with his mouth, claiming the kiss he'd been wanting for so long.

Her hands gripped his arms, sliding up to sink into his hair.

This was probably a line they shouldn't cross, but the thought of her being with anyone else was too much for him. He didn't want anyone else touching her. Cassie belonged to him in every sense of the world, and no bastard was going to take her from him. Sliding his hand up her thigh, then up her body to cup her breast, he heard her gasp.

That little opening had him plunging his tongue deep into her mouth. She met him stroke for stroke.

He squeezed her breast, feeling the hard bud of her nipple against his palm. There were too many clothes between them. He wanted her naked, beneath him.

"Do you think this is a good idea?" she asked, whispering the words against his ear as he kissed down her neck, nibbling on the pulse that was beating erratically there.

"How are you feeling right now?" He moved his hand back down, cupping her ass as he did.

"It feels amazing."

"Do you want me to stop?"

"No. I don't."

"If it feels so wrong, then I don't ever want to be right." He pulled away. Her cheeks were red, and he cupped her face. "Do you want me to stop?"

She shook her head. "I've … I don't want to ruin our friendship."

He chuckled. "We won't ruin our friendship.

We'll just have the benefit of helping each other in our time of need." He moved his hand between her thighs and cupped her pussy. The panties she wore were soaking wet. "I'm going to warn you though, Cassie, I like my sex dirty. I like to fuck and hard, and I love sex. I don't like it neat or clean. I'm not going to turn the light off, and there's no way in hell you're going to hide from me. I like to see what I fuck."

He watched as she licked her lips. "I don't have a problem with that."

"Good."

Slade tore her panties from her body and tossed them to the floor. Capturing her lips, he found her soaking cunt, sliding two fingers inside. He wasn't surprised by how wet she was, nor how tight. He began to stretch open his two fingers, pushing them into her, and out, working her wetness over his digits.

"You're so fucking wet." He shoved her dress up to her hips, and stared down at her beautifully prepared pussy. Her pussy hair was closely cut, and just an outline around the lips of her pussy, looking so sensual. His cock pulsed as another wave of arousal washed over him.

He held her hips and moved her up so that he could lick her pretty cunt.

Sliding his tongue from her entrance to her clit, he swirled the bud, and moved back down to plunge inside her. She tasted fucking amazing. He'd never liked giving oral sex, but there was something different about Cassie. He wanted her taste in his mouth, and to give her the kind of pleasure no one else ever had before.

"Oh, wow," she said.

"You ever had your pussy licked?"

"No."

He smiled against her mound, and then took her clit into his mouth and sucked it hard. Her cries of pleasure echoed around the room, and Slade relished them.

Using his teeth to cause a little pain, he heard her gasp and scream his name once again.

He pushed two fingers inside her as he tongued her clit. Within seconds she came apart, her orgasm coming fast. He'd not expected her to come so quickly, but he wasn't going to complain.

Flicking his tongue across her clit, he eased her back down on the sofa.

Her cheeks were flushed and her eyes glazed. "That felt amazing."

"Do you want me to stop?"

She sat up, and moved so that she was straddling his lap. "Our friendship remains the same?"

He held onto her ass, grinding her down onto his dick so she felt how hard he actually was. "It stays the same."

"We can have anything we want?" she asked, kissing him back, her fingers sinking into his hair.

"Anything we want. You want to fuck down here, or upstairs, in our gardens, I'm all for it. You want to suck my dick until I come down your throat, just say the word. At the end of it, we're still friends. No judgment from either of us. We both get what we want."

He stared into her eyes as she looked down at him. His cock was so damn hard that it was starting to hurt where it pressed against his zipper.

"I've only been with one person, so I don't have a whole lot of experience," she said.

"I told you, no judging. You can practice on me."

Slade would remember the smile on her lips for the rest of his life. It was utter fucking sin, and it was all his.

"Then I want you to fuck me, Slade. I want you to

take me, and make me ache. Get me to make all those noises that women love to make for you."

Chapter Eight

Never in her life had she ever been so blunt. Cassie was used to staying clear of situations like this, and yet, she wanted to play dangerously. Slade wasn't like any of the boys she'd grown up with. When he looked at her, he didn't see a trailer kid. He just saw Cassie, and she liked that.

"You want me to fuck you?" he asked.

"Yes, do you want me to repeat myself and do it slowly?"

He lifted her up, and she gave a little squeal, wrapping her legs around his waist.

"You need to put me down," she said.

"I'm not letting you go until I'm good and ready." He gripped her ass tightly, and she wrapped her arms around his neck, holding on.

Slade didn't wait around, and carried her upstairs toward her bedroom. He wasn't friendly as he dropped her onto the bed, and she gave a little bounce. Pushing her hair off her face, she watched him as he began to remove his jeans.

She noticed he took his time, easing the jeans over his cock. When he turned, she saw why. He was rock hard. The top was red, pulsing, and slick with pre-cum.

"Is this what you want, babe?" He wrapped his fingers around the shaft, and began to move his fist up and down the length.

"Yes." Why wasn't she embarrassed, or trying to hide? The way he looked at her, it was like he wanted to eat her. She'd gladly have his lips on her body, or any part of him even. He'd made her feel oh so good, and she didn't want to lose that feeling.

"Then lie back, and spread those pretty thighs."

"I want you to wear a condom."

He reached into his pocket on the floor, and pulled out a condom.

"You were that certain I'd cave."

"This may come as a surprise to you, Cassie, but I didn't have any intention of fucking you tonight. I've thought about it a lot, but I didn't think I'd be allowed." He crawled onto the bed. "I knew you had a dirty side under all of that pristine cleanliness you seem to keep around you."

Cassie smiled, and pressed a kiss to his lips. It was rather chaste considering less than five minutes ago his face had been between her thighs. "I never once said that I was a prude."

"And you shave your pussy." He glided his fingers over the smooth flesh of her pussy, and she gasped. He slid a finger through her slit, teasing her sensitive clit, and then down to plunge inside her. "You're so wet. I may hurt you."

"You're not too big, Slade. I'm not stupid. I know for a fact you'll fit."

"Oh, you do, do you?" He pushed her down and spread her thighs wide. The tip of him was poised at her entrance. His gaze was on where they were about to cross that line from neighbors and friends to lovers. She wasn't afraid or nervous.

Cassie wanted his dick. She wanted him to fuck her so hard that she couldn't think straight.

Slade never talked about his women. He never made them feel stupid, or small. Yes, he rejected them, but Cassie was going in with her eyes open. If in the morning he didn't want to remember this, she was more than okay with that.

He pressed an inch inside her. "Are you okay?" he asked.

There was a wicked glint in his eyes, and she raised her brow. "Are you even inside me?"

Maybe it was the wrong thing to say, or the right one, as he grabbed her hips, and slammed every inch of his impressive length inside her, making her cry out his name.

Slade wasn't a small man, not at all. In fact, he was a very large, and she wasn't used to his size. However, it wasn't painful at all.

"Fuck, you're so incredibly tight. I can feel every fucking pulse of your pussy, baby. So perfect." He dropped a kiss to one nipple, and then the other, before moving up to poise just above her.

Gripping his arms, she ran her hands up to lock behind his neck.

"You feel so fucking amazing," he said. His hand went from her hip, to her thigh, then back down to grasp her ass tightly.

Slade wasn't gentle. His touch was really hard, and she knew that in the morning she'd have bruises that matched his hands. She didn't care.

"You're not going to fall in love with me, are you?" she asked.

His gaze returned to hers. "No, I'm not going to fall in love with you. We both know you already love me."

She laughed, which quickly changed to a moan as he thrust deep within her, making her gasp. "I'm not in love with you."

"Good, don't even think about falling in love with me." He pulled out. "I'm not the kind of guy to keep promises." He slammed inside her, and when he did it again, she looked down to watch his condom covered cock pull out of her body.

"I'm not the kind of girl to marry," she said.

"I don't want a wife. I'd much rather fuck than love." He slammed inside her, fucking her into the bed. She grasped his shoulders, pushing up to meet every single one of his thrusts.

His cock was rock hard, and the pleasure he was giving her was unlike anything she'd ever felt.

"Push your tits together," he said.

She did as he asked, and he tongued each nipple in turn, nibbling and biting. The pleasure and pain went straight to her clit, turning her on even more.

Cassie felt the start of another orgasm, and she screamed his name, needing it.

Suddenly, Slade pulled out of her pussy, and held her hips up so that he could watch. "Play with your pussy."

"Right now?" she asked.

"Yes. I want to watch you. Come on, Cassie, I thought you could handle being a little dirty."

With him this close, she didn't know if she could do it, but she did. Reaching to her pussy, and with her gaze still on his, she ran her fingers through her slit. She couldn't believe at how wet she felt even to her own touch. Her fingers were completely slick. Pushing two inside her, she felt a little tender even from the few seconds of fucking they'd had. Moving her fingers up her slit to circle her clit, she gasped, her mouth falling open as she teased her sensitive flesh.

Each touch only added the fuel to the already smoldering flame.

"You look so sexy, and ready to take a good hard fucking, Cassie. You want my cock inside you?"

"Yes."

"Then make yourself come, and I'll fuck you until you forget your own name."

She teased her clit, watching as his gaze never

once left hers. His eyes were so blue, and in that moment, she thought he was the sex devil, the way he seemed to read her body, to know what she wanted, and how best to make her come apart.

"I can see how wet you are. Do you love being given orders, Cassie?"

She didn't answer him.

He chuckled, and then bit the flesh of her thigh. "That's okay. I've got enough to say for the both of us." His stubble scratched her thigh, but she didn't mind the bit of roughness as it only seemed to heighten her need for him. "On Monday, I want you to wear one of those pretty skirts that you love. The ones that show off this perfect ass, only this time I don't want to see any lines of your panties. I want you to go bare, so I know that all it would take is my hand under your skirt to feel your pretty cunt."

"Slade," she said, moaning.

"I know what you need, Cassie. Come for me, and I'll give it to you."

She stroked her clit, feeling her orgasm begin to build. She didn't prolong it, and she came, screaming his name, which only got stronger as his tongue plunged inside her. Her pussy pulsed, and it was like she was trying to keep him inside her, clutching at him, not wanting to let him go.

Before the last embers of her release began to fade, he pressed her to the bed, and his cock replaced his tongue. He slammed inside her, making the headboard hit the wall.

"It's a good job I'm not at home right now otherwise I would have to come and see who was taking what was mine."

"I'm not yours, Slade."

"No?" He pulled out of her, and she whimpered,

wanting him back. He thrust back inside her, and she cried out. "You're mine, Cassie. You just don't even know it yet. This body, for as long as we want, is mine. I can do whatever I want to it."

She wrapped her hands around his neck, dragging her nails down his back, scoring the flesh. "Then your body is mine to use, and to do with what I want."

"You want to use me, Cassie, you can use me. I've got no problem being your own little toy. So long as you're mine to do the same!"

"I'm a great believer in being equal."

Slade fucked her hard, and Cassie came a third time, screaming his name. When he finally found his own release, she loved seeing him come apart. The look of total rapture on his face, and how open he was, Cassie knew she had made the right decision, and she certainly looked forward to playing with him.

****

"Blowjob," Slade said.

"You can't have a blowjob," she said.

"Why not? It's seven letters, and it's a word."

"Blowjob is a rude word, and you shouldn't have it."

"You had oral!" Slade pointed at the board, and she shook her head.

"That doesn't mean sex, or anything else. Like an oral examination. What you get at the dentist."

Slade smiled. "You and I both know you were thinking about my mouth on your pretty pussy."

It was Saturday morning, and he had yet to leave to go home. They were both naked. The curtains were still closed, and they were playing a game. He was never one to play games with the women he fucked, and yet with Cassie, it was something more. She shook her head, pulling her hair back, and leaving it over one shoulder.

"I'm not playing anymore, if you refuse to play properly." She got up, grabbed their empty cups, and entered the kitchen.

He got distracted while watching her ass move away from him. He loved her ass. It was so damn full and round. She hadn't made any move to cover up, and he loved that. The confidence only served to turn him on even more. Even with the sun shining, her head was held high, and her entire stance said, "this is who I am, fuck you if you don't like it".

Packing away the board game, he entered the kitchen, to see her making some toast. She had some chocolate spread open, and was already eating a slice.

"I'm sorry. I got really hungry. You want a slice?"

His stomach chose that moment to growl.

He took the slice she was eating, and bit it. "Um, that tastes so good." He licked his lips, and smiled as she glared at him.

"Can't you just take a fresh piece?" she asked.

"Why would I do that when yours look so tasty?" He popped the last piece into his mouth, and moaned again. "Almost as much as your pussy."

Her gaze ran over his body, and she took another slice, licking her lips. His cock thickened, and he wanted those lips wrapped around his cock.

"What are your plans for the day?" he asked.

"Not a lot. You?"

"I'm going to have your lips wrapped around my dick. That's how I'm going to spend the day."

She started to laugh. "There's no way I'm spending the entire day licking your cock."

"You don't have to lick, you can suck." He sat down, and wrapped his fingers around his cock.

Grabbing a spoon, he smeared some of the

chocolate spread onto his dick. "I've even made it taste good." He winked at her, and she just shook her head.

"I cannot believe you've done that."

"Believe it, baby. You know you want a taste."

She moved from behind the island and stood in front of him. Her hands landing on his knees, she leaned in close. "What do I get out of it?"

"You get to taste my cock, and see if you can make me come before the end of the day." He was ready to blow already. With her tits hanging, and her body on display, knowing how good her pussy felt, he wanted her again.

Her gaze moved down to his cock. "I don't think that's tempting enough."

"You do me, and I'll do you." He caught her hand.

She was laughing, tucking some hair behind her ear as she kissed him.

He released a groan as she sank to the floor. Her lips moved over his cock, sucking on the tip. There was no chocolate on the tip, but she licked at his pre-cum. She moaned, giving him a smile, before sliding her lips onto his cock.

"Holy fuck!" He gripped the back of her head, and watched as she sucked his cock. A trail of chocolate followed her mouth, but he didn't care.

She took him to the back of her throat, and then eased up. As she bobbed her head, he felt himself getting harder still.

When all the chocolate was gone, she pulled away, licking her lips.

She stood up, and he watched as she dipped her finger into the chocolate spread, and wiped it on each of her nipples. "How does it taste?"

Gripping her back, he pulled her forward, and

sucked her first nipple, making sure to use his teeth. Each time he gave her a bit of pain, she moaned and pressed her body closer to him.

"It's the best way to eat chocolate." He trailed his tongue between the valley of her breasts, and sucked on her other nipple.

She pulled away from him and went down to the floor, sucking on his cock. Using her hand and mouth, she teased his cock and balls, bringing him closer to the peak. He didn't fall over the edge, and her brown gaze stared up at him.

"Have you ever had a man come on your tits?" he asked.

Cassie shook her head. "Nope. I've not had anyone come in my mouth either."

Slade hated Andrew in that moment, but now he was about to be a lot of Cassie's firsts. She was a beautiful woman, smart, kind, and simply amazing. The passion inside her equaled his. He'd seen some of her erotic books that she liked to hide. There was a kinkiness inside Cassie, and he intended to tap into that, to give her everything her heart desired, and to reap the rewards for himself.

She cupped his balls and sucked him deep, nearly gagging on his length. He pulled out of her, just as the first jet of cum erupted out of the tip. Working his length, he covered her breasts in his spunk, creating a piece of artwork that he wished he could have a picture of.

Cassie was his. It was cliché as fuck, but when he looked at her, that was all he felt.

When the last of his orgasm ebbed away, he fought off the need to just relax, and grabbed her, pushing her to the floor. He spread her legs open, and flicked her clit with his tongue. Plunging two fingers inside her pussy, he fucked her hard with his digits as he teased her clit, bringing her close to orgasm.

"Come all over my face, Cassie. Show me how much you love to get fucking dirty." Reaching up, he stroked a finger through his cum and played with her tits. It was dirty, it was naughty, and it felt so good.

With his finger coated in his cum, he placed it against her mouth. She sucked it inside, and he played with her pussy, teasing her to orgasm.

When she came, he licked up her cream, and held her in place, not letting her escape his touch. He wanted her to come in his mouth, and to taste her. She was perfect.

Lying next to her after it was over, he waited for her words of regret.

"I think I need a shower," she said. "You got me all dirty."

"You don't have any regrets?" he asked, turning so that he was facing her.

"Regrets?"

"I don't know. I expected you to kick my ass out, and tell me all bad shit about treating you like a slut." He took hold of her hand, and locked their fingers together.

"You told me that while we're together like this, there won't be any judgments. You don't think I'm a slut and whore, do you?"

"No. I don't. It's the last thing I'd think."

"Then I don't care. I enjoyed what we had." She squeezed his hand. "I don't think I'd be like this with every guy. I wasn't like this with Andrew."

"You've got to stop thinking about that asshole. He didn't deserve you. You're a beautiful woman, and he's a loser."

She smiled. "You're making me feel better already. He thought I was trailer trash. Something to be used and discarded. Kind of like a toy."

"I always took care of my toys. I never had a reason to put them away."

"That has to be one of the nicest things ever said to me," she said. "And you're not even saying it to get in my pants."

He shook his head. "Of course not. I'm already in there."

Chapter Nine

"Do you really think this is a good idea?" Jessica asked.

Cassie looked over her mug of coffee. "Is what a really good idea?" They were eating in the diner, outside in the sunshine. They had a canopy to give them some shade.

"Screwing your boss?"

It had been nearly two weeks since she and Slade had begun to have sex. Two weeks, of looking forward to bedtime. They had sex a lot. Last night they had screwed six times, seven if the bath exploits were included.

She hadn't had sex so much in her life. Of course, the last time she did have sex had been when she was eighteen and with an asshole. Thinking about Andrew didn't make her feel anything anymore. She also wasn't embarrassed about the sex she was enjoying with Slade. He was so damn hot in the sack, and what was more, afterward, they often talked. Sometimes he'd still be inside her, and he'd make some kind of joke that would make her laugh. When she was with him, everything felt right.

"Technically, he's not my boss. Daniel is."

"You know what I mean. I've seen the way you and Slade look at each other. You pretty much fuck in looks alone."

"Let's stop talking about my love life, and let's talk about your impending move." She was helping Jessica at the weekend to move into their new home. She already had several lasagnas, chicken casseroles, and pies made so that they didn't have to worry about dinner. She'd gotten boxes as well, and she'd be helping.

All she needed to do was convince Slade to help her with his car, and she was all set.

"No, let's not talk about the move. You know that your houses have a long history of the couples falling in love. You've gone from hating Slade, to being friends with him, to now having sex."

The waitress brought out their burgers, and Cassie thanked her before diving in. "We're not in love. It's just sex, Jessica. You told me I needed to lighten up. Consider this my path to enlightenment."

"Now you're just being a pain in the ass."

"I'm not. Really. Slade and I are friends with the whole benefits thing. I'm having a lot of fun."

Jessica sighed. "You know I was messing around with William a long time before we got caught. I knew I loved him, but we had that honeymoon period."

"I'm not going to get pregnant. We use protection," Cassie said.

"I know you, Cassie. I warned you against Andrew, and look what happened there."

This made Cassie pause, and look at her friend. Being eighteen and having the first guy show her attention, she had basked in it. Jessica had warned her so many times, but she didn't listen.

Her appetite disappeared to nothing. Putting her burger on the tray, she looked at Jessica.

"You think he's using me?"

"I don't think he's using you."

"Do you think he'll tell others about what we're doing?" Andrew had gone into graphic detail.

Jessica reached over, and placed a hand over hers. "I don't think any of that. Slade, considering he's a man-whore, is a good guy. I'm worried that you're going to fall in love with him and get your heart broken."

"Oh, is that all?" Cassie asked.

"Yes."

She saw her friend was worried. "Don't worry. I

have no intention of falling for Slade. He's a great guy, but we don't have those kinds of feelings." She finished her burger, and the conversation turned to the move.

Cassie forced herself to show that she didn't care. She *did* care. One of her biggest fears in the past few weeks was that she *was* starting to fall for Slade. Then again, she couldn't fall for him. They were friends, neighbors, colleagues. Nothing was going to come of it, and having some good sex didn't exactly mean anything.

She loved being with him. They watched movies, played video games. He had this awesome one where they competed at each level to shoot or stab each other. She didn't win them all, but she put up a good fight. Then there were the times they spent just having fun. He'd come and perch on her desk, and they'd do the crossword together. They no longer carried two trolleys to do their grocery shopping, and only used one. They even split the bill.

He came and did any jobs around her house that she struggled with, and they had painted her spare bedroom last week.

Entering the sheriff's office, she saw three people waiting, and after making sure they were booked in, and ready to speak with Daniel or Slade, she got to work on any necessary emails. She took care of Mrs. Wilson complaining about cats again, and updated the work timetable that Daniel gave her, along with the necessary amendments for safety during the fair that was coming in three weeks to mark the end of summer.

She tapped a pen against her lip, as she finished the last letter that Daniel wanted her to send to a lawyer.

"How was your lunch?" Slade asked.

He'd just entered the office, and was fanning his face with a file.

"It was good. Yours?"

"Boring without you. However, that pasta salad you made was delicious."

"Did you take the entire bowl from the fridge?" she asked.

"Yep, and I found the lid you tried to hide. Finished it today after talking with one of the Andersons."

This made her pause. "You went to see the Andersons?"

"Yep. It would seem they have been getting some complaints about the noise of their current building. They're constructing a house on their land, and residents are getting pissed with the noise."

"The Andersons are the ones that own a lot of the town." She printed the letter, and placed it on the pile for Daniel to sign.

When she turned to look at Slade again, he was staring at her. Not liking that he was looking down at her, she stood up, and grabbed the letters. "Why are you staring?"

"The Andersons are Andrew? Andrew Anderson?"

"One and the same. It's no big deal though. Just be careful. They can be quite mean to people who step on their toes."

"I don't care about rich bastards. Are you still game for my parents' next weekend?" he asked.

"Yes."

She heard his phone going on his desk.

"When you're done with that, come and talk. I'll take care of this." He left to go and answer his phone, and she took the letters through to Daniel.

"Are these for me to sign?" he asked.

"They are." She placed them on his desk, and waited as he went through them.

"I heard about you and Slade," Daniel said.

She looked at the sheriff, and her cheeks heated. "Erm, I'm sorry."

"You don't need to be sorry, Cassie. I just want you to be careful. I know how upset you got the last time, and I don't want to see you hurt."

"You won't. I promise. I don't intend to get hurt again." She took the letters from him.

"I heard news that Andrew is coming back to town."

She shrugged. "I honestly don't care. I've had a long time to deal with everything that happened. Seven years of it, and I was hurt, but I've come to see that I wasn't sad about him. I was sad about what happened afterward. I'm not a little girl anymore, Daniel. I can handle myself." She moved toward the door, and bit her lip. "Actually, I wanted to thank you."

"For what?"

"For everything you did for me growing up, and I also want to thank you for going and seeing my father's body, and laying him to rest." She hadn't told Daniel that she'd known about that.

Going through some of his old files a few years ago, she had seen the report tucked away. Her father had died and no one had any way of contacting her, so they had gone to Daniel.

"You knew?"

"I didn't know at the time. I found out after." She hadn't cried either. It was hard to cry for a man who told you how much they hated you. "Did he suffer?"

Daniel shook his head. "No, he didn't."

"That's all I needed to know."

She left, going to her own desk, and placing the letters into the necessary envelopes. It was good to finally get that off her chest, and to admit to Daniel that she knew.

****

"If you're giving them food to help survive, why are we helping?" Slade asked.

"We made a bargain, and you're going to live up to your end, and I'll live up to mine." Cassie placed the box on the floor inside Jessica and William's new home. It was big, and the kids were already somewhere, screaming and laughing.

Slade placed his box on the floor, and caught his woman into his arms. Gripping the cheeks of her ass, he nuzzled her neck.

"We don't want one of the kids to see."

"Is putting your ass on the line worth it?" he asked.

She chuckled. "I asked you for help, and you told me it would cost me anal." She pulled away, and cupped his cheeks. She pressed a kiss to his lips. "I thought it was a good price."

She kissed him again, and then left.

Slade watched her ass in the knee length shorts she wore. He wanted to take her home and have his way with her, but he had agreed to help her friends move. He didn't want to be lugging shit about, but he was finding his life a lot more fun being around Cassie.

"I really appreciate you helping us out," Jessica said. "It has taken us a long time to find this place."

"I'm always happy to help." He went to leave the room, but Jessica's next words had him stopping.

"Are you playing her?"

He turned toward Jessica, shocked by her outburst. "I'm not playing her." He wasn't even going to pretend that he didn't know what she was talking about.

She laughed. "William told me to stay out of it. Cassie could live her life the way she wanted, and I had to accept that. She's my best friend. I saw her get hurt by that fucker, and I don't want to see her fall for you."

"I'm not going to hurt her."

"You think you're not going to, and that in itself tells me you're a fucking idiot." Jessica put her hands on her hips. "Do you even realize that you're the only guy she has been with since Andrew? Since she was eighteen? There hasn't been anyone else in her life. You are both acting like this is just some fun. That you'll move on, and still be friends, but you won't be. What happens when she finds someone else? What happens if you get bored? What if you're already in love with each other, and you're pretending that it's not the case?"

Just the thought of Cassie being with anyone else made his gut twist. No one else deserved her.

"I don't know." There were no words that he could give, as he didn't know the answer to that.

"I hate this. It's like I can see this going two different ways," Jessica said.

"What ways do you see?" She was Cassie's friend, and he was giving her the respect to voice her opinion.

"You're either going to both fall in love, and live a happy life."

"Or?"

"Or you're going to break each other's hearts. I know that if this fucks up, Cassie's never going to be the same again."

Silence fell between them. He didn't say anything especially as Cassie and William came in at that moment.

He smiled, and pretended that Jessica hadn't just made him think of all the shit he'd been trying to avoid.

There was no way he could think or even deal with Cassie being with anyone else, or falling for someone else. She had cancelled and removed her picture from two dating sites, and never went with Greg again. He knew, deep down, that for as much fun as they were having, it wouldn't be a forever thing. Cassie was a good woman, and she deserved someone who was going to love her for her.

What he couldn't do was let her go.

He didn't want to.

For once he didn't want to share her either. He'd never had these possessive, protective instincts for anyone else, and yet for Cassie, they were out in full force.

"Are you okay?" Cassie asked a couple of hours later.

He'd been working in a bit of haze, following William and Jessica pointing to where they wanted boxes to go, and just working through his own thoughts.

"Yeah, I'm fine. Why?"

"You're just … acting weird. Has Jessica said something to you?"

"Are you happy?" he asked.

"What? Yes, of course. Why wouldn't I be?"

"I'm sorry, I'm just not in the right place right now. Everything is fine. Don't worry about it."

She caught his wrist, stopping him from leaving.

"Jessica said something, didn't she?"

"It's nothing, and no, she didn't." He lied with ease. "Let's get all this done so that we can go and eat."

"O-kay."

He left the room, and focused on unloading the truck. When all the boxes were distributed around the house, they said their goodbyes to the happy family, and he avoided Jessica's gaze. He didn't like some of the shit that she'd been saying, and especially as it was so close to home for him.

Pulling into the bar, he parked up.

"I'm not cooking?" she asked.

"Not tonight. Steak, potatoes, and some dancing is in order. Come on." He climbed out of his truck, and made his way to Cassie's side, helping her out.

"You're in a real weird mood." They took a seat toward the back of the dance-floor. He nodded at Bethany, who gave him a wave.

"I'm sorry."

"Jessica said something, didn't she?" Cassie asked. "She's already given me the whole you're going to be sad or hurt speech. She's just looking out for me. I wouldn't think too much of it."

"She's your friend, Cassie. Of course she's going to look out for you. I just … she said some stuff, and it just got me thinking."

"Do you want to end it?"

He jerked back, and stared at Cassie. Her face was unreadable. He didn't know what she was thinking or feeling.

"No, I don't. Do you?"

Cassie didn't get to answer as they came to take their order.

"No, I don't," Cassie said, the moment they had their privacy. "You don't have to start freaking out. I know this isn't some kind of love thing, or a happy ever after. I have no intention of springing up words of love for you, Slade."

What if it's what I want?

"I've not been in a real relationship for some time. I didn't want to end up like my parents. Hating each other, and then causing heartache to get away from each other."

"Slade, I'm not like that."

"You've only ever been with Andrew. How do you know if you're even falling in love with me?" he asked.

She sighed. "Are we going to do this now? You want to go and screw one of the women here, Slade? Is that it? You bored already?"

"Fuck no!"

"Then what is your deal? I'm not bored. I've not told you I loved you, and you're acting like I told you I was pregnant. Don't listen to everything Jessica says, okay? She's my friend. She's allowed to do the whole threatening thing, and the worrying. Don't put that shit on me." She stood up, and this time he caught her wrist.

"Where are you going?" he asked.

"I'm going to dance with someone, and it's not going to be you. If you want to be an asshole, you can sit here, and be an ass."

She stormed onto the dance-floor, which only pissed Slade off. He was acting like an ass, and in doing so, she couldn't seem to help her reaction to him. He seemed to get under her skin and drive her crazy.

He didn't know what was wrong with him. Pushing Cassie away was not what he wanted to do. Running fingers through his hair, he forced himself to watch as Cassie was pulled into another man's arms.

Slade's hands clenched into fists as jealousy rushed through him, and then he took the time to watch her. Cassie wasn't open in her dancing. She kept the guy at arm's length, and there was no swaying of the hips, or drawing him in.

She was just having a dance with a person. There was no connection.

Stop being a fucking asshole, and go and get her.

He didn't need to be told twice. Crossing the dance-floor, he wrapped his arm around her waist, and pulled her against him.

"Sorry, man, but this woman belongs to me,"

Slade said.

The guy held his hands up. "No problem."

Cassie wound her hands around his neck, but didn't move. Her back was pressed to his front, and he kept his hands on her stomach.

"Are you done being stupid?" she asked.

"Yes."

"Are we still friends?"

"Yes."

"Do we still fuck?"

"Hell yes."

He nibbled on her neck, breathing in her scent.

You're falling for her.

She's yours for the taking.

Take her.

Slade ignored all of his thoughts, finished the dance, and then made their way back toward their table just in time to eat their food.

Chapter Ten

Entering Slade's home, Cassie giggled. The few beers she had drunk with the steak and potatoes were enough to give her a bit of a buzz. What also hadn't helped was Slade's hands all over her body as he teased her. She was on fire, and it was all his fault.

He didn't even turn the light on. He pressed her up against the wall as soon as the front door was closed, his mouth on hers as he took possession of her lips.

Slade caught her hands, pressing them above her head, and she gave herself to him, without putting up a struggle.

"You're so fucking beautiful. All day and all night I've wanted to bend you over, and fuck you so damn hard."

She pressed her thighs together, moaning as she did. The shorts she wore seemed to press against her clit so that as she closed her legs, it created a nice little pulse that made her ache for more.

Slade's thigh moved between her legs, and she gasped as he rubbed in just the right spot to make her want more.

"You want my cock, baby?"

"I thought we agreed it was going to go in my ass." She grabbed his ass, tugging him closer.

He felt so good.

She wanted him.

"We have on way too many clothes."

"You got that right. We need to get naked." Slade grabbed her shirt, and in one tug, had it torn in two. He pushed it down her arms and dropped it on the floor.

"I liked that shirt," she said.

"You wear it for gardening. It's a shitty, shitty shirt."

She chuckled. Grabbing his shirt, she didn't have the strength to tear it, and he helped as she rid it from his body.

Running her hands down his muscular chest, she grabbed his hips, grinding her pussy on his thigh.

"Does your pussy need some attention?"

"Yes. I'm so wet."

He cupped her pussy through her jean shorts, but it wasn't enough. Within seconds they were both fighting to get naked, and only when they were, did she throw herself back into his arms.

Slade pressed her against the wall, his hands cupping her tits, roughly. He pinched one breast, and then the other, before giving each curve a light slap.

"Mine!"

He claimed her lips, his hand moving up around her neck. His thumb pushed her chin up so she had no choice but to take the kiss that he was giving. His dominance turned her on even more.

The feel of his fingers on her neck made her gasp, and she closed her eyes, basking in his touch. The way he held her, she felt in that moment like she belonged to him. It was heady, amazing, and oh so fucking good. The grip on her hands tightened, and she opened her eyes, to stare at him.

"I didn't like anyone else touching you."

"Then next time, don't let me dance with anyone else." She leaned in close, and smiled. "What are you going to do, Slade?"

His hands released her, and before she knew what was happening, he held her hips, lifted her up, and plunged her down hard on his cock. He had her wedged between the wall, and his body.

They both gasped as he filled her pussy. She wrapped her arms around his neck, moaning as his hard cock took her a few moments to get used to.

"I've not put a fucking rubber on. I couldn't wait," he said.

"I'm … on the pill. I'm clean."

"I don't expect you to believe me, but I'm clean as well."

She chuckled. "Of course I believe you. You polish your boots."

"What does that have to do with anything?"

"You take the time with your appearance, and even though you think my cleaning is funny, your place is always spotless. I figured you were a stickler for health in all things."

The smile on his face was wicked. "You know what this means?"

"Nope. I'm an innocent, deputy. I've never been naughty in all my life."

"If I don't have to use a condom anymore, I can fill you with my cum," he said.

She knew that he liked seeing his claim on her skin. He was a very physical person, and the dirtier the better for him.

Cassie didn't mind. She loved his dirty mind, especially as she always benefited from it. When he got dirty, she got pleasure, and what woman in her right mind would complain about that?

He pumped inside her, and she looked down, wanting to see his cock within her.

It was too dark, and he groaned.

"Upstairs, bedroom, I want what you promised me." He pulled out of her, and she rushed ahead. He gave her ass a little slap, making her yelp.

Running to his room, she bounced on the bed, spreading her thighs open. She had come to see that whenever he caught her playing with her pussy, it always worked in driving him wild, and she wanted him wild. She wanted him at the point of no return.

When she'd asked for his help in moving her friends, she didn't know what he'd want in return. At the mention of anal, her first instinct had been to tell him to fuck off. The thing was … she'd read a lot of erotic books, and they talked in detail of anal.

She was … curious about it.

There was no one else she would ever feel more comfortable with.

Cassie smiled even as she filled her pussy with two of her fingers before pulling them out to tease her clit. The memory of his shocked face would stay with her for a long time.

He stood in the doorway, and she slid her fingers over her clit, watching him, waiting for him to react.

"You know what you're doing to me, don't you?"

"It feels so good, Slade."

"Show me how wet you are."

She held up her fingers, and he moved toward her, catching her wrist, and sucking on the digits, tasting her pussy.

"You want me to collect my debt?" he asked.

"Yes."

"Then get on your knees, and show me that ass that now belongs to me."

She moved to her knees and bent forward.

"Spread your cheeks wide. I want to see you."

Cassie did as he asked, and closed her eyes. He stroked her ass, and she released a little gasp. His touch brought her to life.

His fingers moved down the center of her ass, running across her anus and down. She closed her eyes, enjoying the unusual feel.

She was nervous, but she trusted Slade.

The sounds of a drawer opening and closing filled the air, echoing off the walls. Her excitement was building with every single second.

"You know, you have the nicest ass I've ever seen. It's so round, so juicy, and I've wanted to fuck it for as long as I can remember."

She turned her head. "You have not."

"I have. Don't get me wrong, I wanted your tits first. I saw you bent over, and those beauties nearly fell out of the shirt you were wearing. Thought I had died and gone to heaven. A woman with a nice pair of tits, and a nice juicy ass. My luck knows no bounds. Imagine my surprise to learn you didn't like me all that much."

"I didn't know you. I thought you were like other men I've known."

"Don't ever put me in the same league as Andrew. That guy is a dick for what he did, and I hear he's moving back to town. Do you want him in your life?"

"Hell, no. You keep talking about him, and I'd prefer to put the news on than listen to more stuff about him." She went to move out of his way, but he caught her before she did. "If I didn't know any better, Slade, I'd think you were jealous."

He didn't answer her question, and she gasped as he pressed the cold lube against her anus.

His fingers began to work the lubricant against her ass, working around in circles, and then he started to press forward.

"Your ass is so tight," he said. "I'm going to be the only man that fills this."

She got a thrill from his words, and had noticed all night that he'd been referring to her as belonging to him.

Cassie thought his words of possession would

have pissed her off. They were turning her on. She wanted to hear them, loved them.

She gripped the sheets beneath her tightly as he pushed a finger into her ass. He didn't stop until he was down to the knuckle.

"Do you want me to stop?" he asked, his voice soothing.

"No." It was painful but also … strangely nice. She didn't know if she wanted to push him away, or ask him for more.

He began to pump that finger into her ass, taking his time, working it in and then out, then back in again.

She held her breath as he worked in a second finger. This time, he began to stretch her ass.

"I need to get you ready to have my cock. At this rate, I'll never fit." He worked on her ass, stretching her out as he did.

Some of the feelings were uncomfortable, and some she loved. There was a tightness there, but when she played with her pussy, pleasure took over. The small bites of pain were worth it.

"I'm going to use a condom, baby." Seconds passed as she imagined him rolling it on. This was it, she was going to get her ass fucked.

His cock pressed against her ass, and she gasped as he began to slowly fill her. She had read so much that she pushed out without him even ordering her to as he began to sink inside her.

When a couple of inches of his cock was inside her, he grabbed her hips, and slowly filled her ass until she had the whole of his dick inside her.

Slade held still within her, giving her a chance to get accustomed to his dick.

"Are you okay, baby?"

"Yes. It's … big."

He chuckled, which made his cock press inside her, making her moan.

Slowly, he pulled out of her so that only the head was inside, and then filled her again. His thrusts were slow, and when she asked him to stop, to wait, he did. Slade took his time, drawing her own pleasure from her before continuing.

He brought her to orgasm before he found his, filling the condom. The tightness of her ass made her feel every pulse of his cock as he came.

There was no way she could ever do this with anyone else. This was something she could only ever feel for someone she cared about, or even worse, loved.

Did she love Slade?

****

Slade was going over a couple of reports he'd written up and a few statements over the Andersons' noise complaint when Daniel entered his office, and took a seat.

"Are you here to complain about Cassie and me?"

"No."

"You'll be the first one. I've had a warning from Jessica already. I figured now was your turn." Slade clicked his pen top, staring at his boss. Daniel was a good man, and the town loved him.

"When I heard the news that you and Cassie were together or whatever it is you call it, I thought it was a mistake. Seeing the way you are, I'm happy for the both of you."

This did surprise Slade. He'd figured Daniel would warn him, or say something to him.

"Cassie's a special woman, and I care about her deeply. I only hope that you see that, and don't hurt her, like others have done. It's Cassie that I wanted to talk to you about."

"What's up?" Slade asked, ignoring the warning that Daniel had given. His feelings for Cassie were already driving him crazy.

Daniel sighed, and held up a letter. "It's from her mother. She's very ill and wants to speak to Cassie."

Slade took the letter that Daniel gave to him, turning it around in his hands. "It's addressed to the sheriff."

"Yep, but inside is the letter for Cassie. She didn't care that her mother left. All Cassie cared about was the way it affected her father. Her mother's abandonment set off a spiral with Bill that can never be forgotten. I don't know what to do, but I figured with how close you two have gotten, you'll know."

"I don't—"

"You can fool yourself, son, but not me. You care about her. You probably even love her. It's not hard to do. She's a nice woman, when you get to know her of course. You can fight this all you want, but you can't deny that you have feelings for her. It doesn't make you any less. It makes you more of a man."

Slade turned the letter over in his hands. It had already been opened, but then it would have been. "If I don't give her this letter…"

"I'm going to leave this in your court, Slade. You'll know what to do."

Daniel got up, and Slade watched him leave, feeling like he'd just been given a much bigger responsibility than what he fucking wanted.

Staring down at the envelope his curiosity got the better of him, and he opened it up.

There were three letters in total. One was to the sheriff, the other to Bill, and then there was one to Cassie.

He ignored the others and opened Cassie's letter.

Dear Cassie,

I wanted to open up and say my darling daughter, but I don't know how that will be received. I've not seen or heard from you since you were a little girl. That is entirely my fault. Over the past few years I've come to see that my actions when you were younger, were not those of a mother, but that of a woman who was selfish, attention seeking, and a whore. Your father was a good man, and I don't know how he turned out. I've not heard from Bill after the first year of phone calls where he begged me to come home.

I left because I knew I'd never make it out of that trailer with him. I had ambitions, and he and a child weren't part of that. During the first couple of years, I didn't care. I was living the high life. I was a mistress, not a wife. When I went to certain functions, women hated me, wives mostly. Some of the men adored me, and I didn't see myself for what I really was. I was a home wrecker, a bitch, and most importantly, a whore. In my mind, I didn't take money from the men I was with. Of course, being a mistress, that's all you do. I was wrong, and I didn't realize my mistake until much later.

By the time I realized what I had lost, it was too late. You were all grown up, and I was afraid to come and visit you, Cassie. I know I should, and sending this letter is just an even bigger act of selfishness. If you crumple this up, and don't come looking for me, I understand. I know deep in my heart I'm not worth your time.

I'm dying, and it seems that you're only ever worth something to someone when you're alive and can spread your legs. That's a really cold thing for me to say, right? Well, I've been taught a hard lesson in life. I thought being a mistress was the best of all worlds. I got a man when I thought I wanted him. Clothes, an apartment, everything I could do. I didn't even have to work a day in my life. The reality is, I was at his disposal when he deemed it necessary. I wish I could say I was clever and figured that out all on my own, but that's not true. It's a lie.

He's paying for my care. He doesn't come to visit, and last I heard, he'd already moved in a new mistress. Some young twenty-something with the same life ahead of her that I had. If I had the strength I'd warn her of how cold and lonely it got. I used to pretend that it was better this way. That I didn't have to worry about caring about anyone. The truth is, unless he wanted me, I was always alone. No one wanted to be friends with a woman like me. I made that mistake. The nurse here asked if I had any regrets at all. I have so many, but the biggest one was walking away from you. I was an awful mother, and a nasty wife. Bill deserved better. So did you, my darling daughter. I am sorry for everything I put you through.

I know I can't and shouldn't ask for your forgiveness, but I've never done what was proper.

I love you, and I hope you find a wonderful life, with happiness, and a man who completely loves you. Who doesn't want to sleep in another room because he misses your closeness, your warmth, your fire. I hope you have someone in your life who will love you until your dying breath, and still hold your hand, because he can't stand to be alone.

Your mother,

Trixie

Slade put the letter down, and his eyes were brimming with fucking tears. He was a full-grown man, and shit like this shouldn't get to him. Trixie, Cassie's mother, had fucked around with her daughter's feelings, and he wasn't about to hurt her like this.

He went to screw up the letter, but he could do it. He looked down at the last part again.

Who doesn't want to sleep in another room because he misses your closeness, your warmth, your fire. I hope you have someone in your life who will love you until your dying breath, and still hold your hand, because he can't stand to be alone.

It had been a long time since he'd gone to his own apartment, and slept alone. Even when her cycle had come in, and she'd said it was okay if he wanted to go home. He'd stayed, snuggled up against her, and rubbed her stomach until she felt better. He didn't want to go through life without her in it.

Over the past few weeks, he had found himself craving Cassie's company, and often went to find her. He knew how she took her coffee, and even some of the food she liked.

She was part of his life, and he never wanted to let her go.

The only question now was what the hell was he going to do?

Chapter Eleven

Cassie didn't like the silence in the car. They were heading toward the restaurant where his parents were waiting for them. The few gifts they had bought were already wrapped and in the back of the car. In her purse was the cruise details.

"You're really quiet today," she said.

Slade had been really quiet for the past couple of days, even at work, which was strange. They had spent most of their time watching television, and they hadn't even had sex.

"Sorry. I've got a lot on my mind just lately. Wish I wasn't going to this fucking farce and bullshit. I'm sorry." He took her hand and pressed a kiss to her knuckles.

"It's okay. I know you're under a lot of pressure at work."

The Andersons didn't like that Slade had slapped them with a fine for a breach of the peace with regards to their noise. Not only that, he'd also issued a demand that a building regulator be called in. When he went to the site, and no one could provide him with one, or the manager, Slade had gotten pissed.

She figured that was more to do with Andrew being back in town. The man who had made her life a misery in her last year of high school was back. She'd seen him one day she was coming out of the diner.

He'd been strolling down the street, and at first she'd hidden behind a sign, but then, she'd laughed, and walked out with her head held high. She wasn't a shy little girl anymore. She had been so happy with the way she'd reacted, she'd gone back home to see Ray, and old lady Mary, to tell them. Of course, she'd taken a coconut cake with her, for good measure. She never wanted to go to the trailer park empty handed. Ray and Mary had been happy for her, and she'd told them all about Slade.

A few times over the past couple of years, she had offered to try to help find them a place out of the trailer park, but none of them would have it. It was their home, and they didn't hold a grudge against her for leaving. They said it was never her home.

"Do you ever think about your mother?" Slade asked.

"My mother?"

"Yeah. Sorry, it's a weird question. I know. I just, I was curious."

"No. I don't think about her to be honest. She was never a nice woman. Why?"

"No reason. Did you ever want to be a mother, have a family, lots of kids?" Slade asked.

"Yeah, I did actually." She started to laugh. "It's probably crazy now, but I wanted to be the kind of mother who wore an apron, and baked sweet pies for my kids when they were feeling miserable. The kind of woman that when she approached another parent, they knew they were getting my wrath. I wanted to be the kind of mother her kids knew they were taken care of, loved."

She didn't bother asking him what he wanted. Slade had told her many times that his future was all about the screwing, the fun. There were too many women for him to settle down with one.

His question made her pause. Did he want to end what they had? She knew it would happen one day, and probably soon. He moved from one woman to the next, without looking back. Their time together had been a ticking clock.

"Are you wanting us to end it?" she asked.

She forced herself to stare at him, and ask the

question. On the outside, she hoped she looked calm, reserved, and ready for whatever he was going to say. Inside, she was weeping. Her heart was breaking, and she hated the fact that she had grown to love this man beside her. Slade was not the kind of man she wanted in a husband. Or at least, he hadn't been when they first started this.

Damn it. She had promised herself she wouldn't fall for him, and now Jessica's warnings were rushing through her head, mocking her because the truth was, she *had* fallen deeply in love with Slade. She loved how he snored, which he didn't know about. It was really cute, and he only ever did it when he was exhausted.

Even when he left the toilet seat up, she adored him. He didn't put the cap on the toothpaste, and he often didn't put the phone back into the cradle. He drank milk straight from the carton, and she hated that. But she fucking loved him, and now he was going to leave her broken.

She grit her teeth, trying to keep the lump in her throat. She tried to stay focused on other things, but she couldn't.

"What? No. Do *you* want to end it? Because I thought things were going really well," he said.

Wow, that didn't exactly give her a confidence boost at all.

She just nodded, and then looked out of the window.

Tapping her fingers on her thigh, Cassie wondered what the hell she was going to do. She lived right next door to Slade. He had a bad reputation, and right now, she didn't think she'd ever be able to see him fall for someone else.

"Is something bothering you?" Slade asked.

"No. It's fine. I'm just nervous. This is the first

time I've seen your parents. Why were you asking about my mom?"

"No reason. Just making conversation."

Something felt off, and she didn't like it. There was an awkwardness between them. She let out a breath. When she had reached her limit, she didn't have time to ask him anymore questions as they had finally arrived at the restaurant.

His car was taken, and Slade offered his arm.

The restaurant was really fancy, and she was pleased she'd taken the extra effort with makeup and the cocktail dress.

"You look beautiful," he said, pressing a kiss to her head.

This was one of the things she loved about him. He anticipated her every single need, and right now, it was driving her crazy. Did he know she had feelings for him? Was this why he'd been distant?

He said he didn't want to end things, but for how long?

Fuck! She didn't want to be in this place, and absolutely hated it more than anything else.

She forced a smile to her lips as Slade introduced his parents. His mother was beautiful. She had long black hair, and grey eyes that sparkled. Cassie saw how beautiful she was, and was surprised by what Slade had told her.

His father looked exactly like Slade.

"This is a first. Usually our son never brings his women here," his father said.

Okay, now she was in even more shock.

"Hank, don't," she said. "Forgive my husband. His manners are not what they're supposed to be."

"I didn't mean anything by it. Joanne's right. I have a tendency to put my foot in it."

"Yeah, your mouth isn't the only thing that gets you in trouble."

This was becoming even more uncomfortable.

Slade held the chair out for her, and she thanked him. The waiter brought over some menus while Slade passed the bag of presents to him.

"Here is part of your anniversary gift," he said.

"And here's your other half," Cassie said, handing it to Slade.

Joanne, his mother, took it from him.

Cassie was nervous as Hank kept looking at her, and then at Slade.

"Have you got something to tell us, son?" Hank asked.

"I've got nothing to say, why?"

The hostility was a surprise. Cassie locked her fingers together, and hoped the meal went by without a hitch.

"Oh, look, Hank, he's sending us on a cruise."

"It should keep him by your side at all times, Mom."

"Not this again."

Cassie stayed seated as Hank leaned forward, and she saw how upset Joanne was getting.

"What is your problem?" Hank asked.

"You're my problem, and all of this crap that you pretend. You don't love her. You never have. Instead of letting her live her own life, and to find some happiness, you make her stay somehow."

"Not today," Joanne said. "I'm going to the bathroom, and when I come back, you better have resolved whatever problem you've got going on."

Cassie watched Joanne go, and made her excuses, following the other woman to the bathroom.

"I am so sorry you had to see that," Joanne said.

"I … it's always been tense between those two."

"Slade told me that Hank cheated on you."

Joanne laughed. "He's always had an issue with Hank. So tell me, how long have you been in love with my son?"

Cassie stared at his mother and knew she couldn't lie to her. "Since I've gotten to know him. At first, I didn't like him, and we never got on. When he showed me the real side of him, who could help but fall in love with him?"

Joanne smiled. "That's the best answer I could have hoped for."

****

"You want me to divorce your mother? After all this time."

"You don't deserve her," Slade said, glaring at his father. He'd not liked how Hank had put Cassie into the same group as the women he'd screwed around with. Cassie was worth more than that. He was screwing everything up with her, because the truth was, he loved her.

There, he'd admitted it to himself on the way over. He was in love with Cassie Love, and he wanted her all to himself.

"You think I don't know that?" Hank said. "You think I don't sit here, and see the men look at my wife, and know that I fucked up. That there was a time several years ago when I nearly lost her completely?"

Slade stared at his father, for the first time seeing remorse on his face.

Hank looked around the restaurant, and straightened his suit jacket. "Your mother and I, we're working on a lot of things. I would appreciate it if you didn't spend the rest of this night pointing out my faults. I know I have them. I know you've seen a lot of them.

I've not treated your mother the way she deserved to be treated."

Slade folded his arms and stared at his father. "What do you mean you nearly lost her?"

"You'd not long moved out, when I came home from work, and everything of hers was gone. She hadn't even left me a note. She had just left. One of my old affairs had turned up at our house demanding money. It was the final straw. Since then, we have been to couples' therapy. I realized when she had left me and the divorce papers came, that I couldn't lose her. I loved her, and the thought of not waking up next to her, was unbearable. I'd nearly lost the one good thing my life. She's one of a kind."

Slade thought about the letter he'd read from Cassie's mother. "You're in therapy?"

"We're repairing the damage that I caused. Your mother, she's had to put up with a lot. We've made a lot of progress. I have moments though, like just now, when things get out of hand. I'm asking you to not ... speak of anything else, and for us to have a good meal."

He stared at his father, and he actually saw a good man there. "All right. I'll do it. I won't do it for you though. I'm doing this for Mom."

"Whoever you do it for, just let us have a good meal."

They were silent, and Slade looked toward the bathroom. He'd always had a strained relationship with his dad.

"You're in love with that woman, aren't you?" Hank asked.

He didn't want to talk about his feelings for Cassie with his father. Turning his head to look at him, Slade sighed. "Are you going to bust my balls over this?"

Hank held his hands up. "For part of couples'

therapy we had to talk about you, and how our relationship impacted your life. I thought you were fine. You were just like any other kid. You'd grown up, screwed around, canceled an engagement. Then Joanne said that she believed our broken relationship had caused you not to connect with other people."

This caused Slade to roll his eyes.

"I'm being serious here, son. I was already married, and had a son at your age. I was making mistakes all the time. I thought I was trapped in a marriage that I didn't want. The truth is, I wanted it. I wanted it all, and I had it all. I just didn't see it. That doesn't excuse my behavior. Nothing does. I don't want you to hold people back because you're scared of turning out like us."

Slade tapped his fingers on the table. He wanted to ignore what his father said, but he couldn't do it.

"I'm in love with Cassie. She's my neighbor, and a colleague, and I fucking love her. I'm terrified," Slade said. Never had he been open with his father. The truth was he'd never trusted him with stuff like this.

"Why are you scared?"

He stared at Hank and released a breath. "Because we're just having a lot of fun. She doesn't want to fall in love, or be my woman." He frowned, and hated himself as he said the next thing. "I fucked other women in my yard, and she could hear. The man she first knew wasn't a good man. I was an asshole. I was a … fucker!" He gritted his teeth.

"I know we've got a lot of work to do, you and I. I'd say any woman willing to come and eat with your parents, and go shopping with you, I think there's a lot more going on than you think."

Slade looked at his dad. "You think there's a chance she loves me?"

"Yeah, I really do."

He never expected to feel relief over that, but now he had to work on getting her to admit to it. He loved her, more than anything.

There was no time to ask for more, as his mother and Cassie came back.

She gave him a smile, and it was like a switch went off in his brain. He stared at her, and he saw his future. Was this what the other couples felt that had come before him? He didn't know, nor did he care. All he wanted was Cassie, and a future with her.

He'd not wanted anyone else, and he knew he never would. She was his one true love, and he'd been too blind to see it.

With the revelation, and knowing he couldn't hold it in for much longer, he got through the meal without any other hitches.

Cassie spoke with his father, who apologized for his earlier comments. As Slade watched his father and mother, he saw a bond there that had never been there before, and it give him hope that maybe his mother would get her happy ending that she'd always wanted.

After the dinner, they hugged, and he promised to visit more often, and then he was in the car, driving back home.

"Your parents seemed nice. After ... that little glitch."

"Yeah, they're working on it. I may have judged him too harshly," he said.

"I don't know. I guess people can change."

He glanced over at her. "You think that?"

"What?"

"People can change."

She chuckled. "I saw it firsthand, Slade. I know people can change. My dad went from being a great guy, to a drunk and loser. I spent so much time in Daniel's office that it feels like home when I'm working."

He pulled up outside her home, and followed her. She was unlocking her door, when he reached out and stopped her. Right at that moment, rain began to fall down. It started as a few drops at first before it became heavier.

"Is everything okay?" Cassie asked. "It's raining. Let's get inside."

"There's something I need to ask you, and I can't do this inside. I don't want to do this inside. I need to do it out here, for you to hear."

"I can hear inside, Slade," she said.

"I've done something awful," he said.

This had her turning back to look at him. "What?"

He reached out, cupping her cheek. "I did something I promised I wouldn't do."

She was frowning now.

"I've … fallen in love with you." He felt like a fucking idiot as he had tears in his eyes. His hands were shaking, and he'd never felt so fucking scared in all of his life. "I love you, Cassie. I don't want us to keep on messing around, and having fun. Actually, I want us to keep on doing that, but I want you to know that one day, I want to marry you, and I want you to have my kids."

Her mother was open in shock, and he saw her eyes glisten as well, but that could have been the rain which was soaking the both of them.

"I've known for a little while, but I've not wanted to say anything. I fought it to be honest. I don't want to fight it anymore. Being with you is like the best feeling in the world. You make everything better just by being near you." He stroked her hair, and stared into her eyes. "That's what I did, Cassie. I fell in love with you, and now I don't know what to do next."

She didn't speak for what felt like a lifetime, and then she threw herself into his arms. He held her close, kissing her neck, holding her tightly, and knowing deep in his heart he was never going to let her go.

"I love you, too. I was so scared. I thought you wanted to end it. I didn't even realize that you loved me as well."

"We've both been struggling then."

She pulled away, and he cupped her cheeks, kissing her hard on the lips.

"Let's get out of this rain."

He picked her up, and carried her through her door, up the stairs, where he spent the rest of the night making love to her.

Chapter Twelve

Three weeks later

Cassie stood outside of the hospital room where her mother was being treated. Terminal cancer had caught her mother, and according to the nurse she had less than a month to live.

She had asked for Slade to wait in the car. This wasn't going to be a trip that took long. When he'd showed her the letters the day after he'd confessed his love, Cassie had fought the decision of coming here.

At first, she'd said her mother could rot after everything she did. Now, she didn't want to leave without getting some closure herself. The letter had answered a lot of questions, but she needed to see her mother for herself.

Entering her mother's room, the bed was empty, but the chair near the window had a woman who looked nothing like Cassie remembered of her mother.

Gone was her hair, and she wore a scarf over her head. She looked frail, old, and … lonely.

Trixie turned toward her, and there was that moment where Cassie saw that her mother recognized her.

"Cassie," she said.

Even her voice sounded weak.

For the longest time Cassie stared at the woman that she had hated for most of her life. Even after reading the letter she'd sent to her father, she hadn't felt sorry for the woman. Her mother had written how sorry she was for being a shitty wife and that she hoped he'd found the perfect woman, and he lived a wonderful life.

Taking a seat in front of her mother, Cassie stared at the woman who she felt had ruined her life.

"I'm so pleased you came."

"I don't think I am," she said. "In fact, I wish I hadn't come." Cassie shook her head, even as tears came to her eyes. "Was all this worth it? You're alone, and you don't know anything."

Tears fell down Trixie's face. "No, it wasn't worth this."

"You only regretted it though because you realize how alone you are." Cassie laughed and shook her head, tears running down her face. She felt sad for the woman sitting in front of her, but this didn't make her feel any better. There were no great revelations.

"Where's Bill?" Trixie asked. "I thought ... he'd come with you."

"He's dead. He's been dead for over six years." Cassie stared at her mother. "You left, and he spiraled. Lost his job, his reputation, and turned to drink. He became an alcoholic, picked a fight, and was killed."

Trixie bowed her head, and Cassie wiped away her tears. "This was a mistake coming here. I'm sorry that you're alone, and that you wanted forgiveness or whatever. Fine. I forgive you. If that's what you need, then I forgive you."

There was no connection, no love. If anything, Cassie was angry at her, and she couldn't bring herself to hurt the woman who was dying.

"I'm sorry, Cassie."

"I know you are. I'm going to be getting married," Cassie said. "I fell in love with a deputy, you don't know him." Cassie smirked. The way she saw it, Trixie would have probably tried to sleep with him.

"Can you at least sit with me for a while?" Trixie asked. "I'd really like it if you'd do that."

For the next month, Cassie visited her mother every single day. Slade would drive her to the care home where she would sit with her. They would stare out into the garden, and toward the end of her mother's life, they'd even started the plans for Cassie' wedding.

Her mother picked out the dress, and also handed her the gold band that Bill had gotten Trixie.

"You didn't sell it?"

"I tried to sell it many times. I could never part with it," Trixie said. "I'm ashamed that he died like that. I drove him to drink, and to being an awful father. I'm sorry I can't make it up to you, Cassie, sweetie."

One week later, Trixie passed away, and Cassie buried her body in the same plot that Bill was resting in.

Daniel was there, with Jessica, William, and Slade. They were at her back as she lowered her last parent into the ground. Resting her head against Slade's shoulder, he wrapped his arms around hers, holding her close.

"I love you," she said.

"I wish I hadn't shown you those stupid letters," he said, whispering the words against her ear.

"I'm glad that you did."

"It made you sad," Slade said. "I don't like to see you sad."

She smiled up at him. "I got closure, Slade. There was no way I could have gotten anything else. I was never close to her when she was in my life. At least I got something, and that's all I can ask for."

"You'll always have me, babe. Always."

She closed her eyes, and knew she would never throw him away. She'd cherish him always.

****

Six months later

"Are you going to pass out?" Daniel asked.

"No. I'm good." Slade glanced down at his watch, and then looked back up, waiting. He was nervous. Cassie was five minutes late, and so far there was no sign of Jessica or his mother either.

He was standing near the priest. His parents sat with the guests, and he even saw the Andersons had decided to join the celebration. He'd sent then an invitation but hadn't expected them to actually come. Of course, he'd made sure Andrew Anderson had gotten one.

Slade smirked, thinking about the other asshole. He'd been out taking a walk with Cassie when they had bumped into Andrew.

Cassie had smiled at Andrew, and introduced him. At the same time, Jessica had called her into a shop, leaving him alone with Andrew, where he had made sure that the guy knew Cassie belonged to him, and if he ever heard or saw Andrew saying shit about his woman, he'd personally make his life a living hell.

Andrew had gotten cocky, and said he couldn't be touched. Slade had told Andrew to ask his parents just how difficult he could be.

That had been the end of that, and of course, Slade had won. He had Cassie's heart, her body, and their future would be together if only she turned up.

He was starting to get nervous. What if she had cold feet? He checked to make sure he had the ring she'd been looking at in the jewelers that time. The ring that would bind her to him was nestled in the fabric. Looking up, he saw the clerk was watching. When he went back to get the ring, he'd invited the clerk to his wedding.

Slade felt people looking at him, and when he was about to grab his cell and call her, Jessica came rushing forward, and the music started up.

Only when he saw Cassie did he take a breath. She looked stunning in the white dress that was cut off her shoulders, and enhanced her curves. He was going to have a lot of fun getting her out of that tonight.

Finally, when she was in his arms, he felt like the world was right again.

"What took you so long?" he asked.

"Car trouble. I'm sorry. I didn't know it would take that long." She gave his arm a squeeze, and then they stood facing the priest.

Binding himself to Cassie made Slade feel whole again. She was his, and he was hers, and together they could handle anything.

By the time it came for him to kiss the bride, in front of the whole town, he claimed Cassie as his forever.

Maybe the curse on the house was right. Although, he didn't see it as a curse. No, he saw it as a blessing.

Epilogue

Five months later

Casey rubbed her swollen stomach as she smiled at the house that had changed her life. She and Slade had been happily married for five months now, and they were also pregnant.

A little baby was on the way, and with it, they had picked a new house together. The couples that had gone before them had sold the houses at exactly the same time, and they didn't want to break the spell, the curse, or the coincidence that brought people together.

She thought it was sweet that Slade wanted to give another couple a chance.

"You okay, baby?" Slade asked, coming up behind her. He wrapped his arms around her waist, cupping his child, and kissing her neck.

Closing her eyes, she basked in his attention, and his love.

"Yeah, I'm okay. So do you think we picked the right couple?" she asked.

"You know, it makes me wonder if something was in the cards when I picked this house. I came here after you. You were already settled. Don't you think that is creepy?"

"Three different guys put an offer on your house, but they all fell through. I guess it really was meant to be with you," she said, smiling.

"I have a feeling you're mocking me right now."

She covered her mouth, trying to hide the giggle. "I don't think two houses being together determine if a couple gets together."

"You don't?"

"No." She spun in his arms. "There's so much more to it than just a house."

"Well, Mrs. Coal, I believe this is the last box. I intend to take you home, and we're going to break in our new bed."

"We are?"

"Yes. All this weekend your pussy is mine. We've got a little one arriving soon, and before he or she does, I want to fuck you in every single room of the house and make it yours."

Her pussy pulsed as a fresh wave of arousal hit her. Ever since she'd gotten pregnant, she had found herself more and more turned on.

He nibbled her neck, driving her need even higher.

"Let's get out of here."

"I told you I'd find another reason for us to not unpack," he said.

She chuckled, and as they left their home, she saw the two large trucks heading their way. They already had another place, which they had been taking boxes to throughout the week.

Climbing into the passenger seat, she watched as the woman Slade had sold his house to climbed out and began to carry stuff into the house.

The guy that she had sold to was covered in ink and looked like he was going to be a nightmare to live next to.

"I give it a year," Slade said.

"A year for what?"

"A year before they're a couple."

She rolled her eyes. "You still think the houses bring couples together."

He shrugged. "I've got the love of my life sitting beside me, pregnant with my kid. I've got to believe in something." He took her hand, pressing a kiss to her knuckles. "Come on, I know for a long time I was the fucker next door. It didn't take you long to change your mind."

"Fine." She looked at the couple. The girl was prim, proper, and looked like she went to church. Pursing her lips, she had the time frame. "Six months."

"That's not long."

"I know it's not. But I don't think it's going to take them long either."

"Babe, you've got yourself a bet."

No, she had the man of her dreams, and a future she always wanted. Maybe he was right, and dreams or blessings, do come true.

The End

PRINCESS NEXT DOOR

Sam Crescent

❖

Chapter One

Wynter Griffin gritted her teeth as once again the sounds of loud, heavy rock filled the air. How many parties could her damn neighbor have? He'd only been moved in for a week, and he'd had an excuse to celebrate every single night. She'd only just finished unpacking and was now getting everything into order.

There was no way that her very inked neighbor had already gotten cozy. He had way more stuff than she did—she'd seen it all while he moved in—but he also had a lot of people helping him out, while she only had the help of the moving men. None of her family wanted to help, as they believed she was making a huge mistake.

This wasn't because they didn't want her to move out. No, they didn't like that she'd not gotten married or had a baby. They were great believers in marrying young, raising a family young, so that you can enjoy it when you're older. The guy she'd dated in high school … she cringed just thinking about it. He'd had a mean streak a mile long. She'd dated him because her parents arranged it all.

They made sure she was constantly in contact with him. Inviting him to dinner, making sure they were together for dates out. She was never bored because Carey was always talking ... always. Sometimes, she actually fell asleep listening to him.

Shaking her head, she rubbed at her temples as the music vibrated the walls.

So, all alone, she'd moved out of her parents' house and come here. Her grandparents had left her some money in their will, so she'd made her escape from the constant pressure of being advised to have kids.

She worked with kids Monday through to Friday as a teaching assistant, helping where children needed her most.

At twenty-five years old, she knew without a shadow of a doubt that settling down, marriage, kids, none of that was for her right now. She was still a virgin. There was no way she'd be giving herself to Carey, and when he'd tried on prom night she'd made sure he knew the score. Her body was her own.

Sitting down in the center of her hallway, she rested her hands on her knees and took in a giant breath.

Everything is fine. More than fine. It's just loud music like it is every single night.

The first night, she'd been fine with it. In fact, she'd even danced around her home, crazy because that was what it was, her home. She'd been so excited and so happy that nothing had gone wrong.

She hated being negative but she'd also seen disaster over the years, and she didn't want to think about it.

Feminine screams filled the air, and she opened her eyes, knowing she wouldn't get to sleep tonight.

Determined to do something about it, she opened

the door just as someone knocked.

"Wow, good timing."

She stared at her neighbor of a week and refused to look at his muscular, inked body, which he had on full display as he only wore a pair of swimming trunks. She'd already seen from her bedroom that he owned a pool, and she didn't. The previous owner, Slade something, had told her the pool was perfection, but he'd been in love with his neighbor, and she didn't intend to ever fall for this guy.

"So, I was wondering, you want to come and join the party?" he asked, sticking his hand out toward her. "I'm Zane Webster."

Staring at his hand, she didn't want to be rude, and years of being taught proper etiquette had her gripping his hand, not too hard though. Her mother's constant nagging about a woman not wanting to appear butch and strong kept rolling around her head.

"Hi, I'm Wynter Griffin."

"Pretty name for a beautiful woman. How about you join us?"

She shook her head. "I was, erm, I was wondering…" She really didn't want to think about how good it felt holding his hand, or how nice he looked.

Nice was too subtle a word.

He was fucking hot.

She never swore though.

Often in her mind but never out loud for anyone to hear.

Swearing made men think of the gutter, and like her mother always said, the key to a good marriage is sacrifice, a lot of it, to be a happy bunny. What Wynter got from that was to grit your teeth when your husband pisses you off.

"If you could perhaps turn the music down a

little?"

"It's Friday night." He smirked.

She really didn't like it when men smirked. To her it was like he was insulting her.

Be calm, Wynter. Be so calm.

"You've played it late every single day this week. It has been a party every single day." She kept trying to remain calm. Nothing good ever, ever came of losing your temper.

See, Mommy, I'm being a good girl.

A very good girl.

"Yeah, well, it's been a party all week. These places are designed for partying, right? I mean, we're set back from the street. The trees are large enough that the music doesn't carry, and no one complains."

I'm trying to complain.

"I really need to get some sleep."

"Come on, Wynter, have a little fun. Don't be a stick in the mud."

She glared at him. "A stick in the mud? Really?"

He stared at her, and she saw the hard set of his jaw, which again enhanced his muscular physique. She loved his ink, and had always wanted to get a tattoo, but her parents wouldn't like it.

If anything risked her getting the third degree, she avoided it. The bonus to living on her own, though, was she didn't have to listen to it every single day, just when they decided to visit, which was never right now.

They didn't want to help, so she was all on her own.

"Look, princess, I think we've gotten off on the wrong foot."

"Princess?" she asked. "With how loud and how long you've been playing music, I should call the police and have you arrested, or at the very least fined."

"You got a problem with my music?"

"Yeah, it's too loud, and it's awful. This is not music, it's noise. Can't you have any consideration for other people?" She took a deep breath and completely regretted her outburst.

He held his hands up. "Whatever the princess wants, right?"

"No, don't be like that. I just want it to be a little quieter." She didn't want to start an argument with her neighbor.

She'd seen television shows devoted to how dangerous it could be. This wasn't supposed to be a bad experience, but a very enjoyable one.

"Party's over. Everyone out!"

She watched as Zane ran through his place, and she stood on her doorstep as one by one he kicked everyone out, calling the party to an end.

The music turned off, and she wrapped her arms around herself as guilt rushed through her.

His guests, or friends, or both, all glared at her, calling her names.

"Prissy bitch."

"Stick in the mud."

"Boring bitch."

She'd heard a lot of things in her time, but thirty minutes later, she stood on her very quiet doorstep, and Zane came toward her.

She felt awful and for good reason. She'd totally lashed out.

"Look, princess, I don't know if you understand this, but if you've got a problem with someone, you don't have to go to the police. You can just come right over to my place and tell me. Was it so hard to just knock and ask to turn the music down?" Zane asked.

"I don't mind the music, but you had it on all

week, and I was tired."

"You could have enjoyed the party."

She shook her head, wishing the guilt would disappear. This wasn't what she wanted, not by a long shot.

Turning on her heel, she stepped over her threshold and glanced back. "My name's Wynter, not princess."

"Yeah, I'll remember that, princess. I'll be sure to."

She closed the door, and leaned against it, slumping a little. In the back of her mind, she heard her mom berate her, and she gritted her teeth.

"Shut up, this is my house, and if I want to slump, I'll damn well slump."

Moving away from her door, she went up to her bedroom, stripping down and changing into bed shorts and shirt, she brushed her hair, looking out over the garden. She saw Zane in his, and she couldn't resist watching him as he picked up the trash. He hadn't put on a shirt, and with each movement his muscles seemed to ripple. Biting her lip, she wondered what it would be like to run her hands down his back, to hold him as he drove deep inside her.

She gasped, pressing her thighs together as the erotic thought rushed through her mind, sending fire into her body.

****

"I can't believe she got you to break up the party," Jones said.

"Yeah, and I can't believe how unlucky you've gotten to be put next to a bitch," Riot said.

Zane stared at his friends, who'd stopped by to help him. It was Saturday morning, and he had most of the outside cleaned up.

His friends were his rock, and they'd helped him move in and to put a real stamp on the place. He hated feeling like he was in a moving place, so getting everything set up meant a great deal to him.

His home was his comfort zone, and he'd fallen in love with this place the moment he saw it. Cassie, the woman who owned it before him, had kept the walls a plain magnolia and the ceilings white, all very neutral colors.

"It's fine. She had a point," Zane said, sticking up for his princess next door. Wynter. He liked the name.

"What point was that?" Silas asked. "To ruin your party?"

"We'd been partying for a week straight. I'm not defending her, but I'm sure if she'd been playing some of that shitty pop music and having lame-ass girly parties, I'd complain."

Jones, Riot, and Silas stared at each other. "A bunch of chicks throwing pillows, bikinis, and parties, nah, you wouldn't have complained. You'd be the filling in any sandwiches."

Zane thought about his blonde-haired, blue-eyed neighbor. He wouldn't mind seeing her in a bikini. Her hot, curvaceous body would fill one out beautifully. He'd always been a sucker for a woman with curves, never seeing the appeal of the slender woman. He was always put off by their bony hips showing with a bikini, always hard, and it was kind of painful screwing them.

He liked a bit of cushion for his fucking. In that moment he imagined Princess spread out on his bed, her legs open, begging for him to fuck her.

He'd been hoping she'd knock on his door, introducing herself. He hadn't for a second thought that it would be to hit him with a warning, and looking half-crazed while she did it. Still, he thought she looked hot even when angry.

"What do you know about her then?" Riot asked.

"Know about her?"

"Come on, Zane. You've lived next door to her. You've got to know something. Is she a natural blonde?"

"I have no idea."

"Maybe I should take her out for a test drive. I can let you know if she's a natural or not," Riot said.

Jealousy struck him hard, and Zane shook his head. "You're going to leave her alone." He felt all of his friends' gazes on him, and he didn't give a shit. There was no way any of them were going to be dating or even screwing his neighbor.

"Are you calling dibs?" Silas asked.

"Okay, right now I don't know if you're doing this to just piss me off or if you have a genuine interest in her."

Riot shrugged. "Now I'm curious as to why you don't want me testing her out."

"She's my neighbor, Riot. I'm not having you break her heart. I live right next door. You've heard of a woman scorned and all that shit, right?"

"Nah," Silas said. "He likes her. Like really, really likes her."

Zane ignored them as he grabbed his vacuum and began to clean up the mess. He loved throwing parties, but the cleaning up afterward was always a fucking nightmare. He hated doing it and had no choice, seeing as he didn't like anyone else going through his stuff, so professional cleaners were out of the question, or at least for him they were. He couldn't stand them.

He bet Princess loved to clean and keep everything tidy. Opening up his curtains and window to let some fresh air inside, he paused when he caught sight of that very neighbor in a pair of shorts and tank top, mowing her front lawn. Their lawns weren't much, but she pushed a tiny mower back and forth. When she spun around, he saw her breasts moving with each back and forth motion. Just the sight of her made his dick ache to see what other temptations she hid underneath.

"I'm going to throw this into the trash." Without waiting for confirmation from his friends, he left his home and stood near his trash bin.

She stopped mowing the moment he appeared.

"Hey," he said.

"Would you like me to do yours as well?" she asked.

He watched as she wiped her brow. It was really hot out, and he wished she'd forgone the shorts and shirt. "Sure, if it's not too much trouble."

She shook her head. "It's fine. I didn't know if I should do it or not."

He waited as she turned the mower back on and started to work on his patch.

Heading inside, he saw his three friends in the corridor watching him.

"Admit it, you like her," Jones said.

"Are you guys ever going to grow up?" he asked, shaking his head.

"If you like her, you should totally take her out a cool drink," Silas said.

He glanced toward Riot, who stayed silent. "Do you have any advice?"

"If you like her, you've got to put your mark on her now, as otherwise you're totally going to be watching guys pick her up and leave."

Rolling his eyes, Zane made his way to the fridge. "Would you look at that? Two sodas. You guys will have to find yourself something else to drink."

As he made his way toward the front of the

house, he heard the noise stop. Opening his door, he was tempted to close it, but figured his friends would prank him and lock it, making him look like a complete clown.

"Cold soda?" he asked, holding up one hand.

"Would love it." She reached out, taking one can from him and smiling. He liked her smile. It was warm, and made him think of long summer nights, along with a lot of other dirty thoughts. The long summer nights thought must only be because it was so warm. There wasn't any connection between her smile and the feelings she was stirring up inside him.

"Thank you for doing this."

"No problem. I don't want it to overgrow and look a mess." She pointed at the rest of the street. "When I moved in the guy who owned it before me said that the neighbors may be a little picky if it looks a mess. I like this neighborhood."

"Yeah, I can't do the whole apartment thing. I know there were a few good places, but I've had bad experiences with them."

"What kind?" she asked.

"Let's see. A handsy landlord."

She chuckled. "Really?"

"Yep. He didn't care who you were, he wanted a piece of the action."

"Oh, my, that's just awful," she said.

"Yep, and then you've got the druggies on the top floor. That was a really bad experience if ever I remember one. Then of course I had the leaky roof."

"Leaky roof?"

"I've found apartments are great providing you with lots of people who like their apartment and are not hunting for the next place."

"Gotcha."

He nodded. "What about you?"

"Erm, I lived with my parents up until moving here. We're a big kind of family who believe in staying together."

Zane figured there was more to the tale but she didn't let on anything else, and he didn't pressure her to tell him more.

"This is your first big place?"

"Yes."

"How old are you?" she asked. "If you don't mind me asking, of course."

He laughed. "I'm thirty years old. You?"

"Twenty-five."

He wouldn't put his foot in his mouth and tell her she was a little old to still be living with her parents. She wasn't still living with them, but still, he stayed silent.

"I'm really sorry about last night," she said. "It had been a long week, and you play rock music so loud that my home was vibrating with it, and I just wanted to get some sleep, but the way I behaved last night, there's no excuse. I'm sorry."

"It's fine."

"More than fine, lovely," Jones said.

He glanced behind him to see his three friends standing in his doorway.

"Hello," she said.

"Don't worry, sweet thing, we don't all live here. We're just buddies of this guy here, not that he deserves us," Silas said.

She chuckled. "Well, it's nice to meet you all."

"How about you introduce us, Zane? Stop looking like the grumpy guy you are," Riot said.

Again, she chuckled, and he didn't want her to stop. He loved the sound.

"These are my friends. Jones is the big guy at the back, there's Riot, and that one is Silas. They helped me move in."

She offered a little wave. "Wynter Griffin."

All three of his friends came out, taking her hand and kissing her knuckles.

"You're a delight," Silas said.

"You wouldn't have thought that last night," she said.

"Which has me wondering what keeps you busy all week?" Jones asked, and Zane didn't like that any of them were taking an interest.

"I'm a school assistant. Young children eight and nine years old."

His friends were impressed. Her gaze turned to his. "What do you do?"

"I work in a bar, and on the weekends, we like to pretend we're a rock band."

"Really?" she asked.

"We play a couple of gigs, not a big real rock band, but we get by," he said. He didn't want to brag.

"Maybe one day I'll see you guys perform."

And one day I'll sing for you naked, just the two of us.

Chapter Two

After her embarrassment on Friday, Wynter didn't know if she should bake a pie for her neighbor or if that would be considered a little ... too showy. They'd not gotten a chance to talk with his friends around, and she saw easily that it pissed him off, which she found adorable.

"That's a nice big smile on your face," Tammy said. Tammy was the teacher in the class she assisted. Forty years old, kids, a family, and so nice.

"My neighbor."

"The very same one you were complaining about last week about constantly listening to rock music?"

"Yep, the very one. I totally went crazy at him when he invited me to join, and I felt bad because he broke everything up."

"He did? Sounds like a decent guy."

"I threatened to call the cops."

Tammy winced.

"Then the next day I mowed his front lawn, and I met his friends. He's in a rock band, or they're a rock band."

"What are they called?" Tammy asked.

"I don't know."

"You didn't ask?"

"It's not like I would know. I don't listen to rock music ever."

"So what's got a smile on your face?"

Wynter sighed. "I don't know. It's crazy. Thinking about him makes me smile, and then I think about what I said, and how I reacted. Should I bake him a pie? Then I'm nervous because pies are like a sign, right, that you want something?"

Tammy's brow rose. "You're really thinking about this?"

"I really, really, really don't know what to do. I'm so confused." She dropped her head to the table in time to hear Tammy's snort of laughter.

"Is he hot?"

Lifting her head up, she stared at her friend. They'd met at a barbeque over five years ago, and even though there were fifteen years between them, they'd really hit it off, and been best friends ever since.

It was Tammy who'd suggested she find her own way, move out, and stop putting up with the pressure from her family.

Wynter had been complaining daily about the constant hints of babies and marriage, and she was tired of them throwing up her sisters and her friends. It was all just too much.

Tammy had understood, and once a new place was mentioned, Wynter felt it was a lifeline, a chance to live her own life exactly the way she wanted to without anyone tell her what she could and couldn't do.

"Maybe."

"That's a yes."

"You've not met him."

"And you've not said he's not either. What's he look like?"

Looking past her shoulder, Wynter nibbled her lip. "Short hair, lots of tattoos. I've seen them going around his neck and across his entire chest and back. They're not ugly either, quite beautiful, mesmerizing." She wanted to trace those tattoos, but she shook that thought from her mind. "That's about it. Brown hair, you know."

"He looks like your average bad boy?"

"In a way, yes, but he's really, really nice. I think.

You have to be nice right to, erm, to completely break down your party for your neighbor?"

"I don't know, Wynter. He sounds like a sweet keeper, and someone your parents would completely throw a fit over."

"Nothing like that is going to happen." She tucked some of her hair behind her ear. "The pie?"

"I think you should do whatever you feel comfortable doing." Tammy stared at her. "Have you ever been in a relationship?"

"There was Carey."

"He doesn't count. He's not even in the same league as boyfriend material."

"He was a boy and my friend," she said.

"You put up with him to get your parents off your back. Okay, have you ever just been with a guy?"

Wynter glanced around the room hoping no one could overhear them. Tammy wasn't known for having much of a filter, and she herself loved her for it. After being around her mother, who was a constant advisor for keeping feelings at bay, she found Tammy refreshing.

"It's just us. No one will talk."

"I've never ... been with a guy."

"You're a virgin?"

She nodded.

"What? How?"

Wynter frowned. "Because I've never had sex with a guy, that's how. That's the scientific way of not having sex and staying a virgin."

Tammy waved her hand in the air. "Not even with Carey?"

She wrinkled her nose. "Ew, no. He was fine, but he was always talking about marriage and kids, and to be really honest I zoned out half the time. I knew what I wanted."

"Your parents are so weird."

Wynter leaned forward. "You were married at eighteen, and had a child on the way."

"I know, but that's because I was married to my childhood sweetheart, and even after all this time, we're still together."

They leaned over the table, whispering.

"I've never been interested in just sleeping with random guys." She shrugged. "Call me weird."

"You're very weird." Tammy ate a potato chip as Wynter ran a hand down her face. "Make him the pie."

"You think so?"

"Have you heard the rumors about the houses you and your neighbor are in?"

"His name's Zane. Rumors?"

"You know, about the last few single people that moved in, living together."

Wynter frowned, trying to think about it, and finally shook her head. "Nope. Can't say that I have."

Tammy whistled. "For the past couple of years, every single couple that has lived in those two houses have always ended up together."

"Yeah, okay. I'm not a child."

"I'm being serious here. I'm not joking around. The guy who sold you the house, he was leaving right?"

Wynter paused recalling Slade telling her that he was married to the girl next door. "Yeah."

"Maybe it's fate and you and Zane are destined to be married?" Tammy held her hands up. "If not, you could probably lose that V-card and find out why I love my husband so much." Tammy winked at her. "Enjoy your lunch."

Wynter watched her friend walk away, and she blew out a breath.

Being a virgin wasn't exactly her plan.

She didn't want to remain one either.

Sitting back, she pulled her hair out of the tight band and ran her fingers through the length, closing her eyes, and tried to think.

Slade had been a nice guy, but she'd also seen his wedding photo. So much in love.

There was no way the houses brought people together, and as for her and Zane, it was an absolute no.

She needed to go on a date, or do something.

There was no way she'd get hung up on her neighbor.

Dating sites were out of the question, as she'd heard way too much bad stuff about them. How was she ever going to meet a guy of her own choosing?

Going to a bar!

Finishing off her lunch, she made her way back to the classroom where Tammy was setting up. She'd scrubbed all the chalk off the board, and was joining up some letters.

"I've got it."

"What?" Tammy asked.

"How do you feel about going to a bar Friday night?"

Tammy looked at her once again, brow raised. "You know I'm forty, right, and married?"

"That doesn't mean you're dead. Get a babysitter and bring Marshall."

Tammy laughed. "*You* are my babysitter. My kids have blacklisted all credible babysitters because they're terrors and they only like you. If you want me to go out, you've got to talk to my kids."

She loved Tammy's kids. They were a bit of a handful, but she found bribery with food worked every single time.

"Deal."

"Wait!" Tammy held her hand up. "Where did we go from pie to Friday night? You don't need Marshall and me to be your wingmen."

"I can't go to a bar on my own. Besides, you could totally give me a thumbs-up or a thumbs-down on potential dates."

"I've confirmed that you're a weirdo, right? I say this with all the love in the world." Tammy placed a hand over her chest.

"Come on, you've got to help me with this. I'm not good with dating and talking to men."

"Then you need to use your neighbor. He'll be a good one to practice on."

She shook her head. "I can't practice on him, and besides, this is totally not practice. This is the real thing. I know I can trust you."

Tammy groaned. "I hate doing these things."

"Please, please, please, if you love me. You're my best friend in the whole wide world, and no one would take care of me like you." She wrapped her arms around Tammy, hoping her friend would cave.

"Yes, fine!"

****

Serving up beer, Zane looked around the crowded bar and nodded his head to the beat of the heavy rock music the live band was playing.

His friends were in one corner, tuning up his guitar for him. He sang, played the guitar, and occasionally smashed the drums.

"You playing tonight, Zane?" a brunette asked.

"You betcha."

There was a time the pussy in the bar would have appealed to him, but for some strange reason he couldn't get a little blonde in conservative shorts and tank top out of his freaking mind. Even last night he'd woken up with some serious wood, and it had taken him half an hour to deal with that shit.

Every single morning, he was awake in time to watch her climb into her car and drive away. His life was becoming stalkerish with his obsession to know more about the princess living next door.

"Three beers," Jones said.

"You driving?"

"Nope, you are." Jones winked at him. "It's a big crowd tonight."

"It's always a big crowd."

"I don't mind. We're going to smash the shit out of it either way." Jones took the beer, handing him some cash. "Well, well, well, it must be your lucky night. Look who just walked in."

Zane looked toward the door and gritted his teeth.

He shouldn't have thought about her. Work was the only place he wasn't tempted to see her, and now here she stood, in his damn place of work, the bar. She wasn't alone either. He saw a much older woman and man beside her.

"I wonder if she's stalking you," Jones said, winking at him.

His friends had been riding his ass over his little obsession with her. Not that it was all that much of a problem or anything. Watching someone wasn't a crime, or at least he fucking hoped not.

Wynter headed toward the bar, and Zane ignored Jones, making sure he was the one to serve her.

Princess spotted him first. "Zane, I had no idea you worked here."

"Yep, been working her a few years now." He nodded at her and glanced at the other two people.

"Stop being rude, honey. Introduce us," the woman said.

"Zane, this is Tammy and Marshall. They're both really great friends. This is my neighbor I was telling you about."

He held his hand out. Marshall shook his hand firmly. "Nice to meet you."

After he nodded at Marshall and then at Tammy, his gaze returned to the blonde bombshell. Her hair fell down around her in ringlets, looking sexy as fuck. She reminded him of sin and sweetness mixed together. *The things I want to do with her.*

Tammy took the lead, ordering a round of beers, and he got them in the nick of time.

"Enjoy," he said.

He couldn't linger as another customer was already signaling to him that he wanted a refill.

For the next hour he kept them all in his sights. They took a booth, and he watched as they all talked, leaning over the table and looking out onto the dance floor.

Finally, after about half an hour, Princess and Tammy got up and joined the others in the center of the room. He saw a couple of men interested in his very sexy neighbor. He understood exactly what they were all seeing … fresh meat. There was no way anyone else could deny she was temptation in their midst, and he felt like calling dibs first. Ignoring his instinct, he kept on serving at the bar, noticing Jones, Silas, and Riot all kept an eye on her as well.

He wanted to be out there to ask her to dance rather than the stuck-up prick that actually approached her. Watching the scene, he wondered if that was Tammy's idea all along. To get out there and dance until someone hit on Princess because her husband was there to take her in his arms the moment Princess smiled up at the other man.

"You okay, man?" Riot asked, stepping up to the bar.

"Yeah, why wouldn't I be?"

"You're holding those scissors like your life depended on it." Riot nodded at his grip. Zane hadn't even realized he'd picked them up. Putting them down, he grabbed three beers and placed them in front of Riot.

"Make sure no one else dances with her," he said.

Riot glanced behind him just as another man stepped up, and he had to watch as she laughed and began dancing with another guy. He didn't like it. No one should be dancing with her.

Why not?

She's young.

Free.

Single.

Ugh, he hated that word.

"Get up, rock your thing, and she won't be looking at any other guy by the end of the night."

He simply shook his head. "Do this favor for me. Please."

"Holy shit, are you begging right now?"

"I asked nicely."

"Yeah, and I've known you for years, and in all that time I can't recall you ever, ever, saying please. Give me one good reason why." Riot held the bottles in his hands while also having that no-nonsense look about him, which only served to piss Zane off more.

"I like her. I don't want any other man to be with her. Is that enough?"

"It'll do for now. I'll let the guys know."

He noticed her coming toward the bar, and he quickly urged Riot away. When the two passed she gave Riot a big smile.

"Three more beers please, Mr. Bartender."

"You having fun?" he asked.

"Yeah, a whole lot of fun. I had no idea how amazing this would be. It's not weird though, right? Me being here? We're only like neighbors and stuff."

He smiled. "It's fine."

"Totally awesome."

She jumped up and down a little, the action making her tits bounce just a bit more, and his dick really liked seeing it.

Three beers, she handed him some cash, and before he could make her linger, she was already gone, heading back to the booth to sit with Tammy and Marshall.

So, once again, he watched the same routine. Tammy and Princess would head out onto the dance floor. Only this time when a guy meant to approach to dance, Riot slid in and asked to.

He saw Princess's sparkle, and she danced first with Riot. Silas didn't get there in time, so Zane waited as another guy took the lead and danced with her. Glaring at Silas, he watched his friend hold his hands up in surrender.

"Not good enough." He mouthed the words, and unfortunately, he had to keep serving others.

This time, Tammy came up to the bar to order beer.

"Did she make you a pie?" Tammy asked.

"What?"

"Oh, nothing."

Confused by her question, he looked toward Marshall, who was dancing with his neighbor, only they were not close, just two people enjoying the same space.

Tammy glanced behind her. "You like her."

"Why did you bring her here?" he asked. Friday nights always had the guys looking for a fuck, and

Princess looked like the kind who was also looking for that, too. In the few days he'd known her, she'd not struck him as the kind of girl who liked to fuck and leave, so it stumped him seeing her dancing with a bunch of random men.

"This was *her* idea. You want my advice? If you like her, take your shot, because you may never get another chance." She winked at him and left.

What the fuck is that supposed to mean?

By the end of his shift, he was really pissed off, and tired of seeing a bunch of horny men hitting on her. They didn't have a right to be drooling over her, and he hated the jealousy that kept slipping through.

His friends intervened when they could, and instead of demanding they go straight up on stage, he hit the dance floor, taking a seat with his buddies.

"You're totally whipped. You know that," Silas said.

"Bite me."

"You look like you want to bite a certain someone. I think you really need to talk to someone you feel that possessive over rather than just glaring at them. If she looks this way, and sees your face, you're so not getting any," Riot said.

He wanted to know why she was there at the bar. Why she was dancing with a bunch of random men, and also why it really fucking bothered him.

Chapter Three

On the way back to the dance floor from visiting the ladies' room, Wynter hit a hard, muscular chest, and when she looked up, she saw that she'd bumped into her very hot, very delicious neighbor.

"You know, I really need to bake you a pie."

"You're not the first person to mention this to me."

She smiled. "Did Tammy tell you I was going to bake you a pie? I've been thinking about it all week, you know, to say thank you, and now I don't know if I should bake you a pie or not. What do you think?"

"How much have you had to drink?" he asked.

"Three beers, and Marshall seems to think they make me very, very talkative. I don't know. Do you think I seem talkative to you?" She tilted her head to the side to watch him.

"Just a smidge."

"Well, I guess in a way they're working then."

She went to brush past him, but Zane stopped her.

"Why is it working?"

She crooked her finger for him to move closer to her. He leaned in, and when she was near his ear she whispered. "I'm a virgin and I struggle to talk to guys, so I'm here to pick one up to show me a good time. You can't say anything though because it's all very quiet. Tammy and Marshall are here to point out the good guys, and the ones they don't like. The preppy guy already got a thumbs-down."

"You're a virgin?" he asked, lifting his head up.

Covering his mouth with her hand, she told him to hush. "You can't say that out loud."

"Why not?"

"It's like totally illegal, and besides, I don't intend to stay a virgin all that much longer. I've got a cunning plan."

She moved past him, and this time, he didn't stop her. With every step she took, she knew she shouldn't have spoken, and that beer had that effect on her. Dropping down in the booth, she was there in time to see Tammy and Marshall making out.

What she found so incredibly sweet was that even after over twenty years of marriage, they were still very much in love.

Tammy pulled away, and Wynter saw the flush in her cheeks, and in that moment, she wished she was her friend. Not for Marshall or anything, but just to know what it felt like to be so loved that she couldn't imagine being with anyone else.

"Do I talk more after a couple of beers?" Wynter asked. "I think I do because I've just bumped into Zane." She turned to Marshall. "The guy at the bar you met. He's my neighbor."

"You already introduced us."

"Yeah, and I just told him why I'm here, and that I'm a virgin." Marshall choked on his beer, but she kept on going. "And that you guys are here to help me pick the perfect guy."

"Whoa, whoa, whoa," Marshall said, turning to Tammy. "You didn't tell me I was here for this."

"We're not. We're here to keep an eye on Wynter while she has a good time because she doesn't trust her taste in men."

"That's the truth. I wanted to meet people, but I was too scared that I'd judge them all wrong, and before we knew where we were, I'd be like totally in the wrong place at the wrong time. This is easy for you guys, and it's so not for me."

"Wynter, hunting for a guy in a bar to lose your virginity to is not the way to go," Marshall said. "No one, and I mean no one, should do that, and especially someone like you."

She pouted. "What's wrong with me?"

"You're twenty-five years old, and the last thing any of us want is for you to be filled with regret. It's not fair to you or anyone else. You've saved it."

She shook her head. "No, that's the thing. I didn't save it. I just wasn't going to give it to Carey." She shivered, recalling his hands all over her body.

"Wynter…"

"I just want to have some fun, and I know you and Tammy care about me. I know you think this is a mistake, Marshall, but I really don't think it is."

"Come on, honey, we'll dance, only this time no one will intervene." Tammy took her hand and led her onto the dance floor.

"Do you think I'm making a big mistake?" she asked, wrapping her arms around her friend.

"Yes, I do."

She pulled back a little, shocked with her answer.

"What? You think I agree to you picking up some random guy. I lost my V-card to the love of my life, and that night still fucking sucked, and Marshall hated it. It's a … vulnerable time in a woman's life. For some it can be over, and they're happy with that. With me, I was emotional."

"You were?"

"Yes, I had tears, and I was scared. I didn't see what the big deal was with the whole sex thing because it wasn't that good. The first time, it's never good, honey. No matter who you pick, do you really want to risk losing a part of yourself to some stranger?"

"We're not in the Middle Ages or something. It's

not some gift."

"And that's where you're wrong. It *is* a gift. Your body is your own special gift, Wynter. It's not to be thrown at anyone, not your first time." Tammy sighed. "I know you just want to get it over with, and you know what? I completely understand your frustration, I do. What I don't want is for you to call me tomorrow, crying because you can't stand the fact you slept with some faceless man you can't remember or at worst, you're never, ever going to see again."

"Why do you have to be the voice of reason right now?"

"I'm a teacher. It's ingrained for me to always guide the young."

She rolled her eyes and finished her dance with her friend. This time when they went back to the table, she apologized, and said she needed to get some air. She didn't want them to feel like they were babysitting her. They should be allowed to have a good time as well, and if they didn't, she'd feel even guiltier.

Stepping out into the warm night air, she took several deep breaths and stared up at the moon. Closing her eyes, she kept on taking deep breaths.

"Couldn't think?"

She turned to see Zane sitting on the hood of a truck, smoking a cigarette. "I didn't know you smoked."

"It's a bad habit, but I always have at least one before heading in to sing."

"You're performing? Tonight?"

"Yep. I work the bar, and perform at it. I told you I was in a rock band." He winked at her.

"I believed you."

"And now you're going to get to hear me play."

"I'm looking forward to it."

He patted the space beside him, and she climbed

on, feeling really clumsy as she didn't want to ruin the paintwork with her heels. Zane helped her up, and she stared over at the bar. It was crazy to think how quiet it was outside rather than inside.

She could at least think here for a few seconds.

"How is your manhunt going?"

"I've been told that my manhunt is not going all that well. In fact, I've been told that I shouldn't be hunting for a guy in a bar. Can you imagine that?"

"I can, yes."

She ran fingers through her hair. "It's tough you know. Being a girl, and then being a woman. I mean, what do men really want?"

"Sex. Freedom. The chance to come and go as they please. Oh, and to be told they're the greatest lover in the world."

She laughed. "I don't think I could lie to someone like that."

"Now that is no way to be getting a man. You have to point out exactly how handsome, sexy, and so right for you they really are." He nudged her shoulder, and she closed her eyes.

Every single time he touched her, she felt this fire ignite inside her.

Wynter felt drawn to him in a way that no one had ever appealed before. He was totally the opposite of everything her parents would like in a guy.

First, he'd covered his body in ink, and they really didn't like it when anyone did that. She recalled a conversation she'd had with her father over a woman at the bank. How she'd ruined her body by having a little tattoo around her wrist.

Her parents weren't religious or anything, although the way they talked, everyone would think they were.

No, they were just really, really opinionated, and that sucked. They wanted people to stick to their way of life, and putting ink on their body was not "the right way" to go.

Pushing thoughts of her parents aside, she focused on the bar.

"I've got to head back in. I'll save a spot near the front for you, and you can cheer me on."

"Okay. This is so going to be my first rock concert."

****

Princess stood at the edge of the crowd as he began to sing. He and the guys had written a couple of their own songs for some fun, but it wasn't that big of a deal. They'd been performing for years together, since they were in high school. They'd had a chance of making it big, but they completely blew it. Now they were keeping their feet firmly on the ground, keeping their focus right.

They just loved to perform.

To get the crowd wild.

Of course, if the big time ever came around again, they'd all jump at the chance to take it. No doubt in his mind that he'd take the opportunity. Throughout the entire half hour they were on stage, he struggled not to sing his heart out to Princess. The crowd was rocking them tonight, and he for one was loving the energy, but he also liked having her attention completely on him.

Any of the guys that approached hoping to dance, he saw she turned them down, and her attention would once again come toward him.

He winked at her often, and she shook her head, smiling.

When they were finished, he found her sitting at the booth with Tammy and Marshall.

"That was awesome. You guys are, like, totally awesome," Princess said, throwing her arms around them.

"I was wondering if you'd mind if I took her onto the dance floor."

"No, go ahead."

Taking her hand, he led her onto the floor, signing napkins as a few people stopped them. "You're like a celebrity now."

"It'll all go in the trash tomorrow," he said.

The music changed to a slow song, and he pulled her into his arms, loving the scent of vanilla that filled his senses for having her close.

"I like dancing."

"You've not danced a lot."

"I went to dances all the time. The only problem was I had to go with my parents' approved boyfriend, and dancing as you know, requires touch. I hated his touch." She gave a little shiver. "I always pretended that I couldn't dance or that I hated it so I didn't have to dance with him. Am I rambling?"

"Nah, I like that you're talking. It beats totally being glared at by you."

She sighed. "I was such a horrible neighbor to you, wasn't I? I was so horrible, and so mean."

"I had celebrated for a week straight. You had a right to complain."

"I don't like your taste in music. If you'd played some of the stuff you sang tonight I totally wouldn't have had a problem. Your voice rocked, by the way." She chuckled. "You get it? You sang rock music and you rocked. Totally so cool."

"You're a weirdo, right?" He laughed, and found her so utterly adorable.

"Tammy says I'm weird. I have a question for

you."

"I'm all ears."

"Where do you think that statement comes from? Do you think someone wanted to like make a statement to an entire bunch of people, and everyone lifted an ear? We're all ears?"

"How many beers have you had now?"

"Five, I think."

He glanced over his shoulder to see the couple she was with dancing and looking all loved up.

She followed his line of sight. "They're an amazing couple. They've been together since they were eighteen."

"They married young."

"Yeah, I know. My parents were so young as well. That's what they believed and wanted for me."

"Your parents?"

"Yeah. They think you should marry young, have kids, raise your family, and be there for them always."

"You don't agree?"

"I'm twenty-five years old, and they think I'm already too old to marry and have kids. They wanted me to marry Carey, the guy I was telling you about."

"Handsy Carey."

She chuckled. "Handsy Carey, I really like that."

He loved seeing her smile and the chuckle on her face as she relaxed in his company.

"I like this," she said. "You're a good dancer."

"You're not so bad yourself, Princess."

When an upbeat song came on, they took a seat with his friends. Tammy and Marshall joined while he went and got a couple of beers for all of them.

Marshall came with him.

"Do you like her?" he asked.

Zane laughed. "You don't need to do any of that

kind of routine with me. I know you're her friends and I'm just her neighbor."

"Really?"

"Yep."

"Last time I checked, getting jealous at a bunch of guys dancing with a girl, it doesn't mean 'nothing' to me." Zane stared at Marshall, who held his arms out. "You looked a little … put out by it all."

He glanced back at Princess and saw her laughing at something Silas had said.

"I'm not in love with her."

"I can see that, totally. Getting your friends to dance with her as well. I'm a guy. I was an asshole once as well."

"You're a bit much, calling me an asshole."

He glanced over at Tammy. "I nearly lost her for being an asshole. I thought I didn't want forever with her, so she went on a date with one other guy. It's why I know why you're feeling what you're feeling. Don't worry, kid, you'll grow up soon enough."

"I'm thirty years old," Zane said.

"And the moment you think you don't need to grow up, is the day you're going to need to do that the most."

Zane laughed. "I like you."

"I get that a lot. Do you have a pet name for her yet?"

"Pet name?"

"Something you call her that no one else does?" Marshall asked.

He looked toward her. "Princess."

"Do you know her real name?"

"Yes. Wynter Griffin. Princess suits her better."

This time Marshall laughed. "You're totally whipped, and right now you don't even see it. I can't wait to see how this unfolds."

Zane ordered himself a soda, and designated himself as the driver for the evening. Marshall was already onto coffee, and he imagined he was the one driving him and Tammy home.

The rest of the evening he listened to his friends tell them all stories about some of the tours they'd been on. Nothing big, just booking bars and clubs, and getting rowdy. He liked watching Princess as the guys told their tales. She seemed to really enjoy them, and he just couldn't get enough of being close to her.

He made sure to glare down any guy who approached with the hope of getting her to dance. That shit wasn't happening, not on his watch.

By the end of the night, they all left the bar. His friends took off in their truck, and he looked at Marshall.

"I live right next door to her. I can take her home."

"Come on, Marshall. It's time to go before the babysitter charges us triple."

"You better not hurt her."

"I have no intention of ever hurting her," he said. "It makes no sense driving out of your way when I'm going in exactly the same direction."

"He'll be fine, Marshall. I'm not so far gone that I can't kick him in the balls like you taught me to."

"See, I'll even let her do that."

Marshall nodded. "Call me as soon as you get home."

"I will." She threw her arms around Marshall, kissing his cheek. "Have a nice night, and thank you so, so much for bringing me out." She moved away, and linked her arm with his. "You're so sweet offering to take me home."

"A real gentleman would do that."

He nodded at Marshall, and took Princess home with him.

"I really enjoyed tonight. I was worried that I'd hate it. I begged Tammy to come with me. They really struggle to get a babysitter. Their kids like to tease and torment all of the people that look after them. I normally babysit for them if they want to go out, and I had to bribe them, offering ten dollars and a week of pizza."

He loved listening to her talk.

"Could you pull over?" Princess said.

"What is it? What's wrong?"

"I think I'm going to be sick."

Before he had the chance to pull over, she leaned between her legs, and he cursed as she hurled vomit down onto the floor.

He rolled down his window and pulled up. She was still vomiting, and the stench was putrid.

Easing her out of the truck, he held her as she kept on vomiting.

"I've got you," he said.

"I feel awful. This is not normal," she said.

"Is this the first time you've drunk?"

"Yeah, I think it could have been the wings I ate on the way out tonight."

"You made them?"

"No, I bought them. I didn't have time to cook myself anything."

When she stopped, he got her in the truck and put his foot to the gas to get there faster.

By the time he pulled up, she was about to vomit again, and he got her upstairs to her bathroom before she did it on the floor. Not that it mattered much, as she was covered in vomit. Holding her hair out of the way, he grabbed her cell phone, dialing Marshall.

"You got home already."

Before he spoke, Princess vomited.

"I've got it under control, but it seems alcohol really, really doesn't agree with her. It's all over my truck. It okay if I get her to call you tomorrow?"

"Crap, do you want us to come over?"

"No, no, I've got it. She's in safe hands."

"I'll talk tomorrow," Princess said, then vomited.

He heard Marshall wince. "Good luck, man."

Five minutes later, Princess was crying. "This is so wrong. My stomach is cramping real bad, and I think I got vomit down my boobs."

Turning on the shower, Zane didn't see himself getting home to his bed.

Holding her in his arms, he stripped her down to her underwear, and even as he wished he had the chance to admire her, he was in no mood to be thinking anything sexy. His car stank, he had vomit on himself, and now he had a very ill Princess on his hands. Getting her washed and dried took him nearly an hour, and when he had her in bed, he took a shower. Gathering up their clothes, he was about to do some laundry when she appeared in the bathroom and began vomiting again.

He was starting to think it wasn't the beer but the food she'd eaten.

"I'm never eating takeout again."

So many people had said the same old thing.

It was going to be a long night. Instead of being pissed about that, though, Zane found himself smiling as he headed to her laundry room. There were worse ways to spend an evening.

Chapter Four

Wynter woke with the worst feeling in the world. Grabbing her head, she groaned and turned to see Zane lying beside her. She gasped, sitting up in the bed.

"There's some painkillers and water by your lamp." He held onto her pillow, and she stared down at him, startled to see him in her room.

"Erm, what are you doing here?" she asked.

"Give yourself a moment and last night will all come flooding back, and you won't need to ask another question."

She'd gone out drinking, and slowly, she recalled being in the bar with Zane. Dancing with him, listening to him perform with his group, and then she winced. "I vomited in your car."

"Yes, you did, and I'm sure there's a nice big puddle out there as well. Not to mention all the vomiting you did in here last night. Those wings you ate must have been really nasty." He held onto the pillow, and she chanced another glance at him.

He wasn't wearing a shirt, and with a quick look underneath her sheet, she saw he was also in boxer briefs.

Nibbling her lip, she looked at him. "Did we, erm, did we…"

"Have sex?"

"Yes."

"No."

"Oh."

He laughed. "Don't sound so disappointed. Believe it or not, Princess, I don't screw a vomiting body, nor do I screw a corpse."

"A corpse?"

"You were completely out of it last night, and the idea of being with you didn't appeal, not at all."

"That bad?"

"Yep, that bad."

She rubbed at her eyes. "I'm so sorry."

"You also vomited in my truck, and I've not even gone down to check how bad that is."

"I will totally clean it. I promise."

"You feeling any better?"

Her stomach felt tender, but her head was easing, and besides being completely embarrassed, she felt fine. "Yes."

"Good. You need to call Marshall. I told him you would in the morning. You were too busy hurling last night."

"I will. I will totally do that."

He held out her cell phone. "Here you go." He snuggled back into her bed.

"You slept here last night?"

"I was worried that you'd fall asleep with vomit in your mouth, and that image wouldn't leave me, so I decided to be a gentleman and stay. I hope that's okay."

"It is." She held her cell phone. "I'll go make the call."

"Take your painkillers first. It'll help with the bad head."

She took the painkillers and entered her bathroom, closing the door silently behind her.

Stepping in front of the mirror, she winced. She looked awful. Her eyes were all dark from the small amount of makeup she'd worn last night.

She didn't stink, which she was happy about.

Dialing Tammy's number, she waited for her friend to answer.

"It's about time you called. How are you

feeling?" Tammy asked.

"I'm feeling … okay."

"Marshall said you were vomiting last night. You didn't have that much to drink."

"I ate some takeout food, and believe me, I won't be doing that again anytime soon. That stuff was just disgusting." She wrinkled her nose. "Zane took care of me. Like … all night."

"You sound surprised."

"That's a sweet thing to do, right? Take care of someone you don't really know?"

"He still there?"

"Yes. I need to clean his truck."

"You threw up in his truck?"

"Yep."

"I'll be telling Marshall about that. He felt so guilty leaving you with Zane, but he loves his car."

She laughed. "It was fine. Zane didn't hurt me or anything, and I feel really comfortable around him."

"If you ask me if that's normal, I will slap you," Tammy said.

"Okay, okay, I won't say anything." Even though all she wanted to do was ask the question.

"Have you ever just thought about trusting your gut with something like this?"

"No, absolutely not," she said.

"Zane seems like a nice guy, and he could have just left you last night. I think you need to stop overthinking everything, otherwise you're going to drive yourself insane."

"Noted, and I hate to say this, but I am already there," she said. She rubbed at her head. "Do you think I should make him breakfast?"

Tammy laughed. "Why don't you think about fixing his truck, and then how he took care of you?

Maybe there's truth in that little rumor after all."

Wynter snorted. She couldn't help it. "Houses don't bring people together. There's no truth in it."

"We'll see. I can hear wedding bells in the distance."

Saying goodbye, she hung up. Then she freshened herself so she looked like she could at least join the land of the living rather than staying camped out in her bathroom.

When she opened her door, Zane was already awake and stretching. He stood in front of her window, and she couldn't help but admire the dragon tattoo on his back. The blue and black ink coming together as one was mesmerizing.

"I'm going to clean your truck, and I'm also going to say thank you so much for taking care of me. You really didn't have to do any of that, and yet you did."

He laughed and turned toward her. "I'm a real hero."

"So as a real hero, do you want breakfast?"

"Bacon, eggs, and waffles?" he asked.

"I can make all of that if you'd like."

"Count me in. I'll check on our clothes. I did a load of laundry last night in between you vomiting."

Once again, another reason to really appreciate him. He was not even rubbing it in her face, which she was pleased about.

Heading downstairs, she began making breakfast, settling for a bowl of fruit and some toast for herself.

She was nervous as he came out and began looking around her stuff.

"Did it take you long to move in?" he asked.

"Yeah. Tammy and Marshall helped when they could. They have a family of their own, so they didn't have much free time."

"Your family?"

She wrinkled her nose. "They didn't even agree with me moving here so they didn't help."

"Are you far away from them?"

Shaking her head, she placed their food on the dining room table. It was only a small table, one she'd gotten from a flea market. She'd cleaned it up, and now it was good as new. "No, they're about twenty minutes away, but they weren't going to help me because they didn't see what I was doing as a good thing."

"That fucking sucks."

"It's the way it is. All the time I was looking and while the papers were going through they were trying to talk me out of it."

"Wow," he said.

"What about your family?" she asked, not wanting to talk about her own.

"They disowned me years ago. I didn't want to join in the family business of real estate. They own an empire, so I went out on my own when I was eighteen and never looked back."

"You don't miss them."

"None of them were all that interesting to miss. I've got my guys, and they're all I need in the world."

She sipped her tea.

"If you'd have come knocked on my door for help, we'd have helped you move in a lot faster."

She still had a couple of boxes in the laundry room to unpack. For the most part, she was moved in.

"It was okay."

"I can't stand having boxes around, and all the moving shit. I can't think with it lying around. It's like a job that always needs doing."

Wynter watched him eat, and she liked having

him at her table, even without his shirt. No one in her parents' house was allowed downstairs unless they were completely dressed.

She was a rebel, in her pajama shorts and shirt, eating breakfast with a man she'd spent the night with.

"Now that wicked smile on your face is telling a whole of stories right now. You're going to share?"

"I'm just thinking about how different I'm behaving right now." She shook her head, tucking some of her blonde hair away. "Ignore me."

"Were your parents strict or something?"

"Not really. Just set in their ways. I'm now the black sheep of the family. Going out and living on my own." She shrugged. "I like it. It's freeing."

"There is something to be said about just being yourself. We spend way too much time worrying about what other people think and feel."

"They would be having a huge fit right now if they saw me last night."

He reached out, taking hold of her hand. "You've got nothing to worry about."

She gave his hand a squeeze, liking his touch.

"I am curious though," he said.

"What about?"

"Why did you think for even a second finding some faceless dick in a bar would be the key to losing your virginity?"

She groaned. "You remember all of that."

"I've discovered, Princess, that with a few beers inside you, you get very, very talkative."

She covered her face, and when she dropped her hands he was still sitting there, laughing at her.

"Don't laugh. That is so not fair. There should be some kind of rule where friends don't laugh at other friends after vomiting."

Zane didn't stop, not once. "I've heard of people making a lot of mistakes in my time."

"Could we please just stop, and really not talk about this? I don't even want to think about what was going on inside my head." She leaned her elbows on her arms and stared at him. "How did you lose yours?"

He raised a brow. "You really want to know?"

"Yes. You've seen me at my worst. I may as well keep on going."

"I had an older lady friend many years ago. Her husband traveled a lot, and of course she got lonely." He patted his chest. "She taught me everything I know."

She stared at him. "Do you miss her?"

"Nope, but I appreciate everything she ever did for me. She's the one who listened to me play, and told me I was good."

She saw the fondness in his eyes, but not love.

"Your first time is going to be crap, Princess. The least you could do is save it for someone special."

****

"How can you even bear to look at me right now?" Princess asked, opening each door of his truck.

She'd gotten changed, and Zane had left her long enough to take a shower and change into clean clothes. Princess wore a pair of rubber cleaning gloves, a shirt, a pair of shorts, and some kind of coverall.

"Quite easy, actually."

"This is gross. It stinks so bad."

He kept a good few feet away, aware that with the sun up, and his car baking in it, the stench wouldn't be all that good.

"Do you want me to help?" he asked.

"No. Absolutely not. It's bad enough that I made this smell. I can't—no, stay back."

Zane watched as she slowly cleaned away her

vomit, only she didn't stop at the floor. She cleaned the entire seating area, wiping everything down, spraying some kind of smelly, flowery odor stuff, and in the end she spent two whole hours cleaning his truck.

"There, I'm going to leave the windows and doors open. Do you want some lemonade?" she asked.

"Yeah, sure."

She left him alone, and he climbed into the driver's seat. The truck was as good as new. He was shocked by how good it looked and smelled.

Princess joined him outside. They sat together in two deck chairs he'd brought out and watched their neighborhood go about its business. A couple of kids several doors down were arguing over a ball.

Parents were cleaning their cars, and not one of them approached them.

This was what he liked about this street. Even the deputy sheriff had told him that they were left alone when Slade and Cassie lived here.

"I really do like this place," she spoke up.

"I do as well."

"It's warm. It's cozy. This is probably going to sound crazy, but I've even driven down this street during Halloween and Christmas. I love the decorations that people do. It just feels like home."

"I get that. I love this place as well. I couldn't believe when my house went up for sale. It felt like fate, you know."

"Yeah, and I was able to use my inheritance to afford it as well. It felt good." She pushed some of her blonde curls off her face. "I think my grandparents knew that I was a little different from the rest of my family. They left me enough to get started on my own and live my own dream."

"They sound like good people."

"My family is nice. They just like to judge everyone and everything."

"Sounds like every single person in the world." He finished off his glass of lemonade, and felt so calm, so relaxed.

It had been a long night. He'd spent most of it awake, babysitting Princess, but he couldn't recall a time ever feeling so at home.

"Can I trust you?" she asked.

"I cleaned vomit from you. I spent the night. You can trust me, Princess. There's no one I'm going to spill your secrets to."

"I want to lose my virginity." He tensed up and turned toward her. She stood up, placing her hands on her hips. "Do you like the way I look?"

Okay, his dick just got hard in the fastest time he'd ever known it.

"Yes."

"Well, you were taught by an older woman, and well, you're an older guy."

"Princess."

She bent forward so that her hands were on his knees. "Please, listen. Don't say no yet. I know this is completely crazy, and it's only because we've been friends such a short time, and I will probably regret this, but I don't want to just lose it. I want to have experiences. Sitting here, watching the street, thinking about my family. I don't want to save it for marriage. I don't want to just be with Mr. Right. I want to have fun. That's why I moved here. I came here to have fun, to learn how to live, not just to exist." She stopped, biting her lip, and he just wanted to suck that lip right into his mouth. "I know it's asking a lot, and I was a real bitch to you when we first met, but I'm not. I promise."

"You're asking me to teach you how to have

sex?" he asked.

"Yes."

"You don't think that's weird that you're asking a stranger about this?"

"Well, of course it's weird, but I can't think of anyone else I'd trust with this. I trust you." She squeezed his knees. "You took care of me when you didn't have to. That says something to me."

He glanced over her shoulder and saw they were getting a little attention. "I think it's time we moved this inside."

Her shoulders slumped, but she didn't argue with him. He didn't know if he was happy with that or not.

Closing up the car, he followed her inside her home, making sure to lock the door behind him.

Once inside, she stopped in the sitting room and turned toward him. "I'm asking way too much."

"You're not asking too much. You're just asking … a lot, but you know what, it's fine. I don't mind you asking, and I don't mind any of that."

His dick was more than happy with the idea of helping her. He wanted to get her naked, spread those pretty thighs, and be the first and only man to taste her creamy pussy. She would be so wet by the time he got his hands on her.

Not right now.

He needed to keep his head in the game; the one he actually used to think with.

"I need to think about this," he said.

"Okay."

"You know what, I've thought about this." He stepped up close to her, intent on kissing those sexy as fuck lips only to stop. "I want to kiss you right now."

She nodded. "I'd like to kiss you, too."

"I don't want you to say things you don't mean,

or what you think I expect you to say."

"I'd never do that."

He pressed a finger against her lips. "I also don't want you to keep playing nodding heads as we're kissing."

"Nodding heads?" she asked, frowning.

He moved his head from side to side in the way he meant, and she covered her mouth laughing.

"I've never seen that before."

"It happens. Just close your eyes, no tongue, okay."

She held her hands up. "Fine."

He waited as she stood, closed her eyes, and puckered her lips.

"Don't pucker."

"I feel like I'm taking a test or something."

"Consider it a test." She stopped puckering, and he took a step toward her. He touched her cheek, and when she opened her eyes, he told her to close them.

She did as he asked, and he tilted her head back. Her skin was flawless, smooth, and he stroked his finger over her cheek, moving around her ear, and back down to her chin. Her lips parted a little, and he slid his other hand up from her hand, cupping her face.

Moistening his own lips, he took possession of hers, and listened as she sighed his name just before he did.

The moment he kissed her, he felt like his world had been turned upside down and inside out. He lost all focus apart from her.

His need for her was so great, greater than anything he'd ever experienced before in his life. He wanted her, craved her, felt consumed by his need that rivaled his love of music.

Sinking his fingers into her hair, he deepened the

kiss, and his cock thickened. Moving her back, he pressed her up against the wall, relishing her hands on his body, and he held her close.

He didn't want the kiss to ever end, but a knock on her front door halted it.

Pulling away, he stared into her eyes. Her cheeks were flushed, and there was no way he could ever let another man taste her sweetness.

"I'll teach you everything you need to know, Princess."

Chapter Five

On Monday, Wynter left for work early, wishing she'd gotten a few moments to speak with Zane. After his kiss on Saturday, all she'd been wanting to do was talk to him. Tammy, Marshall, and their kids had been the ones to interrupt their kiss. She'd seen the questions in Tammy's eyes, but there hadn't been time to talk.

Zane had left, and on Sunday he'd been working all day, and now *she* was heading to work. There just wasn't any spare moment to talk, and she found it so damn frustrating.

When she arrived to class Tammy was already there getting everything set up.

"Close the door and tell me everything."

She did as instructed, and when she turned back, she saw Tammy had already gotten them both some coffee. School wasn't due to start for another half hour.

"Come on, spill. I'll not get through 'til lunch for you to tell me everything."

"There's not much to tell."

"The look on your face on Saturday told me straight something had happened, and I'd interrupted it. Come on, spill."

"He kissed me." She licked her lips, and smiled. "And it was so amazing. He's one hell of a kisser."

"And?"

"And I kind of, sort of asked him if he'd teach me about sex."

This time Tammy's mouth did open. "You did?"

"It just blurted out. We were watching the neighbors, and I was thinking about my parents, and I didn't want to be proper in that moment."

"You're attracted to him?" she asked.

"Yes."

"Well, that's good then. It would suck if you're asking a guy you couldn't stand," she said.

"I've not spoken to him though. Not since he agreed."

"He agreed?"

She nodded. "Right after the kiss."

"Well, I think the time has come for you to at least bake him a pie."

"You think so?"

"You've asked this guy, a stranger, to teach you about sex, and you've already told him you're a virgin."

"Alcohol does not go well for me."

"You still didn't swear," Tammy said.

"I didn't?"

"Nope. You were every bit the perfect lady." Tammy patted her hand, giving her a funny look.

"What is it?"

"You don't think that your houses have something to do with it?"

Even before Tammy finished her question, Wynter rolled her eyes. "They're houses, Tammy. Not people, just things."

Tammy shrugged. "If you think about it, it's a little coincidental that you're asking a complete stranger to have sex with you, and at the same time, you're kissing him. Both things I know you'd never dream of asking Carey."

She shuddered. "Stuff like that is not real. It's a fantasy."

"Life's made of fantasies, sweetie. It's what helps get us through the really crappy times."

They finished their coffee, and then the day was about to begin. She didn't have time to dwell on anything Zane related as she helped the children with their spelling, drawing, and of course coloring. Tammy always took the lead, and the classes were filled with so much joy. They were going have a parent-teacher evening very soon, so Wynter had lunch all to herself, which wasn't fun as she found her nerves getting the better of her.

What if she'd made a terrible mistake?

She had to live with Zane.

What if you like him a little too much and he ends up with lots of groupies?

She really hadn't thought this through enough, and now there was no time to think as she'd see him that evening.

Even though her attention was on the kids, she couldn't stop for even a second thinking about Zane and his kiss. He'd completely taken over and kissed her in a way that had her begging for more. Not only had she not wanted him to stop, she'd been more than ready for more. So much more.

Her pussy had been so wet, and she wanted him to touch her, to make her orgasm.

Those feelings had never happened, not with a guy.

Pushing them to the back of her mind, she finished her day at school, lingering in the evening to help with the last of the preparations with Tammy, who happened to hate parent-teacher day, before heading home.

His truck was parked in his driveway when she got home. Grabbing her groceries, she made her way into her home. Before she'd even put the bag on the counter, there was a knock on her door. She closed her eyes for just a few seconds to find some kind of peace, any peace. When nothing came, she had no choice but to make her way toward the door, opening it up.

Both his hands rested on the frame, and his smile

caught her completely off guard.

"Had a good day at work?" Zane asked.

"Yes." Any of her doubts left her as she looked at him. "You?"

"Wrote a couple of really crappy songs, but everything's set up at the bar."

"Would you like to come in?"

"Love to." He entered her home and she stood, watching him, not really knowing what to say or do. "I'm wishing you had a beer right now."

Surprising even herself, she started to laugh.

"You don't have to start freaking out. I'm not going to jump on you or demand anything. We're just two friends here hanging out."

"Yeah. Do all of your friends ask you to take their virginity?"

"Not really. It was touch and go with Riot."

She threw her head back and laughed again, walking back to her kitchen. He'd put her completely at ease.

"I'm not going to be able to look at him without picturing that."

"He deserves it. Always thinking he's a gift to women."

"Want a drink? Tea? Coffee? Soda?"

"Beer?" he asked, winking at her.

"I don't keep it in the house."

"It's like a truth serum for you."

"I was thinking a 'never shut up' kind of serum." She tucked some stray strands of hair behind her ear, and she gritted her teeth as nerves kept getting the better of her.

"I'm not going to jump you. This isn't a rush for me to rid you of that pesky little V-card you're so desperate to let go of."

"I'm not desperate. I just want to know what all the fuss is about. I've never really been all that interested in sex and guys."

"Cheers," he said. "I'll take a cup of coffee."

She nodded and began to fill her kettle.

"You know I've got a pool, and I was wondering if you'd like to go for a swim. It's been a long day, and you really need to relax before you totally hurt yourself."

"I'd like that. It has been ages since I went for a swim."

"I'll even show you a little access into my garden that the woman showed me," he said.

"Access?"

"Yes. Did you know these two houses have a rumor attached to them?" he asked.

"Not you as well?"

"What?"

"Do you really think that two homes can bring two people together, and the two that are living there at the same time will magically fall in love?"

"With how sarcastically you're saying that I'm going to take a hunch and say you don't believe in it?"

"It's a bunch of bull. It has to be."

"Okay, what if I can say that I know for certain the last three couples here are all married and happy settled?"

"Well, I know Slade and Cassie are. They're in town."

"Yes, but the couples before that as well. They moved away, but they're still together."

She finished making them both a cup of coffee. "Say I believe you, what does that even mean?"

"It means that one day soon you're going to find yourself completely and totally in love with me."

"Well if that's true, then it means you're going to

be the same with me. You're going to think of nothing and no one but me." She placed a hand on her chest and smiled. "Would that be pure torture to you?"

"Not at all. I quite like thinking about you." He took a sip of his coffee, staring over the rim of the cup, which made her stomach twist, and she had no choice but to press her thighs together. Damn, this man was good.

"In all seriousness, I won't hold you to anything about what I've asked you to do. You're your own man, and I don't expect anything from you."

"Just my dick."

Her cheeks heated. "It's … why is this so hard?"

"You're the one that asked me, and soon it will get hard. I promise. Right now, it's kind of soft. You make really nice coffee."

She knew he was teasing her, and the moment he talked about his cock, she couldn't help but look.

"You'll get to see it soon enough, Princess."

Something must be happening because she didn't even mind it when he called her Princess.

"How was your truck?" she asked, moving onto a much safer topic than sex, Zane's penis, and the possible rumor their houses played Cupid.

"It doesn't stink; it's really clean. You need to vomit in my truck more often. I think it's cleaner than when I first bought it."

Her mouth and beer had already gotten her into this. There was no way she'd ever risk it again.

****

Zane waited for her to change into her bathing suit. Cassie, the previous owner, had a pool, which he'd just recently paid to get clean. Princess, now dressed in a bathing suit, followed him out to the back of her garden. When Cassie had been at a hospital appointment because of her baby, Slade had showed him around and also told him about the loose fence panel.

"Why didn't anyone fix it?" she asked as he showed her how to slide it open, and keeping it there as they entered his home.

"I don't know. Maybe they didn't feel it needed fixing? Our houses being connected and all that."

Cassie had told him about the house rumor when he moved in, and of course he didn't believe her.

It was total bullshit.

Houses didn't control emotions, people did.

He pulled off his shirt, then removed his jeans, walking all the while. "And here is the little darling that I had cleaned especially for you." He held his hand out. "You may remove your robe."

She rolled her eyes, opening up the robe and handing it to him.

Placing their clothes on the deck chair, he jumped in without waiting for her. The day was so hot that even the water was warm.

Breaking the surface, he saw her standing there. She wasn't trying to hide her body, and the bathing suit she wore shaped to her curvy figure to perfection, and even seemed to push her tits up and together. He focused on other parts of her body rather than the pure beauty of her breasts.

She had a touch of cellulite on her thighs, but they were full, juicy, and he wanted them wrapped around his waist as he slammed his dick deep inside her.

She's a virgin.

Rubbing his hands down his face, he watched as she slowly climbed into the pool, her hands gliding over the surface.

"It's not going to bite. I don't have a shark hidden beneath waiting to eat you up or anything."

She smiled. "It has been a long time since I've

been in a pool."

"Is this something to do with your family?"

"Nah, just … pools." She leaned forward, and he watched as she began to swim, moving from one end of the pool to the other.

It wasn't a large pool, not like a proper full length, but it was a nice size to stretch out, or take a short swim.

Moving toward the edge, he stretched his arms out and simply watched her. She floated on her back, staring up at the sky. Treading water, he moved toward her side and placed a hand on her stomach.

She jerked up but didn't push him away. Her head turned toward him.

"Have you changed your mind?" He ran his thumb back and forth over her stomach.

"Yes and no. I've not changed my mind."

"Tell me your thoughts."

"I've felt guilty for putting you in this position. I shouldn't have, and I'm really sorry."

He smiled. "You don't have to apologize."

"Do you want to?"

Staring into her blue eyes, he nodded. "Yes. I want to." He took her hand and placed it over his dick, which was already rock-hard. "This is what you do to me, even when you're driving me crazy. I want you. That's never going to stop."

She slowly rubbed him through his pants, and he closed his eyes, enjoying her touch. Her feet touched the pool bottom, and she stood, staring at him. "I don't know what I'm doing. I don't believe that our houses are connected, and I have no intention of telling you that I love you any time soon."

"I don't either."

"I've never had sex before. I've never done

anything but touch myself, and even as I'm sharing this with you, I'm feeling crazy because I don't know why, but I feel safe with you. Is that normal?"

"Define normal for me."

"I knew there was a big reason why I liked you."

He rested his hands on her hips, and neither of them spoke for several seconds. Her gaze kept going to his lips then back again. "Do you want me to kiss you?" he asked.

"All I can think about is that kiss."

"Close your eyes."

She did as he asked, and he stared at her. He didn't know if their little house rumor was true. He only knew his own feelings when it came to this woman, and how much he wanted her. He'd never known anything like it before in his life. It was like a consuming need.

His thoughts were dominated by her. He constantly wanted to know if she was okay, if she was happy. She'd gotten under his skin, and now he couldn't seem to shake her, not even when he was writing, which always took him away from his troubles, and yet this seemed to only give him trouble.

Pressing his lips against hers, he squeezed her hips, knowing that small touch wasn't enough. His cock thickened even more, pressing against the front of his black briefs, demanding attention. He ignored it, focusing on the woman in his arms.

As he slid his tongue across her mouth, she opened up, and he plundered inside. At the same time, he began to move her backwards until they were at the wall.

Moving his hands from her hips, he slowly stroked her body, moving up as if to cup her tits, but then gliding down to rest on her thighs.

She wrapped her arms around his neck, holding him close.

Running his fingers in a pattern, he caressed up until he cupped her large tits. Her nipples were already rock-hard as they pressed against his palm.

He rubbed them in a circle before cupping them even more.

She pulled away, breaking from their kiss first.

With her gaze still on him, she slid each strap of her bathing suit down until it fell to the surface, exposing her large breasts.

She had tiny, red-tipped nipples, begging to be sucked.

Leaning forward, unable to resist, he lifted up her breast and sucked on one nipple before moving to her other. Having two tits to choose from, he alternated between the left and right.

Pressing her tits together, he laved each bud with his tongue, loving her moans as he did.

Finally, releasing her tits, he pushed her suit down even more before it hit the floor of the pool.

Sinking under the water, he picked up her swimsuit and placed it on the edge of the pool before claiming another kiss.

He removed his boxer briefs, holding them up for her to see and placing them on top of her bathing suit.

Naked.

Princess didn't try to cover up. She stared at him, and he gripped her hip, pulling her against him. Her gaze widened when she felt his cock.

"I'm not going to fuck you or make love to you today. You're going to get used to seeing me like this, and I'm going to enjoy watching you naked. I made lasagna. Will you stay for dinner?"

"You made dinner?"

He smiled seeing her little blush. She wrapped her arms around his neck.

"I have a great deal of skills, baby. Just let me know which one you'd like to see me show off."

"Why don't you show me all of them?" She raised her brow, and he found it so cute when she did that.

"Whatever you wish."

He slid his hand around to cup her ass, but he didn't stop there, moving around to cup her mound. She had a small dusting of hair, and he slipped a finger through her slit. Even with the water all around them, he could tell that she was aroused, her cream coating his finger.

She moaned.

Her grip around his neck tightened as he touched her clit.

No man had ever touched her.

She was a virgin.

His to do with as he pleased, to show her exactly what he liked, and to get her used to his touch.

Just the thought of that alone was making him ache to claim her there and then, but he held back.

"I want us to get out," he said.

"Why?"

"I want to see all of you, and I want to show you another skill I have, and I know without a doubt you're going to love."

She smiled, and he watched as she moved to the edge of the pool. He followed her, groaning as her ass came into view.

He wanted to bite her ass, to slap it as he fucked her hard. There would be time for that, so much time, but for now, he kept his hands to himself.

She stood at the edge of the pool with her hands clenched.

Taking the lead, he walked her toward one of the

lounge chairs, getting her to lie down.

She stretched her arms out and he put her legs on either side, spreading her wide. When she kept trying to cover herself, he winked, and got her to put her hands on the arms of the chair.

"You've got to learn to trust me."

"I don't see how me being spread-eagled like this is going to show me any of your skills."

"That's because you have no faith in me whatsoever."

She rolled her eyes, and he cupped her pussy, silencing any protest from her. He changed in position so that his face was just above her pussy.

Her gaze was on him, and he spread the lips of her pussy open, and licked across her clit, flicking back and forth, watching as she gasped, and her body shake as he teased her.

"Holy ... oh, my."

His mission was to get her to cuss, if for no other reason than to get him to fuck her, or at least to say it.

Sucking her clit into his mouth, he gave it a gentle tug before releasing her and licking her, going back and forth, teasing her until she was shaking with her need.

With just a few minutes of his tongue on her mouth, she came, crying out his name, her entire body quivering.

He was surprised at how quickly she came apart, but he didn't mind, not at all.

"You taste exquisite," he said.

"You really are talented." Her gaze moved to his aching dick. "Could you show me?"

"What?"

"Show me how you like to do it." She nodded at his dick.

Wrapping his fingers around his length, he began to stroke himself. They'd known each other such a short time, and yet it felt endless. He felt like he knew her, and there was no pressure.

She moved forward, wrapping her fingers around his cock, working with him.

Her lips brushed his, and as her hand took over, he played with her tits, pulling her close as she worked his dick.

The pleasure was intense as he came, holding her while he did.

Chapter Six

Standing in the grocery store Wednesday evening, Wynter looked at the carrots, trying to figure out which ones would be better, the short, dumpy ones or the long ones. Cooking for one was a nightmare, but tonight she was determined to cook for two.

So far Zane had taken care of their meals for the past couple of nights, and he could cook. His lasagna was the nicest she'd ever tasted, and he'd even offered to give her the recipe. She'd wanted to watch him cook, and he'd agreed but for another night. Last night he'd done some other concoction with shrimp and pasta, which made her mouth water for more.

Tonight was her turn, or tomorrow seeing as he was working late, and she wouldn't see him tonight.

Picking up several large carrots, she placed them in the basket she held over her arm and moved on to some peppers. Her thoughts were constantly moving back to Monday night when he'd showed her exactly how wicked his tongue could be.

After they'd enjoyed their meal, she'd insisted on going back home to get some sleep and giving him a chance to rest. When she'd been at home, she'd started to do some research on how long it took for a woman to reach orgasm.

Much to her embarrassment, everything she'd watched and read stated at least thirty minutes. She'd not even lasted five.

She didn't know if that was normal or not, so she had no choice but to ask Tammy. Of course, asking your friend for orgasm time hadn't been the most comfortable conversation.

"He clearly rocks your boat."

"Is it normal?"

"What's normal? When Marshall has me going, it takes a few seconds, but we're talking a buildup."

Tammy had then told her about the buildup, the caressing and teasing that brought them to their knees.

She finished her shopping and was making her way toward her car when someone shouted her name.

"Wynter, Wynter."

Carey, her ex, was rushing toward her. Holding her shopping basket in her arms, she forced a smile to her lips.

"Hey, Carey, how have you been?" she asked.

They'd been friends, not much else, not that they needed to be much else. She also wasn't a believer in being rude. She'd been the one to end things with him, and he'd not been heartbroken. He'd shrugged and said there were more girls out there.

"I've been great. I've just seen your parents." He held up a shopping list. "Asked me to pick some things up for them."

"Great." She'd not seen her parents since she moved, and even though she'd been tempted to call them, she just hadn't.

The point of moving away had been for her to flesh out her life on her own.

"Your parents are worried about you, you know."

"Not *that* worried. They could come and visit me anytime if they really wanted." She hoped they didn't.

He chuckled. "They're pissed that your grandparents left you enough money to start over. They feel they undermined their authority."

She forced a smile. "I really need to get going."

Wynter turned in time to see Zane's truck pull into a parking spot. His friends and the man himself spilled out. They were laughing, and she smiled.

Glancing back at Carey, she saw the sneer on the guy's face. Before she could make her excuses, Zane moved up beside her.

"Hey, Princess," he said, placing a hand across her shoulders and kissing her head.

Carey looked like he'd seen something crazy.

"Hey. I was just picking up some things."

"Yeah, I'm about to get some supplies to show you how a mean lasagna is made." Zane looked toward Carey. "Hey, I'm Zane."

"Carey."

She watched as they both shook hands, and seemed to linger on their handshake, which didn't make her feel uncomfortable at all … *not!* She'd told Zane about Carey the night she'd had one too many beers.

"You two are together?"

"Yes," Zane said, answering before she got the chance. She smiled and rested against him.

"He's my neighbor."

"Do your parents know about this?" Carey asked.

"You mean the ones that couldn't even get off their asses to help her move?" Zane asked.

Okay, she was enjoying this moment a little too much.

"I've got to head home. I'm going to be cooking your dinner for tomorrow."

Zane kissed her head. He waited for her to say her goodbyes, and then walked her to her car, taking the groceries from her hands as he did so.

"You don't like him, do you?" he asked.

"How could you tell?"

"You looked annoyed, as if you were waiting for an excuse or a reason to leave."

"He's the guy my parents wanted me to marry. They picked him out in high school, and I had no choice but to date him. Believe me, it wasn't fun. He's so full of himself." She stood by her driver's side door, and smiled. "You saved me."

"I'm always here to serve my damsel in distress."

"Have fun tonight."

"I could stop by later. My shift ends at eleven."

"What about performing?"

"The bar's fully booked. I'm dropping the guys off at home before I head in for my shift. I'm only covering for someone else who left."

"Then I'll be waiting." She suddenly couldn't wait to get home.

He stepped in close. "This is not about showing who you belong to for that loser. This is about me." He cupped her face and slammed his lips down on hers. She couldn't resist wrapping her arms around his neck and holding him close.

Her body ignited as if he alone held the flame, and she kissed him back with a passion that rivaled his.

"I'm not going to want to go to work after this," he said.

"I'll see you tonight."

He stepped away from the car, and he stood watching her as she drove home. The moment she got home, she unpacked her groceries quickly and rushed up to the bathroom. Undressing, she ran herself a bath, and took the time to shave and wash every single part of her. It had been a long day at the school, and also a really warm day.

Once she was done, she settled on a sheer negligee that she'd been saving for something special.

She'd seen it years ago in a store, and she'd picked the last one in her size and hidden it away for only herself. She loved the feel of the silk against her skin, and how sexy she felt. Glancing in the mirror, she pinned her blonde hair up and wondered if she was going too far.

She shook her head. No. This was being herself, and since seeing Carey, she was determined to live life her own way, and that meant being with Zane.

She liked Zane a lot.

He made her laugh and smile, and he'd made living next door to him a pleasure.

She still didn't like his taste in rock music, even though he kept trying to turn her to the dark side as he kept calling it.

It was just funny to her.

Making her way downstairs, she saw she still had some time before he got home, so quickly putting on an apron, she grabbed some of the shrimp she'd bought for herself, knowing they'd stretch to at least two people.

Marinating them, she assembled the salad, made the dressing to go with it, and then placed a batch of brownies in the oven.

By the time Zane arrived, her nerves were getting the better of her. The moment she opened the door, he pulled her into his arms, and she found herself becoming addicted to his kisses.

They were like a drug, filling her with so much need that she didn't want him to stop.

"I think your mouth is a skill all on its own."

He chuckled. "You've not seen anything yet."

"I made you some dinner." Her stomach chose that moment to growl.

"You didn't feed yourself?" he asked.

"I was waiting for you." And now she was starving and embarrassed. Her stomach was making so much noise.

Zane took the lead, entering the dining room, helping her sit down, and he'd not even seen her sexy negligee as she still wore her apron over the top.

He served her up some food, and ordered her to eat as he served himself.

The food was delicious, but her stomach still kept making noise.

"I think you could be a better cook than me," she said.

"Wait until you taste my grilled steak. I'm a master at it, and I like mine rare."

She wrinkled her nose. "I love mine pretty much burned and rock-hard."

He started to laugh. "Wait until you taste mine. You know you're going to have to try it."

She took a bite of the shrimp and smiled. "I may just do that."

He winked at her. "You'll love it."

"How was work?"

She listened as he told her about his day, and then he asked about hers. It wasn't long before they were both laughing at each other's stories. He'd grab her hand, giving it a squeeze. She loved watching him laugh.

He didn't hold anything back, and she adored that about him.

When it came to the brownies, he decided she was the better baker though.

"I can't even get a boxed mix to work. It's always sunken and gross."

She smiled and stood up, taking their dishes into the kitchen. She was washing them when he moved up behind her, placing his hands on her waist.

His lips went to her neck, and she gasped.

"I want to see what you wore for me."

She didn't deny it, and drying her hands on the nearest towel, she tossed it aside and removed the apron, dropping it to the floor to let him see.

"You make it impossible for a man to wait for the right moment." He pulled her close, kissing her neck, and she gasped, arching against him.

"Then don't."

She was tired of waiting.

****

Zane had spent a great deal of time thinking about Carey, the guy he'd seen talking with Princess. There had been judgment in his eyes, and he hated it when people did that. She'd told him about the kind of life she'd lived, and even though it had been a good life, she'd been met with expectation from her parents. Expected to marry, expected to have kids, her life to be entirely different.

If she'd followed their rules, he wouldn't have her in his arms right now.

"Once we do this, there is no turning back," he said.

"I don't care about turning back, Zane. I don't want to turn back the clock. I trust you, and I want you. I know it's going to hurt, but there's no one else I want to be with." She took his hand and placed it against her breast. Her nipple was hard as it pressed against his palm. "You make me feel so much, and I don't want that to stop. I want this with you, Zane. I'm not going to regret it."

Gripping the back of her neck, he took possession of her lips, and like every single time before, she melted against him, her arms wrapping around his neck. Running his hands down her back, he squeezed her ass and tugged her up into his arms. She wrapped her legs around him, and he carried her from the kitchen.

He didn't break the kiss as he took her to her room. Easing her down onto the bed, he switched the light on.

"Don't you want to turn it off?"

"Nope. I want to be able to see all of you, and I don't want you hiding from me." He pulled his shirt over his head, tossing it to one side, and next removing his jeans.

The hard line of his cock was easily outlined in his boxers, but he got rid of them quickly.

"Oh, I got these." He watched as she moved up the bed, opening the drawer. "Do you have any idea how many different condoms there are? I was so confused." She placed a couple on the bed, and he lifted a few up. "Did I get the right ones?"

"Yes."

She knelt on the bed, and he reached behind her head to take the pin holding her hair up. He watched as her hair fell around her in waves, and he ran his fingers through the length, pulling her up so that he could claim a kiss once again.

Princess moaned, holding onto his arms, and he didn't want to let her go.

"I've never bought condoms before."

"There's always a first time for everything." He kissed her lips once again and closed his eyes, breathing her in.

He wanted this to be so damn perfect for her. She'd gotten under his skin in more ways than he could deny. Even his friends said that he was different.

"Are you nervous?" he asked.

"A little."

"If at any point you want me to stop then you've got to tell me and I'll stop."

She nodded.

Slowly, he slid his hand down her body, cupping her pussy. Pressing a finger through her slit, he felt how wet she was. Teasing her clit, he watched her as she began to thrust onto his fingers.

"Do you want my mouth on this pretty pussy?" he asked.

"Yes."

He moved her onto the bed, and he crawled over her, kissing her lips, and trailing down to take one nipple and then the other, sucking them hard. He bit her, and she cried out. Soothing the pain with his tongue, he began to kiss his way toward her thighs.

She had the prettiest cunt he'd ever seen. Spreading her legs, he circled her nub with his tongue, gliding down until he got to the point just at her entrance when he moved back up, and began to suck on her.

Princess writhed on the bed, and he caught her hands, locking them at her sides. Her body arched as he drove her to her first orgasm. He didn't want to stop sucking her pretty pussy, but he also didn't want to wait another second.

Kneeling between her thighs, he tore into the condom and rolled the latex down over his shaft.

Staring into her blue gaze, he pressed the tip of his cock at her entrance and began to slowly sink inside her.

She tensed up, and he had no idea the kind of pain she must be feeling. Her nails sank into the flesh of his arms, and he slammed every inch of his cock inside her. She cried out, and he took hold of her hands, wrapping his arms around her, kissing her.

Her cunt clenched around him, and he wasn't in any rush to move. Her pussy was so tight. He felt every ripple as she became accustomed to him.

She's yours now.

Zane kept on kissing her lips, refusing to let her go, wanting to take care of her, to hold her.

"That hurt," she said, gasping.

"I'm so sorry."

Tears glistened in her eyes, and he felt like the worst bastard imaginable for hurting her.

She nodded. "I knew it would hurt."

He released her hands, and pushed some of her hair off her face. "I'm not going to move. I'm not going to hurt you."

"I'm being a girl."

"I really like that you're a girl." This made her laugh.

Zane stared into her eyes, and he couldn't understand the twisting in his gut, or what it all meant. She was part of him now, and all he wanted to do was to give her everything she ever wanted.

Time passed, and he felt her wiggle and suddenly arch up. "It doesn't hurt so much now."

Easing up, he pulled his cock out, taking his time, watching to make sure she wasn't hurting. She gasped, and he stopped. "Do you want me to stop?"

"No. I don't. Please, I want it."

Thrusting back inside her, he did several slow thrusts, seeing that the pain was no longer in her eyes. Rocking inside her, he began to speed up, feeling her pussy tighten around him, and he went deeper, feeling his own orgasm begin to build, spreading through him.

"Oh, wow, that is so … amazing."

"I'm not going to last, Princess." He groaned as the pleasure went to the next level. His balls tightened, and he thrust deep within her, and his orgasm spilled into the condom.

He dropped his head against her shoulder, holding most of his body weight off her so he didn't squash her.

She ran her hands up his back.

"That wasn't one of my finest moments," he said,

kissing her shoulder.

He pulled away to look at her.

"You don't think that was a finest moment?" she asked.

"No." He stroked her cheek. His heart was pounding, and even though all he wanted to do was slump down and go to sleep, he didn't. "I can do much better."

"I really enjoyed it."

"Now you're just crushing a guy's ego here."

She giggled. "You were wonderful, oh great and wise one." She winked at him.

He found her utterly adorable.

"Any regrets?"

She shook her head. "None. I've got no regrets at all. I'm no longer a virgin."

"I know. Are you done with me now?" he asked, teasing.

"Not even close. I hear there's a lot to enjoy yet, and I don't know if you know this, Zane, but I rather like you."

"Not bad for someone who wanted to call the cops on me."

"You do have hideous taste in music, but I have since learned that I was mistaken and have no intention of calling the cops, not ever." She cupped his cheek. "Can I ask you a question?"

"I'm balls deep inside you, Princess. You can ask me anything you want."

"Do you even know my name?" she asked.

"Yes, I do. I recall it started with a W. I like calling you Princess."

"Why?"

"You just remind me of one."

"Okay, I'm not going to touch on that."

"Was that what you wanted to ask me?" he asked.

She shook her head.

"What did you want to know?"

"Are you good to go again?" she asked.

Her cheeks heated, and she looked so adorable, he couldn't help but chuckle. "It'll take me some time to get going, but give me half an hour and I should be good to go again. I'll even last long longer this time."

Taking her lips once again, Zane felt her pussy tighten around him, knowing in the back of his mind that he was royally fucked when it came to this woman.

Chapter Seven

"I've woken a temptress," Zane said. "Don't you remember a time when you wanted more from me than my dick?"

Wynter laughed as she pulled him down for another kiss. She was completely addicted to his lips, and he made her ache all over. It had been over a week and a half since he'd taken her virginity, and in that time, she couldn't get enough of him. She thought about him all the time, even at work.

When she got home, she'd spend at least an hour preparing so that she'd have the confidence to seduce him.

"My cock needs a rest."

She chuckled. "You're the one that invited me to the bar tonight. I was only showing you how I was dressed." She wore a pair of black jeans that molded to her hips, and dipped in at the waist. They always made her feel sexy wearing them. She'd partnered it with one of his shirts, leaving a couple of the top buttons unfastened. Pulling her hair into a ponytail, she'd not even bothered with makeup, but she felt sensual.

Zane gripped her ass, squeezing the cheek, and making her recall how he'd taken her from behind the night before, spreading her ass as he teased across her anus. Everything had been delightfully sinful, and she'd loved every single second of it.

Tammy had pulled her aside that day, and asked how things were going.

"They're going great," Wynter said.

"And Zane?"

"He's amazing."

"You're falling for him."

"Don't be ridiculous. I'm not falling for him."

"What makes you think you're not?"

"You have to have time to fall in love."

"You've spent more quality time with him than you ever did with Carey. You're falling for him, and you don't even see it."

She didn't have time to dispute her friend. There was no way she was falling for Zane. Falling in love took time, right? It took a lot of time. Knowing each other, and sharing everything, dates, and other stuff.

Her nights were spent at either his place or hers. When they weren't working, they were with each other, enjoying some good food and a lot of laughs.

"You've gotten that serious look on your face. Have I upset you?" he asked.

"No, not at all. It takes more than you not seeming impressed by my dress sense." She pulled out of his arms. "Come on, we don't want to be late for work."

Zane and the guys were also performing tonight, and she looked forward to seeing him sing again. He had all their equipment in the back of his truck, so he was driving. She was free to drink but after what happened last time, she had no intention of letting alcohol get the better of her.

He held her hand, and she stared at his inked arm compared to her own.

"Do you like my ink?" he asked.

"Yeah, I do. Why?"

"You've been staring at it since we got in the car."

"I've always wanted to get a tattoo. Like a rose or something."

"Why don't you?" he asked.

She paused. It had been on the tip of her tongue to say her parents wouldn't approve. "I think I will."

"I know a great place. I go to him every single time I want new ink. I can book it if you'd like."

"Could you show it to me? I wouldn't know what to have, and I'd prefer to know in advance if that is possible?" she asked.

"How about tomorrow?"

"Yeah, I can work with that." She smiled. "I'm feeling all rebellious right now."

He burst out laughing. "You're amazing, you know that, right?"

"I certainly hope so." She rested her head on his arm. The angle of the mirror caught her attention, and she got a good look at the two of them together. Zane was the sexy, bad boy kind of guy, his arms and body heavily inked with his short hair, and she didn't imagine he'd ever be in a suit and tie. She liked that about him, and had no desire to see him in something like that. It wouldn't work, not even once.

He kissed the top of her head, and she closed her eyes.

Against him, she seemed out of place. Even staring at her reflection, she knew she was different from him.

"Do you like me, Zane?" she asked, suddenly struck with insecurity.

"Yeah."

She glanced up at him. "You don't think I'm boring and a stick in the mud?"

"Princess, I think you're a lot of fun to be around."

"Even though we've stayed in all that time?"

"I don't need to go out to have a lot of fun." He parked the car outside of the bar, which was already heaving with activity. She'd never seen it this busy before. The hot weather they were having drew more and more people out.

Zane cupped her cheek and forced her to look at him. "I don't know why you're doubting yourself, but you've got nothing to fear at all, baby. I like you. You like me, and there's nothing for you to worry about."

She smiled, shaking her head. "Ignore me. I was having a crazy insecure moment."

"Every time you have them, tell me. I don't want you hiding anything from me." He leaned in close, and took her lips. "Are you ready to go inside?"

"Yes."

"And you're free to drink whatever you like."

"Totally not happening."

Riot, Jones, and Silas were there when she turned to open her door. Their faces pressed against the glass, making her jump and laugh. "They're crazy."

"Yeah, it just goes to show you can never take the kids out to play."

Jones opened the door, and Silas helped her out. They all embraced her before Zane came to her side and gave them all a shove. "Know who she belongs to."

She liked that he was possessive of her. Snuggling against him, she felt safe, warm.

"Do you want to piss on her as well?" Riot asked with a smirk.

"Just remember who has to work tonight," Jones said. "We'll be keeping her occupied."

"I can sit at the bar and keep you company all night," she said, snuggling up against him.

He kissed her lips and shook his head. "Nah, you should have fun. They'll dance, and just know I'll be the one that wants to be with you."

"Don't worry, hot shot. We'll take care of her," Silas said.

Zane reluctantly let her go, and she made her way

inside with his three friends. There was no room inside the bar, so they had no choice but to find a chair out back where the overflow was.

Jones found them a table and went to get a drink. She watched the dancing, as the song was sexy and drew people together.

"So, do you like our guy?" Silas asked.

She returned her attention to the two men. Jones still hadn't returned. "Yes, I do. He's amazing."

Silas and Riot shared a look.

"What is it?" The look they each had didn't look great, and she started to feel nervous.

"Zane likes you, and he's not been himself since you both moved in next to each other."

She didn't like the way her stomach twisted.

"Are you wanting me to break up with him?" The thought of not being with Zane filled her with absolute sadness. She loved being with him.

Silas held his hands up, but Riot spoke first.

"No, we don't want that at all. Zane's writing more songs now than ever before, and they're not all shit either," Riot said.

"We ... he's never fallen for a girl. He's never been one to settle in one place, and we know this time it's different. He's different with you. No woman has ever captured his attention, and he never cooks for them."

She nibbled her lip, staring at them.

"He's our best friend," Riot said. "We don't want him to get hurt, but with you, we think there's a risk."

"I have no intention of hurting him."

"We think he's falling in love with you. Do you think there's a chance you could ever, ever fall in love with him? We know your family wouldn't approve of him, and even though you're being a little rebellious now, what about in five years' time?"

"You don't know anything about my family," she said. "I would never let anyone hurt him, and my family has no right to come near him."

"We all know who Carey is. Ask around and the right people will tell us everything we need to know. Your family wouldn't approve of Zane, and if you get over your problem, you're going to break his heart."

They stopped speaking as Jones came to the table. "They're all worried that you're going to hurt our boy. Ignore them."

"I'm not going to ignore them. I'm not going to hurt Zane, and if you heard the rumors about my family and Carey, then you know I left everything behind. I have no intention of going back to them, and I'm not going to hurt Zane. I care about him a lot."

Neither of them spoke again, but the damage had already been done. She sat back in her chair, wondering what the hell to do.

This wasn't some rebellion.

This was the real deal … wasn't it?

****

By the end of his shift, Zane was desperate to spend time with his woman. He found her sat at the table while the guys were setting up their equipment. She didn't look happy, and taking hold of her hand, he led her onto the dance floor, not caring that he was due to perform.

"Hello, Princess."

She smiled, but he saw that it didn't quite reach her eyes.

"What is it?" he asked.

"It's nothing."

"When I left you earlier, you were happy. What's changed?"

"Nothing. It's nothing. I'm just being silly."

He gripped her chin and stared into her eyes, seeing that it wasn't just nothing. There was something wrong, and he intended to find out what the fuck had gone wrong.

"Tell me, Princess. You can tell me anything."

"Are you falling in love with me?" she asked.

He stopped and stared at her.

"Your friends seem to think that you're falling in love with me, and that I could break your heart. I don't want to break your heart, Zane. That's the last thing I want to do."

Cupping her face, he forced her to look at him. "I'm not falling in love with you." It may be the first lie he'd ever uttered to her. "We're having some fun, right?"

She nodded.

Kissing her lips, which he could never resist, he smiled at her. "I've got to head back to get ready. Will you be at the front of the stage? Cheering me on?"

"Yes."

He hated leaving her, but before he went on stage, he was going to deal with his friends. Riot, Jones, and Silas were waiting for him, and he grabbed Silas. He just knew it had to be him. Slamming him up against the wall, he didn't feel anything. "Who the fuck do you think you are?"

"Whoa, Zane," Jones said.

"Back the fuck off. I brought her along so that she could have a good time, and you go saying shit that you don't have a right to say."

"We're all worried about you, Zane."

"This is not your fucking business. It never has been."

"You want me to apologize for pointing out the fucking obvious."

Zane shoved him against the wall again, wanting to do a whole lot more, but holding himself back. "You had no right."

"We have every right," Riot said. "This isn't just about you."

"She inspires you," Silas said. "In the past couple of weeks, you've done nothing but spend time with her. When you're with us, you're constantly talk about her. You've got your own name for her, or don't you know her real name."

"It's Wynter," he said, snapping the word out. Why were people so hung up on the fact he called her Princess?

"You're falling for her, Zane. You saw that guy she was talking to. We did some digging, and we know her family."

"She's told me about her family. It's not a big fucking secret!" His anger was building once again.

"What happens when she goes back to them? What happens when the bad boy next door no longer appeals and she wants the marriage and kids? You're not her forever man, Zane."

He glared at his friend. The urge to slam his fist against Silas's face was strong, but he reeled it in. Stepping away from Silas, he stared at his friends.

The need to play was no longer inside him.

"We're just thinking about you, Zane," Jones said.

"I may not be her forever man, but I'm her man right now."

Grabbing his guitar, he turned on his heel and began to walk away.

"Man, what are you doing?"

"Right now, I really can't play." For the first time ever, he turned his back on playing and went straight to

Princess.

"Zane? What's going on?"

"Do you want to go for a drive? Just be away from here, away from everything."

"What about work?" she asked.

"Forget work. Just you and me. No one to interrupt us. No trouble. Nothing."

"Yes."

Taking her out of the bar, he rode out of town, not even heading toward their homes.

"What about clothes?"

"This is an adventure, right? You've got to trust me, and right now, clothes are the last thing we need."

She stayed silent for several minutes, and every time he glanced her way, she stared at him. "What? What is it?"

"Have you ever missed a chance to play before?"

"No."

"What's going on, Zane?"

"Nothing is going on. The guys and I are having a disagreement. It's not anything serious. We'll resolve it when I get back."

"Is this because of me? Of my parents?"

"No."

He gripped the steering wheel even tighter, hating the fact he'd lied to her.

"You don't have to lie. They don't think I'm the kind of girl that's staying around, right? They think I'm going to leave?"

He glanced over at her, and sighed. "They have their opinions of your parents, and that you're not going to stick around."

"That sucks. I was starting to really like them."

"They're worried about me. Let's not talk about them, okay? Let's put everything else to the back of our mind and just focus on our drive right now. A little adventure. Is there anything you've ever wanted to do?"

"Get a tattoo. Go to a fairground. Eat candy without worrying about the calories. Make love all night underneath the stars."

He clicked his fingers. "I know exactly what we can do."

Making a quick turn, he headed toward the mountain. He and the guys had been there several times. There were often kids around that had raves or at least a small bonfire and pretended to be rebels.

Parking up in the abandoned space, he climbed out of his truck and grabbed a blanket.

"Where are we?" she asked.

"It's not such a secret. Let's consider it make out lane."

"What? You've brought me to where a bunch of teenagers get it on?"

"And adults. You'd be surprised how many couples just want to feel like teenagers again. This is a very prime spot."

She took his hand, pressing her body against his arm. "You want to take me to make out?"

"Yes."

"Will you bring your guitar? You can sing one of those songs you've been writing. I'd love to hear it."

He didn't have to be told twice. Grabbing his guitar, he took her hand and followed the well-worn path to a small picnic area. The moon high in the sky lit his path, making it easy for him to follow directions.

Once he found the secluded spot he was looking for, he placed the towel on the ground, waiting for Princess to sit before doing the same.

He'd not gone out like this with a woman … ever.

She crossed her legs and pulled from her hair the

band that held up those golden locks. "Sing for me, Zane."

Resting his guitar on his knee, he stared at her. She ran her fingers through her hair, and he was caught once again in the feelings that she kept inspiring inside him.

If he didn't know any better, he was starting to believe she was his muse.

"Where do you see yourself in five years?"

She smiled. "I have no idea. Where do you see yourself?"

"I don't know." He saw *her* in his future. Everything he imagined always had Princess with him. She belonged to him in a way that he couldn't even fathom.

Strumming his fingers across the strings of his guitar, he tuned it up, and then began to play. It was a slow song, not something rock and roll.

When he began singing about a woman who'd opened the door, she'd rocked his world, and turned him upside down. It was a song he'd written the day after he first met her. He sang about her fire, her passion, and also how she was trapped within herself, begging to get out, calling to him to be the one to unlock her.

Glancing over at her, he saw the tears in her eyes, and he didn't stop playing. He spilled all of his love and happiness into the song, every single emotion that she inspired within him, and he did it without guilt.

He didn't care if she didn't feel the same, but the truth was, he'd fallen for her faster than anything he could ever recall.

When he brought the song to a close, she leaned in close and placing a hand on his knee, she sank her fingers into his hair and claimed his lips.

Cupping her face, he didn't let her go, feeling his

dick begin to ache as her kiss awakened his arousal. Plunging his tongue into her mouth, he loved her moans, and knew he wanted to hear them for the rest of his life.

"I lied," she said.

"What about?"

"In five years, I know where I'll see myself."

"Where?"

"I see myself sitting here again, listening to you play."

Chapter Eight

Zane put the guitar down, and Wynter crawled into his lap. He moved back a little so that he rested against a large stone. Straddling his waist, she kissed from his lips down to his chest. It was still really hot outside, so she tugged off his shirt.

"You're only going to take advantage of me."

"You'll love it," she said, chuckling.

He didn't stop her as she trailed her mouth down his chest, stroking her fingers across his many tattoos, and then down to cup his rock-hard dick.

She moved off his lap and released his cock. Wrapping her fingers around the length, she saw in the moonlight that the tip had copious amounts of pre-cum. Licking her lips, she flicked her tongue across it, swallowing him down.

He groaned, and his fingers sank into her hair, wrapping the blonde locks around his fingers. She loved his touch in her hair, and she covered the whole head of his cock with her mouth, sinking it down and swallowing him up. When he hit the back of her throat, she pulled off his cock, swirling the head, and then taking him down again.

She hummed as she sucked him. Bobbing her head, she loved the feel of his hand on her head, guiding her, getting her to increase her speed, showing her with his actions exactly what he liked.

He tasted so good, and she didn't want to stop. Licking the length of his cock, she glanced up at him and saw his gaze on her.

Wynter didn't want to think of what his friends had said, or the doubt they'd placed. She didn't know what the future held. Her parents had always been part of her life, but in the past few weeks, she'd not missed them, or their meddling. Seeing Carey, she hadn't been struck by guilt at not seeking them out.

Having her own place, being her own person, she was free, and that meant way more to her than anything else.

She was exactly where she wanted to be, and Zane, he was something special to her. He made her laugh when she didn't think it was possible. Her days were far more exciting with him than without.

The song he'd just played had been about her. There was no way he or she could deny it. That song was about how they first met, and what it meant to each of them.

Sucking his cock into her mouth, she felt that slight change in his moan and the jerk of his hips, letting her know he was close.

She didn't stop. Taking him deeper, she moaned as more and more of his pre-cum leaked into her mouth.

"Shit, fuck, babe, you're going to have to stop."

This was about him, and she didn't stop. Sinking onto his cock, she sucked hard, and he came, spilling all of his cum into her mouth, and she swallowed it down, moaning as she did.

When she licked his cock clean, Zane flipped her onto her back, and began to tug on her jeans.

She laughed. "What are you doing?"

"You really think you're going to get away with that? I want a taste of your pussy, and then I'm going to give you one of your wishes."

He had her jeans off along with her panties within seconds. She cried out as his tongue latched onto her clit, and he sucked hard. His fingers circled her pussy as he slid them inside, teasing her.

"You're so wet. Did you enjoy sucking my

cock?" he asked.

"Yes!" She arched up, wanting his tongue back on her pussy, but he wouldn't do it. He teased her, making her wait, and she whimpered, desperate for more of what only he could give her.

He thrust two fingers inside her, and she cried out, the pleasure intense as he curled his fingers around and began to stroke over that special spot that had her burning for more. The fire within her was so intense that she couldn't think straight.

"Please, please," she said.

"You want to come?"

"Yes." She felt that was the only word that she screamed at him, and he chuckled, nibbling on her clit, setting her alight even more.

He licked her nub, stroking his tongue back and forth, making it harder for her to focus, to think, and she didn't want anything else but his touch.

She stared up at the sky as he brought her to orgasm, fucking her with his fingers at the same time, and she was on fire.

She cried his name as she came, her mind flooding with pleasure and need, and everything in between. She couldn't stop, and knew in that moment there was no way she could ever let go of Zane. He was inside her, in her heart and her mind, and there was no way she could ever give him up.

He brought her down from her peak, and she watched him tear into a condom, rolling it down his already stiff cock. When he moved between her thighs, she knew without a shadow of a doubt that she actually loved this man.

The man with the tattoos all over his arms and down his chest. The man who loved rock music that she couldn't stand. Who worked in a bar, and had the cheekiest smile on his face, who'd never look right in a country club, or even in a tux.

She loved him, and she didn't care what anyone thought, because he was hers, and she belonged to him.

No one, not his friends or her parents, could ever take that away from her.

He slowly slid inside her. She felt every single inch and gasped as he filled her, seeming to touch her in places that took her to the stars and back.

Zane took hold of her hands, pressing them either side of her head, and staring into her eyes as he began to make love to her.

She felt … everything.

The passion within him that he kept at bay as they made love.

The love in his eyes as he stared down at her. She felt everything, and she didn't want him to stop or to let go.

Once again, he took possession of her lips, and she knew without a shadow of a doubt that she was addicted to Zane, her sexy neighbor, the man that at times drove her crazy.

Thrusting up to meet his cock, she took him deep, hoping that he at least felt something for her.

"You're the most beautiful woman in the world to me, baby. I don't give a shit what anyone else says. You and I both know that the moment I claimed your virginity you became mine."

She didn't confirm it, nor did she deny it.

After having an overload of emotion, she couldn't focus on anything other than the pleasure he inspired.

He brought her to another orgasm and kept her poised at the peak, desperate and begging for more. He didn't give in, and only when he was ready for her to release did he come, and they came together, crying out each other's name. His cum was inside the condom, but he filled her deeply as he thrust.

She felt each wave and every pulse of his cock as they came.

When it was over, they lay on the blanket, and she stared at him, tracing her finger up and down his arm.

"What are you thinking?" he asked.

"I don't want to leave this moment."

"You don't have to. We can stay here forever."

"You promise?"

"Haven't you realized yet that whatever you wish for, I'm going to make sure comes true?"

"Are you my guardian angel?" she asked, teasing him.

"Nah, I'm a man who wants to give you the world."

She didn't deserve him.

He was so good to her.

"I want to give you everything you desire as well."

He took her chin and kissed her lips. "You already do just by being you."

They stayed curled around each other on the blanket. As the night wore on, a chill began to fill the air, and it wasn't long before they had to move on.

"I'm not going to have you getting sick on me right now. Come on, I saw a hotel just a few miles back."

Getting dressed, Wynter knew they'd come to a turning point in their relationship. They'd known each other a matter of weeks, and still thinking about how short a time they'd known each other, she was in shock. She'd never felt this way about anyone, and she couldn't deny it either.

Whatever happened, she'd given her heart to Zane, and there was no way she saw of her ever getting it back, nor did she want to.

****

"What are you wanting, Princess?" he asked.

"I don't know. There's so many to choose from."

Zane watched as she scanned all of the walls of the tattoo parlor he'd taken her to. The guy, Ray, was an expert, and had done most of the work on him, which was why he'd brought his woman in. He trusted the guy to do a good job, to not hurt her, and to not fuck it up.

"Where did you find her?" Ray asked.

He'd been standing by Zane as Princess stared at the walls.

"She's my neighbor."

"It must be special for you to bring her here. I don't recall ever meeting one of your bitches before."

"She's not a bitch. She's my woman."

Ray held his hand up. "Okay, fine. You're protective of this one, I get it."

She stood on her tiptoes looking at the highest rose across one wall. The flower was blue, and he didn't ever recall seeing a blue rose before. It looked beautiful as the main rose was blue with red flowers coming out of the stem.

"I like this one," she said.

"I've not had any woman or man ask for that one." Ray moved toward his books and opened one up, showcasing the design so that she could get a good look at it.

Another customer came in, and Zane stood beside Princess as she stared at the strange design.

"You like it?"

"I know it's weird, but I don't know. It just … it's really striking, don't you think?"

He stared down at the book, and saw the intricate design of each flower.

"It's beautiful." He didn't lie either. The flower didn't have any real design on an actual rose, but it stood out, the colors, sharp, vibrant.

"You sure you want to do this?"

"I'm totally not sure. I'll probably cry like a baby, but we only live once, right? I want to do this. It could be a whole lot of fun."

Resting his arm across her shoulders, he kissed her temple and waited as Ray finished dealing with another man before coming back toward them.

"You're sure this is the one you want?" Ray asked.

"Positive." She held the book out and gave him a big smile.

"Where would you like it?" he asked.

She turned to the side and lifted up her shirt. "Could you do it trailing from my hip up to underneath my breast?"

"Are you sure about that?" Zane asked. "It's pretty big for your first time."

She smiled at him. "I may never do this again. Go big or go home, right?"

"Right."

Zane didn't like it as Ray stepped forward and looked at her side, his fingers pressing against her skin. Ray wasn't doing anything untoward, but it pissed him off that another man had his fingers on her skin.

"I don't see a problem with this. Do you want to get started?"

"What do you think, Zane? Do you think it will look good?" She held the design of the book against her, and he thought she looked so cute.

"It's going to look epic. No backing out though. Now is your last chance."

"Why do you keep thinking I'm going to chicken

out? I want a tattoo."

Following Ray into the room, Princess was adamant that he join her.

She got comfortable on the chair, moving so that she was on her side, and she held his hand as Ray prepared the area.

"It feels so weird being here," she said.

"Why?"

"I never thought I'd get a tattoo. The rebel inside me is totally winning. Do I look hot right now?" she asked.

He chuckled and kissed her lips.

"No sexy time in my office. I have to keep everything clean."

"Sorry, Ray," she said.

"I'll be good and keep my hands all to myself."

He took her hand, which she squeezed a little tighter when Ray began to work. Throughout the work, she'd close her eyes, and he watched her as the ink marked her skin. Neither of them spoke, leaving Ray to work without any interruptions.

Staring at her hand, he kept their fingers locked together. Her fingers were much smaller and paler than his. In his mind, he saw their hands getting older, and still, he kept on holding them, keeping her against him, binding her to him for the rest of his life.

He'd never really known what love was.

His family had disowned him, and the women over the years just wanted to screw him. Nothing and no one besides his friends had stood out to him.

Princess was the only exception to that.

They were the complete opposites, and yet, they matched somehow. She was his fire, his passion, his inspiration. He knew he gave her strength, and helped her to live her life rather than just existing.

"Are you okay?" she asked.

"Yeah, I'm fine."

"You seemed to disappear on me there."

He waved a hand. "Just thinking about a song."

"You need to call your friends."

"I will."

"I'm not going anywhere. You can call them. Please, Zane. You know you want to."

Ray nodded at him, and he left the room, heading outside. Pulling out his cell phone he saw several missed calls from the guys.

He dialed Silas's number, waiting for his friend to answer.

Zane didn't have to wait long.

"Man, we've been trying to call you all night."

"Yeah, I'm sorry. I ... I was with Princess, and we decided to get away for a few days."

"We're worried about you. We've never seen you this devoted to one woman, and it's *you* we're thinking about. We don't want you to get hurt."

"I get it." He turned so that he stared at the wall. "You're right. I do love her. She means more to me than anything else I can remember." Just saying the words gave him a sense of peace. "I shouldn't have attacked you like that though, Silas. I shouldn't have attacked you at all. I know you guys are worried, and you're going to have my back, but I can't give her up. I won't."

"Zane?"

"She may not want me forever, and that's fine. I know she'll be my girl forever. Stepping out when we had to play was wrong. I'll handle everything so that we play this Friday, okay? We'll meet up in a few days."

"You don't want us to come out to you?"

"No." He wanted a couple of days with just him and Princess.

Saying his goodbyes, he called his boss next, and lied about not being able to do the show. He arranged everything so that on Friday the guys would be playing again. When he got back inside, a great deal of her ink was completed.

She smiled at him, holding her hand out, which he took. "Did you resolve everything?"

"As much as I could over the phone." She didn't ask him anything more, and within an hour, Ray was done. He covered the ink and gave her some ointment, along with a list of instructions on what to do over the next few days.

He paid for her tattoo and they left the parlor, heading toward the hotel room that they'd booked. They stopped for some food before heading inside. Sitting on the floor, he opened up several boxes of takeout food, mostly burgers and fries.

"I'm not going to go back to my family," she said, making him look at her.

"What?"

"I know your friends are worried, and they think I'm going through this little rebellion that will lead me back home, but it's not like that. I'm not sad or angry with them for being worried and carrying about you. I care about you, Zane. I've always been a little different from my parents, which is why my grandparents set me up in their will and allowed me to live my own life. They saw something different inside me. I'm not going to go back to them."

"They're your family, Princess."

"So? I like to think that family can be the ones we choose to have, not the ones we're forced to have." She took his hand. "I love spending time with you, being with you. Nothing is ever going to change that."

"Even my awful taste in music?"

"I'm not sure about that yet. That seems a little touch and go for me." She laughed. "Don't be angry at your friends for caring, Zane. They're your friends, and you always need them in your life."

He gripped the back of her neck and pressed his lips to hers. "I won't. I promise. We're going to play on Friday night. Do you want to come and watch?"

"Yeah, totally. I'll be in the front, jumping up and down."

They finished their food and he brushed his hands off, standing up. "Now, show me that tattoo. I want to make sure it totally looks awesome."

She stood up and lifted her shirt. The ink looked amazing, and he saw how beautiful it was even with it covered.

"It drove me crazy watching him put his hands on you."

She rolled her eyes. "He didn't have much of a choice. It would be impossible for him to ink my skin without putting some hands on me." She turned, wrapping her arms around his neck. "Now you get to put your hands on me, and no one is here to stop you."

He liked the way she thought.

Chapter Nine

Late Friday afternoon, Wynter was still at the school going through the grades that she and Tammy were dealing with. The kids were going to be off for a few weeks, and Tammy always liked to get everything in order. Her trip with Zane had lasted until Tuesday night when Tammy called her and asked for her to please come to work.

She felt so bad about leaving her friend to deal with everything that she'd cut her and Zane's trip short. They'd been planning to stay away until Friday when he needed to be home to perform.

"Are you angry at me?" Wynter asked, stamping the book and closing it.

Tammy glanced up at her and frowned. "What?"

"You know, for abandoning you?"

This time her friend chuckled. "Nah, I'm not angry at you, honey. I think it's been good that you're doing stuff for yourself. Since you've moved out, I've seen how happy you are. It always drove me crazy watching you not really enjoying your life. I know Marshall and I settled down and had kids young, but we also had a really good life together. You deserve to have a little fun with Zane. He makes you smile."

Wynter nodded, sucking on her lips and staring down at the book in her hands. It wasn't just fun, at least, not to her. It had stopped being just fun last week when she realized that she loved him.

"It's not just a little fun," she said, not looking at her friend.

"What do you mean?"

This time she took a deep breath and stared up at her friend. "I've fallen in love with him."

She expected Tammy to laugh or to ridicule. Instead, her friend just stared at her.

"You're in love with Zane?"

"Yes. I'm in love with him, and I don't need you to tell me how much my parents would—"

"Screw your parents. They don't even count. They've not even come to see that you're okay. They don't get to decide everything in your life."

"But—"

"No buts, Wynter. This is your life, and you can't keep living it like your parents are going to judge you every second of every fucking day. They wanted you to live a certain way, but you chose differently. Don't feel guilt over that. Feel fucking inspired by it." Tammy held her hands up. "I'm sorry. I tried to be nice about it, but you shouldn't feel guilty for not wanting the same things. You and Carey didn't match. You and settling down young didn't match. I've never seen you so happy since you started seeing Zane. He's good for you."

"His friends think I'm going to dump him and run back to my parents."

"Prove them wrong. Friends are there to look out for their friend, Wynter. I'm there to look out for you. I had my doubts. I'm not going to lie. You were always bitching about him that first week, and his music. Then it's like something changed. I'm beginning to think that little thing about your houses is so real."

She rolled her eyes. "It's not magical. Not at all."

Tammy laughed. "You keep telling yourself that." She slammed closed the final notebook she was working on. "Done. I am done, and now I get to spend the week with my husband and my kids. Sounds … dreamy."

Wynter laughed as she looked like it would be anything but dreamy. Tammy often teased that being a teacher of other people's kids spoiled her.

Hugging her friend, she stepped away. "You're the best friend I could ever have."

"Yeah, and I'm older than you, think about that." Tammy winked at her.

Leaving the school, she stopped off at the grocery store to collect some stuff. Zane had given her a list of everything he'd need to show her how to make that lasagna she loved so much. They'd been so busy with other things that it was only now they were getting to it.

She rounded a corner and came to a stop when she saw the deputy Slade and his very pregnant wife, Cassie.

"Hey, Wynter," Slade said.

"Hey, guys. Not long to go, is there?" she asked, looking at Slade's hand on Cassie's stomach.

"Not much longer." Cassie patted her stomach. "I'm becoming really impatient." Cassie looked at Slade, and they shared a look before turning toward her.

"How's the house?" they both said in unison.

"Erm, my house is great."

"What about mine?" Cassie asked. "I mean Zane's?"

"It's going good."

"And you and Zane?" Slade asked. "How are you two getting on?"

She stared from one to the other. "We're doing good."

"And?" Cassie asked. "Has anything happened between the two of you?" She spoke really slowly, and Wynter frowned.

"Are you okay?"

"Are you and Zane a couple?" Slade asked.

She stared at the happy pair and wondered what the hell was going on. They were staring at her intently.

"We're seeing each other."

Slade groaned, and Cassie fist-pumped.

"You didn't win," Slade said. "It hasn't even been six months."

"But I was totally the closest, which means I win."

Wynter continued to stare at the couple, and she was struck by how much in love they were. She thought about Zane, and how she felt when she was around him.

"Does this have to do with that crazy notion that the houses in some magical way bring couples together?" Wynter asked. She was getting tired of hearing about this.

"You know about it?" Slade asked.

"My friend told me about it." She looked between the two of them. "You don't think it's real, do you?"

"How can you think it's *not* real?" Cassie asked.

"Houses are not magical. They don't bring people together."

"I think you're denying a little too much. We came together," Slade said.

"And I hated him to start off. Believe me, I'm married to him, and we've got a kid on the way. There's something about those houses, and we've seen the other couples as well." Cassie rested her head against Slade's shoulder.

Glancing down into her cart, Wynter really didn't know what to say, so she made her excuses, grabbing the last few items from her list and making her way out of the store.

By the time she got home, Zane was waiting for her. He opened the door and helped her with the groceries. She followed him into his home, where she stood at the counter watching as he put stuff away.

Pushing some hair off her face, she was struck by

how much she loved being with him. The moment she saw him, she couldn't help but smile, and watching him put food away, there was a warmth with him.

"You got everything," he said.

"Of course. I also bumped into the people that lived in our houses before us."

"Cassie and Slade?"

"Yep. They kept asking questions of how we were getting on, and if we were together."

Zane burst out laughing. "Is this going back to the houses bringing people together?"

"I don't believe it, do you?"

He shrugged. "I don't really think about it. There's an easy explanation. We're two houses set back from the rest, we're close, and that close proximity brings about feelings."

She had feelings, a whole lot of feelings. In fact, in the past few days she'd begun to unravel, and little things were starting to really catch up with her. She recognized tiny things like him opening the door for her, helping with the shopping. He also put the seat down on the toilet. He always asked about her day, and actually seemed interested in knowing what was going on with her life. She loved listening to him play, strumming his fingers across the guitar, filling the room with his music.

Every single thing he did, from wearing slippers as he didn't like to get footprints on the floor, or his weird fetish with hats. He'd even posed in several for her, making her laugh as he did so.

In such a short time she'd shared so much of herself with him, and she didn't, not once, want to ever let that go, or let him go.

"Do you believe in a mystical house?" he asked.

She shook her head. "Nah, I don't. Anyway, moving on, I better go and get dressed."

"Yes, you'd better. I left something sexy out for you to wear." He gave her ass a little slap.

Shaking her head, she made her way upstairs, and found a pair of jeans, some boots, and a shirt. All of them she'd worn before, and it wasn't the first time that she was aware that he found her particularly sexy in and out of them.

****

The crowd at the bar roared to life as he began to sing the song he'd dedicated to Princess. It was titled that, and he saw her laughing as she danced along. He'd made up with his friends, apologizing to Silas, who'd shaken his hand. They'd been friends a long time, and tensions like that never ruined their friendship.

She winked at him as she threw her hands in the air and shook her ass from side to side, teasing him from the stage. Zane loved her, without a doubt in his heart. While singing to her, and only to her, he had to wonder if the miracle houses were real. Cassie and Slade had fallen for each other, and several other couples before he moved in.

Now he'd fallen for Princess, and there wasn't a thing he could do about his feelings, not that he wanted to.

After finishing one of the songs, he took a bow and climbed down from the stage, going straight to her. She threw her arms around his neck, and kissed his lips.

"That was, like, totally incredible. Did you see the audience? They were totally drooling over you."

"I only saw your drool." He wiped her mouth, and she laughed.

"I can guarantee that they totally, totally loved you."

"It doesn't matter." He gripped her ass, pulling her close and claiming her lips as he led her outside.

"Now, now, now, you've got people with eyes here," Jones said, slapping him on the back.

His three buddies followed them outside, and they sat on the hood of his truck. He and Princess had a soda while his friends drank a beer.

She'd sworn off beer ever since she'd discovered she had a rather loose tongue with the stuff.

"You guys are on fire tonight," she said. "Your own songs really put you on the map."

"I couldn't agree more."

Zane turned to see a man that he didn't recognize, wearing a suit.

"I've been coming to your shows for the past couple of weeks, and I found you guys compelling but not great. Tonight, you really showed me that there was something to see."

"And you are?" Silas asked.

He pulled a card out of his jacket handing it to Zane. "Rufus James. I manage bands. I help to get them on the map, and I know for a fact that you guys have what it takes to make it big. No more bars, or clubs. Just concerts that are sell-out tours. I'm not in the market for prissy little boys who want to cause a scene. I'm looking for hard-working men, willing to make a name for themselves within music. You want to take a chance, give me a call."

Zane couldn't believe what had just happened, and watched as the man in question left in a really nice car, not one he'd ever like. He rather loved his truck.

"That just fucking happened, right?" Jones asked. "Did we just like ... get offered a deal?"

Princess gave a little squeal. "Oh, my God! You're going to be a rock star." She hugged him tightly, and Zane held her close. "I'm going to grab us all a beer to celebrate because this is totally worth it." She clapped her hands, and he watched her leave.

"What's with the shitty face, man?" Silas asked. "This is a big deal."

"We've been down this road before," Zane said. He'd never told Princess the story. They'd been found a few years ago, and asked to go on tour with another rock band. They got pushed out, and ended up having to make their way home with no money. They hadn't been at their peak then either, so it had rocked and changed their entire world.

"This is different, man, we're different," Riot said. "You heard him. He wants actual artists, not fuckups. We were fuck-ups."

Running fingers through his hair, he glanced toward the bar, and knew the one thing he couldn't give up. "She's got to come with me."

All three men groaned.

"Look, I know you're not her biggest fans, but I love her. I'm not willing to give her up. I don't want to give her up. I'm never going to get a chance to feel like this again."

"And if she doesn't want to come?" Riot asked. "This isn't just your dream, Zane. It's our dream."

"I know." He saw her coming back. "Let me talk to her. I can at least tell her how I feel, and see how she feels."

All the guys agreed, and they all put on a smile as Princess approached.

"I want to make a toast. To you guys' many talents, and success is yours." She clinked her bottle with his, and he pulled her against him. He didn't want to let her go, not ever.

After they celebrated with a drink, it was time for them to go back inside and finish their set.

By the end of the evening, he couldn't wait to sit

down and just relax. When he and Princess got home, he took her up to his bedroom, stripped her completely naked, bent her over the bed, and began to caress the cheeks of her ass.

"This was a little … unexpected." He slid his finger down across her anus, circling her ass before using his other hand to stroke her soaking wet pussy.

"There's something I want to tell you, Princess."

"Okay."

He plunged two fingers inside her cunt and moaned as her pussy tightened around him. Running his thumb across her ass, he began to stroke her, which made her even more slick.

"This isn't the first time that a guy has approached us about a possible deal."

She glanced over her shoulder looking at him. "There's been other times?"

"Once before, when we were younger. We fucked it up, and we weren't that good either. Of course, we thought were the best, and we weren't. We were soon put in our place."

"What happened?"

"We had no money left, and we'd drunk most of it away. We had no choice but to start again. I think what sucked for me was that I couldn't remember any of it. Most of it was in a drunken haze of feeling on top of the world, and it wasn't long before that top of the world came crashing down all around us."

Using some of her cream from her pussy, he coated her anus and began to push his thumb against that tight ring of muscles. She tensed up but didn't stop him. She didn't say a word, slowly relaxing as she grew accustomed to his touch.

His dick was rock-hard, wanting inside her, to fill her pussy and claim her ass. He felt a need to make every single part of her his.

"After that we decided to keep our feet firmly on the ground, and our heads in the right game. If we ever got another opportunity like this, we wanted to be prepared."

Pulling his fingers from her pussy, he held onto his cock, and began to sink into her pussy. Her wet heat surrounded him, sucking his cock in deep.

They both groaned, and he stroked the cheeks of her ass, at the same time thrusting his thumb inside her anus.

"Oh … that feels so good." She moaned each word out, pressing back against him.

"Princess?"

"Yes?"

"I want your ass. I want to fuck your ass."

"Yes, Zane. I trust you." She stared at him over her shoulder and offered him a smile. "I know you won't hurt me."

He pulled out of her tight pussy and grabbed some lubrication that he'd purchased. Opening the cap, he spread lots on his cock and moved back up behind her. Making sure her ass was prepared for him, he threw the tube onto the bed and placed the tip of his cock at her anus.

So very slowly, he began to work the tip past the tight ring of muscles. He got her to push out, and as she did, his cock filled her ass.

Zane didn't rush, giving her the chance to get accustomed to the feel of him inside her. Once she had all of his dick in her ass, he held onto her hips and began to rock.

Her ass was so tight, just like her pussy.

Reaching between her thighs, he stroked her clit, feeling her ass tighten around his cock as he teased her.

She felt so fucking good.

Every single part of her was his.

Princess, Wynter Griffin, was his woman in every single way that counted.

His thrusts increased, and he fucked her a little harder, going deeper inside her. She cried out his name as he brought her to orgasm. Seconds after, Zane joined her, filling her ass with his cum as he held her tightly against him. He didn't want to ever let her go.

Collapsing behind her, he wrapped his arms around her as they lay on the bed, their breathing getting back to normal.

"Does this mean you're going to be gone for a long time?" she asked.

"Yes, and it's why I want you to come with me."

"What?"

"I don't want to live without you, Princess. You're my heart. I want you to think about coming away with me. To consider it."

Chapter Ten

A couple weeks later

"This is what has you looking so sad and down in the dumps?" Tammy asked.

Wynter stared across the table at her best friend. They were in the coffee shop in town, and she was struggling with what Zane had asked her.

No, she wasn't struggling at all.

She wanted to go with him, more than anything.

"I've not been down in the dumps."

"You've not been your usual chirpy self."

She'd not seen Zane in a couple of days as he and the guys were finalizing the deal of signing with a company for their music. They'd been in some studio in the city organizing a demo, and a rush had been put on it. The title of the track was called "Princess." Zane had played it to her, and she knew it would be a hit for the guys.

"I'm fine."

Tammy sighed. "Don't you want him to be successful?"

"I do."

"Look, honey, I don't know what the problem is here. I've said this before. You've never been so happy before in your life, and I know it's because of Zane. He doesn't want to leave you behind, but he wants you to be part of his life, and I don't know which part of that you're struggling with."

"He's not said that he loves me," she said, biting her lip and feeling the guilt.

"Have you told him you love him?" Tammy asked.

She shook her head. "I don't know what to say. I

want to just blurt it out, but then I start to panic. What if he doesn't feel the same way, and this was only supposed to be some fun?" She rubbed her eyes and groaned. "Ugh! I can't handle this."

Tammy giggled. "You think you're the only woman on the planet that has been in this position?"

"No, of course I don't. I just don't know what to do, and everything is moving so fast. He'll have tour dates and other dates, and I'm worried. What if he doesn't love me, and he just wants me to come along for a bit of convenience?"

"I've seen the way he looks at you. You're not that, Wynter."

She ran fingers through her hair.

She'd not even put it up for her coffee date with Tammy. They'd only been able to say a few words in passing over the phone, and she didn't have anyone else to talk to.

"Have your parents been to see you?" Tammy asked.

"No. Why?"

"They stopped by the house last night. They asked some questions about you and Zane."

Wynter sighed. "What did you tell them?"

"Marshall told them if they wanted any information on their daughter, they were to go and ask. He doesn't play with gossip, Wynter."

She leaned her head back, looking up at the ceiling.

"If they came around, you know they wouldn't like Zane."

"I don't care what they like, Tammy. I've spent way too long caring about what they like." She rubbed the side that had her ink, and she smiled. This was her life now, not theirs. She hadn't once missed her parents, and it probably made her sound like a bitch, but she didn't care.

Zane was part of her life, and there was no way that she'd give him up. She loved him more than anything else in the world.

Her nerves were getting to her. The feelings she had for Zane were not little or insignificant. They were everything.

Tammy chuckled. "You know you could just tell him. Just go up to him and say, 'Zane, I love you.'"

"Can we just do that? I thought it was supposed to be something special. A dinner? A declaration?"

Tammy took hold of her hand. "Just relax. Be yourself, and let the words flow from you. Tell Zane how you really feel. What it means to you. If you don't, you could lose him."

They finished off their coffee, and on the way out of the shop she picked up a chocolate chip muffin for Zane. She knew they were his favorite. She'd walked all the way to the coffee shop, so she began the walk back to her home.

Zane was due back later today, and she wanted to tell him how she felt.

It was important to her for him to know that she'd fallen in love with him. She'd tried to put her finger on when exactly she'd fallen for him, and each time, she came back to that first night when he was at her front door.

He'd looked cocky, and so confident and sure of himself. She'd been at her limit, and still he didn't lose his temper, but he got his house under control, bringing the party to a close.

Glancing around the neighborhood, she felt happier. Regardless of what Zane said to her, or how he felt, she knew this was what she wanted.

She wanted Zane.

She loved him.

Making her way toward the end of her street, she came to a stop when she saw her parents, along with Carey, standing in her driveway. She spotted Zane in her doorway and from the noise along with the neighbors being nosy, she knew she'd missed something. Rushing across the street, she walked straight past Carey and moved in front of her parents to stand by Zane's side.

She was surprised to see them on her doorstep trying to cause a scene.

"Who is this man?" her father asked.

"What is he doing inside your house?" her mother asked, staring down at him.

"What the hell are *you* doing here?" Wynter asked.

"Watch your language, Wynter. We taught you better than that."

Just like that, Wynter felt the sting of her mother's words, and she realized after seeing them right now, why she hadn't missed them at all. She didn't want the constant insults about her language, or the way she looked, or how she should perfect herself.

Not once since she moved had she thought about them, or cared what they were doing, what they were getting up to.

Her life had been perfect.

With Zane.

"Now, I knew my parents leaving you some money would be ridiculous and look what you're doing. Allowing strangers into your home," her mother said.

"He's my boyfriend," she said, making both of her parents pause.

"Don't be so stupid, Wynter. You've been dating Carey."

The man in question stood at the back, looking bored.

"No, I can't stand Carey, no offense. I don't want him." She moved toward Zane, who wrapped his arms around her. The moment he touched her, everything in her world felt ... complete. "I love him."

She stared into his eyes, and she saw that she'd surprised him.

"I've been wanting to tell you."

He pushed some hair that had fallen off her face, and she realized how much she loved it when he did that to her.

"I love you, too."

"This is just plain stupidity. I will not have a daughter of mine dating this ... this ruffian."

She smiled. "There's nothing you can do, and he's not a ruffian. He's a rock star. I'd be careful, Mother. You wouldn't want all my neighbors to know what a fucking bitch you are."

With that, she took Zane's hand, walked back into her house, and shut the door.

He pulled her into his arms, kissing her head, and she held him tightly, never wanting to let him go.

"I can't believe I just swore at my mother."

"I can't believe you love me."

Just like that, her focus went back onto Zane. "I've been wanting to tell you for some time now. I was so worried." Then she realized he'd said the same thing back to her, but insecurities hit her hard. "I understand if you don't—"

He silenced her with his lips, pressing her up against the wall, holding her hands above her head as he ravished her mouth.

She opened her lips, and he plundered inside her.

Zane released her hands and sank his fingers into

241

her hair, tilting her head back, and she lowered her arms to grip his hair.

"I love you," Zane said. "You're my reason for everything." He pulled away, and she stared into his eyes once again. "You're my muse. My inspiration. I've never known a woman like you, and I don't want to ever find anyone else."

Tears filled her eyes, and she stared at the man she loved, and for some strange reason she thought about their homes. "Do you think it's real?"

"What?"

"The crazy idea that our homes bring people together."

"That all depends," he said.

"On what?"

He went down on one knee and held up a velvet box. "Only if you say yes to my next question."

Her heart pounded, and she didn't have a clue what to do. He opened up the box, and inside rested a small diamond ring.

"Wynter Princess Griffin, would you please do me the honor of becoming my wife?"

"You know my name," she said.

"Of course, I know your name. I just prefer Princess a lot more." He held the box up and chuckled. "You're really making a man wait here."

"Yes. A gazillion times yes."

He took the ring from the box and slid it onto her finger. Kissing him back, she cupped his face, and knew this was where she was meant to be in the world.

"I want to come with you. When you're on tour. I don't want to miss a moment."

"You're sure?"

"I've never been more sure of anything else in my life. I know what I want, and I know it's you," she said.

"I'll be happy listening to you and watching you guys. I know your friends don't really approve of me."

"Fuck 'em."

"What?"

"My friends will come to adore you, but it'll be me that will love you until the end of time." He pressed his lips against hers, and she moaned.

This was exactly what she wanted, and she knew without a doubt she'd never look back.

Epilogue

One year later

After touring for the past year, and having a number one release, Zane and Princess had no choice but to head back home to deal with their houses. They couldn't leave them vacant for much longer, and they had both recently sold. Leaning against his truck, he watched as Princess handed over the keys to two men who'd decided to purchase the house. They were two good-looking men as well. Muscular, strong, and Zane noticed quite a few of the women on the street made a point of putting out the trash when they came around.

He wasn't taking any chances with his woman, who was smiling as she came toward him.

"They're charmers. Asked if I'd stay with them."

He pulled her into his arms and watched as the girl he'd sold to came out of the house just as a movers' van appeared.

"Do I need to go and kick anyone's ass?" he asked, holding his wife as he watched the three people move in.

"Nah, I told them straight. I come with a plus one."

They'd gotten married while on the road. They'd been in Vegas on a break when they decided to tie the knot. Jones, Silas, and Riot had all been there. They'd called Tammy and Marshall, who'd been there on a video call to watch the event.

He'd loved it, and now he had Princess all to himself.

Kissing her neck, he chuckled.

"What is it?" she asked.

"Well, if we're to believe that our houses bring

people together, which I'm more inclined to believe…"

"Yeah?"

"Well, there's two men there and one woman."

He saw the smile spread across her cheeks.

"Oh, my, you said she was so nice. They're great guys as well. I wish we were sticking around to see this, Zane."

"Yeah, well, we've got a plane to catch." He gripped her ass, turning her toward him. "I love you more than anything in the world, Mrs. Wynter Webster."

"You love saying that."

"I'll never get tired of saying that. Come on, let's get out of here just in case our presence spoils the magic of the house."

Maybe, just maybe, there was truth in it, and another couple of people were about to find theirs.

The End

SAM CRESCENT

 TWO HOTTIES NEXT DOOR

Sam Crescent

Copyright © 2018

Chapter One

"What do you think her deal is?" Ace Campton asked as he sipped at his cup of decaf while watching the neighbor as she tried to sketch whatever it was that seemed to have captured her attention. They'd been moved in now for three months, and since then he'd not been able to get a real introduction to the woman. She always seemed so busy, so preoccupied, even when carrying in the groceries.

His best friend, Brett Voss, came up to the window and looked past his shoulder to the lawn. There had to be a hundred crumpled-up pages of paper. She looked frazzled, annoyed, pissed off, and everything in between.

"You know it's freaky how much time you spend watching her," Brett said.

"What? I can't be curious about our neighbor, especially when on the first week here she was tearing everything up and throwing it out the window? I thought she'd been robbed." When Ace realized it was the actual neighbor, he'd simply gone back inside and waited as someone came with a huge truck and began dumping everything inside. "You're not the least bit curious about her?"

Brett sighed. "I haven't thought about it, to be honest."

"You're lying. You've got to be." Ace was completely obsessed with the new neighbor, and it made no sense.

"We've moved in, and we've been making changes. They've been way more important than the chick next door. Sorry, but it has. Also, it's really creepy how much you watch her."

"We're in our own little world all the way back here, Brett. Come on, man, you've got a dick. You can't tell me you're not curious about her? She's like a little fairy with her green eyes and red hair." He also noticed that she was constantly wearing dresses, the kind that stopped at her knee and had thin straps. She had a fuller body, curvy with nice, rounded hips and stomach. He also loved the shape and size of her luscious tits.

Running a hand through his hair, he felt fucking wired, and all he wanted to do was talk to her. They'd been inside redecorating for weeks. Work had come first, obviously. As personal trainers they were completely booked up and constantly in demand. They worked six days a week most of the time, so getting to their home had been a constant battle.

It wasn't that the previous owner did anything wrong, but the person who lived here before was a chick, and they needed to make their love den a bit more male.

"Why don't you take out the trash?" Brett asked. "You can see if you can talk to her, or how about just doing something other than staring out a window?"

"You make it sound bad."

"Dude, it *is* bad. You're constantly looking out of it." His friend smirked.

"You don't think it's weird taking the trash out on a Sunday?"

"If you don't do it, I will, and I know you've got a hard-on for her."

Ace wanted to deny it, but he was curious. It was a Sunday, the trash needed emptying, and the mystery woman next door was outside sketching away. He didn't see a better time to reach out than now.

On the way to the kitchen, he stopped at the mirror to check that a single hair wasn't out of place. He looked good, felt good, and as he grabbed the trashcan, he kept going over the different kinds of conversations that could happen.

Instead of panicking, he decided to play it cool. When he got to the trashcan, she was still sitting on the front lawn sketching away. He didn't know what to say, or how to approach her. Did he just come out and blurt it?

"Nice weather we're having," he said.

She didn't even acknowledge his presence.

Seriously, dude, the weather?

Taking a deep breath, he glanced over at her, and again, she didn't even notice that he existed. This was so fucking embarrassing. Women flocked to him all the fucking time. In fact, they were always around him, giving him their number. He didn't have a fucking clue as to why it was any different right now.

Clearing his throat, he tried again.

"It certainly is good weather we're having."

Dude, what is it about the weather?

Clearing his throat, he saw that she was still doodling.

He didn't know what the hell to say.

Finally, crossing the lawn, he stuck his hand out. "I'm Ace Campton, nice to meet you." He had stepped in front of her and thrust his hand at her.

"Oh, my," she said, jumping back. "You were totally in my light."

"Excuse me?"

"Who does that? I mean, seriously. Didn't you see I was doing something?"

He quickly stepped out of the way, and the woman glanced around the space that she'd clearly been sketching and growled.

"Sorry."

"Great, just great!" She stood up, brushing down her dress. "Who are you?"

"I'm your very friendly neighbor. We moved in on the same day."

"That's supposed to mean something?"

Her lips were a shocking pink, and her outfit completely screamed that it didn't go together. Her red hair stood out in contrast against her pale skin. She'd even painted her eyelids green. Even though it shouldn't work, on this woman it totally did.

"I'm sorry for standing in front of your light and all that. I just wanted to introduce myself. It has been three months, and to make this work I figured we should get to know each other." He withdrew his hand, thrusting them into his pockets.

He watched as she took a breath.

"I'm so sorry for … reacting like that. I was in the zone, or trying to be in the zone, and it was wrong of me. I've been trying to get the perfect light for this damn picture, but it's just not working for me. I don't think pristine neighborhoods are my thing, but I'm trying. I like to try new things."

"You're a photographer?"

"Artist." She held up her sketchpad. "The name's Meredith Snow."

"A pretty name to match a pretty lady."
****

Meredith hadn't meant to snap at the man for simply introducing himself. In fact, she'd been hoping to meet the two neighbors for some time now, but it just didn't seem to be happening. Between trying to work, attempting to work, and failing to work, she'd been completely consumed by what she couldn't do.

That was the reason she'd moved into the small, quaint house at the end of what appeared to be a suburban road. Everything looked so perfect, and yet for her, her house seemed like the best place to cause a little chaos. For the past year she'd been unable to complete a single personal project, which was fine as none of the projects she'd started were for anyone, but she needed to get back into the swing of things, otherwise the world was going to remember Meredith Snow as a two-trick wonder. Yes, she knew it was only supposed to be one trick, but she'd had two amazing, sell-out shows, and now, well, she couldn't even finish commission work. It had been so bad that she wouldn't even talk to new clients yet. She wanted to get back to her old self. She missed that flair that always took her, and right now, she didn't have it. She needed it.

Moving away from the city seemed like the right thing to do, especially as she hated it. The loud noises, the crime, the danger, she had lived in a bad part of city, and then when she made it big, the better part of city, but each one had its constraints. She hated both.

Pushing some hair off her face, she smiled at her neighbor.

"So, what is it that you do?"

"Brett and I, we're personal trainers."

"At the local gym?"

"Yeah, do you go there?"

"Not a chance. If I go anywhere it'll be for a swim or to relax. Not to get all sweaty staring at whatever is in front of me." She tilted her head to the side just as another man came outside.

Were they gay?

She didn't mind at all.

Well, her lady parts would certainly mind come nighttime, but that would just make for a more interesting show in her fantasies.

"I take it you're Brett."

"The very one."

Ace had dark hair while Brett had brown hair. While Brett had brown eyes, Ace had blue. They were both tall, muscular, and she could clearly see without knowing they were trainers that they worked out. Their muscles were huge, and that wasn't an understatement. It was indeed a fact. They were ripped all over.

She introduced herself and hoped that she didn't drool. These guys were over six feet tall, and while she was happy being five-foot-six, she actually felt small in comparison.

Out of the corner of her eye, she noticed several women walking out carrying their trash, and she couldn't help but smile. Even on the day they were moving in, this was something she recalled seeing. The women, married or not, were trying to garner the boys' attention.

"So, how are you finding our little spot of heaven?" she asked, liking that they were talking to her.

She'd never been one to crumble under pressure. Being known as a weirdo in school, she'd embraced her quirks, and enhanced them. She had never allowed a bad word to get her down, and in fact, when someone would say mean things about her hair, the next day she'd put it in a more flamboyant style.

Fight fire with fire was what she believed.

Never had she gotten into a fight. She didn't believe in violence, but she also didn't believe in allowing people to walk all over her, so she would fight every single day if she had to, just in a different way. There was no way anyone was ever going to step on her; she wouldn't allow it.

"We're getting by. Little creeper here couldn't stop looking at you," Brett said.

She saw Ace's face go red, and she laughed. "Your curiosity got the better of you?"

"Yeah, it did, but Brett is overexaggerating."

"I kind of like the idea of you watching me. It seems a little strange, but I like that. I love strange." She watched the two of them. They were nice, she could tell that instantly. "I feel like I've been a very bad neighbor here." She glanced down at her books. "How about I order us some dinner? We can sit out in the garden, have some food, wine, talk. You guys do drink wine, right?"

"We're more for beer," Brett said.

"Don't worry. I've got a few bottles I'll put in the chiller. Chinese?"

"Sounds good." This came from Ace. "I am sorry for stepping into your light." He pointed at her sketchbook, and she simply smiled.

"It's okay. It's not that good anyway. I completely overreacted, and I was forcing it anyway. I just panicked, and I really shouldn't have done that and yelled and been a bitch. Lovely to finally meet you both and I'll see you around seven?" It would be nice to have some company, and not wallow in self-pity for another day that hadn't gone well.

"Count us in."

They said their goodbyes, and she walked into her home. It had been a simple place, plain walls, but it had that male vibe, which she'd not liked. When she had her own space, it had to be *hers*, so for the first few weeks it was about changing everything, making her space, and now it finally was.

As she shut the door, the scent of vanilla filled the air, and she closed her eyes, enjoying the fragrance as it relaxed her.

She needed this space. Her manager, agent, whatever Will liked to call himself, had insisted on it, especially as he'd come to her studio a year ago and seen all of her half-baked projects.

When she was drawing, creating, designing, she had to connect with each piece. To give a part of herself, otherwise it was just another drawing in a long line of them. She didn't want them to feel like mass-produced trash.

Getting away, changing her scenery, doing something different, Will had believed would help her find that spark once again. Right now, it didn't seem to be working.

****

"I can't believe you said that shit!" Ace stormed into their place, and Brett simply smiled.

"What? She found it funny."

"And if she didn't?"

"Then it was no big deal to me. Come on, have a laugh and a joke. It was funny." Brett watched as his best friend paced the main living room. It had been so hard to resist, and then seeing as their little neighbor was giving Ace the flirtatious eye, he simply couldn't *not* mention it.

What had surprised him was her amusement. It's not every day a woman would find a stalker funny, but he had a feeling she wasn't like every other woman.

"What's her name?" he asked.

"Wouldn't you like to know?"

"Yes, I would. Stop being a pain in the ass."

"Her name's Meredith Snow." Ace dropped down on the sofa. "What do you think we should wear tonight?"

"Clothes."

"I'm being serious. She's an artist, and I want to make a good impression."

"You do, do you? After what, five minutes of chatting?" Brett asked.

"I like her, okay? I don't know. She's nice. Got a pretty smile but a word to the wise, do not stand in her light. She tends to go a bit crazy."

"As all women do when you affect their light." Brett rolled his eyes.

"No, this wasn't because of makeup or taking a selfie or shit like that. She was drawing, sketching the neighborhood. She held onto that notebook like a lifeline. I don't know. I'm curious about her. She has no sense of style at all, but she owns her shit. You know?"

"You figured all this out in five minutes?"

"I'm a people person, Brett. It's why all the chicks like coming back for more."

Again, Brett rolled his eyes. They were both personal trainers at the local gym. The difference between the two of them was Brett wouldn't back down. When he got a client who gave him boundaries to work under, and a guideline for what they wanted, he worked to it. He made sure they met every single one of their goals, and he wouldn't take complaining or whining, or whimpering. If a woman started to bat her eyelashes at him and beg for him to stop, it wasn't going to happen. He also didn't allow for relationships. That was a big no.

Now, Ace on the other hand, a woman batted her

lashes and he stepped back. His friend had never been in a relationship with a client, but he knew that Ace's kind heart and good nature tended to put him in tricky situations, which was why he always had a helper on hand to be there so nothing could be mistaken, nor could Ace be accused of anything.

"Are you coming tonight?" Ace asked.

"Yeah, I'll be there."

"Good. Try and keep your bad attitude at the door. You know, she's our neighbor, so we want to make a good impression."

Brett grabbed a bottle of water from the fridge and moved back toward the sitting room where Ace was flicking through one of the fitness magazines they had delivered. "Be straight with me right now. Are you trying to fuck the neighbor?"

"That's just so … crude. What's wrong with just wanting to be nice?"

"Cut the crap, Ace. Be honest. You want to bang the neighbor?"

"I wouldn't be averse to, you know, getting to know her. She has got some rockin' curves, and fuck, she is so hot!"

"So that's a yes."

"Yeah, fine. Sue me. I like the neighbor. She's different, and you know what, we came to this neighborhood for different. What's the deal?"

"I just need to know what you were hoping to achieve tonight so I don't throw up in my mouth over dinner."

Ace stood up and laughed. "Please, you can't tell me you weren't affected by her. I know you saw the ink that was on her thighs, just peeking out of the dress. Don't tell me you didn't imagine slowly pulling the straps of that dress down, watching her tits appear, and having a little taste."

Brett wasn't about to deny it. For the past three months, where Ace had been completely blatant in his watching and stalking of their neighbor, he'd been subtler. Instead of standing at the window, he would watch her from his bedroom, completely out of line of sight. She liked to garden, and she wore shorts that molded to the curves of her ass. Watching her, seeing her, he knew she was confident in her body, and it was refreshing to see. Being in the gym, around so many different personalities, he knew insecurity when he saw it.

Meredith didn't have that at all.

She was who she was. She knew herself, and he found that sexy as fuck. With the heat of summer fast approaching, her clothing had gotten less. He had even seen her in just a bikini top and shorts the other day. Ace hadn't been home, but Brett had seen the ink that trailed up her hips, across her stomach, and along the base of her back. Roses, thorns that seemed to have a wildness like the woman herself.

"You know, there's nothing wrong with us sharing her," Ace said. "I can take her Monday to Wednesday, you have her Thursday through Saturday, and we can let her rest Sunday."

"Some days I wonder how you're not a virgin, Ace. You sound like a total dick."

"But a dick that you love, and you always have my back."

Yes, he did. For all of Ace's faults, he was loyal, determined, and an amazing friend. He just wasn't the brightest man around, but that was fine.

"I'm going to go and get ready. Figure out what color you want your bedroom. We're painting this weekend," Brett said.

"You sound like a wife, Brett."

"Whatever."

Chapter Two

"It's too nice to eat indoors. I hope you guys don't mind. I love being outside, especially now that it's so warm. I miss it," Meredith said.

There were lights hanging around the back porch, even the steps which led to the lawn. Her garden was also beautiful, flowers, roses, all in different stages of bloom looking stunning. Ace hadn't even realized the changes to her garden, but it worked.

The table had several Chinese cartons on the top. He loved Chinese food so much. Of course, he was used to cooking it himself. Part of being a personal trainer, for him, was also telling his clients how best to eat, and what alternatives to take. Chinese food, at least takeout anyway, wasn't a good idea. One night, however, wouldn't hurt.

"You know, I was worried that you guys would want, like, quinoa or something like that. I don't do that, I'm afraid. I think it tastes so bland," she said. "I love Chinese food, and it has been way too long since I ordered all my favorites."

"I make a mean quinoa salad. You just got to know what flavors to add to it. That's only if you want to know, though," Ace said.

"Thanks, sweetie. Some people were born to eat healthily. I don't think I'm one of those people, I'm afraid." She shrugged.

He didn't have a problem with that, not at all. In fact, he rather liked not having to constantly be a good boy when it came to his diet, but that was for another day.

His mouth watered at the scents coming from the food.

Beers were in a bucket with ice, and he saw plates

with chopsticks on the side.

It looked … different.

"Please, have a seat."

She touched his arm before heading back inside. He didn't know what she was doing, but he caught Brett checking out her ass.

"Not interested, huh?"

"Did I say that?"

"Pretty much."

"You just don't listen to me."

"I listen to everything," Ace said. He raised a brow as Brett stole a dumpling. "What if they're for her?"

Brett closed his eyes. "You know, you really need to try these. They're fucking amazing. I mean, seriously, right now I can't even think."

"Started without me. Are they good?" Meredith asked, coming to stand in front of them. She held a bottle of wine. "I forget to get something for me to drink. Dig in, boys. I didn't order all of this for myself." She took a seat at the table, and Ace took the seat closest to her.

Using his chopsticks, he began to serve himself up a generous portion. He wasn't dieting for anything, and he'd be able to work off any calories he got in the gym. He closed his eyes and moaned as the flavors exploded on his tongue.

"How long has it been since you ate Chinese food?" Meredith asked.

Opening his eyes, he saw her smiling and glanced over at Brett to see him smirking. "What is it? Do I have something on me?"

"No. You were moaning as if you were having an orgasm. I know the place I order from is damn good but not as good as chocolate."

He chuckled. "I think it has to have been three or

four years since we indulged."

"He won't even allow us to order anything unless it's vegan," Brett said.

"Ah, so you two do take your job seriously."

"Our job is kind of boring," Brett said.

"It can be. The same old routine, but we have different clients."

Meredith wrinkled her nose. "I went to a gym once when I was, like, twenty-one and doing the whole New Year's resolution thing. It lasted for, like, one day. I hated it. I got all sweaty. My thighs hurt, my legs hurt, everywhere hurt, and I decided it wasn't worth it. Now, I speed walk, which is fun. It helps to clear my head, you know. Also, we live one life, and I think we should live it any way we want, you know."

"You're an artist," Ace said.

"Did you search me?" Meredith asked.

"I did, and it turns out you're sought after. You've filled two gallery shows, and your work has even gone up for auction to help raise money. You're rich."

She laughed. "I wouldn't call myself rich. I'm doing well, but I have to be careful."

He saw the nerves shining in her eyes.

"Why do you have to be careful?" Brett asked.

"Wow, invasive much?" Ace asked.

She chuckled. "Nah, it's all fine and great, you know, when one is actually working. But when that creativity seems to stop or there's a wedge between you and that need to do your job, it can be quite frustrating."

That explained the article he'd read about her being a two-trick pony. There had been several news items that said she'd gone into hiding, or was at a retreat or something. Instead, she was here, his trusty little neighbor.

"You're having a few problems?"

"Pretty much. I can't seem to focus on a project. I've been completely dedicated to my work for so long now. I've not had a break, apart from this past year when I've been forced to, because at the moment I suck. At least my manager or agent likes to think so, well, not the suck part. If not, then I've got to start looking for a career change. Enough about me, though. How are you finding the neighborhood? Any of the desperate wives asking for you to come and fix their plumbing or something?"

Ace laughed. "It's not that bad."

"Seriously, on the day we moved in I saw them all. They were not looking at me, and they were, like, drooling. It was so bad I was sure there was a puddle on the ground."

Ace enjoyed her straight talking. She didn't hold back. Her hands were expressive, she smiled, she was just full of life. He'd not been with a woman like her for so long. He couldn't think of the last time he'd known a woman who was just so confident, happy, outgoing. She was filled with this energy that just sparkled from the inside out.

He found her completely charming, and he didn't want to leave. No woman had ever affected him like this in such a short amount of time.

****

Three glasses of wine later and Meredith felt buzzed. Brett and Ace were incredible company, and so much fun. She loved the way they were with each other, their friendship shining through. They often teased each other, and she liked that.

Their love for each other came through.

She'd never been close to many people, often preferring her own company or that of her sketchbook. People often had opinions, judgments, and she found listening to them always affected her craft. Being a bit of a loner helped her a lot.

Brett and Ace though, they were nice. They didn't seem to care that she loved having twinkling lights all around, or that her garden wasn't color-coordinated. She hated it when she went to places and they had to have all white rose bushes or pinks.

A splash of color was the way to go as far as she was concerned. She loved to see everything. Life was too short to have greys, dullness, and order. She wanted everything to be alive, to feel part of it all.

She couldn't live inside a closed box. Many nights as a child she would sleep in a treehouse outside in the back yard rather than stay cramped in bed. Even now, she had times when she'd sleep outside.

Camping was something she enjoyed, and considering she usually avoided strenuous activity, camping was something she found refreshing and completely rocked her world.

"So, are you two, like, together-together?" she asked.

Ace laughed, and Brett chuckled. "That's not the first time we've been asked that," Brett said.

"It's not?"

"No. We're best friends. Not lovers," Ace said. "What about you, sweetheart? You got a man you're pining for?"

"Nope. No man in my life. Hasn't been for some time, actually." She hadn't been in a relationship for about three years. Her career had always come first. She'd been on dates and shared some one-night stands, but nothing that had screamed long-term, not for a long, long time. She leaned back in her seat. "I doubt I'll meet anyone here."

"Why not?" Brett asked.

"I don't know. This is a family neighborhood.

Besides, I really need to be relaxing."

"If you're not seeing a guy, who is that dude that has been visiting you?" Ace asked.

"Ah, you mean my manager, Will. He comes around once a week to see how I'm doing. I think I'm totally stressing him out."

"Would you like us to see some of the work you've been doing?" Brett asked.

"Nah, I don't like sharing my stuff. When I work, until it's complete, I kind of have to … leave it."

"But Will?" Ace asked.

"He's different. He's been with me since the beginning. He was the first guy I actually painted. At his desk, yep. He was so surprised by what I drew that it kind of made him want to help me."

"What did you draw?" Brett asked.

"The corporate world. The fact that he had a picture of his family but in their faces I drew numbers and charts. It kind of worked him up. It's what I love about drawing, painting, just anything really. You can see something every single day, and then all it takes is another person's viewpoint of that exact same thing and it's, like, bam, totally different. They wake up. I helped to wake up Will to what he was missing, and in doing so, he helped me." Will was twenty years older than she was, a friend to her, a father, a guide, and just a best friend she'd never had.

He didn't have expectations of her.

When he came to visit to check on her work, she knew he was worried that she'd lost that flair he enjoyed and that others loved. She'd find it again. It wasn't lost, not at all. She felt that urge, that passion. It was still there bubbling beneath the surface. She just had to find the metaphorical glass or ice that was keeping her inspiration locked down.

She glanced down at the time to see it was a little after ten, and she was shocked. "Oh my, time has, like, totally flown by. Can you believe how fast it has gone?" she asked.

"Shit, we've got an early shift," Brett said.

"I'm so sorry to have kept you guys. I mean, this was fun."

"Honey, this was the best evening we've had since moving in. Seriously, we have to do this again sometime. How about I be the one to cook you dinner?" This came from Ace.

"An invitation to dinner? I'm intrigued. Is this going to be your way of turning me on to quinoa?"

"I've got a few recipes up my sleeve that I think you'll love."

She turned to Brett, the bigger of the two with more ink. She loved getting ink herself and was working on a design for her back, but seeing as she wanted it to be permanent, it had to be perfect. She didn't rush anything like that.

"What do you think? Think I should risk it?"

"He's a damn good cook."

"Okay, I'm sold."

"Really?" Brett asked.

"You look like the kind of guy that doesn't give compliments easily," she said. She liked Brett. He was serious, and yet there was an edge to him that she couldn't quite read. Ace was fun. He was boisterous, loving, passionate. They were both suited for each other as friends.

"He doesn't," Ace said. "Always complaining about something."

"Okay, okay, let's get out of here. She doesn't need to hear our life history," Brett said.

She walked them through her house and said her

goodbyes, sad to see them go even though it was only next door.

Closing her own, she leaned against it and smiled. Both men were amazing, and that was the most fun she had experienced all year.

****

"I'm really impressed with these test results, Max. You've lost over forty pounds since we started this new, healthier lifestyle," Brett said, smiling at one of his favorite clients.

Max had come to him last year when he discovered he was a type two diabetic. It had woken him up to the damage he was doing to his body through lack of exercise and simply eating all the wrong kinds of food. After they sat down together with a nutritionist, they'd come to an agreement where they could control his diabetes with medication, diet, and exercise.

"This is all because of you, Brett. Honestly, I know you've been busy with moving house and everything. I really appreciate you not missing a single appointment."

"I'll do anything to help. I'm sure you know that." Max was one of his few clients that was doing this for health reasons. Some were there to stay on target, and others just wanted to look sexier, but Max was a family man. He'd been honest. He wanted to do this for his wife and kids, so they could have him around as long as possible.

Brett liked Max, and even when he wasn't feeling one hundred percent, he never missed an appointment.

Shaking Max's hand, he saw him out. Ace was at the front desk signing some paperwork.

"Good appointment?" Ace asked.

"The best. He's doing well."

"Good. I know you care about that one."

"He's determined, Ace. You know what that's like. Sometimes you need someone to give you a pat on the shoulder, you know. It'll be okay. I'm here."

"I get that. So, I'm thinking, you, me, our sexy little neighbor. I'm heading out now. Got no more clients. My shift ended ten minutes ago. Signed on a new client, and now I'm out. I'll grab a few things from the grocery store. Will you promise to have your sexy butt at our place around six?"

"Yeah, you got it."

"Awesome. Enjoy."

He didn't linger to watch his friend. Heading back into the gym, he spent the next couple of hours of his shift trying not to think of his sexy little neighbor. It was next to impossible though. Since their dinner at her place, he'd found himself thinking about her more and more. It had only been a couple of days, but still, his thoughts were dominated by her.

No woman that he could recall had ever made him feel this way, this fucking wired, and so hungry for more. The time had been getting on the last time they had dinner, but he'd not wanted to leave, not even for a second.

"There is a little secret I think I should tell you," the cute blonde said. *"These houses are kind of special in their own way. Now don't laugh, because I didn't believe it either, but you see, the last several couples actually, well, it is believed that the houses help people to fall in love."*

He couldn't remember the previous owner's name, but her words had stuck with him. Ace had burst out laughing, and Brett had simply found it sweet that she thought the houses were responsible for love.

Now, however, he couldn't help but wonder if there was a smidgen of truth to all of that. He wasn't in love with Meredith; that would be completely crazy. He barely knew her, but his thoughts about her in the past few days had been nonstop. Even Ace, his best friend, never chased after a woman, and yet here he was, wanting her, desperate for her, ready for her.

Ace didn't cook for women. No matter how much it would impress them, he never went to that extra effort unless there was a guarantee of getting laid. With Meredith that wasn't the case.

By the time his shift ended, Brett was still no wiser as to what the hell was going on, nor did he want to try to figure it out. Clocking out of the gym, he made his way toward his car, climbed in, and headed home. He didn't make any pitstops anywhere. When he arrived home, he heard the sound of laughter coming from the kitchen.

Entering the room, he saw Ace in the kitchen tossing some vegetables into the air and catching them.

"Hey, it's my BFF. He's home," Ace said, winking at him.

Meredith was drinking from her glass, and she smiled toward him. "Hey, I had a bottle of wine left over and I thought why not."

"I've got you some beer," Ace said.

Brett caught the beer that Ace tossed toward him.

"So, how was work?" Meredith asked.

"It was good. Is he showing off?"

"His very impressive cooking skills. He certainly is. I'm even a little impressed."

"Just a little?"

"I lie. A hell of a lot impressed," she said with a giggle.

He loved that sound.

"How was your day?"

"I did some changes to my art studio. I'm

working on little doodles and patterns on the wall. It's not canvas, so I feel a little more freedom to express myself." She smiled at him.

The worry seemed to have faded away.

"So, I have to ask," she said. "The one day I went to the gym, I came home and slept for, like, twelve hours straight. How do you two handle it?"

"We're big, strapping young men. We can take on anything," Ace said, flexing his muscles.

"That is cute."

"We've been at this a long time," Brett said. "It's our work, so we pretty much have to be able to do anything that our clients throw at us."

"Is the experience different with a personal trainer as opposed to going solo and just winging it?"

"I couldn't tell you. I'm a guide. I make sure people don't push their boundaries or their limits."

"What if someone likes to have their limits pushed? To experience that bite of pain?" she asked.

He stared at her lips, wondering what they would be like around his cock. "Everyone has a point where they need to be brought back from the edge, Meredith. I'll throw you in a free session if you want? Show you what you've been missing."

"I'll think about it."

Chapter Three

"You were both flirting, and I made the perfect quinoa salad. The entire time she was glancing toward you," Ace said.

He glanced over at his friend. Brett was putting some pictures up on the walls, giving their home a more personal touch. They'd been living together now for well over ten years, and in all that time, he'd not wanted to leave, not once. He enjoyed living with Brett.

From the moment they met each other in high school, they'd been inseparable.

"You're still going on about that?" Brett asked. "You made quinoa three days ago. We're still eating it from the fridge."

"That's because I made enough so we had lunch."

"Yeah, well, I'm getting bored of eating it all the time."

"I could fry you up some shrimp that you love in some spicy sauce if you'd like."

"Nope, I'm good. Just sit on your ass while I attempt to make our home, ours."

Ace glanced down at his magazine. It was getting to a good new exercise that he'd heard about. "Nah, you're doing such a good job. You know, looking all sexy. I'm quite happy to sit here, do nothing. Relax. It was a long day at work."

"Suit your lazy ass."

"Oh, I will. I love it." He wriggled in his chair and sighed. "This is the life."

Brett just chuckled. "You ever thought about what that lady said who lived here before us?"

"Wynter."

"What?"

"The girl that lived here before us. Her name was

Wynter, why?"

"How do you remember all these names?"

"Because I'm awesome and it's polite. How do you not?"

Brett shook his head. "Anyway, that's not the reason I wanted to talk."

"It's not?"

"No."

"Then what?"

"Shut up for, like, a second and I'll tell you."

Ace smirked. Brett was so easy to rile up. He also got a kick out of it as well.

"You remember what she said about the two houses."

"About them helping couples fall in love? Yeah, what of it?"

"Have you noticed you think about Meredith a lot? Like, a whole lot."

Ace paused. The words on the magazine faded away as he thought about Brett's question. Yes, he thought about Meredith a lot.

Actually, it was more than that. From the moment he first saw her, his obsession had been in place. He wanted her, no doubt about that. That didn't mean he loved her.

You wake up wondering about her.

You go to sleep thinking about her.

"I don't think we're in love with her." He looked up at Brett to see his friend's brow raised.

"You're thinking about her all the time?"

"Well, yeah, but that doesn't mean much. I think about watching cartoons."

"Okay, when you think about her, is it just sex?"

Ace gritted his teeth. He'd passed a floral shop on the way home three times this week, and each time he'd seen some red roses that reminded him of Meredith's hair and also her rose garden. He'd even stopped by her house to give them to her. She'd been so sweet, inviting him in, and he'd watched her plant them. Why buy a bunch of roses when you can buy a rose bush?

"What?" Brett asked.

"When I think about her it's not always sexual. It's crazy to think that the houses have any such control over our emotions. We're guys. We've had a stressful year. Moving is pretty chaotic. We've not dated, and you know, we're just, everything is fine," Ace said.

"All right. Tell me how you feel right now about the thought of going out on a date with anyone other than Meredith?"

Ace squirmed in his chair. His stomach twisted, and he didn't feel comfortable.

"It's not possible, okay? This is crazy. We're two guys here. There's no way that can happen," Ace said.

"We've shared women before and enjoyed it."

Of course they'd shared women. They'd been in high school, and the head cheerleader had said how amazing it would be to have the chance to be the filling in their sandwich. Then they'd experimented in school. Played a few games along the way. Even experimented themselves.

Yes, they'd attempted to kiss, seeing as they could handle touching the one woman, but it had never been right to kiss each other. Brett was his best friend. He didn't imagine being with him or anything.

"We've never spoken about it being long-term," Brett said.

"Look, we don't even know if Meredith would go for something like this, okay? For all we know, she doesn't have a clue what this is about. We're crazy right now." Ace stood up, rubbed the back of his head. "I'm going to bed."

He moved out of the living room and made his way upstairs to his room. He went straight to the window, and there Meredith was. She sat in the garden in the middle of her yard, bent over a sketchpad. There was a lamp near her to give her light. She wore a bikini, which displayed her ink to perfection. Her body moved this way and that, and he loved watching her.

Her curves were all on display, and she seemed not to have a care in the world as she worked away at whatever had taken her fancy. He didn't love her.

He wanted her.

There was no doubt in his mind that he wanted her.

Love between houses.

The thought of sharing her with Brett didn't sicken him.

It turned him on.

Could they do it? Was there a way for them to share this woman between the two of them without causing trouble?

Stepping back from the curtain, he laughed.

The entire idea was ridiculous. He had thought so when Wynter told him about the whole curse. Clearly, they needed a drink and a relax.

Love didn't exist because of two houses.

It simply wasn't possible.

Then why is it, I can't get her out of my mind?
****

"Stop looking so panicked, okay? The world is not going to forget you anytime soon, but they will if you don't start to focus," Will said. "You're supposed to be here to work. I'm doing as much as I can."

She bit her thumbnail, which she hated doing as it was a habit she got into as a kid. "This isn't about that, and you know it. I don't care if they remember me. I'm nothing without my craft. You know that."

"You've hit one or two snags."

"It has been over a year since my last commissioned piece, Will. Not only that, I can't seem to focus." She glanced around her studio and felt completely lost. The walls were decorated with words, some hard, some soft. They were passions she felt.

Will picked up one of her sketchbooks, and she was so busy looking at her failure that she didn't stop him.

"What about this?" he asked.

She glanced over and gasped. "That's nothing." Rushing toward him, she was about to take the sketchbook from him, but he wouldn't release it.

In her spare time, she'd been sketching Brett and Ace. They were the only two people she seemed to be able to get right. Whether it was them mowing the lawn or carrying their stuff into the house, she'd committed everything to memory so that she could sketch it.

There was even one of Ace behind the kitchen counter, cooking away. He'd made a mean quinoa, and she'd been totally turned to the idea of actually giving it a try.

"This is all pretty good stuff."

"They're my neighbors, Will."

"Then you know what you've got to do."

She did, but she winced. "Look, a lot of people don't like sitting in for this kind of stuff."

"Meredith, the point of you getting away from the city and being here in the first place was to relax. You're not relaxed. You look far more tense than I can recall ever seeing you."

She fanned her face and walked away from him, taking a deep breath, and turning toward him. Breathing deep, she looked at him. "I'm trying. It's kind of hard to relax when everyone keeps telling me to do exactly that."

Will put his hands on her shoulders, and together they breathed deeply. "You're awesome."

Meredith rolled her eyes.

"No, say it with me."

"You're awesome," she said.

"Meredith!"

"I'm awesome."

"I'm talented."

"Do I really need to keep saying this?"

"Do it," Will said.

"I'm talented."

"I can do this."

"I can do this."

"Just ... relax."

She copied everything he said, and at the end of it, she did, in a weird way, feel calmer.

"I'm not going to go anywhere. People still want your commission work and are willing to wait, even though they have not even given payment and you've not accepted any, or even taking any orders. I do get regular phone calls asking if you're taking any contracts. They're still talking about your paintings. You don't have to be constantly present for people to think about you, not with the internet. I'm taking care of that. Now, relax." He picked up the book. "I think you should talk to these two men. You're inspired by them. They've got a lot more passion than the women you've watched putting out the trash."

After another hour of chatting, catching up with the family, Will left, and she stood in her home ... alone. She rubbed her arms, took a deep breath, and wondered what to do. Heading back to her studio, she picked up her sketchbook and looked at the few drawings she'd done.

She wouldn't know if she didn't ask, and even though Will was being considerate to her, she knew she had to get her stuff together. Time was running out, and she didn't want to ruin her career.

Picking up a new sketchbook, she was determined to get this over with. If they were willing, she'd make sure it worked. If they were not, then she'd continue to work in secrecy. She could chop their heads out of the pictures so they didn't know it was them.

Making her way next door, she lifted her hand to knock.

Like so many times before, Ace was the one to answer.

"Well, hello, my sweet little neighbor."

"I can promise you, honey, there's nothing sweet about me." She placed a hand on her hip and pouted. They both laughed.

"Come in. I was just about to eat."

"What?" she asked.

"Some quinoa."

"Do you have enough for two?"

"I certainly do. My little roomie doesn't like my food anymore."

She laughed. "I'm sure he does. Where is Brett?"

"He's still at work. He has clients that don't always come in during the day. They prefer more private times."

"Oh." She didn't like that jolt of pain at the thought of him being with anyone else.

"They're special cases to him."

"I guess so." She pushed some hair off her face.

"What's with the book?" he asked, pointing at her sketchpad.

"Well, actually, I wanted to ask you and Brett something."

"I'm here. You can ask me."

She nodded.

Why did she suddenly feel so nervous?

"So, I've been hitting a few snags lately when it comes to my work. Will, my manager, came by today, and he saw some of the sketches I've done of you and Brett." She flicked open the page and pushed the book toward him across the counter.

He picked it up, and her hands got clammy.

What if he didn't like her work?

Would he laugh?

Her art was a part of her soul. She didn't like the thought of anyone laughing at her. For weeks before her first art exhibition, she'd had repeated nightmares of being laughed at.

"Wow, this is really good. I look hot cooking."

She smiled. "I was wondering if you and Brett would mind being models for me. In your spare time, of course. I'm willing to throw in food, and I can pay if I turn the sketches into paintings."

"I like this," he said.

"You do?"

"Yeah. I can't speak for Brett, but count me in. Food and money sounds pretty good to me. To be honest, I'm in it for the food." He winked at her.

"Thank you." She felt like he'd just given her a lifeline.

****

"I really do appreciate the both of you doing this," Meredith said.

They were in her studio and she'd opened up a window. It was nice and cool as there a through breeze. Her studio seemed to be the biggest room in the house. Brett glanced at the walls, seeing the many different kinds of art.

Fuck you.
Beautiful.
Beauty is only skin deep.
See into souls.
Home.

In between the words were drawings. There was a face with scars down it and a kindness in her eyes. The next was a woman so beautiful and yet within her eyes was evil. It amazed Brett how much he saw. The room seemed to represent Meredith. It wasn't just one color but a variety. There was nothing that put her into a box. She was a free spirit throughout.

"What would you like us to do?" he asked.

"You could sit. Relax. I know. I hate it when someone tells me to relax, but if you could do it, I would appreciate it."

He walked toward one of the chairs and sat down. Spreading out his thighs, he was curious about the room, about the woman.

In his world, everything had to be in order. He didn't like clutter, but when he was around Meredith, her organized chaos enthralled him, as did she.

Her hair was bound up on her head today. No makeup, and she wore a simple yellow sundress. Her feet were bare, and the dress ended just above the knee so he got a glimpse of the thorns coming up her thighs. He loved her ink and had wanted to see it up close and personal for some time.

Ace sat down. "Do you want me to be serious?" He placed his elbow on his knee, resting his chin on his hand and looking serious. "Or cool?" He leaned back in his chair. "Hey, good lookin'." Suddenly he sat up. "Or completely still." He held his chair and didn't move a muscle.

Brett chuckled along with her.

"No, just be yourself. This is about expressing yourself in any way you see fit. I'm not going to control who you are."

"Okay then." He sat back in his chair, and Brett smiled. "Hey."

He shook his head as Ace went for the coolness that he liked to portray.

Meredith grabbed a book from off her shelf and a small case. She opened it up, sat down on the floor, and looked up at them. She tilted her head to the side.

"You can smile," she said.

"I will. You just go right ahead and do what you need to do."

She nodded. Brett watched her, listening as Ace every now and again said something about her décor.

"Did you always want to be an artist?" he asked.

Meredith shook her head. "No, not at all. The first job I wanted to be was a nurse. I liked the idea of helping people. You know, of being there for them."

"I get that."

"Then of course I'd sob and panic whenever I saw the sight of blood on myself. Skinned knees and stuff. That went out of the window. Then came the whole hairdresser phase."

"You wanted to be a hairdresser?"

"Yep. I'd cut off all the hair off my dolls. Drove my parents insane."

"You don't speak about your parents," Ace said.

"They're still alive. I go and visit them when the need arises. We have creative differences. They wanted me to enter the corporate world like my two brothers. One's a lawyer, and the other is the head of a bank. I didn't want to do that. We tolerate each other. I know they're proud. They just think the art world is a fickle industry." She shrugged. "It doesn't matter though. Will has always been my support."

"I can't speak for Ace, but I can for myself. If you ever need us for anything, let us know. I'd love to help you," Brett said.

She smiled at him. It wasn't a fake one. She liked what he said. "Thank you."

"I can speak for myself. You want anything. A perfect model, a gardener, cook, booty call, I'm your guy."

They were all laughing. "You two are very sweet to me. Thank you."

The rest of the afternoon went by slowly. Between conversation and Meredith sketching, everything felt relaxed. He loved watching her.

Throughout the day she went from sitting to sprawling on her stomach. The dress she wore moved up the backs of her thighs, tempting him with the rounded globes of her ass. He wanted to reach out and touch her, but he couldn't.

You want to.

He held himself back, staying in his chair, watching her, waiting. She looked so beautiful. Her hair came out of the clip that she'd bound it up in. Her tongue rested against her full, kissable lips. He imagined removing her dress, taking her to the floor, and tasting every single inch of her, spreading her thighs wide as Ace came up, kissing her mouth.

In his head, it felt right for Ace to be there. He'd sit back, watching her, desperate to see the pleasure on her face.

Ace's stomach growled, drawing Brett out of his arousal. His cock was rock-hard.

"Food. I will go and order it now. Be right back," Meredith said, getting to her feet. The way she stood up he got a glimpse down her dress, showing off the rounded globes of her tits.

His erection wasn't going to go away anytime soon.

"You okay, man?" Ace asked.

"Nope. I'm not okay."

Brett stood up and paced the room, trying to contain his composure.

"Wow, you really do want her."

"Don't," he said.

"I've got the same problem, buddy."

It was going to be a long evening.

Chapter Four

One week later

Brett was once again working the late shift, and Ace was inside Meredith's house. She'd been in the shower when he arrived, and, seeing her slick and covered in only a towel, restraint was so fucking hard.

The past week, he'd spent many nights with his hand, getting really fucking acquainted. Constant thoughts of Meredith filled his mind. He couldn't get her out of his head, and imagining her naked, between himself and Brett, well, it was keeping him in a constant state of arousal.

No other woman would do though.

The only time his dick didn't seem to play was during work. None of the women he worked with could get him excited or even the littlest bit interested in them. He knew some were pissed at his complete lack of desire when it came to them, but he didn't care.

The only person he wanted was upstairs getting dressed.

Entering her studio, he saw several canvases set up. One had a splash of color, but it didn't showcase any of the work she'd been doing.

He and Brett had been helping her all week for the sketches.

"I'm so sorry about that," Meredith said. "I went out to the park, lost track of time." She entered the studio dressed in a pair of shorts and plain white vest shirt. He could clearly make out that she wasn't wearing a bra. Her tits bounced with every step that she took. His dick went from flaccid to hard in the blink of an eye.

"Don't worry about it." He cleared his voice as it went high-pitched. "Brett should be here soon."

"Great." She turned her back on him. The vest

was sheer enough that he got to see the dark ink of her tattoo. The outline was doing shit to him. "Are you okay?"

"Look, Meredith, there's only so much a guy can take."

She tilted her head to the side.

"I like you," he said.

"I like you too."

"Right now, I need to go home."

Her gaze ran down his body, and she paused at his dick, which seemed to get harder.

"Me being dressed like this affects you, Ace?"

"Yes."

She didn't take a step back. She moved closer. Within touching distance. Her hair was still slightly damp, and she was the kind of woman who didn't need makeup. Her face was clear, and there was a glow to her, an energy that he couldn't look away from.

When she lifted her shirt up over her head and tossed it to one side, he was fucking shocked. Especially as her shorts followed soon after.

"Do I make you nervous?" she asked.

"You don't make me nervous."

"Good." She placed a hand on his chest. "They're just clothes, Ace." She tugged his shirt, and he helped her to pull it off. "No ink?"

"I don't like needles."

"I hate needles, but I did it anyway. I don't like being afraid." She touched his stomach, tracing one of his abs before taking his hand. She placed it on one of the designs curving up her stomach toward her breasts.

His cock strained against the front of his pants, and he wanted her.

"Do you like what you see?" she asked.

"Fuck, yeah."

Unable to resist another moment, he sank one of his hands into her hair, pulling her close. Smashing his lips against hers, he slid his tongue across her mouth. She gasped, opening up for him, and he plunged in deep. Her hands went to his shoulders, stroking down his back. Her nails felt so good against his skin. Walking her back until she hit the wall, he captured her hands and locked them above her head.

She moaned.

"You've felt this as well?" He pressed his cock against her stomach.

"Yes."

"I want to fuck you, Meredith. I want to drive my cock so deep inside your tight pussy that I can't think straight."

"Then let go of my hands. Let's get you naked."

He let her go and she attacked his pants, releasing the belt and the zipper, pushing them to the floor. He kicked them away, groaning as she wrapped her fingers around his length and began to work his dick.

Pre-cum leaked out of the tip, and he gritted his teeth to stop himself from coming, thinking of anything that would stop the excitement from building.

Pushing her hand away, he took her to the floor, spreading her thighs. Then he slid two fingers between her slit, feeling how wet she was.

When he touched her clit, she cried out his name, squirming against his touch. "Feels so fucking good."

"That's right, baby, so good. Yeah." Thrusting two fingers inside her cunt, he felt how tight she was. She fucked his fingers, and he teased her clit with his thumb.

Within seconds she came, screaming his name, begging for more.

Kissing the pleasure from her lips, he pulled his fingers from her pussy, grabbed his cock, and placed the tip to her entrance. Breaking the kiss, he stared into her eyes, and slowly began to sink inside her wet heat.

They both cried out, and as he was getting to his last couple of inches, he filled her hard. Their bodies slapped together, echoing off the walls along with their cries of pleasure.

"Feels so fucking good. I knew you would."

She wrapped her legs around his waist, and he pulled out of her only to drive back within her. Over and over he fucked her, feeling her tight heat swallow him. His balls felt heavy, and he stared into her green eyes, completely lost to everything but her. She was a beautiful woman.

Taking her hands, he locked their fingers together, and he fucked her hard, driving in deep. He couldn't contain his desire for her.

Meredith had become a need that he no longer wanted to deny.

****

"Ace, you okay?" Meredith asked. He had this weird look on his face as she stared at her. It was like he was seeing something else.

She continued to dry her hair on the towel. The park was one of the rare places that still held the magic of when she was younger. Before her parents had moved to the city to continue to pursue their careers, she'd lived in a small town, not too different from this one. She'd hated living in the city. The parks were always too crowded and loud. The streets were always filled with people who didn't care about anyone but themselves.

To Meredith, the city had been a slow and painful death. Sitting there in the park today, watching the few mothers and fathers with their kids had brought back so much love, so much happiness that time had simply slipped her by.

Ace, however, was concerning her. He'd not looked away from her clothing. She wasn't wearing a bra as the one she wore today was a little tight and left red marks that were itchy from rubbing.

He shook his head, and she frowned. "Are you okay? Do I need to call Brett or something?"

"Sorry, I completely zoned out there and not in a good way."

She saw his body was flushed, and one look at the front of his jeans, and she figured out straight away that he was aroused. "Would you like me to go and change?"

"No, no, it's fine. Just ignore me."

Meredith only wished it was that easy. She'd found herself thinking more and more about her two hot neighbors. Watching them, sketching them daily, her nights were filled with all the hot delights that a woman like herself craved and yet she was repeatedly let down with no follow-through. She was filled with constant need. Right now, her pussy was so wet, and it pulsed as she moved, and the seam of the shorts grazed her pussy.

She loved to cleanly shave her pussy as she liked not having anything in the way, and also, it made her hornier throughout the day, desperate. The vibrator she kept in her drawer was getting a lot of use, and even though she came, it wasn't earth-shattering or even helping her in any way. She found herself aching even more, wanting more, desperate for more, begging for more.

"Are you dating anyone?" he asked.

"No. Are you?"

"No."

She stared at him. "I've never been good with these guessing games, Ace. Tell me what you want."

He stepped closer toward her, the intent clear in his eyes. Her nipples hardened, and as he stepped close, his gaze was on her lips. She purposefully licked her lips, giving him a glimpse. The heat built in the room.

"You know what I want."

"I'd like to hear it."

"Am I interrupting something?" Brett asked.

She didn't turn to look at the other man, keeping her gaze on Ace the whole time. "No, you're not interrupting anything."

"I want to fuck you," Ace said.

"Ace! You can't speak like that to her."

Again, she didn't look away. There was no need to. "Is that why you zoned out? You imagined fucking me?"

"Yeah, I did." He reached out, cupping her cheek. "And I want to, so badly. I want to feel your tight cunt wrapped around my dick." He ran his thumb across her lips. "I want these on my cock, sucking me."

"Ace, seriously, buddy, this is…"

"I don't mind," Meredith said. "Actually, I kind of like it."

She finally looked toward Brett. Both men were hot. Her "two hotties next door" was what she labeled the sketchpad that she was using to draw them.

"I guess I'll leave you two to it," Brett said, stepping out of the room.

"Why do you have to leave?" she asked.

Looking from Ace then to Brett, she raised a brow and smiled.

She'd always been open about her sexuality, willing to try new things. She'd never been with two men at the same time, but Ace and Brett featured together in her fantasies. "What do you say?" she asked.

"I don't know what to say right now. I don't have a clue what I've stepped into," Brett said.

She smiled and grabbed Ace's hand, leading him

close to Brett. Taking his other hand, she pulled him in.

This felt completely natural to her as she took their hands and placed them on her breasts.

"I'm saying that we don't have to put a label on anything and that if you want, we can just have a bit of fun. It's just the three of us."

With their hands on her breasts, she cupped their dicks. Both men were hard, and it felt so good to have them there, exactly where she wanted them. Their cocks were long and wide. Brett still wore his workout clothes, so she slid her hand inside his pants with ease, feeling his silken hard cock. The moment she wrapped her fingers around his length, he moaned.

Ace opened the button of his jeans, helping her ease inside.

Holding both of their cocks, she turned her head, left, then right, staring at each of them. She was so wet, so horny, and she wanted both of them, without a doubt.

This felt right to her. It didn't matter how long they'd known each other. She needed them.

"I'm yours for the taking if you want it," she said.

Brett was the first one to cup her tit, his thumb tracing across the beaded nipple, sliding it back and forth, twisting the bud through her vest. She cried out at the pain but also the pleasure as it seemed to go straight to her clit. Ace followed, teasing her breast.

The strap of her shirt fell down her arm, and both men pulled the shirt so that her breasts appeared over the top. This time, Ace sucked on her nipple while Brett ran his fingers down her stomach, the tips of them resting against her shorts.

She wasn't above begging if that was what it would take to get him to touch her.

****

Walking in the room to see Ace and Meredith so

close together, Brett had been overtaken by arousal. He'd not been jealous, but he'd wanted to watch, to see what happened. He should have known something would, seeing as they'd all been coming together a lot over the past week or so.

Meredith was such a wonderful woman.

So alive. She laughed about everything and was willing to take chances. He'd seen some of the pictures that she'd taken from her life in the city and the few bits of traveling she'd done, going from city to city, promoting her work. There really was no stopping her. Inside, he saw a caring woman, a loving woman.

He found her a joy to be around and also sexy. He wanted to fuck her, no doubt about that. It was more than that, though. There was no way for him to explain it.

These feelings were just there, and he couldn't stop it.

With her fingers wrapped around his dick, he closed his eyes, enjoying each touch and every stroke. He had to look at her, to see what she was thinking. Her eyes were dilated, her cheeks flushed. She wanted this. Running his hand down her body, he toyed with the edge of her shorts as Ace licked and sucked at her nipples.

He pushed past her shorts and found her wet, silken pussy, shocked to find her completely bare. There wasn't any hair present on her pussy. Cupping her mound, he slid a finger between her slit, plunging one inside her, feeling how tight she was before pulling back, and stroking her nub.

Meredith opened her legs wider, and he teased her clit, watching her and at the same time feeling her touch on his dick.

Needing her naked, he pulled his hand from between her thighs. Quickly tugging his clothing off, he kicked it toward the corner. Ace started to remove her clothing, and in no time at all, all three of them were completely naked. The studio room had so much space, and Meredith smiled as he and Ace stood side by side.

She sank to her knees before the two of them.

"Tell me, boys. Have you ever shared a woman before?"

"A couple of times," Ace said. "You want to be our little toy?"

She raised her brow. "That depends. Do you think you can handle me?" She covered Ace's cock as she worked his balls. He watched her hand running up and down his length. She pumped him into her mouth before moving to him, taking him to the back of her throat.

Back and forth she worked, sucking on each of their cocks. It wasn't enough. Brett wanted to taste her pussy.

Pushing her hand off his dick, he moved toward the floor. "What are you doing?" she asked.

"Sit on my face. I want to taste your pussy."

"Brett, you do surprise me."

He helped her so that she was kneeling over his face, and with his hands on her hips, he moved her into position so her creamy cunt was right above his lips, the scent of her already driving him wild for a taste. Spreading her pussy lips open, he stared at her pink hole and swollen clit.

Sliding his tongue across her nub, he heard her cry out. With the way he was lying, Brett couldn't see what she was doing, but it wouldn't be hard to guess that she had her mouth on Ace's cock.

His friend was moaning, encouraging her to keep on going, to keep licking his dick.

Pushing two fingers inside her cunt, Brett began to pump them in and out, feeling her walls tighten around his digits. He wanted so badly to thrust inside her, to stick his dick deep, but he held himself back.

Sucking on her clit, he used his tongue and his teeth to build her pleasure. Every time he did something she liked, her pussy would get even wetter, which he loved.

"That's right, baby. Fuck yeah, that's it. Shit, baby, if you're not careful I'm going to come."

He bit her clit, causing her to cry out, and he soothed out the pain at the same time thrusting his fingers inside her, driving her to the edge of bliss.

She came with a few strokes, and he loved the sounds of her cries. Not long after her orgasm ended, he heard the sound of Ace coming as well, the male hiss and grunt as he filled her mouth with cum.

Brett's cock was fucking lonely.

He didn't have to wait long, though, before Meredith moved down his body. She licked her lips, and he looked up to see Ace on the chair, his cock flaccid and spent. "I need a minute."

Meredith smiled down at him. "What do you want?" she asked.

"Your pussy."

She lifted up, and he gripped his cock, aligning the tip to her entrance. She sank down on his dick, and she was so wet from her orgasm that he slid inside her with ease. He wasn't a small man, and without the extra lubricant of her release, it would have been a tight fit.

Running his hands up her stomach, he cupped her tits, teasing her nipples, playing with her. He loved her body, couldn't get enough of it.

Sliding his fingers across her tits, he moved down, stroking her clit.

Glancing down at where she was fucking him, rocking up and down, he saw how slick his cock was from her. It had been so long since he'd been with a woman that within a few thrusts, he felt the need to come.

He tried to hold it off, to count sheep or to do something that would mean he wouldn't come, but it was too much.

Gripping her hips, he slammed up inside her, drawing her down onto his dick as he erupted his spunk, filling her to the brim.

It was the best three minutes he'd had in a long time, but it certainly wouldn't be the last.

Chapter Five

"That was incredible," Meredith said.

Ace stared down at where she lay next to Brett. His best friend hadn't lasted long at all, which kind of made him feel just a little better knowing that he'd been unable to resist his own orgasm.

He'd been wanting Meredith so badly that he'd even fantasized about fucking her and she'd been drying her hair.

Climbing out of his chair, he lay down beside her so that she was between him and Brett. She smiled up at him.

"Hey, you." He winked at her.

"This was not what I thought we'd do tonight," she said.

"It wasn't on my mind either," Brett said.

"I've not been able to think of anything else," Ace said, admitting the truth.

Him, Meredith, Brett, fucking, making love, it was all he could think about, even in the gym with clients or supervising them.

Meredith chuckled. "You think about sex often."

He turned over, facing her, and rested his head on his arm. Tracing a finger across her stomach, he slowly teased her flesh. "All the time, actually."

"I think about the two of you. I'm going to admit I've never done two men before." She looked up at him, then turned to Brett. "Never."

"We've shared women. Nothing has been long-term though. It has always been over before it has begun, to be honest," Brett said.

"So, what do we do now?" Meredith asked. She moved so that she was kneeling. Lying back down, Ace rested his head on his hand, watching her. He was distracted by her tits. They were nice and big, just the way he liked them. "I don't want anything to change. We're neighbors, and sex can complicate things. I'd hate for that to happen."

"Wait, are we having a talk now?" Brett asked.

She laughed. "Yeah, I guess we are. I like both of you. You're awesome to hang out with, and you're doing me this huge favor with my work, and I appreciate it so much. I don't want us to lose that, you know?"

Ace sighed. "She's using us for our looks and our bodies."

She rolled her eyes.

"I'm in. If we get to have sex then I'm all for it."

"I have one condition," Brett said.

"Great, mister boring pants is going to ruin it."

"Conditions can be fun," Meredith said.

"Name one?"

"When it's hot out no clothes at all. That's a good one."

"You know what, I'm intrigued. What's your condition? You know, it's not going to be as good as your suggestion. I've known this guy so long now he doesn't even know what fun is." He kept on talking, not giving Brett time to answer.

"Why don't you shh, so he can answer. You'll never know otherwise."

Ace turned to look at his best friend. "Go on with your conditions."

"It can only be with me and Ace."

"Sex?"

"Yes."

"I like that condition," Ace said. He looked toward Meredith.

"I know this is going to sound mean, but if I'm only getting you, then you both only get me."

She pointed to her chest.

"I don't have a problem with that. We're all agreeing to remain faithful to one another. Let's fuck," Ace said.

Meredith placed a hand on his chest now. "Patience, Ace. We're all friends here, and we're all adults. We know what we're doing."

Ace looked toward Brett. "Any more demands?"

"Yeah, we both get one night a week of you to ourselves. No sharing, just each other," Brett said.

"Oh, okay. I wasn't expecting that one," she said. "What nights were you thinking?"

"I get Saturday," Ace said. "I get off work earlier that day, and I'm guessing Brett was going to pick Friday. He finishes that day early as well."

"I was, and that works for me," Brett said.

"Wow, erm, okay, yes, I can do that. Just the two of us?"

"Yes," Ace said.

"That's not going to be weird for the two of you?"

"Nope." They both spoke in unison.

"Now, how about we get to fucking?" Ace said.

Before anyone else could speak a loud rumble came from Brett's stomach.

"You hungry, baby?" Meredith asked, placing a hand on his stomach.

"He can wait, I'm sure," Ace said, his cock already rock-hard.

"How about you two move this to my bedroom and I'll go and order some more Chinese food?" Meredith asked.

"We shouldn't eat more takeout."

She pressed a finger to both of their mouths. "While you're in my house, you don't get to complain about the kinds of food you eat. That's my condition. I grew up with all that bullshit, and I promised myself I wouldn't stand for it when I was an adult."

"Consider it done."

"Excellent. I'll go and order."

She didn't put on any clothes as she got to her feet, leaving the room completely naked.

"Why do you want a day alone with her?" Ace asked.

"You don't want to invade each other's day, do you?"

"Well, no."

"I thought this was the best solution. If you don't like it, why didn't you speak up?" Brett asked.

"I do like it. I want to spend time with her."

"I know you, Ace. What's up?"

"What if she doesn't like me as much as she likes you?" Ace asked. He hated sounding vulnerable. "I like Meredith. I don't think I could handle the two of you being together if it doesn't work out."

Brett stared at him, and he felt like a bug under a microscope.

"This is brand new, Ace. You've got to give it time. Nothing is going to move faster than it needs to be. Please, don't worry about it." His friend patted him on the shoulder.

They'd gone from being models, to fucking within the space of a night, and he knew things could move fast as they already were.

****

"I think you're just better suited to other work, honey, you know that."

Meredith listened to her mother on her cell phone as she continued to walk down the long town road. She'd already been into the florist and ordered more daffodil bulbs to plant. Then she'd gone to the supermarket to look for a nice bottle of wine and some beers. It was the first Friday, and Brett had already said that he wanted to cook her dinner. Since Ace had somewhere to go, Brett had given her a list of things to buy, and she'd been working her way through them when her mother called.

News had gotten back to her parents about her canceling another gallery show and that she wasn't taking orders anymore. On her website, Will had also told her he'd put "creative vacation" down as her reasoning for not being available.

"Mom, I'm not going to work for some advertising agency where they'll want me to doodle little pictures about their products. I don't know how many times I've told you this."

"Why do you have to be so damn stubborn? Your brothers don't cause this kind of stress. Do you have any idea what you're doing to me?"

For the next five minutes she listened to her mother's pains. How she just wanted her little girl to be happy, and that she wouldn't listen to reason. Then of course came the talk of the husband that Meredith didn't have, the children she still hadn't given birth to.

"Mom, I'm thirty years old. I'm not dead. There's no rush for me to have kids."

"What about me being a grandma? You want me to be old? To not be able to enjoy my grandkids?"

"It's not happening right now or even ever, okay? I don't want to argue about this. I've got to go."

Her mother wasn't ready to finish the conversation, so Meredith had no choice but to listen to a little more complaining. Close to an hour later, she finally hung up, and Meredith was back home but feeling anything but inspired.

She threw her cell phone onto the table beside the

door and made her way into the kitchen to put away her things. By the time that was done, she didn't feel any better. In fact, she felt annoyed, angry.

Grabbing the daffodil bulbs, she made her way out into the garden. Kicking off her pumps, she sighed as the cool grass slid between her toes and she was finally able to relax.

Everything was fine now.

Her mother would make her demands.

Her father would agree, and she'd be the rebel child that wouldn't conform.

It was totally fine.

She didn't know why she was close to tears. It wasn't like anything had changed in her life. There was no way she was ready to start a family or settle down. She'd just come to a damn agreement with two men. There was no way her parents would ever accept that.

"Are you okay?" Brett asked.

She looked up to see the man she intended to date tonight standing in her yard. "I didn't even hear you come in." She'd given Brett and Ace each a key to her place so that they could make themselves at home. They'd given her a key to their place.

"You're crying."

"What?" Using the back of her hand, she swiped the tear that was so close to falling, hating herself even more for allowing anything to get to her. "I didn't even realize I was crying."

"Would you like me to go?"

"No, no, no. Believe me. This is not about you or Ace or our agreement. I'm just … I don't know what I am. Everything seems to be falling apart right now, and I'm so sorry." She stared down at her hands, which were covered in dirt. "I garden when I want to relax. I had a bad phone call with my mom. It didn't go well."

"Oh."

"Yeah, oh." She bit her lip. "You're home early."

"My last client canceled. You want to tell me about your problems? I'm a good listener."

"It's not important. I'm starving. Let me go and wash my hands. I got you everything you asked for."

They made their way into her home. Brett went toward the kitchen as she used the bathroom downstairs. Washing off the mud, she quickly sanitized her hands before making her way back to find him rummaging through her cupboards.

Everything was nicely ordered within. Cans were dated and labeled. She did like some order. Also, she hated losing time trying to find something that was stuck behind a can that was completely useless. Why store tomatoes and peaches on the same shelf? One's a dessert, the other savory?

No sense.

"Did you need me to do anything?"

"Nah, you sit your cute little ass down and I'll cook."

"How was work, honey?" she asked.

Brett opened up the bottle of wine, and today she didn't care what time it was. Taking a sip of the fruity liquid, she sighed. This was the life.

"It was busy. You?"

"It was busy. I was doing okay, and then my mom called. It would seem they've heard about my difficulties. She'd already got me an interview with someone that I really didn't want to work for. I know she means well. You know, her being my mother and all, but she doesn't seem to get that I don't want that. I don't want to sit behind a desk all day, making the same pictures to help sell a product I don't believe in." She slapped a hand over her mouth. "I'm so sorry."

"Stop apologizing." He rounded the counter and removed her hand. He cupped her face, tilting her head back before pressing a kiss to her lips. "Feel better?"

"A little? I think I need a longer kiss."

He chuckled, and that just did things to her. Screw dinner, she wanted dessert.

****

Dinner went off without a hitch. After Meredith unloaded on him about her troubles and a couple of glasses of wine, she was relaxed again. They made their way outside to the garden. It was late, and he knew Ace would be home, but his friend would get his day tomorrow, while he enjoyed today.

"This is nice," she said, curled up on the chair beside him.

"I'm glad you think so." He stroked her hair back from her face, wanting to look into her pretty eyes. She stared up at the stars. "You know you'll get your passion back. Your parents are wrong. You don't need to go into the corporate world."

"You think so?"

"I know so. You're too good to not get over this little bump."

"I sometimes wonder if it's a big bump at all."

"I checked you out online, Meredith. Your stuff is amazing. Critically acclaimed and they are truly beautiful." He patted her arm. "Come with me."

He took her hand and led her upstairs to her studio. Standing behind her, he stared at the two women, the one with the scars on her face and the beautiful soul, the other that was the complete opposite.

"You *see* people, Meredith. This right here is proof of that." He held her tightly before moving to stand in front of her. "Now I want you to paint me."

"Come on, for real?"

"Yes. I want you to, but I warn you, I'm going to be naked. I've heard all about these artists. They have affairs with their subjects, break their hearts. You've got to stay strictly professional now." He removed his clothes, ignoring the hardness of his dick as he turned to face her. She had already set up a canvas.

Brett didn't like how nervous she looked. "It's just you and me. Whatever you do, no one else is going to see. Just be yourself."

"Well, seeing as you agreed to be my guinea pig, I suggest you get comfortable. Painting someone can take a while."

He pulled a soft chair toward the center of the room and sat down. Leaning back, he put his hands on the arms of the chair, legs out, relaxed, and watched her. "I'm all yours to do with as you wish."

"If I could do as I wished, I'd be riding that sweet dick of yours," she said. "You don't have a problem with me being a little naked, do you?"

Before he'd even answered her dress was off. He had no problem with that. His cock thickened, but he didn't even stroke himself. Staring across the room, he waited.

"It's all on you, sweetheart."

She took a deep breath, her nerves back.

She'd been like this in the beginning with him and with Ace.

"You can do this. Don't think."

"Tell me about your work," she said. "What do you love about it?"

"I have a love/hate relationship with my job."

"Talk to me."

So he did. He told her how much he loved helping people reach their goals, especially those were struggling with health choices. How he wanted to make a difference in someone's life. He also talked about the clients that believed they needed to lose weight when they didn't. The challenging cases.

He opened up to her in ways he'd never done for another woman. Throughout it all, she started to paint, taking her time, and their topics changed. They talked about their childhoods. Her life growing up in the city after being in a smaller town. He talked about growing up without any siblings, of finding Ace. Their friendship.

They talked until she finally put the brush down and smiled.

"Can I see?" he asked.

She shook her head. "No, not yet. I'm not finished, but I … want to work on it." She glanced over the canvas, her green eyes sparkling back at him.

She moved from the canvas. "So, would I still be taking advantage of you if I come and say thank you?"

"I'd rather like for you to come and say thank you."

He watched the sway of her tits as she came toward him, her hips moving seductively. When she was standing in front of him, he couldn't resist. Reaching out, he banded an arm around her waist and pulled her down onto his lap.

Cupping her cheek, he brought her lips to his, and he kissed her.

Her hand landed on his chest but started to move down, gripping his cock. She worked the length, going from the base up to the tip then back down again.

He broke the kiss, trailing his lips down to her neck where he sucked on the pulse. She gave a little gasp, arching up. Sliding a hand between her spread thighs, he stroked her pussy. His fingers moved down to her cunt, filling her, gathering her cream to stroke over her clit.

"I need to feel you inside me."

He lifted her up, and with her back to him, he worked his cock into her tight cunt. Meredith was the one in control, able to fuck him as he teased her pussy. He wished there was a mirror so he could watch her fuck him. Instead, he watched his cock, seeing it appear before sinking inside her.

He couldn't get enough of her.

Maybe the houses *were* cursed.

As she came on his cock with his name spilling from her lips, he didn't care. If the houses were cursed then he was going to be a happy man regardless.

Meredith continued to ride his dick until he couldn't contain his release any longer. Grabbing her hips, he pulled her down and flooded her cunt with his sperm, wave upon wave filling her.

Afterward, sated, she tilted her head back, and he kissed her. She was pure perfection as far as he was concerned. He wouldn't change her for anything.

Chapter Six

"And I used to run around the yard all day completely naked. No one could get me in trunks, or clothes. I think they were just thankful I didn't start swearing and cussing." Ace laughed along with Meredith as he told her tales from his childhood.

It was late. They'd gone to the movies to watch a romantic comedy, which he admitted he did enjoy, unlike Brett. They had both had a meal afterward and now were walking back toward their homes.

He'd been worried at first that she wouldn't enjoy the walk back, but it would seem Meredith didn't have a taste for heels. She wore a pair of flat shoes even with her beautiful red dress.

"You sound like a handful."

"Believe me, I was, and not much has changed. Brett would easily tell you I drive him crazy all the time."

She linked her arm throughs his, and he heard her sigh. "This has been amazing."

"What?"

"This date. I've not been on many, but this has been right up there." She rested her head against his arm. "I love the stars at night, you know."

"They're beautiful."

They paused at the end of their street and simply looked up at the sky.

"I'm used to a lot of people not really getting me or understanding me. It's nice to know someone out there appreciates the quality things in life. You and Brett both. You're amazing."

"We do our best."

She placed her hands on his shoulders and slid down until she held his arms. "So, how is this night going to end?" she asked, brow raised.

"I was hoping you had coffee."

"I do."

"And maybe we could go inside, talk, and maybe do … something else." His cock was already liking whatever that "something else" might be.

"I like the sound of that." She took his hand, and he followed her, watching the curves of her ass while she walked with purpose. He'd been wanting to touch her all night long but knew the moment he did, he wouldn't be able to stop.

The instant she entered her home, he closed and locked the door, pressing her up against it. Taking the leftover food they had, he placed it on the cupboard beside her door where she kept her keys.

Removing her jacket from her shoulders, he let it drop to the floor. Still staring into her eyes, he took the straps of her dress, reaching behind her back to catch the zipper, lowering it, and dropping it down onto the floor. She stood before him in the same color lingerie set. All red, lace, tempting him with what was beneath.

Flicking the catch of her bra, he removed it and cupped her tits, pressing them together. "These are the nicest tits I've ever seen."

"Speaking from experience?"

"I was a guy that read a lot of magazines when I was younger. Believe me, I've seen a lot, but these beauties." He flicked his tongue against the peak and watched as she moaned. He loved that she didn't hold anything back. She gave everything to him and took as well. She was so fucking perfect and beautiful.

Moving onto the next nipple, he licked the hard, red bud as he teased the other with his thumb. When that wasn't enough, he dropped down to his knees and helped her out of the panties.

She stepped out of them and kicked them across the floor. She'd already toed out of her shoes.

Her hands were on her hips. "Okay, Ace, what do you want to do with me now?"

He picked her up in his arms, loving her squeal. Carrying her upstairs, he loved the way she wrapped her arms around his neck, holding on.

"I'm going to take you upstairs and make love to you. Think you can handle it?"

"I can take whatever you want to give me."

Kicking open her bedroom door, he placed her on the edge of the bed, and pressed her down until she was flat. Grabbing her hands, he placed them above her head. "Stay."

"What happens if I move?"

"Then I won't let you come. You move those hands and I won't give you what you're really wanting."

"Oh, you're being a little dominant."

"You'll love it, I promise."

Sliding his hands down her body, he pressed her tits together, stroking the hardened buds with his thumbs before moving down, taking his time until he got to her waist. Down further still, he gripped her thighs and spread her legs wide, staring at her glistening pussy.

"Have you been like this all night?"

"Yes."

"Good."

Down his hands went, and he opened the lips of her pussy to see her glistening cunt and swollen clit. Using his thumbs still, he stroked between her slit, grazing across her nub before moving to slide in deep.

She cried out, arching up against him as he did this. He watched her, completely enthralled by her as she took his thumb. Her tight cunt squeezed him, wanting more already, and he was willing to give it to her. In fact, he wanted to. Pulling his thumb out, he replaced it with two fingers, then a third, watching her hole open up just a little, taking his fingers.

His cock pressed against the front of his pants, wanting inside her, desperate to be within her.

Pumping his fingers inside her pussy, he released his cock, running his hand up and down the length. He wanted a taste of her, and leaning forward, he took her clit into his mouth and sucked hard. She screamed his name, her back arching up off the bed.

Meredith worked her pussy onto his fingers, taking him as deep as she could go, and he loved watching her take her pleasure. She didn't hold back for a single second, and he didn't want her to, not at all.

"You're so fucking beautiful, Meredith. Come for me. Come for me now."

****

Meredith had never been the kind of woman to come on demand, but hearing the order spill from Ace's lips, she couldn't help it. Her body seemed poised and ready for whatever he wanted. The way he licked her clit, teased her pussy, drove her higher and higher, so that by the time he ordered her to come, she couldn't stop herself. She came, screaming his name, begging, desperate, aching for more, needing more, wanting more, unable to control herself.

"Yes, baby. Fuck, you feel incredible." He pumped his fingers inside her, and she watched him as the last of her orgasm began to ebb away.

She wasn't done though, not by a long shot. Reaching out, she wrapped her fingers around his length, covering his hands with her own. The tip was already slick with his pre-cum. Covering the head, she licked it away before taking him all the way into her mouth until he hit the back of her throat.

If someone had told her months ago that she'd move into a house and begin to date and fuck the two neighbors, she would have thought they were mad. There was no way she'd do something like this, and yet here she was, sucking on Ace's cock after last night having Brett balls deep inside her.

She wanted them both together.

Her days were filled with all the delicious fantasies that any woman would have if they were in her position, and she wasn't embarrassed about that either. Far from it.

Ace wrapped her hair around his fist, and he held onto her, making her take his length deeply, forcing the head of his cock to the back of her throat so she had no choice but to gag on the length.

"Fuck, that feels so good."

She took more of him, wanting to give him this kind of pleasure. Glancing up his body with her mouth full of cock, she watched him hiss as he began to thrust his hips forward.

Once or twice he hit her throat, causing her to gag, but she didn't stop. She'd already tasted his cum and wanted it again.

"Your mouth looks so perfect wrapped around my dick like that. So pretty, so fucking hot. I want to come in your mouth. No, I don't. Fuck, I want everything."

He pulled out of her mouth, and the strength he showed surprised her as he moved her so that she was on her knees before him. His hands curved around her ass before giving it a little slap.

She cried out, which quickly turned to a moan as he filled her hard with his cock. They both groaned, the sound echoing off the walls. Gripping the white sheets beneath her, she pushed back against him as he thrust forward, driving deep inside her.

Ace stroked up her back, pressing down so that her tits were flat to the bed. He ran his hands up, cupping her ass and spreading the cheeks.

"Do you ever think about Brett and me taking you together?"

She closed her eyes as she thought about the other man that she was dating.

"I'd say with how wet your pussy has gone, that's a yes." He teased across her anus, making her gasp as he played with her. "Imagine it, baby. One of us fucking your tight pussy and another right here." He pushed against her asshole, and she moaned.

Arousal flooded her as she thought about it. She'd been taken in the ass before and knew she liked it, but to think of either Brett or Ace, it was so good.

"Damn, your pussy is on fire. Yes, baby, fuck my dick. That feels so good. Yes, yes."

She wanted to come again. Reaching between her thighs, she stroked over her clit, teasing herself, needing to come, wanting it. She'd already come from his mouth, but as he was teasing her asshole and fucking her, she needed more. Hungry, desperate, aching.

"That's it, Meredith. I love it when you take what you want. That's it, play with your pussy."

He pushed a finger into her ass, and she cried out, the burn only making her hornier to feel Brett inside her right now. To have both men take her, she wanted it, craved their touch so damn much.

Ace added a second finger as he began to fuck her hard.

Her orgasm started to build for a second time. He kept on working her ass and pussy, and she was putty in his hands as he took her body to new heights, talking about Brett, what they could all do together.

She couldn't contain it, not anymore, and when she finally came, she did so with a cry of pleasure, both Ace and Brett's names on her lips.

Ace filled her pussy, pumping wave upon wave of release inside her.

Afterward, he pulled out and disappeared to the bathroom, and she moved up the bed, resting against the covers.

She'd shower later. For now, she was tired and wanted to rest.

Minutes later, he returned, lying down on the bed behind her. He wrapped his arms around her waist, pulling her close.

"I love your ink."

"Thank you."

"Does it mean anything?" he asked.

"Not really. I got it because I knew it would drive my parents crazy to know what I'd done." She shrugged. "Not a lot they can do now."

"You don't get along with your parents."

"They like to control things all the time, and I hate that." She tilted her head to the side. "They want me to be something that I can't be. I'm not interested in following the rules or being held in a box and doing stuff like that just to make them happy, you know?"

"I get it, I do."

"You do?"

"My parents wanted me to be a lawyer."

"They did?"

"Yep. Behind this very hot body, there's a good mind as well."

She chuckled. "I'll believe that when I see it." She winked at him.

****

Brett finished mowing the lawn in his yard,

glancing across the space to see a bikini-clad Meredith still on her hands and knees across the fence border. The woman who lived here before him liked to do the occasional yard work, and some of the plant beds had gotten full of weeds.

He could mow the lawn and cook a good steak in the barbeque pit, but flowers and weeds, they were not his forte. But the bonus for him, they happened to be Meredith's.

She'd driven to the florist shop and one of the yard centers the other day, and came back with so many plants and flowers, he'd been shocked.

Heading inside, he saw Ace was still on the phone, dealing with the gas company about their current bill.

Brett grabbed a pitcher of fresh orange juice he'd squeezed that morning, handing Ace a glass before making his way toward Meredith. She wore gloves, and perspiration covered her body.

"Hey, beautiful," he said. "Thought you could use a glass."

"Does it have vodka?" she asked. "Kidding. I don't drink vodka." She took a sip and sighed. "I stink. Are there flies around me?"

"No. You look cute." He sat down on the grass beside her. "You didn't have to do any of this for us."

"Please, it's nice to have a place where you can sit down, relax, and just enjoy the view. Besides, I love getting my hands dirty. It makes me feel alive. I will need to take a long, hot shower later though. This day is just crazy."

She was working near the shade, but as the day wore on, that shade was disappearing fast. The gym had to close today to deal with some new regulation, so they had a rare day off on a Tuesday. It felt good to just have a day, to get a handle on the work, especially with the yard.

"How come you've not filled your pool?" he asked.

It wasn't a large pool she had in her yard, but it would fit a small family to just have a game. It wasn't the size of the one at the gym to swim.

"The previous owner said it needed some repairs, and, seeing as I don't make a habit of spending so much time in water, it didn't seem like a big deal. Getting my studio working, you know, the house. The pool can wait. Besides, we'll have a couple more weeks of good weather, I'll get it fixed, and then rain all the time." She shrugged. "I'll get it done soon."

"You know the previous owner?"

"He was in a rock band or something. I don't know. I like the classics, you know. I can handle some pop now and again, but yeah, I met him. I didn't know him, know him, if that makes sense."

"It does." He patted his thigh.

"Why do I feel like there's something else you want to say?" she said.

"I just wondered if you were aware of the history of this place."

She burst out laughing. "You mean with the whole falling in love thing?"

"So you do know it?"

"The guy who owned the house mentioned it. Seeing as I was a woman, he thought it was only right to mention that there was a risk of me falling in love with whoever moved in next door."

"What did you think when he told you?"

"It was complete bull. Come on, Brett. You have to admit it. Houses do not have the skill of making someone fall in love."

"Why not?" Ace asked, finally coming outside to them.

"Any luck?"

"Yeah, they're sending someone out to check the meter. Now are you pleased I take pictures of the numbers every single week? Stupid assholes wanted to overcharge us. Anyway, back to the house thing. Why couldn't it be real?"

"Are you telling me you believe that in some miracle way, our two houses that are at the bottom of the street have magical powers that can help couples fall in love?" she asked.

"Said like that it seems crazy."

"The couple before us got close. I don't even know who lived here before."

"The old deputy and his now-wife," Brett said.

He saw her pause.

"They did?"

"Yep, and if you go grocery shopping enough you'll see that they are very happily married with a couple of kids," Brett said. "You see, when Wynter, the previous owner, told me about this place, I did a little digging. Both of these houses for the last owners have ended in their sale and the current owners married, living a long, happy life."

"How far back did you go?" Ace asked. "Is this, like, an obsession?"

"I'm really curious now. I figured it was just a ploy to get me to buy the house," Meredith said. "You know, being a single woman and seeing as we're all after Mr. Right. Now I am curious." She patted Brett's arm. "Come on, let's go and see."

They ended up at his computer.

Meredith stood on one side of him as Ace did the other. Bringing up the old newspaper archives, they went toward the matrimony section. The town always liked to print the couples that had married.

"How will this help?" Ace asked.

"There you go. 'We wish Zane and Wynter Webster all the best as they are married.'" Meredith leaned past him and pointed at the address. "Can you cross-reference that address?"

He typed in the address in the newspaper search and at least twenty files came up, going back seventy years.

"Wait, seventy years?"

"That's when the houses were first built," Meredith said. "It has to be."

"Okay, is anyone else finding this creepy?" Ace asked.

"Look, it's just a coincidence. Single people moving in and finding love. It happens all the time. They make movies about it. Besides, we're all good. Not anywhere does it say that one woman marries two men," Meredith said.

"They wouldn't write it," Brett said. "Even if she stayed with the two men it would be illegal."

"I'm going back out to weed. This is why the internet is dangerous. It makes people think things that are just stupid."

Chapter Seven

Ace glanced around Meredith's studio. She'd completed a couple of projects, both of which featured himself and Brett. They were really good as well. He was impressed. She was downstairs talking with Will, her manager.

The guy was in his late fifties but seemed to care for her a lot. Pushing his hands into his pockets, Ace paused at one of the half-finished sketches. It was of him in bed. One of his arms rested behind his head, and he looked completely relaxed. He didn't pose for this one.

"She has a real talent, doesn't she?"

He spun around to see Will there. No sign of Meredith.

"Yeah, she does."

"I remember when she sat in my office, and no matter what I said to her, she just kept drawing until she was done. When she showed me what she saw, I was blown away. Up until that moment I was all about work. The extra hours, the lack of vacations. I couldn't even remember my kids' ages, and I knew something had to give. She saw all of that, and overnight, I quit my job and helped her instead."

"She certainly has a way of making you do crazy things for her." Ace didn't think for a second that he'd be sharing her with his best friend, much less enjoying it, but he did. Having her between him and Brett, it was … amazing. They hadn't taken her at the same time, but she certainly loved it whenever he teased her tight little asshole. Not that he was going to tell this man that.

They were close but not *that* close.

"You and this Brett, you care about her?"

"We do."

"You've given her back her passion, which I

love." Will moved toward one of the finished paintings. "It was her family, you know."

"What?"

"It didn't matter that she had a sell-out gallery or that her website was overrun with requests for her work. So long as they stayed away, she could do anything, be anything. Her work was always flawless. The energy seemed to be held within the painting. I was ill for two weeks, so I wasn't able to be there to help. She went and stayed at her parents' house for three days." Will scoffed and shook his head. "I should have known. Whatever they did or said, it got to her. The first painting I saw after that was like an amateur was copying her with no real passion at all."

"You think her parents ruined her mojo?"

"It's one way of putting it. Until that moment, no one could touch her. She was on fire. That's how passionate she was, and to see her in front of a canvas… The last year has been tough. She's been worried, scared, and that sparkle hasn't been there. Now though, I see it flaring up again. She's right there in this painting. You and Brett, I want to thank you both for doing whatever it is that you do. Meredith is not herself without her ability to draw like this, to lose herself in her art."

"She's a firecracker. You were lucky to find her."

Will smiled. "I have a feeling that she found me."

Meredith came back, smiling. "Sorry about that. My supplier wanted to try and give me a bad deal on something. How are you two getting along?"

"I'm telling him how good you've been doing since you moved here," Will said.

Ace didn't say anything.

"It's the fresh air. You know, and the neighbors, they keep me sane."

He followed them out of the studio.

Ace stood back and watched as she hugged Will and waved at him. Closing the door, she leaned against it. "Did he say anything to you?"

"Like what?"

"I don't know. He can be very protective."

"Exactly how much does he know about our situation?"

"He doesn't know everything, but he knows that I'm seeing both of you. Besides, he looked at the paintings I did, and it's not exactly hard to see."

"Very true." He pulled her into his arms.

"What are you doing home early anyway?"

"My last client canceled on me, and instead of waiting around for Brett, I decided to come and see you. Wondered if you needed help with anything."

"I do, actually." She took his hand, and he was hoping they were going to where he thought they were going, but they weren't.

The last bedroom at the end of the hall was open, and the window was unlocked.

"Will you help me decorate this room? I know it's small, but I don't like that I've left it. I don't need it or anything, but it seems wrong for one place of the house to be deserted."

Pulling her against him, he kissed her neck. "I'll help."

"Good." She handed him a wallpaper scraper.

"You don't want me to paint over the walls?"

"No, I want the paper down. I don't like it. I've got an idea I want for the room."

"Okay, then." He took the scraper from her hand and started getting the old wallpaper off.

Meredith grabbed his hand, turning him toward her. Before he could say or do anything else, she kissed him. Cupping his face, she meshed her lips against his.

Holding the back of her head, he kept her in place as he took the kiss.

"What was that for?" he asked.

"For being you and for helping me, and I don't know, for just being everything."

He smiled, stroking her cheek with the backs of his knuckles. "It's always a pleasure to help you."

****

Meredith walked around the DIY department store, looking at different colors of paints. She had opted for a pale, yellow color, but that didn't seem good enough at the moment. She didn't want baby boy blue or baby girl pink. White just screamed bland, so she was opting for the yellow.

"What about some furniture?" he asked.

"No, not yet."

She was having really weird thoughts and feelings right now.

"What is it?" Brett asked.

Ace was working today, so Brett had taken his place in helping her get the room right. For the past couple of nights, she'd been dreaming about that room. Not in any way a nightmare, more like what she knew it had to be. The way it had to look.

She wasn't about to tell Ace and Brett that she intended to fill it for a nursery. It was crazy, completely so. Stupid even, but she felt it had to be ready for a child, for a baby, for something.

While she was thinking this way, she was kind of freaking out.

Who prepared for a baby she wasn't even close to having?

She couldn't get it out of her head, and rather than freak out her two current boyfriends, she'd ordered the furniture online and it should be delivered on one of the days that they were both working.

"It's nothing. I don't want to buy something that is going to sit around for some time."

"Ace told me about his visit with Will. Your manager seems happier with what you're creating."

"I'm happier with what I'm drawing. It does make all the difference, even if at times it makes me nervous."

"Why?"

"You and Ace may not be around forever, and I guess that worries me right now. You're helping me, and I don't want you to stop doing that."

"We're not going anywhere." He cupped her hips and kissed her neck. "Why would we want to leave you?"

She sighed, melting against him and closing her eyes. Ace and Brett both had this power over her. It helped her to forget and to relax, and to feel calm.

Opening her eyes, she looked across the center and saw a couple of women from their street watching them. They had probably seen her kissing Ace just last week.

"Oh, no, I have this horrible feeling I'm going to be the talk of the town," she said.

"Let them. If Ace catches wind of it, he'll give them something to talk about."

She chuckled, and she saw a rug with dog prints on it. "I want this." She picked it up off the shelf.

"Do you have a dog?"

"Nope, but it is needed."

"Anyone ever tell you you're strange?" Brett asked.

"All the time."

She chuckled.

They paid for their goodies and headed out to

Brett's truck. He unloaded all the paint and her purchases into the back seat as she climbed into the passenger side. Turning over the ignition, she put the AC on, and a blast of cold air hit her in the face.

It was too hot outside but the perfect weather for decorating the house, especially this small bedroom, which was in the cool side of the house.

Brett climbed inside after returning the trolley to the bay, and they pulled out, heading back to her place.

She tapped her thigh as she watched the houses go by. Everything was so perfect in the street, each home looking exactly the same. A single car in the driveway at the end of the day. One or two of the houses had a basketball hoop.

Sometimes she hated the conformity of something like this, but today, it felt right. The street seemed like the best place to be.

"Did you do any more research on our homes?" she asked.

"There were a lot of myths and legends online," he said, pulling up onto the driveway.

"Tell me about them."

"The one that really stuck out is what this land was prior to the houses being built," he said. "There's a tale that there were two lovers that came from different worlds. I'm guessing the rich and poor."

"Okay."

"The girl was poor, and the guy was rich. The land was owned by his family, and she worked there from the time she was a little girl. They grew close, and it wasn't long before that closeness turned into love. The problem was, he was destined to marry a woman with money, who would help them grow stronger."

"Oh no, this is sounding tragic."

"So anyway, they decide to run off, to marry

anyway, and to have a life together. He always loved the simple life with the sweet things, and she never wanted anything more than him."

"This story is not getting a happy ending. Is it?"

"Nope. According to sources when they were running away, they were caught, but for whatever reason, he ended up shot, and was dying. Completely swamped with grief with her love dying in her arms, she took his gun, pressed it against her temple, and shot herself. He didn't die straight away. The tale is that they were found together. He was still alive when she shot herself in the head, and he'd pulled her into his arms, holding her, and before he passed away, he wrapped her arms around his so everyone would know that he loved her."

"Wow, that story sucks, but that is incredibly detailed. How does that have any relevance to us though?"

"They died in this exact spot where our houses join. We're the only houses in the street that are joined together as a terrace house. I even checked the planning of this. Our houses are not built the way they were meant to be designed. No one can explain what happened. Clearly a builder or contractor read it wrong, which is why they have the trees and why it's at the end of the street, so it doesn't look odd."

"What a sad tale. Do you really believe this?" she asked.

"Think about all those couples before us, Meredith. You tell me."

"I wonder if we're going to be the three to break the cycle."

****

"What do you think about the future?" Brett asked Ace a couple of weeks later.

They'd been with Meredith for a couple of

months now, sharing her and enjoying her together. They still hadn't taken the chance and made love to her at the same time, but it was close. Whenever he was inside her, he felt that need building within Meredith, how she'd either look at him or Ace, and it was in her thoughts.

"Is this about the house again? I checked your computer, and you've been going crazy with this whole thing."

He wasn't about to tell him that he reached out to Wynter and to Cassie, who had lived here before them. They believed in the magic of the houses.

"It's not about the houses."

"Then what is it?"

"Meredith."

Ace stopped his press-ups and sat on the mat. They'd been teaching a class, which was a new thing the owners of the gym wanted to try. Some people didn't like one-on-one treatment, but they needed guidance on how to work out themselves. He and Ace had opted to teach the class together. They knew what they were capable of, and as such, their class had been a huge success, so much so they were now doing two classes a week and the owner wished to up that to three within the next month.

"What do you feel for her?" Brett asked.

It was the only thing they hadn't talked about when it came to Meredith. Sharing her felt natural to the both of them. They'd shared girls in the past but never to this degree. Not only that, he actually looked forward to seeing and hearing about their dates. He wasn't jealous of Ace or the way she was with either of them.

Meredith didn't choose favorites. She adored them both.

Ace stared at him, and he knew he wasn't going to like what was about to be said.

"I love her," Ace said. "I know she's different

and she has this fire and shit like those creative sorts do, but I love her and I don't want to live in a world that doesn't have her in it."

"How long have you known?" Brett asked.

"Hey, before we get into the whole, 'how long have you known,' why don't we figure out your feelings as well? I'm not stupid, buddy. I know you ask this shit for a reason. Let's have it out."

They had never fought over a girl.

"I love her as well."

"So we both love her. We're both having fun. What's the big deal?"

"I want the whole thing. Kids, family, a wife."

"Wow, so you want me out of the picture?" Ace asked.

"No, I don't."

"This is kind of confusing me here. You want me to leave or what?"

"No, I don't want you to leave. I'm telling you exactly what I'm hoping to get. That I love her and that I want to one day start a family."

"But?"

"I see you as part of that family. Don't you think about it? The three of us together. Having a family, being fucking happy."

Brett couldn't deny that it was something he thought about a whole lot, no matter the time or day. He'd watch Meredith and Ace playing around in the yard, and he always saw a couple of kids dancing around their feet, laughing, joking, having fun.

"I haven't really thought about that, you know."

"I know. I just thought you should be aware of what I want is all." He slapped his friend on the back.

"You're going to have to tell her."

Brett sighed. "Do you really see her as the

settling down kind of girl?"

"I see Meredith as the kind of girl that doesn't get told what to do. She does what she wants, and no one will be telling her any differently. It's the way she has always been. Neither you or I will change that."

They'd never spoken about family or what they'd do for one, or how it would be.

Rubbing the back of his head, he left the gym and made his way toward the shower in the private men's changing room.

Removing his clothes, he stepped under the cool spray, closing his eyes, and trying to think of something, anything that could possibly take his mind off what was going on in his world.

Everything was so fucked up right now, and he was not in a good place.

A family. A future. He'd never wanted anything like that. In fact, he would normally ditch anyone who started talking about that shit. What was it about Meredith that made him even consider something that he normally hated?

His cock hardened as he imagined her in the bikini she loved to wear, her red hair bound up, curves on display, only this time her stomach was full, rounded with their child. He didn't even care if it was his or Ace's, just that it was one of theirs. Her ink, which she still hadn't finished because it had to be right. So much to adore and to love. There wasn't a single part of her didn't enjoy. Her laughter always made him smile.

Listening to her tell the worst jokes always made him laugh. Sitting and watching chick flicks even though he hated them, he did so just to be close to her. She'd either rest against him or Ace, with her feet across the other.

They were the inspiration for her art.

He even liked Will, as he'd met him a couple of times now.

"Get a grip, Brett. Don't ruin this."

Either way, he'd have to tell her soon. The only problem he had then was how she'd take the news once he did.

Chapter Eight

The following Saturday

"Are you on a diet?" Meredith asked.

"No, why not?"

"You're twirling your pasta and not eating it. It's kind of rude not to eat the food they served you. Just a little hint there."

"Right, of course." Ace continued to twirl the pasta.

It was their date night, and since Brett's revelation, Ace couldn't get the idea of them all living as a happy family out of his head. *Thanks, Brett.*

Meredith, as usual, looked stunning. Tonight, she'd gone more formal than he was used to. Her red hair fell in ringlets around her body, and she wore a simple black dress. Red, shiny heels finished off the outfit. There was not much in the way of a splash of color.

He loved to take her out for their dates rather than stay in. There wasn't a single decent movie playing in the theater, so he'd opted to come here, to the Italian restaurant as he was getting a little tired of Chinese food.

"Ace, something is going on. Please tell me."

"How was your day today?" he asked.

She took a deep breath, her lips pressing together. He knew she hated when he kept things from her, but right now wasn't the time to start spilling his guts, not yet anyway.

"It was good. I've got a few more paintings to complete, and once they're done, Will thinks we can start to pull in some prospective buyers."

"What about another show?"

"I've been talking with him about that, and we're in agreement to keep holding back. I've done two, which is amazing, and they've been sellout as well. Leave them wanting more, he said. So that's what I'm going to do. I'm working on individual work and building up my collection. When I'm ready I'll go back to doing commissioned work. It's happening. I'm so relieved to say that it is. I'm getting it back, and it feels so amazing to *be* back."

"That's great news. I'm really happy for you."

"Yeah, it's great, but I don't know what's going on right now, Ace. You're different, and I thought we were all friends here. Have you and Brett got something to tell me?" she asked.

He ate the mouthful of pasta, not really tasting it.

"Do you ever think about the future?"

"You mean like what we're all going to become and planning for the worst-case scenario?"

"Something like that."

"No."

"Why not?"

"I don't want to. Simple as that. I hate to think or to plan about a future that may never happen. Do you do that?"

"I've always got a plan in place. I know not many thirty-five-year-old men spend all their time with their best friend. Brett and I have been with each other forever, and it's almost hard to think of a time without him."

"I understand that."

"You're one of the few women that do."

"But?"

"Have you ever thought about kids? Family? Something other than just living life by the moment."

"Oh," she said, pushing some hair off her face.

Ace watched her reaction and saw that she was a little uncomfortable. "What is it? I didn't mean to ruin this date."

"Erm, kids was, were, are, I'm not really sure. They were in my plans. Erm, I … when I was eighteen I had a serious boyfriend. We'd been together forever, to be honest. From the time we were kids we were the friends that somehow came together and were in love." She took a deep breath, and he saw her hand shake as she reached for her wine. "Before I went to college I discovered I was pregnant. About two months."

"Oh. I'm so sorry. I didn't know you had any kids."

"I don't." She tilted her head to the side. "Erm, I thought we were in love, and then one morning before I decided to quit college, I went back to our apartment without telling him, and there I found him sleeping with who I thought was my best *girl*friend."

"Ouch." He winced.

"Needless to say, the hormones, everything, it … I ran. We were in an apartment block that had no elevator. The stairs were a nightmare. I didn't watch where I was going, and then, I woke up in the hospital. I had fallen down the stairs, and in doing so I had lost my baby," she said.

He saw the tears in her eyes, and he was in shock. What the hell was he supposed to do?

"I was going to marry this guy. My best friend and my best *girl*friend had been cheating on me. They were going to tell me on the same night that I found out I was pregnant. I had fallen in love with my baby though. I didn't know if it was a boy or a girl, and I was devastated. You could say that I flung myself into my art, and since that moment, I don't plan. I allow things to happen. I planned for a family. I planned to be in love, for a husband, and look what happened." She put down her fork. "The greatest pain I ever felt was touching my stomach and realizing *it* wasn't there."

Ace moved. He went on one knee and cupped her face, pressing his head to hers. "I'm so sorry."

He didn't care if they were drawing attention. All that mattered was that she knew she wasn't alone. He wanted her to know that he was there, and that he cared for her, and would always care.

"It's not your fault. I love kids so much. Family means a lot to me, even if mine sucks at times. I do like a family, but please don't ask me to plan anything, Ace. I can't do that."

"I won't ask you to plan. I promise you." He kissed her lips, knowing this story was for her to tell Brett.

****

Ace and Brett both knew the truth, and Meredith had seen the shock on their faces. It wasn't exactly easy to hide. She had been on the verge of motherhood. To think that was nearly twelve years ago. Her son or daughter could be screaming the house down right about now.

Both her men were at work, and she was all alone. Will had just left with another finished picture. She was on a roll at the moment. She refused to take any calls from her parents, and Will had even asked for any proposed visits to go through him.

She wasn't afraid of her parents, but they didn't exactly fill her with confidence. The last time she saw them, they'd had nothing but bad things to say. Not just about her work but they spoke of Lucy and Jess. The ex of everything in her life.

Talking about her past with Ace and then with Brett had been … revealing. Not just because she'd told them part of her story, but also because of how she felt inside. Losing her daughter or son, whichever one it was, that still hurt. The pain would never go away. Over the years it had simply lessened. Going to her closet, she pushed her clothes to one side, and in the back was a basket. Pulling it out, she carried it to the bed. No matter where she moved, this basket always came with her.

Untying the hooks, she pushed it back and glanced inside. Lifting out the white teddy bear, she stared at it. The feet had the word "Expecting" on them. It was the first Jess had gotten her after she told him.

Looking back now, she should have been able to spot the changes inside him. The fact he didn't hold her as tightly as he once did, or there was judgment in his eyes as he did so. He'd always been good at keeping secrets. Seeing Jess and Lucy together, she truly believed at the time that there was no way she'd ever be able to get over that pain. She had though.

Jess and Lucy didn't mean anything to her anymore. They'd done what they had. The only thing she wished was different was that she hadn't run. That she'd stayed and maybe her baby would still be alive.

Picking up the band that hospitals put around a patient's wrist, she saw the writing had faded. So much of who she was back then had faded as well. She liked to keep her own company. Jess and Lucy had been the two people who would respect her space, and not force her to conform to what they wanted.

She didn't think about them now.

This was the first time in a long time she had thought of them and the past. She did think about the baby she'd lost, but it was so random. There wasn't a gravestone to remember her by. Just the memory of once being pregnant. She didn't even have the chance to feel her baby move.

Putting everything away, she closed the basket up and put it all back in the closet. It felt good to talk to Brett and Ace about it.

Kids had been part of her plan, and after she lost her baby, she'd vowed to never plan for anything ever again. Her life was her own, to live each day and to make it count.

Leaving her bedroom, she made her way toward the small one where Brett and Ace had repapered, painted, and even laid a new carpet. They'd made light work of what she wanted. Breathing in the fresh air, she opened up the boxes of furniture that had been delivered and began to read through on how to build it.

There was no way it should be that difficult. One hour later, she had assembled a plain white chest of drawers.

"So this is why you were so secretive," Brett said, standing in the doorway, his arms folded as he watched her.

She smiled up at him, twirling the screwdriver in her hand. "I know this is going to sound crazy, but putting this place as a nursery seems really the right thing to do."

"It looks good. Yellow is a neutral color, right?"

"It is. Yes." She took a deep breath. "It feels right. Do you ever have that feeling?"

"Sometimes. Isn't it bad luck to get furniture?"

"The crib and stuff I think. Also clothes. I'm not pregnant or anything." She got to her feet, brushing some of the dust off her body. She'd clean up in a moment. "You're home early." She moved toward him, wrapping her arms around him. "Not that I mind that at all."

"Good. I wanted to come home. Check on you. You're not answering your cell."

"Shoot. I forgot to put it on charge."

Brett ran his hands down her body, cupping her eyes. She closed her eyes, loving his touch.

"Have you been thinking about me?"

331

"Maybe just a little."

"Do I get a little something before Ace gets home?"

"It's not a competition."

"I know, but you also have seen how he gets."

She chuckled. Ace liked to compete for who gave her the most orgasms. It was cute and exhausting, but she loved it. Moving Brett out of the nursery she was creating, she walked him back to her bedroom.

"I guess the biggest question is how much time do you have?" she asked, removing the clip from her hair.

He groaned, running his fingers through her length. Before he could hold her still to kiss her, she sank to her knees before him. Tugging on his zipper, she pulled down his pants, easing out his impressive dick. When she ran her tongue across the tip, they both moaned. She loved it when they couldn't resist her. The way he touched her, the sounds he made; she was addicted to him.

The problem was, it wasn't just Brett, it was Ace as well. She had fallen for both of these men, and there was no way she could pick just one. She didn't want to.

****

"I see you've started this party without me," Ace said, entering the room.

Brett wrapped Meredith's hair around his fist, working his cock in and out of her mouth. His friend's eyes looked fucking possessed as he watched her. Moving her hair out of the way so that Ace had the perfect view, Brett raised his brow.

"She's only just getting started."

He'd have to tell Ace at some point about her fixing up a nursery, but that didn't need to happen right now.

With her mouth around his dick, he couldn't really think all that clearly, not that he wanted to. Her lips on him was what he'd been wanting all day long, and now that he finally had her where he wanted her, he wasn't giving that up anytime soon.

"Help her out of her clothes," he said.

"With pleasure."

Ace stepped up to Meredith, and with her mouth on Brett's cock, his friend began to remove her clothes.

"No, your mouth doesn't leave my cock. Ace can get your clothes off you without you stopping."

"Damn right I can." He worked her vest top off, going down her hips along with her shorts. Her pumps came off next, followed by her underwear. Within minutes she was completely naked, her mouth still working his cock. Brett kept his hand in her hair, holding her in place as he pumped his dick deep between her lips.

She gagged on his length, and he pulled out. His shaft was completely covered in her saliva. Thrusting back inside, he looked over at Ace and saw his friend already naked, cock in hand, ready.

"So, I've been thinking, Meredith. Ace and I, we want you. You belong to us, and I think it's time that we fucked you together. One of us in your ass. The other in that tight little cunt of yours. What do you think?"

He gritted his teeth as she moaned around his dick, the pleasure vibrating up his spine. Damn, he wanted to come, to flood her mouth with his spunk, but he held back, keeping himself in check.

They'd been teasing her ass, using that vibrator she loved so much to work her tight little ass open for one of them.

"I want it," she said, her mouth still around his cock so her words were muffled, but he knew what she wanted.

"Ace, see how wet she is."

His friend moved up behind her. He couldn't see what he was doing, but the moment he touched her pussy, she took more of Brett's cock into her mouth.

"Fuck, that feels so good," he said.

"She's wet, Brett. So wet. You like the thought of two cocks inside you. One in your pussy, the other in your ass, riding you. Making you come."

"Yes!" Again, it was muffled, but that was okay. Pulling out of her mouth, Brett lifted her up off the floor, and carried her to the bed. Placing her in the middle, he spread her legs wide and licked her pussy. She cried out his name.

Ace joined them. He presented his cock to her lips, and Brett watched as she took him, swallowing down, licking his cock, cupping his balls.

Lifting her legs up, he pressed them against her stomach so that he could see her asshole clearly.

Working his fingers between her creamy slit, he slid them down to coat her anus. She groaned as he teased her asshole, working her natural arousal over the puckered hole.

"We've got to decide who takes her ass."

"Seeing as I got to fuck her first, you want the honors?" he asked.

"Yeah, I'm not going to turn down a chance to feel her around my dick. I want it."

Brett smiled. "I'll get her nice and ready then."

He worked a finger into her ass, and she cried out. He took his time getting her accustomed to the pain. "Hold her legs," he said, looking at Ace. With his cock in her mouth, Ace held onto her legs. With his hand free, Brett teased her clit, providing the pleasure that would equal if not surpass the burn and pain of her asshole.

With his thumb on her clit, he slid his fingers

inside her as he worked another into her ass at the same time.

She cried out, and Ace groaned.

"I don't know exactly know how long I can hold back. Her mouth is fucking heaven."

"Keep on going until I have her nice and ready." Pumping two fingers inside her ass, he continued to play with her pussy, working her to the point of orgasm but not letting her go over the edge.

When they took her together he wanted her to be completely on fire for the two of them. There would be no holding back, not for a second. He'd give her everything she ever wanted and then some more.

Ace pulled out of her mouth and began to suck her tits.

"Please, I need to come," she said.

"I love it when she begs. She sounds so damn sexy."

With a third finger in her ass, Brett nodded at Ace to get ready. He'd stretched her ass, and it was now time. He wanted to be inside her, to feel how tight her pussy was when Ace filled her ass. Pulling his hands out of her, he quickly went to her bathroom, to wash them but to also grab the lubricant that he'd stored there, just in case. Her wet pussy would only help so much, and he didn't want to hurt her.

Tossing the tube to Ace, he climbed on the bed.

Meredith was already crawling toward him, looking like the goddess that she was. She was the woman for them, and what was more, he had no intention of ever making her pick. This was the family he wanted. Screw normal, screw conformity. This was all he wanted, Ace and Meredith.

Chapter Nine

Ace watched Meredith's full, rounded ass, and it was a fucking dream. He'd spent many hours massaging those cheeks, spreading them, imagining her open and ready to take his cock, and now he was going to get her.

Not only that, he was going to share her with his best friend.

There was no one else he loved in this world more than Brett. Together they made a good team, and it suddenly dawned on him that they had, in their own way, become a family. Their own little threesome unit.

He didn't want to give any of them up.

Since Brett had started talking about kids, and knowing what she lost, Ace had found himself seeing more children and babies with their parents. He'd even taken a walk through the park, and there he'd watched a man, not much older than himself, lifting a baby girl into the air and kissing her cheek.

It had struck him so hard.

He wanted that.

To have a baby, a daughter or son.

Anything, so long as it was with Brett and Meredith.

Brett cupped her ass, and he watched his friend guide her down his length, taking all of him until she was sitting with it inside her. She glanced back and smiled at him. "I'm all yours."

Opening the tube of lubricant, he smeared it all over his dick, getting himself nice and slick before climbing on the bed. Placing a hand on her back, he held her in place, and stroked more gel into her anus. She released a gasp and then a whimper as he put his cock to her asshole, and slowly began to fill her. He took his time, allowing her to become accustomed to his sheer length.

He wasn't a small man, and she was taking all of him. Her ass was so fucking tight. There was a thin wall that separated him and Brett, but he felt him just as he felt the fluttering in her asshole. She was turned on and wanted this.

That only served to turn him on too, and his cock seemed to swell a little more. Gripping her hips, he pushed the final inch inside her so that he was balls deep, and they both moaned.

"Fuck!" Meredith cried out the word.

He kissed her neck, and they all stayed still, giving her time to get used to the two of them.

"How does it feel?" Brett asked.

"I feel so full. So full." She repeated the word a third time.

"Want me to pull out?" Ace asked.

"No, just give me a minute." She took a deep breath, and he continued to stroke her body, waiting for her to get accustomed to the feel of the two of them.

"Will one of you move, please?" she said.

Brett did so first, lifting her up then slamming her back down on his cock. He settled into a pace that Ace caught onto, and he took his chance, easing his length out of her as Brett filled her.

Working together, they fucked her body. Sliding a hand between them, he touched her pussy, not caring as his hand got crushed between Brett's and Meredith's bodies.

Each stroke of her clit seemed to drive her wild, and she wriggled on his cock, thrusting back against him, and riding Brett.

"I think our girl likes this," he said.

"I think you're right."

He brought her close to the edge of orgasm but

not allowing her to go over the edge. Keeping it at bay, he worked her pussy at the same time he thrust inside her ass. His own arousal had started to build, and he knew it wouldn't be long before he came.

Glancing over her shoulder at Brett, he saw his friend wasn't long from coming either.

Biting her neck, he sucked on her pulse before whispering in her ear. "Come for us, Meredith. Scream for us."

He was relentless on her clit, and she came, screaming both of their names. The sounds echoed off the walls, and he rode her ass, taking her harder than he ever had, driving in deep. Brett came first, his groan filling the air, and Ace felt the kick of his cock even as he worked her ass. Kissing her neck, Ace closed his eyes as he found his own release, his cum filling her ass.

His orgasm seemed to go on forever, and he didn't want it to stop.

Afterward, they collapsed on the bed. He eased his cock out of her ass and wrapped his arm around her waist.

He'd run a bath for her in a moment, but for now, he had to feel her against him.

"That was incredible," she said.

"We'll be doing that again," Brett said.

"My sore ass." She burst out laughing.

"I think I need to sleep," Ace said.

"Oh, dear, did we wear you out?" Meredith asked, turning her voice soft. She rolled over and snuggled up against him.

He wasn't even close to sleep, but he knew saying how tired he was would get her attention.

"I'm more than good right now."

"Babe, I think you just got played." Brett chuckled against her skin.

"That is so not fair." She pouted. "You shouldn't use my kind nature against me."

"I got what I wanted." He pushed some of her hair off her face. "I'm going to run that bath though. It'll help soothe you for tomorrow."

"What would I do without you?" she asked.

"Not a lot. Remember that. Your vibrator was a waste of time," he said. "It would never have been able to handle your needs."

"It was doing okay," she said.

"It would never give you this." He held her tightly and kissed her on the lips. "It doesn't care, whereas we do. That's the difference, and no matter what you say, Meredith, I know deep down, you want to be cared for."

****

"These are your best yet," Will said several weeks later.

"Thank you." Meredith tucked some hair behind her ear and watched as the last of her paintings were tucked away safely in the van that Will had come in.

"I knew this place would be amazing for you."

"You did?"

"Yeah, you needed to get away, find yourself. You'd become too trapped in your memories."

"Yeah." She smiled and stared down at her hands. They were covered in paint as they were most days just recently.

"Why do I feel you're not as happy as I'd hoped you'd be?"

"It's nothing."

"I can read you like a book, Meredith. You're happier than I've ever seen you, so what's with this mood? You're sad."

She shrugged. "Just thinking about a lot of things

lately."

"Such as?" He sat down on the chair opposite her.

"You know, stuff."

"Does this have to do with those two boys next door?"

"They're not boys. They're a little older than me."

"Still, they're younger than me."

"True," she said, laughing.

"What about them?"

"I don't know. I'm just trying to figure a few things out, you know. Trying to see what the future holds." Being lost in her painting, she'd realized how much she loved both men. There wasn't a favorite, and this wasn't just a bit of fun to her.

She loved Ace and Brett with all of her heart. They were the two friends she didn't want to give up, not ever.

"You're in love with both of them?" Will asked.

"What makes you think that?"

"I know you. Your parents don't approve of your life right now. You know deep down they'll never be happy with you being with two men."

She took a deep breath. "It's not just that. It's everything."

"Such as?"

"Do you think I'm a slut?"

"I thought you didn't care what people think."

"I don't. I don't. You're important to me, Will. You're not like everyone else."

"True. I am special." He sighed. "Honey, I don't care, okay? You have given me a chance to see my family before it was too late. I was working all the time, never saw my kids. Couldn't even remember their ages or names half the time. You love two men, and from what I've seen both of those men, they love you, Meredith. More than anything."

"They do?"

"You don't know?"

"We don't talk about things like that. I told them about losing my baby and how that affected me. They both started talking about babies, but nothing else has come from it. I don't know. Maybe I'm reading too much into it or something."

"The last time I checked, the only way to know for certain how a person feels is to ask them, or better yet, propose."

"Is that what you did?" she asked.

"Yep. I didn't have a clue how Sarah would feel about me, so I decided to give it a go as the saying goes. Now I live happily ever after with my wife, and we've got beautiful children, Meredith. You deserve happiness. Those men will grant it you. Your private life is your own, but I will always be here for you, regardless of what happens. Not only do I think you're extremely talented, you're a good person. Inside and out. I'll do anything for you."

"I love you too, Will."

"I know, honey." He hugged her close.

"Thank you for not giving up on me and for not freaking out about … you know."

"Your lack of productivity?"

"Yes, that."

"I *was* worried, Meredith. This is your life, and I know you're talented. What I didn't want to do was give you more stuff to stress about. I will handle that part of things. I just need you to find the love that makes you draw, that makes you paint."

"Thank you."

"I never for a second doubted that you'd find that

spark again that makes you you. I better get going. Think about what we talked about."

"I will."

She saw him to the door and watched him leave. He gave a final wave before turning off the street. Closing the door, she leaned against it, taking a deep breath. Everything was going to be fine. Of course, it would be fine.

For nearly twelve years she'd avoided anything as serious as she'd had with Jess. Her work always came first, and now, for the first time, she wanted something more.

It was unconventional, different, weird to a point, but it was what she wanted more than anything.

Stepping away from the door, she made her way upstairs toward her studio. Ace and Brett spent just as much time as she did in this space. They were always posing for her, making her laugh, showing her how to have some fun. She loved every second of her time with them.

This house was purchased in the chance of her finding her love of her art once again after she had lost that fire. She had found her way back to what she loved. Ace and Brett had been part of that.

They'd been her reason for getting up some mornings, just to see their smiles. Her sadness wasn't part of her anymore. It was nothing more than a distant memory. She was more than what she had been, and she knew it was because of Brett and Ace.

She stared at the piece she was working on. It showed Brett and Ace in bed. This one clearly showed their faces, and on the end of the bed was her, a blanket thrown across her ass, her leg lifted in the air. No one saw her face, but she knew it was her. Her hair was bound up on top of her head.

She loved both of those men, and there was no way she could choose one.

"What have you gotten me into?" she said, touching the wall of the house. She rested her head against it, and then laughed. "Great, now I'm a crazy person talking to walls as if they hear me."

Meredith didn't believe in the tales of houses drawing people together. It was a nice thought, sentimental and a bit scary, but she truly believed that it was single people who happened to live close together, learning about each other, and then falling in love. Houses didn't have a way of making people fall in love.

They brought people together, and then time helped people to fall in love.

****

"Did you get it?" Ace asked, sitting opposite him at the café.

"I got it." Brett pulled out the engagement ring he'd picked up and showed it to his friend. They'd both made the choice a few days ago but needed some time to finish the payment, as it had been a little out of their budget.

"It's beautiful," Ace said.

"So, do you have the plan in place?"

"Garden is nearly complete. I've got the table. You've got date night tonight, so you need to distract her so that I can finish setting it up."

"I don't usually go out for date night."

"Well do. I don't want her to check on me or anything."

"We've already picked the music, right?" Brett asked.

"Yeah. I've got dinner cooking right now. It's in the slow cooker, and the wine is chilling in the fridge."

"So all I've got to do is distract her."

"I would, but I think she'd get a little suspicious as it's your date night."

"I know. I know."

"You're sure about this?"

"I've never been more sure about anything else. We're in agreement though?"

"Our date night stands, but for the rest of our life, we all want to be together, yes?" Ace asked.

"Yes."

"You're nervous?"

"Wouldn't you be?"

"All you're doing is distracting her. I don't see a problem with that."

Brett smiled. "This is the first time I've ever proposed to anyone, at all."

"I get it. Don't forget I've never proposed either."

"Will gave us his blessing."

"He did?"

"Yes, I asked him the last time he visited."

"Shoot. She's seeing him today. You don't think he's talked, do you?"

"Nah, he wouldn't do that." Brett ran a hand down his face. "We are really going to do this."

"Yeah, we really are." He snapped the box closed and handed it to Ace. "You keep hold of that."

"I will."

With their lunch over with, their plan in place, Brett finished with his last client of the day and made his way home.

The scent of whatever Ace was cooking filled the air and made his mouth water, but he wouldn't allow himself to get distracted.

He took a quick shower, thinking about their proposal tonight. He'd never done anything like this, and his nerves were fraught. Once he finished in the shower, he made his toward his bedroom, dressing casually in a pair of jeans and shirt.

There was no backing off now.

He walked next door and found Meredith in the kitchen, pouring herself a glass of water. Her hair fell down around her in waves, and she wore a pair of jeans and a white blouse.

The warm weather had started to leave them, making way for fall and winter. With it, the summer dresses and bikini had been put away.

"Hey, babe," she said, coming toward him, carrying a glass of water. "How are you?" She kissed his cheek and smiled.

"I'm doing good. So, I thought we'd go out. The fair is having its last day tonight, and I've not been to one since I was a kid."

"A fair?"

"It'll be fun. Rides, cotton candy?"

"You had me at fun, sweetie." She finished off her water, putting the glass on the counter. "I'll grab my bag."

"How was Will today?" he asked.

He watched her tense up just a little, and he couldn't help but wonder why. Had he said something? Had he told her he and Ace intended to propose?

All of his carefully organized plans started to unravel, and he didn't know what to do. Shit, he wanted tonight to be special.

"It went well, actually. He's really happy with everything that I've produced lately." She tilted her head to the side as she turned toward him. "He likes you guys."

"He does?"

"Yes."

"Well, that's good. We like him."

"Good."

He took her hand and walked outside, helping her into the car.

"This isn't like you. Taking me out for your date night."

"I know. I wanted to try something new."

He strapped her in, and when she giggled he realized what he did. She placed a hand to his head. "Are you feeling okay, Brett? You're acting a little strange."

"Yeah, sorry. I guess I'm more excited than I thought."

"Yeah, I guess you are." She spoke so softly he almost didn't hear it.

She looked sad for a few seconds, but that disappeared the moment he climbed behind the wheel. Starting up his car, he pulled out of the driveway and headed toward the fair, which had been set up near the high school.

Parking was a nightmare, and the drive was quiet. He didn't know what to say for fear of alerting her to what he and Ace had planned.

"You're quiet today," he said.

"Just thinking. You know, about things."

"It is important to think about things."

What the hell are you doing and saying?

She's going to know.

Glancing over at her, he forced a smile as she was looking right at him.

"Okay, what is going on, Brett? Are you going to break up with me tonight?" Meredith asked.

"What? No."

"Really? Because you're acting really guilty and it's kind of worrying me. I don't need to go to a fair to be broken up with."

He was so taken aback that he pulled in against

the side of the road and turned toward her. "I don't want to break up with you. Neither does Ace, so get that out of your mind right now. Okay? We're not breaking up with you."

"Then what is this, Brett?"

"This is me taking you out on a date. We've got a surprise for you later and rather spoil it right now, we're going to have some fun, and then there will be a big reveal. You're not getting dumped."

"Oh."

"Not even if you wanted to," he said, pressing his lips against hers.

"I don't want to get dumped," she said, laughing. "Wow, I sound like a teenager."

"And you were acting like one. Now, stop panicking okay."

"I will."

He took her hand, locking their fingers together and kissing her knuckles. Tonight had to go down properly. He wouldn't accept it any other way.

Chapter Ten

"I'm screwed!"

"He's going to fucking kill me."

Ace had everything set up. The garden was a romantic paradise. The food was perfection. When Brett texted him, he'd cook the pasta, toss the stewed sauce, and everything would be perfect.

Rushing upstairs, he rummaged through his bag and found nothing.

He'd lost the fucking ring!

How was that possible? He had it right on him, and it was not there anymore.

"Don't panic. Don't panic. Shit."

If he left it at the gym, he wasn't getting that tomorrow.

"I didn't leave it at the gym. I had it on me today." His bag was clear, and then he moved to the bathroom. "No, I brought it home with me. I put it on the counter."

"The counter." He ran back downstairs, and the counter was bare.

Standing in the kitchen, he felt fucking nervous. This was their big night. They had picked the damn ring together. "I'm screwed."

As if that wasn't the end of it, his cell phone chimed to let him know to put the pasta on.

Running his hands down his pants, he quickly started trying to figure out not to get killed before the end of the day. Of course, Brett was going to kill him. The ring was expensive, and this was their night.

How could they not have the damn ring?

He knew it was in the house *somewhere*, he just forgot where.

The water came up to the boil for the pasta. He

seasoned it, and then dumped the pasta inside.

Just as he was draining it, he heard them pull into the driveway.

"You had fun, baby?" Ace asked.

"The best kind. What is all this?"

"We've got a nice surprise planned for you," Brett said.

She kissed Ace on the cheek.

"Why don't you go out into the garden?" Ace said. "I'll finish up in here."

"Okay."

He grabbed Brett's hand. "I lost the ring."

Brett's face dropped. "What the fuck, man? You had one thing. One thing and you lost it?"

"I didn't mean to lose it."

"I don't even want to talk to you right now. How did you lose it?" Brett asked.

"I put it down somewhere, and now I can't find it." He smiled, and Brett shook his head. "It's not completely lost. I just got to find it."

"I gave it to you so you wouldn't fucking lose it. Damn it. Don't worry. We'll figure something out." Brett patted him on the arm, which made him feel a million times worse. Yep, he'd screwed up, like, completely screwed up.

Heading back into the kitchen, he added the parmesan, pasta cooking water, and a drizzle of olive oil to the sauce. If he was going to eat something like this, it was going to be done right.

Serving it up into three bowls, he quickly put the parmesan back into the fridge, and paused. There, glaring at him, was the velvet box, near the cream.

He laughed, and quickly pulled it out. Opening the box, he saw the ring still perfect and slid the box into his pants pocket.

He was saved. The night was saved.

Clearly, he'd been so preoccupied with getting this meal right that he'd not even noticed that he packed it into the fridge.

Putting their meal on the tray, he carried it out. Brett and Meredith were dancing to a slow tune that was playing. "Your dinner awaits."

"This is date night, and you're both here. This is curious."

"I stopped her eating a lot of cotton candy," Brett said.

"You told me I'd throw up going on one of the rides." She looked between them. "What's going on?"

"Why don't you try your meal first? It's lovely," he said.

"Okay." She put her fork into the food and twirled it around.

He couldn't take his gaze away from her as she took a bite of the pasta. Her eyes closed, and a moan escaped her lips. "Oh, that is so good."

"Excellent." It was a beef rib sauce that had been slow cooked all day with onions, carrots, celery, and lots of tomatoes and herbs. It was one of his favorites but took some planning to get it all right. He also liked to skim off most of the fat. The meat on the ribs was so tender, but greasy. He didn't want to weigh down his sauce. He glanced at Brett, who was still glaring at him.

Ace winked at him, and he watched Brett visibly relax.

Diving into his own meal, he closed his eyes, and enjoyed the taste. Watching Meredith and Brett, Ace knew without a shadow of a doubt that he could get used to this life. Of being with his best friends, falling in love, having a family.

He really liked the idea of having kids around.

They wouldn't live in these two houses forever, if she agreed. He hadn't told Brett yet, but he was already looking at places for them to move to. He loved Meredith and his best friend. She hadn't said anything to either of them, but he knew she loved them as well.

He finished his bowl first, leaning back in his chair. "That was good."

"And no quinoa about," Brett said.

Meredith chuckled. "You're still not over that?"

"I had to have quinoa for a long time. Lunch and dinner, I got a bit bored."

"You hear him complaining, but you don't see him rushing to the kitchen to cook."

****

Meredith watched the two men, not exactly sure what was going on but also knowing something was.

Brett had been strange all night, and Ace, well, he looked super happy with himself. Taking a sip of her wine, she stared at the two men she loved so damn much. How could she have ever thought of a life without either of them? They completed her in so many ways, and being between them, it all felt right.

Love filled her, and she just couldn't hold it back any longer.

"I love you two," she said.

The entire table seemed to freeze. She didn't care.

She had held back from her feelings, and she was done. She wanted to shout it from the rooftops, to scream it.

"What?" Brett asked.

"I know we've never really talked about the future or what it would mean, but I love you ... both. I know it's messed up and that it should only be one of you, but I love you both the same." She glanced down at her plate. "I didn't want to go another moment without telling you guys."

Looking up, she saw them both looking at her.

Suddenly they started scrambling around, and she watched as they both got on one knee. She frowned as Ace started to pat down his body and pulled out a velvet box.

She knew what that was.

"Meredith, we love you," Brett said. "We know we come as a package deal—"

"Which is great because that means you have me, and everyone knows life is better with me in it," Ace said.

"Anyway, we come together, and being with you, it showed us both that we don't want anything to change. We love you, and we will always love you. Who cares what the outside world thinks? This is our business. We live one life, and I know, we both know, it is with you."

"So, Meredith Snow, will you do us the honor of becoming our wife?" Ace asked.

She was in shock.

"You want to marry me?" she asked.

"Brett and I have already decided. You'll marry him, and we'll have a private ceremony."

They opened the lid, and she saw the two rings bound together.

"We thought this would show that you belong to the two of us."

"It's beautiful."

"Hold up, you've not even said yes yet," Ace said. "Only a yes gets the ring."

She burst out laughing. "Yes, yes, of course, yes."

Brett took the ring and slid it on her finger as Ace kissed her. The ring fit perfectly.

"You do know what this means, don't you?" Ace asked.

She kissed Brett before turning back to look at Ace. "What?"

"We're going to have to sell the houses. We can find a place of our own, and then we can let this bring two unsuspecting people together."

"You're kidding, right?" she asked looking from Ace then to Brett.

"You've got to admit, it's pretty telling." Brett stroked her cheek. "We found each other."

"Just think about the little magic that's clearly there."

She tilted her head to the side and smiled. "Then whoever is next, I hope they find someone special."

Brett lifted her up, and she released a squeal as he carried her through to the house. "Now, we're going to make this a night to remember." He took her to his bedroom.

"There are so many things for us to get through. How are we going to work this? Where are we going to stay?" she asked.

"When we find the house," Ace said, removing his shirt. "We'll have a bedroom big enough for all three of us."

"There has to be a studio," she said, gasping as Brett placed a hand between her thighs.

"Of course, and a gym for us. We also need to be close to town so we can continue to work," Brett said. "We love our job, and also, we love helping you, inspiring you."

He removed all of his clothes, and she watched as Ace moved up behind her. He ran his hands up from her stomach to lift her tits up.

Brett leaned forward, taking one of the buds into his mouth.

He trailed his tongue between the valley to suck

on the other. "And we're going to need a couple of spare rooms for our kids."

"You want kids?" she asked.

She wanted loads of them, so many, to fill the house with the sound of laughter

"Yes," Brett and Ace said together.

"I've love to have a little Meredith running around," Ace said before sucking on her earlobe.

"I want that too, so many." She moaned as Brett pushed her back. Spreading her thighs, she cried out his name as his tongue started to stroke her pussy, driving her wild with need, wanting more of him. His mouth wasn't enough; she needed his cock.

Two fingers thrust inside her, and Ace worked his cock into her mouth. She sucked him as if she couldn't get enough of him, and she couldn't.

These two men, her neighbors … she'd come here seeking peace and a place to find herself again. She'd discovered the loves of her life, and they were two men.

If the houses were indeed cursed then it wasn't a curse at all. What it was, was a gift. Whoever stayed here, whoever found their love, they were being given a chance, and for that, Meredith could believe in it.

As Brett thrust inside her, Ace fucked her mouth, and she gave herself over to these two men. They accepted her for who she was and didn't try to change her.

She didn't even realize that she'd been looking for love when it finally landed in her lap, but she was going to take this second chance and hold onto it for the rest of her life.

****

Three months later

Meredith's parents didn't come to the wedding.

None of her family did. Brett's family did, as well as Ace's. They knew they were marrying the same girl, even if his and her name would be on the marriage certificate.

To them, they were all married together, and that was all that mattered.

Making his way home, he saw Meredith's truck parked in her driveway. She must have gotten home early after being with Will. Her paintings had been a huge success, but Will wasn't interested in making her do another gallery showing again anytime soon.

The demand was there and her creativity was there, but Will didn't want to press her. He'd been there at their wedding as well.

He liked Will.

Brett was careful as he parked his car as the real estate hadn't done well with putting the sign out, and he'd knocked it down three times. Now it had "SOLD" over the sign.

Both houses had sold together, which was a shock. They expected time between each. They already had a down payment on a new place and were just finishing up some paperwork.

Moving in was a matter of days, and most of their stuff had been packed up. They were living in her place so that they were ready to move everything out.

He entered their home, and he didn't hear the soft classical music that she sometimes liked to play.

"Meredith, you home?" he asked, walking upstairs.

No answer.

He went to her studio first, but there was no sign of her. Then he went to their bedroom, and with still no sign of her, he opened up the bathroom door. She sat with her back against the sink, holding a white stick in her hand.

A pregnancy test.

"I haven't taken it yet. I'm kind of afraid to."

"You've got nothing to be afraid of."

"I don't?" She licked her lips and stared down at the stick. "I've not had a period in over two months."

He sat down beside her, taking her hand and locking their fingers together.

"I didn't realize how badly I wanted a baby until now. What if it's negative?"

"Then we keep going," he said. "You, me, and Ace, we keep going. If it says no, then that is not a problem."

"What if I can't have any more after the accident?"

"Did the doctor say that?"

"No."

"Then stop worrying your little head off, okay? You're fine. We'll deal with whatever life throws at us, remember. We're in this for life."

"I'm being silly."

"You're not. This is a big deal. Not just for you, but for all of us."

"Ace has to be here."

"I'll text him." Brett quickly typed out a quick text and sent it off.

She rested her head against his arm. "I love you."

"I love you, too."

"I really want to have a baby. I'm thirty-one. I want to start a family."

"We will do so, together." He cupped her cheek and stared into her eyes.

"Together."

The front door slammed, and Ace ran up the stairs. By the time he got to them, he was panting. "What did I miss?"

"Nothing. I was going to take this pregnancy test. We thought you'd like to be here for the result."

"Fuck, yeah. I'm ready to be a dad."

They gave her space while she peed on the stick. When she was ready, she called them both back in. The stick was on the counter, waiting for the two minutes.

"I want a boy or a girl, I don't care," Ace said.

"I just want a healthy baby," she said.

Wrapping his arms around her waist, he pulled her in close, and all three of them stood, watching the pregnancy test.

The two lines appeared, and Meredith grabbed the box, reading out the results.

"We're pregnant. This is going to be totally awesome. We're going to have lots of kids," Ace said, holding her tightly.

He saw the tears in her eyes, and he smiled. "Are you happy?"

"Yes, I'm really happy. There are no words for how I feel."

Brett was going to be a dad.

Ace was going to be a dad, and Meredith was going to be a mom. He had never felt happier in his entire life.

His family, his future, his love, all together.

Epilogue

Six months later

"There, all done," Meredith said, putting the last teddy bear on top of the wardrobe.

The nursery had been her project for the last few months, and she finally had it perfect.

"I think we should have taken the furniture from the old place. You did buy it," Ace said.

Meredith chuckled. They lived a little closer to town, with a nice yard, and it was in walking distance of the park. This was where she wanted to stay. The city life wasn't something she wanted to go back to, and she would rather stay as far away from it as possible.

Leaving their homes had been hard, especially when she discovered she was pregnant. She couldn't stay there, though, as she'd already signed the documents over. The man who had moved in was a single dad with a little baby girl. The nursery had seemed really appropriate for his situation.

He'd found it strange at the time that she'd created a nursery without having a child. Brett and Ace had sold their house to a single woman straight out of college. She'd been looking for a first-time house, and she finally got it with Ace and Brett's bargain.

"What are you thinking?" Brett asked, moving up behind her, wrapping his arms around her waist and putting his hands flat on her stomach.

"I'm wondering if they're together yet? You know, our old houses."

"Ah, you want to see if the magic still works?" Ace asked.

"Aren't the two of you curious about it?" she asked.

Brett shrugged. "I was when I lived there, but

now, I'm just happy. No matter the reason why. We're here. We're together, and we're happy. We're going to have a little boy very soon."

Ace moved to stand in front of her, his hands on her stomach. "We all made this. I can't believe it. We're going to have a little boy running around the house very soon."

As they both leaned in to kiss her, she smiled, moaning, and then gasped.

"Shit, what was that?" Ace asked, jumping back.

"I think my water just broke. I just cleaned these carpets, and my water broke," she said.

"We've got to get her to the hospital," Brett said.

Her two men jumped into action, but she was pissed that her water had broken on the beautiful carpet she laid. Why couldn't they have broken on the wood floor, or outside? She wanted to cry, but there was no time.

With Ace and Brett prepared, she was urged into the car where she started to have contractions.

Ace and Brett were yelling at each other to help her or to drive faster. She didn't care. She focused on the pain, on doing the breathing techniques she'd been advised. In and out. In and out.

"I love you," Brett said.

"Why are you saying that? She's not dying," Ace said.

"I love you both as well. Please, I feel I need to push." She tried not to push, but as Brett pulled into the hospital parking lot, she couldn't contain it. She really needed to push, and there was no way she was moving.

Ace stayed with her, holding her hands as Brett rushed to get a nurse.

"This is just the story of my life. Giving birth to our son in the parking lot."

Seconds later Brett returned, and she was suddenly covered and crowded as she kept on pushing in the back seat of the car.

There was a doctor and nurse between her thighs, telling her what to do, not that Meredith needed help. She just wanted to push.

The sound of a baby's scream filled the air, and she gasped at the sound.

"Holy shit," Ace said.

The doctors and nurses were saying something to each other, and she didn't understand it. They must have brought out a kit to cut the cord as their baby was wrapped up in a blanket.

She was helped from the car and placed in a wheelchair very gently. The doctors and nurses were fussing, and she saw her baby boy in Brett's arms.

Ignoring the questions, she held her arms out. Brett placed their son in her arms. Ace stood one side of her, Brett the other.

Their son.

The start of their family.

"Hello, my precious boy." She kissed his head. "Welcome to your family."

The End

www.samcrescent.com

www.ingramcontent.com/pod-product-compliance
Lightning Source LLC
Chambersburg PA
CBHW021437240626
47153CB00001B/186